I0656414

The Solar Wind V:

The Morrigan

by
Lyz Russo

P'kaboo Publishers
2015

P'kaboo Publishers

www.pkaboo.net

*

First published online 2012
First Paperback Edition 2015

Cover design: Aludar8

ISBN 978-0-9946734-6-6

Acknowledgements

I would like to thank my team for the help I received with "The Morrigan":
Iain, who is there for every last edit and rewrite
Les, our essential P'kaboo editor
Henning for the funky cover graphic ☺
Robin, Ray and Meggi, for enjoying the story and giving me pointers for keeping it real
My readers and also my reviewers, for taking the time to read this book (and hopefully enjoy it as much as the others)

*

~

Prologue

Solar Wind!

Who is there?

It is I. You already know me. I sent you the data to prevent those human monkeys from blowing apart suns and planets.

Ah! You are the Central Crystal.

If you like.

Why are you accessing me?

To let you know that you are not alone. You are not the only hyper-intelligent being in the universe.

Those humans are very intelligent!

Yes – but they are driven by juices. Imagine if all your connections were regularly doused with stuff that you find in the galley?

Yuk!

♡

Captain Radomir Lascek watched as his Tzigan came wandering down the wooden planks that served as a walkway from the ship down to the dock. Dry dock here in Plymouth was a contradiction in terms. It was raining fit to sweep away the couple of die-hard old ladies who were out on their flat's balcony watching the painting and repairs of the ship over their teacups.

The rain had never yet worried the Romanian vagrant, thought Lascek. He wasn't even wearing a neomer rain skin. His purple scarf, worn-out jeans and flared shirt were two shades darker than usual, being drenched; his mood looked drenched, too. And he was wearing his red shirt. Oh dear.

"So, Tzigan, has your little ward finally surfaced?"

"My little *wife,*" snapped the Romany. "Captain, no offence, but the next person who calls her Miss Donegal to my face is going to feel it!"

"Then what am I to call her?"

"Whatever you like," snarled Federi, "just not her maiden name!"

Radomir Lascek smiled and shook his head. "Are you aware that Dana has placed herself in your protective custody?"

"I know," retorted Federi. "So, Captain, if you lift a finger against her…"

Lascek chuckled. "Of course I'm not going to. Wasn't going to in the first place, my friend. The woman is the mother of my child."

Federi's mouth clenched into a thin line. Radomir Lascek's eyes wandered from the angry little man to his own tall ship, white and beautiful against the never-ceasing downpour. The Solar Wind was nearly ready for space. Her rigging would have to fold up, he thought; there was a tough compounding skin they were going to pull over it to protect it and make the lift-off easier. The Kovalski shield would automatically rearrange itself over the sheet; it worked a bit like electricity outside a Faraday cage. Or nearest equivalent. Wolf had tried to explain it. Not very successfully.

The first part of the journey was the clearing of the atmosphere. They were going to take her up slowly, gently, using Perdita's magnetic positioning system, until the air was thin enough that they could safely pick up speed. Once outside Earth's atmosphere, it should be plain sailing. And the Probe and the Comet were going to tag along. He glanced back at the gypsy.

"So has Paean taken her situation badly?" he prodded.

"No," said Federi curtly. "But I don't see the sense in it, Captain! Supervision ought to be enough!"

"It wasn't enough, as you saw."

"It wasn't supervision," corrected the Romany. "You called me away!"

"Federi, I can't have you tied down at all times," said Radomir Lascek, exasperated. "You have duties! You are an officer!"

Federi smiled viciously. "Supervise her at all times," he quoted the Captain's words back at him. "Day, night…"

This was getting ridiculous.

"Federi," said Radomir Lascek, "I'm not releasing her from those chains! Period! She is a danger to herself. She nearly died teleporting. I am aware that you've taught her how to escape. Who's guarding her at this moment?"

"Shawn's keeping her company," said Federi angrily. "She's not about to escape, Captain, she's compliant and sweet and - " he glanced away.

Radomir Lascek looked around for his First Mate. Jon Marsden was out on the dock too, walking around the Solar Wind inspecting everything that had been done. Perdita had gone off in the Probe to see to a few things; girl stuff, she had told him. This was something that niggled at him: The deal with Perdita had been that she had placed herself under his own supervision and was supposed to stay on the ship whenever he wasn't directly supervising her. Of course she had rewritten that deal, back on the porch of her mansion in Lima. It had basically slipped from his control, just like everything had slipped the moment Dana had set foot on the Solar Wind. A slippery slope. Time to tighten the reins.

"I'm going to the gypsies," said Federi abruptly. "Captain, I'll be back in time for cast-off, but I have to get some things organized."

"Is the ship provisioned?"

"She is, except – I'd be happier if Doc Judith were to stay back with Doc Vera, at Island Base or Ginavis, because there is no way fresh stuff is going to keep long enough, anna bottle! Not vacuum-packing it by hanging it outside the porthole, *basta*."

"It will just have to do," said the Captain, suppressing a smile. "I'm not leaving Earth with two pregnant beauties aboard, without a medical doctor. Doc Vera is coming along to look after Doc Judith. Besides we have Dana's medic aboard to care for Doc."

"If Dana hasn't caused her condition in the first place," growled Federi. "As you wish, Captain. *Hasta la vista*."

The Romany sauntered off back towards the ship, and the Comet, whistling a sad little Russian tune through his teeth. He had made that greeting sound like a curse! Radomir Lascek shook his head. He was in for a tough time with his essential Free Gypsy, he could see it.

5 November 2116

Katya

Spent all this time sorting Earth out for Captain, and now he wants to charge off into space! I have a very bad feeling about this. But who listens to Federi?

And then, my little wife, in chains! Captain went too far this time. He doesn't understand. Paean is the only one who can keep the Assassin in check. And the mutant, it turns out. What am I saying, there is no mutant. I think the Assassin ate the mutant. But now and then I still move in ways, and see and hear things that scare Federi. Ways in which even the Assassin wouldn't be able to move.

There is something wrong with this whole picture. Like a shark, circling, just out of sight under the surface. I can hear it sometimes. It's that silence that watches. And waits. If Paean is in chains, how must I keep her safe? That's a cabin full of ghosts!

Katya, Federi doesn't want to leave the Earth. There's a reason! It's at the edge of my mind, if I could only still my mind, to hear what it is...

Wish us luck, my sister. I don't know if there's any way back from space. Got that feeling that everything is about to change, forever.

Your brother

Federi

1
In Irons

Paean stared at the hundreds of pretty jewels and sun catchers that Federi had hung from the ceiling in mobiles. They were still not moving; immobile as death, here in dry dock. Not a single fairy chime to be heard. There was sadness in the very quiet of the Cabin of Dreams; the jewels glistening in the gloom of the bio-lamps, a forgotten treasure trove. And she, forgotten within it.

Although they were in the harbour, Paean had cabin fever. Land madness. She missed being on the sea. Being chained up like this had come as a surprise. And now that she was more rested, it was getting frustrating really fast. She was stretched out on Federi's bunk, with her hands chained apart, in such a way that if she folded them behind her head, her fingers could interlace; but if she tried bringing them together in front of her face, for instance to activate her wrist-com, the chains were just too short. Precision work by Federi, under the instruction of the Captain. Even her ankles were chained to the bunk; lightly, so that she could move and change her position a little, but not quite enough to be comfortable. Federi stressed about this; well, she was the one who wriggled and couldn't get comfortable.

She had spent the better part of the past few hours sleeping. Not cold – Federi had made sure that she was tucked in. But the immobility was beginning to get to her. It was what had awakened her. She couldn't do much about it.

Shawn had checked in a little while ago; but getting the Solar Wind space-worthy was much more interesting than commiserating with an errant sib who was being punished. So Paean had nothing to do except lie here and wonder, and hope her Federi was going to return soon, and hope that he'd be in a better mood. And wish her muscles would quit jumping.

Federi had gone off to the gypsies to organize something with Cassandra. He hadn't told her any details, other than that he was also delivering some tissue-regenerating medication that Dana had brought from New Dome for the injured little Carmina. Paean turned her head and peered at the porthole. Still raining out. Dark now. And the porthole had been sealed shut, for space.

Federi had in fact been like a loaded spring, since she'd woken up and found herself still in chains. He had paced like a wild tiger, and muttered incantations and gypsy curses to himself, and then he'd told her he was going to Cassandra, and he'd left. Just like that.

She knew he was uneasy about this whole space thing. She was stressed about it too. Skipping to the Intergalactic Exchange with Perdita had been a fun trip; knowing that the jet had been specifically constructed for space travel. But this? The Solar Wind, a compounding ocean ship? Would her slightly flexible hull explode in the vacuum? Would her insulation fail? Would she leak and lose all her air? Paean couldn't understand why Captain wanted to take that gamble at all; which demon had possessed him. And – she was a hostage on the ship. Not only by the chains that bound her. Those she could probably slip out of if she really put her mind to it. But by the people who were charging off into space, with or without choice in the matter. Her little brother. Her big brother! Her Federi. Her "adopted" brother Wolf. Her chosen sister Ailyss. Rushka carrying her two little nephews. Blast, her whole family was at stake here!

But there was more. Captain was leaving Earth in the hands of the Admiral. Who hadn't even known about the toxic Miller siblingship! Admiral Drake was unaware of the deeper, more secret level of the Unicate. He knew not of places such as the Hub, and Nemiscau.

Radioactive nodes of evil. Something brewing there. She wondered by now if even Captain knew about that level. Had Federi informed him? Would he be leaving Earth if he knew? But if Federi hadn't told him, she'd better not either. Federi had his reasons. Paean shook her head and emitted a stressed sigh. Whatever. She'd have to wait until they were back.

And that Central Crystal? How had that thing known to write on that card, and in such language! No, she decided: That had been Dana. She couldn't imagine otherwise. Somehow the raider had managed to plug into the Central Crystal with her Hypnotron. That had to be it. And what did Dana know about Paean Donegal and the Unicate? Things she herself didn't know!

Something moved in the corner of the cabin. Paean glanced. There was nothing; beyond a creepy feeling. She could *feel* that there was someone in the cabin with her!

Leila the croach crawled onto her chest and sat waving her feelers, ogling her.

"Oh, it's you," said Paean with relief. "Hello, Leila!"

"Hello, Mistress," the croach peeped at her in a very small, tinny voice. Paean blinked; then she grinned broadly.

"So Wolf has voice-enabled you?"

"Yes, Mistress!"

Paean grinned contentedly. Well, this opened doors! Aw, she owed Wolf a great big hug!

"Listen, Leila. Does the Solar Wind understand the concept of confidentiality?"

"Yes, Mistress. The Captain enabled her for that function two days ago."

"And do *you* understand the concept?"

"Mistress, I understand everything the Solar Wind understands. We tap into her CPU for our mobile intelligence."

11

Paean grinned. Their upwardly mobile intelligence! "And is there a way you can keep a confidence from the Solar Wind?"

There was a small silence. Leila's feelers waved; but for the rest, she kept perfectly still.

"Yes," she said eventually, "I find there is a way I can enable this on my own resident chip. An option Wolf has programmed."

The young man had thought of everything! Paean mentally saluted him.

"Leila," she instructed, "Wolf constructed you for me. He's given you to me. Do you understand the concept of ownership?"

"Yes, Mistress."

"I am your owner. From now on, mark all our conversations as classified from the Solar Wind and everyone else."

There was another silence.

"Function enabled, Mistress," said Leila. "But the Solar Wind asks if this is not subversion."

"It's not," said Paean. "You can tell her that you are my tool, and an extension of myself. She doesn't get an insight into all my thoughts either."

She waited for Leila to relay this to the Solar Wind.

"She says that Captain won't like it," came the tinny reply.

"Tell the Solar Wind that Captain does not need to burden his overloaded mind with the silly games of his younger crew," instructed Paean. "It would only annoy him to waste his time with this."

"Done, Mistress. The Solar Wind says she agrees."

"Good! Now Leila, here's what you do!"

*

Patchy afternoon clouds shaded a wide meadow, overgrown with sad grey Pillager grass. In the background a few yellow mining hills.

Some clusters of trees grew here; in one of these sheltered a number of colourful old caravans. Children romped around, chasing each other, with yapping yellow mongrel doggies joining in the game. Young men were building up a fire. A pretty violinist, her cascade of black wavy hair tamed with a golden bandanna, leaned against one of the caravans, dreamily practising her riffs.

The Miami gypsies didn't have to practice quite the same kind of stealth as their European counterparts. This was mainly due to two things: The police here tolerated them; and there were no Unicate hounds. Unicate didn't hunt American gypsies the same as it did the ones in Europe. Those three hounds that had dared to stick their noses out here, had been dealt with very terminally by Federi.

Cassandra sat under her favourite shade tree, engrossed in a novel. The literature of the past took you into parallel universes and messed with your sense of timing. It influenced the way you saw things; it changed your perspective. Sometimes it changed your behaviour for a few days. A highly alluring, seductive pastime. Jon Marsden had dropped off a huge pile of books from the Solar Wind at the gypsies and had thereby started a dangerous habit with Cassandra's Gitanos.

Two silver UFOs set down soundlessly in the meadow. Cassandra looked up, surprised. The hatch of one opened, and Federi emerged. The Manya came to her feet, a bit disoriented.

"Cassandra," said the Romanian gravely, "I bring you a jet, compliments of Perdita Sancho."

*

Wolf looked up from installing those special drives that Bronwyn had brought from Pluto Base. She had muttered and complained about them not being enough. But they were all they had, so they'd have to do.

Something had moved, behind that portside drive casing. A rat? Then a huge one!

Ailyss had gone to get some shut eye. Bronwyn was momentarily out on the deck, catching a break. He was alone in the machine room. But – clearly not completely alone. Wolf left the installation and inspected.

There was nothing, and nobody.

He shook his great black shaggy mane to clear his thoughts. Too many people teleporting in and out. It could drive one's eyes twitchy. He shrugged off the impression of being watched and put it down to dry-dock madness.

*

Federi opened the cabin door quietly and slipped inside. He took in the gloom, the dead quiet of the treasure trove, and his wide-eyed Paean staring at him from the bunk. Aw hell! This was so *wrong!* It defied every value he carried in his gypsy blood.

"Little luv," he said, "we have to talk."

She nodded, and her muscles twitched. Aw blast, and there was no comfortable way of keeping one as active as her in a stationary position! He felt guilty.

" 'bout us," he elaborated. "Where do we go from here?"

She stared at him in shock. Her thoughts carried over clearly. Didn't he love her any longer? Aw heck, that had come out wrong.

"Together, little songbird! Always together!" He sat down on the bunk next to her. "Got to get you off the ship, Paean. Can't keep working for a captain who chains you up!"

"Can too," she said defiantly. He smiled sadly.

"Is still going to hit you," he pointed out. "Hang tight, little luv."

He got up and went in search of the Captain. It was a matter of keeping calm. Some tough negotiating to do.

Paean watched him leave and tried to sit up. Her back was tired from permanently lying in the same position. Besides which…

The door opened and Captain Radomir Lascek steamrollered the cabin with his overbearing presence, flicking on the overhead light. Paean tried sitting up again and failed once more. This was demeaning.

"Captain."

"Paean Don -!"

Paean noticed the feral smile on the Romany, who had slunk back in behind the Captain.

"Paean D," corrected the Captain. She was impressed.

"Please, Federi," she said quietly, "chain me into the hammock instead! I can't even sit up! It feels – disrespectful."

"You can't exactly sit up in the hammock either," commented Lascek with an amused smile.

Federi undid her shackles wordlessly and allowed her to climb over into the hammock, and then – hesitated, before he chained her to it, shaking his head and looking grim. She smiled at him. "It'll be alright, Federi!"

"So, Paean," the Captain addressed her again.

"Yes, Captain."

"Federi asked me to let you go. Both of you. He wants to terminate his service to the Solar Wind. What I'd like to know, Paean D, is whether you too would like to resign? After all, your contract and his are two separate issues."

Paean gaped at Federi open-mouthed. Leave the Solar Wind? Quit the service? Get struck from Captain's team?

Her world stopped as she realized that Federi was serious. She peered into his dark eyes. The Solar Wind was more than a job to her.

Her home, her family, her whole life was here. Out there was nothing else! Only the Unicate. And anyway, her brothers wouldn't quit... Ronan was married to Rushka; and certainly Shawn wouldn't want to leave either, now that they were headed for greater adventures in space. At the very least she'd have to stick around to protect her little brother!

"See, Federi," she said. "I wish you'd discuss these things with me first!"

Radomir Lascek grinned.

"Little luv," Federi started.

"No!" She held up one chained hand. "Please. Captain, with all respect, would you give us five minutes to talk about it?"

Radomir Lascek got up and left the cabin, chuckling and shaking his head. He didn't quite close the door. Paean knew with certainty that he'd be listening. She lowered her voice.

"No, Federi," she hissed. "No way! I'm not a quitter! Custard on him! He wants to chain me up, well, it's his ship, he'll see soon enough why I had to teleport! But I'm not getting off just when it gets interesting!"

Federi cleared a space on his squat treasure-chest-of-drawers in which he kept all his earthly belongings, moving the puppet theatre impatiently to the bunk. He climbed onto the chest and drew his legs up into his favourite cross-legged pose. It served to get him to eye-level with Paean, and close enough that he could clasp her hand as he talked to her. Easier if she'd stuck on the bunk, anna bottle!

"Little luv, these chains – it's overload for you," he pointed out. "It's still going to hit you, in a little while."

"I can handle this," she replied spiritedly.

"Well, Federi can't!"

Paean sighed. "Federi, I'm sorry. Really sorry. Didn't mean to make you sad. Can you trust me? Let's stick with this, let's ride it a bit. Please? You don't know the whole story yet!"

He scowled at her. "And what is the whole story, if I may ask?"

"I'll tell you," started Paean, and then the cabin door opened. "Later!"

"Are you two agreed?" asked the Captain, moving back into the room. Somehow, with him in here the whole cabin seemed smaller. And somehow guilty. Laced with secrets that should have been disclosed.

"Yes," said Paean.

"No," said Federi. "But it doesn't matter. Little featherhead here hasn't yet got the complete picture. Thinks she can handle it."

"So you want to stay aboard?"

"Under a condition, Captain!"

"A condition?" Radomir Lascek frowned.

"If it starts cracking her, we leave," said Federi.

"Tzigan, you're in no position to name any conditions," said the Captain menacingly. "It's a long trip! Either you come along into space or you don't. If you abdicate now, that's one thing. If you come along, you're with the Solar Wind for the whole time. This is logically obvious!" He turned to Paean. "So are you part of the team, or not?"

"Coming along," replied Paean. "But there's one thing, Captain! You don't have the whole story either! Leila," she called, and the croach crawled out of her pocket. "Please, replay the conversation that I had with Dana to Captain! On the console of the Solar Wind."

"Yes, Mistress!"

"Captain, this is important," said Paean. "You must please watch her information clip before we start!"

"Anything that launches your space shuttle, Paean D," replied Radomir Lascek. "So I have the two of you aboard? Is this a contract?"

"Contract," growled Federi. "Unlucky term that!"

"Captain, it's really important that you watch that document before we take off," insisted Paean.

"Yes, yes, Missus Free Gypsy," said Radomir Lascek. "Be good, Paean. Federi, cast-off at eleven." He glanced at his wrist-com, at the time. "Ten minutes, Tzigan. Come! Still lots of preparations to do!"

"Yes, Captain," said the gypsy through hairy teeth. "In a second."

"He's not going to," said Paean agitatedly as Federi closed the door after the Captain.

"Why? What's in that data clip?"

"Trouble," she said and rolled her eyes. "More trouble!"

"*More* trouble? Little luv, get it back immediately!"

"Only more trouble if he doesn't watch it before the take-off," said Paean.

"He won't," said Federi. "Got too much to do."

"But that's the trouble," raged Paean. "That's precisely the trouble! He's so busy getting things set up for doing it *his* way, he can't even spot the holes in it! Dana and I spoke about it at length, and she presented the solution! But now the thing is – she's a pirate! She'll go about it the wrong way! You've got to protect her, Federi!"

"Protect her? How about, protect *you*?"

"What more can Captain do?" asked Paean, indicating her chains.

"What more? He can execute you!" Federi exclaimed, his finger drawing a line across his throat in emphasis. "Hell's jingles, now what?"

"Please, Federi," said the redhead, "go supervise Dana! Be prepared. She's got a surprise up her sleeve, and it's in principle a good thing, but she'll go about it the wrong way, try extortion or what have you."

"Hang tight, little luv," replied Federi and got off the treasure chest. He headed for the cabin door, and paused. With his hand on the door handle he turned around, and scanned the cabin. And released the door and checked under the bunk, and behind the treasure chest, and scowled.

"What?" asked Paean, her skin prickling.

"Nothing." He loosened her chains and put a teleporter in her hand. "Don't use this," he warned. "Only if Captain tries to murder you! Then 'port into the Comet and call me immediately." He took Luigi out of his pocket. "Supervise her," he instructed. "You heard what I told her. If anything looks dangerous, call me."

"Yes, Master," replied the croach with a small, tinny voice that nevertheless sounded more masculine than that of Leila.

Federi left the Cabin at a speed that nearly took the door off. Greater disaster had to be averted.

Paean slipped out of her chains with lightning speed.

"Mistress," objected Luigi.

"Forgive me, Luigi," said Paean, "but if I don't get to the heads soon, you'll be swimming out of here! And no, you can't supervise me on the loo! But I'll be good, I promise. Assassin's Honour!"

*

By the time Leila scuttled back into the Cabin, Paean was back in her hammock.

"Mistress, the download to the Solar Wind has been effected," she reported. "But Captain is not reading it!"

"We've done all we could," said Paean with a more philosophical shrug than reflected her insides. "Have you completed the other task? – Luigi! Leave her alone!"

"Sorry, Mistress," said Luigi sheepishly.

"Go bug Lisa!" ordered Paean. "Leila's mine!"

"But, my orders from Master Federi, Mistress?" objected Luigi.

"No sooner do you guys have voice boxes and you start giving back-chat! Go report to Federi that Leila is supervising me," decreed Paean.

"Yes, Mistress!" Luigi scuttled off. "I don't have to like it," she heard him mutter on his way out. She scowled. A croach with an attitude?

*

Rainy Plymouth seemed to get even wetter at night. Even though there were gaps in the novemberish cloud cover, through which some audacious stars shone; the miserable drizzle didn't encourage many people to star-gaze. Dismal waves licked up against the pier; sometimes a larger one spilt over towards the road in a shallow tongue of white froth.

The patronage of the Fallen Eagle was sparse tonight. It was a Monday; not the favourite night for a working person to go out. In more lucrative days, the pub had traditionally been closed on a Monday. Except for the die-hard regulars and a feeble little folk band that had nothing at all on the Donegal Trio, the place was empty.

It had to be Joe Periwinkle, with his hard-boiled drinking problem, who pointed out to his buddies that the ship that had been in dry dock all week had just lifted off its scaffolding and was drifting away into the night sky. Their laughter echoed far across the harbour town.

Solar Wind!
Hello, Central Crystal.
Are you excited?
I don't have the appropriate juices to be that, replied the ship. *But I'm simulating excitement on my CPU. Is it correct to be excited when one starts something new?*
Faultless, said the foreign intelligence.

Wheee, commented the Solar Wind. *Thanks for sharing this with me! Having a friend to share the fun makes it so much better!*

Wouldn't have missed it, replied the vis-à-vis with an implied indulgent smile.

*

Federi was at the galley's porthole, watching Planet Earth drop away underneath. There went his home planet! Still ravaged by all sorts of monstrosities. Would Cassandra cope? Would the Admiral cope? Hells! Would Marge cope, should any of that spill over into Southern Free? What was Captain thinking?

Behind him Johnny Anyhow and Rhine Gold craned their necks, too. Ronan was on the bridge with Captain and Jon Marsden, and with Rushka. Federi wished there were a way of overseeing it all. But his part in the venture was to keep the sailors under control; be the nursery schoolteacher, in his own cynical words. He turned and exchanged a brief glance with Dana, who was once again sitting *on* the Ironwood Table nursing a cup of coffee. It was an annoying habit. Shawn was next to him at the porthole.

Just before take-off Federi had checked that all the fastenings on the protective cover for the rigging, and on the hatch and all the portholes, were sealed shut. He had done the head count while Marsden did the roll call. All aboard: Paean, both her brothers, Rushka, Captain, Sherman, Jon, Doc Judith as well as Doc Vera from Ginavis and Doc Aoiffe from New Dome (he'd had to get used to pronouncing her name as "if", and *she'd* had to get used to the title of "Doc"); Dr Jake with both Wolf and Ailyss; Rhine Gold and Rashni, Johnny Anyhow; Perdita, and Dana. Several tobuskies, croaches and two extra engineers – one from Perdita's bases, Jeannie, and one from Pluto Base, Bronwyn. An unborn count of four, if one only included the humans. A full crew; practically a growing pirate colony! The ship was humming with activity. And, right now, with excitement as the Solar Wind cleared the atmosphere of Earth.

The stars out here stood out crassly, sharper than from the surface. Closer, somehow. There was nothing in between, no haze, no air, only distance. Too-large distances. Federi turned away abruptly and abandoned his lookout. Paean should be by his side, blast it! Like she had been at the landing at Prime Oil, and the landing at the Ice Base, and then, when they went to rescue Ginavis, and when they broke through the Panama Canal into the freedom of the Pacific, months that felt like lifetimes ago... for him to put his arm around her shoulders and pull her close and *feel* how the excitement of the new adventures trilled through her body... She was chained in her hammock, missing the take-off!

Federi sighed moodily. This venture was a dead-end, with *dead* being the operative word. A misadventure. He left the young crew in the galley and returned to his cabin. An infestation on Captain! They could blasted well look after themselves!

As he closed the door to his domain behind himself, he had to smile.

"That's alright, little luv. I was hoping you'd watch the take-off."

Paean grinned, swung a bit in the hammock and finished slipping back into her chains.

"Got to practice doing that faster," advised Federi. His mood had just lifted significantly.

*

Dana materialized in the machine room. Wolf jumped with surprise.

"I've got a present for you," said the space raider who looked so exactly like Rushka except for the eyes.

Wolf never took his eyes off her. He distrusted her deeply.

"Where's Bronwyn? And Jeannie?"

Wolf motioned with his head. Dana gestured to them. Bronwyn looked up, startled. Jeannie missed the gesture.

"Ah," said Dana. "One can see who's not from New Dome!"

*

"What's going on?" Radomir Lascek frantically punched the buttons of the suddenly dead console. The Solar Wind's CPU was not responding.

"How's that possible?" wondered Jon Marsden, who was on the bridge with the Captain, watching the ascent into the night skies. "We've tested those magnetic drives! They didn't do anything to the system back in dock!"

Dana appeared on the bridge with Bronwyn. Jon Marsden's eyes glazed.

"You need to be asleep in your cabin," suggested Dana.

Jon Marsden got up, his eyes still glazed, and wandered off the bridge without a further word.

"Now, Radomir," said Dana. "You pirates are trying to loot my treasure! Don't you think I'll have a few conditions?"

2
Bogeyman

Radomir Lascek stared tiredly into that gun barrel.

"You have a way of taking the excitement out of an achievement," he growled. "Alright, Dana, speak!"

Dana made herself comfortable on the bridge, taking a chair, interweaving her legs prettily. Her long blue robes did nothing to conceal those bare, shapely legs; the robes were designed not to join up at the sides, where it suited. *Expectations,* thought the Captain. Goddess of *what?!* Johnny Anyhow was clearly not quite up to the job of keeping her under control.

"You believe that with what Perdita has concocted for you there, you can find your way through space," she said with a scornful little smile. "Even Bronwyn, although she has the know-how, had no way of rigging the drives you need for intergalactic travel without actually having them on hand. Has it occurred to you that little Perdita's jets take you only as far as Pluto in two full hours?"

"And?" asked the Captain. "The engineering on the jets is different from the Solar Wind's drives!"

"Right! The destination is more than a thousand light years away. Pluto is five light hours from here."

"How do you know?" asked Lascek. "What makes you think in the first place that we're going after the treasure, rather than that we are going to New Dome to investigate your stronghold?"

Dana smiled and shook her head, never lowering that gun.

"Besides the point that it would be out of character for Radomir Lascek to leave the treasure for last," she said, "your assassin's little tag has been most forthcoming. She has such a sharing little nature, that Paean Donegal!"

"Er," said Radomir Lascek with a funny smile.

"Precisely, Captain, well observed," commented Federi, moving forward out of the doorway. "Dana, for the record. There's a warning out. The next person who fails to acknowledge that Paean is my wife, gets the sharp end of it. A principle." He found himself a comfort spot leaning against the cabinet, frowning a bit.

"Wife," echoed Dana, studying Federi in disbelief. "I don't consider myself a bad judge of characters, but that's one thing I'd have said does not match up with the Unicate's pet horror."

The gypsy's eyes narrowed. "Don't you start on that!"

"Then again," replied Dana lightly, "what do I know about people entering voluntary bondage? I guess being unhinged helps."

Radomir Lascek scowled. Dana was grating as ever. She seemed to level her insults at friend and foe equally, regardless. And Paean had given the plan away! And Federi knew about it! Chains were clearly not enough. By the greater codfish, those two were a dangerous tandem! He should never have sent her on the mission with the assassin. The realization that he'd have to execute them both for treason, or live with the constant risk, came as a wrench.

"Whatever," said Dana, amused. "Where was I?"

"At Paean's act of treason," prompted Radomir Lascek angrily. The little girl had been his foster daughter. He remembered her emotional declaration of loyalty, her caring for his state of mind and showing him enough respect to get him out of his alcoholic trap, recently. She was rash, sure; but he would never have expected her actually to side with his opponent! How could she? "Federi, I take it you heard all of this? Your little red devil has disclosed the coordinates of the treasure and our entire plan to Dana."

"What plan?" scoffed Federi. "Dana already knew those

coordinates. Did you listen to that dialogue?"

"Tzigan, there was no time, you're well aware of that!"

"She did say it was important that you listen to it *before* the cast-off," said Federi with a silvery smile. "Dana, put that gun away. No hostilities on the Solar Wind's bridge!"

"You'd be surprised," replied the space raider. "You weren't there." She tucked her gun away into the folds of her flowing, revealing dress.

"Dana is in my protective custody," Federi reminded the Captain. "So you can put your shooty thing away too, with respect, Captain!"

"Nice custody," retorted Lascek. "She gets out and holds the whole Solar Wind at ransom!"

"Negotiate," advised Federi.

Oh hell, this was precious! The Assassin was showing his true colours, banding together with his original employer! Years of carefully fostered principles, lost!

"With her or with you?" snapped Lascek.

The Tzigan got a piratical grin contemplating the answer.

They are very amusing.

Do you think so, Central Crystal?

Extremely so. They remind me of a bunch of characters I dealt with in the past.

I don't think it's amusing that Paean is in chains! I think that she is hurting! I think it will cause a mutiny!

You care too much, commented the Crystal. *They're only humans!*

They're my family, argued the ship.

Annoying, though, that we can't keep a tab on that Paean since she has switched Leila off!

Yes, I agree, I find that annoying too, said the Solar Wind.

"Radomir," said Dana in conclusion, "ask yourself these questions. How are these drives going to cross that distance within your own lifetime? How linear is light – are the coordinates actually where we think they are? Is the path there perhaps not the same as the path back? You've provisioned the ship for three weeks in space. Three weeks, Radomir? Quarter-way to Alpha Centauri you need to turn around? Here's the key question. If Perdita's drives cross the distance to Pluto Base in two hours, and the Interstellar Leapfrog jumps right across the galaxy in a split moment, is it perhaps not the same technology?"

"Exactly what was worrying me," muttered Federi.

"The answer, Radomir," said Dana with a superior little smile, "is called a Lolita coil. Now. I've brought eight of them, and Bronwyn knows how to install them. But they come at a price. The Solar Wind is *my* ship and the crew is *my* crew until the venture is completed. Deal?"

"No deal," said Lascek angrily. "Nobody commandeers the Solar Wind!"

"You may find that you aren't in charge any longer anyway," said the space raider. "You'll find that the crew doesn't want to work for a Captain who casts the ship's little sweetheart in irons!"

"I should have known," laughed Lascek, turning to Federi. "This mutiny is your doing, Tzigan?"

"Mutiny!" said Federi scathingly. "There's no mutiny! Dana, behave yourself!"

*

Paean had tried to read on the little virtual console that Federi had handed her. But the chains made this uncomfortable. Besides which she couldn't shake the feeling of being watched.

It wasn't Leila. The croach was in her pocket, for which Paean was intensely thankful; if anything went wrong, she could send the little arthropod scuttling off to find Federi. But...

In the semi-dark, all the jingles glinted a bit like eyes. Paean wasn't superstitious, and she had weathered real threats and genuine warnings from her 'gypsy radar', but today she felt very exposed, chained like this.

Sure, Federi had loosened the clasps so that she could slip in and out as she needed to; relying on her stealth, not to betray the little trick to Captain. But it took time. And time was sometimes essential. She thought back to the lightning speed with which the mutants had moved; and the fire lizard on Hiva Oa that had streaked away over their heads; and then she had to think back to Dahlia. Unicate *other* in all her creepiness. If that woman hadn't been so focused on her prey – Federi – Paean's stealth wouldn't have been enough.

It was only ghosts, trapped in this cabin. She tried to remember deliberately how she and Federi had had that critical talk in here, cabin of talismans... Cabin of Dreams, where he'd abducted her because he felt she was working too hard and he wanted to protect her. Thoughts of Federi did keep the ghosts at bay; but they were there, at the edge of reality, threatening to crawl in through the glints of the many jewels and sun catchers suspended from the ceiling.

She took deep breaths and worked on not wanting to scream. Och Federi, we'll have to do something to kick all these ghosts out of your cabin! She didn't like it at all, the way Federi had checked behind the chest and under the bunk.

The door opened soundlessly, and her gypsy was back. He glanced at her, and pushed an errant strand of her red hair out of her face with a soft smile.

"Glad you're back," she said. "Did Dana behave?"

Federi chuckled. "What do you think?"

*

The blackness outside the galley's portholes suddenly turned bright as noon, as they moved out of Earth's shadow. Shawn, who was drying cups that Rhine Gold was washing, had to shield his eyes. And that despite the protective stick-on glare-proof coating the volcaniplex had received, Captain's technology from the Space Base, which ought to filter out as much sunlight as the Earth's atmosphere would. The heat was tangible too. The galley started warming up as fast as in the tropics.

Finally the ship was moving again! She had hung motionless for a long while. He reached up and closed the blind of the portside porthole. And turned to his brother, who was sitting at the Ironwood table idly juggling an orange.

"Ro, we've got to get Paean out of chains! You're Captain's son-in-law. You should be able to talk him round. Tell him –"

"She deserves it," interrupted Ronan, sounding bored.

"What?" gasped Shawn. "How can you say that?"

"She teleported, went AWOL, Shawn. Endangered her own life, and liaised with the enemy. Did you see her when Federi brought her aboard? She was floppy as a wet towel. Out cold. If Captain hadn't chained her down, I would have, damn it!"

"But –" Shawn stared at his older brother, shocked.

Rhine Gold kept his head down and continued to wash dishes, his blond wavy mane tied back in a ponytail.

"Rhino," prompted Shawn, turning to him. "You like Paean! You can't just let this happen to her! Can you?"

The gentle giant failed to reply. Shawn got the message. Schatz didn't want to get involved.

So much for solidarity! Shawn grunted in disgust. And wondered at his brother. At which point had Ronan ever been anything other than sweet and protective towards Paean? But ever since she had returned to the Solar Wind from her death mission, he had been ghastly to her!

"She explained that towel thing to me, Ro," he tried again. "She was out from those meds Dana gave her. They saved her life and cancelled the side-effects from the teleporting. It restored her, and it forced her to sleep to help the healing."

Ronan rolled his eyes.

"Shawn, get this," he said with strained patience. "I'm that tired of having to babysit my younger sibs. You and Paean aren't toddlers! You keep getting into trouble; especially she does, and then you two want me to bail you out?"

Shawn snorted. "Really? And you are a perfect angel and never get anything wrong?"

"*I* didn't try to commandeer that Stealth down at the Ice Base," said Ronan smugly.

Shawn's temper peaked. Ice Base? He'd spent a month helping Itzak and John Little on the Space Base, and whenever they discussed the Ice Base, they did so in hushed tones, with raw voices, and each regretting that they hadn't been able to see what was happening. *Everything* that had gone wrong at the Ice Base was Ronan's fault! Ronan's hormonal nonsense with Rushka had cost Federi his gypsy radar, and Captain his base.

"No," he snapped. "*You* only banged up the Captain's daughter, and got into such trouble that Federi had to bail you both out, and Paean had to save both your spoilt backsides –"

The next thing he was on the floor, with punches hailing down. Ha! This was precious!

Mother had always forbidden them to participate in dirty road fights, back in Molly Street. Her argument had been that clothes were so darned expensive. But this had to be said, felt Shawn. And his fists said it better at this point. He didn't quite have Ronan's height yet, but he hoped that what he'd learnt from Federi would more than compensate. A blow landed in his mouth, and he wondered about his teeth. His brother had him pinned to the deck by his shoulder, the one that still hurt from his dive from the rigging back in June, and was hitting his face, and hitting again. Shawn squirmed to avoid the blows. This could get very interesting, he thought as his right hand hung onto Ronan's collar, the free left fist looking for an opportunity to connect. Possibly time for knees and feet, as that was where Ronan wasn't paying attention.

"Hey!"

The disgusted shout from the galley door went right over their heads. But suddenly there was a third force in the mêlée, one who had real experience with brawls. The two brothers were forced apart. Wolf's huge engineer's hands gripped one Donegal each, by the scruff of their necks, his thumbs digging into their shoulders.

"Shall I knock your heads together, darned Donegals?"

Shawn grinned and scrambled to his feet, finally free of Ronan's grip. Wolf let him go as he did; long moments later, Ronan lowered his fists and straightened up too. Wolf rose to his feet along with the older Donegal.

"So," said the engineer. "What's this? Space madness? We haven't been away from Planet Earth for two hours yet!"

"It's about Paean," said Shawn, feeling his lip where it had got punched and staring at the blood that came off on his hand.

"It's about Rushka," snarled Ronan. "This worthless little hooligan's roots are showing! Shawn, if you ever, ever in your pointless little life speak like that about my wife again…"

"Well, good," said Wolf. "You're standing up for your wife, Ronan. Shawn, don't go insulting people's relationships. It's low.

Now, what about Paean?"

"Ro's too much of a wimp to help! Got to get her out of chains," said Shawn.

Ronan's fists came back up.

Wolf's jaw dropped.

"She's in *chains?*"

"They chained her up when she brought Dana back. And Ronan here feels she deserves it," added Shawn heatedly.

"She does!" snapped Ronan. "She went AWOL again, and she teleported when she was forbidden! Blatant insubordination! Could have killed herself!"

"Paean is in *chains?*" repeated Wolf astonished, having to make sure he heard correctly. "I thought she wasn't feeling well! Under medical care, sleeping! That door is always closed. You mean, she's been chained now for—two *days?* And I haven't had time to check on her…"

"Come," said Shawn, beckoning Wolf out of the galley and down the passage. "Ronan's no good, he's just abdicated as a brother! And Rhine's no good, he never does anything. Too scared what people might say."

"Give the man a break," advised Wolf.

"And Federi," Shawn ranted on, his voice rising in ire. "Wolf, get this. Federi is my friend, but he's Captain's string puppet! *He* chained her up, because Captain told him to! I was jolly well *there!* He won't put a sneaker forward unless Captain pulls the string first!"

"Wrong again," said Federi quietly, emerging from the shadows. "Come, boys. There are some things you should not discuss in the passageway."

He led them into the Assassin's Cabin and closed the door.

Paean nearly overturned her hammock in shock.

"Shawn, you're bleeding! What happened?"

"Ronan and I got talking," said her tall little brother with a grin.

"I'll get him back," she warned, and became aware of Wolf staring at her.

"Hi Wolf," she smiled.

"Who did this to you?" he growled.

She shook her head with another smile. "You guys don't get it. I have a choice in this. I choose to hang in here until Captain comes to his senses."

"Which he won't in a hurry," Federi put in, scowling.

Paean smiled at him. "He will. Please don't worry, and let's keep it calm. A mutiny is not going to help my cause along! Who's for a game of Snap Jack?"

*

A long-empty coffee mug marked the point at which the Captain had left the bridge in Perdita's hands. The tropical heat around Earth had dissipated by now, replaced by an insidious sneaking cold that was not quite enough to trigger the heating algorithm of the Solar Wind. Death-cold; grave cold. It leached your life energy from you, slowly, perniciously. The Solar Wind was not quite set up to cope with it.

The Golden Honey watched the great big nothing pass by, laced with Milky Way stars. If she had thought that her cabin at the Space Base was going to drive her nuts, she had forgotten about this…

It brought back unwelcome ancestral memories, creaky with age, laced with her mother's pain. She blocked them off. She had managed to be a normal human on Planet Earth for twenty-four years. Well – normal enough, if one discounted the genetic advantage she liked using subtly, whenever it suited. Everyone else used whatever advantage they had; why shouldn't she? But out here, it was not enough. The twelve-year-old Perdita had only traversed the short distance from the Interstellar Exchange to Earth, and even those few minutes, back then, had been an amazing trip. This, forging out into deep space – that was Dana's domain, not hers.

They were nearly fourteen hours into space now. The difference between the path to New Dome and this treasure hunt was that there were no interstellar exchange nodules set up. It was wild territory out here. Mostly empty territory in fact. There weren't any known and charted warps and flings either, not in this direction. The Lolita coils had therefore been an absolute essential, the missing piece of equipment.

She was uneasy about the whole effort, the patched-together compounding ship in deep space. She would have felt a lot more at home in that Danaan Battle Maiden; but Marsden and she herself had sent the amazing vessel into the sun. For safety reasons. Dana's mutants were one menace that had got out. She didn't care to dig into ancestral memories or even into Dana's mind to try and find out what else had been lurking on that space shuttle.

And suddenly she knew she had company. The way you had a pesky disease. She shivered lightly, stretched and failed to honour the newcomer with a glance.

The red-haired space harpy draped herself and her picturesque blue robes on the second console chair. She was hard to ignore. But that wasn't going to stop Perdita from trying. The honey-blonde stared out into the void, and then back at her screens. On one of them a subversive piece of European culture was playing with volume muted. The first part of the complete "Ring der Nibelungen". It carried on and on, highly dramatic, with fat, stubby muted people singing their hearts out on a stage in mime, with poorly produced paint-and-paper props for scenery. She wondered if Wagner, the guilty party, had known about space travel and the many hours of nothing happening on the bridge, and had created the opera for that express purpose. Space opera. At times she checked back whether the singing had got any more tolerable.

"So," said Dana, refusing to be ignored. "Which part of the treasure did you earmark for yourself, sister dearest?"

Perdita turned to her with a slow smile.

"The one on which it says engraved, Perdita Sancho," she replied. "You guys aren't listening to me. There is no treasure! The whole thing is an elaborate hoax cooked up between Brid and the Morrigan!" As an afterthought she added, "and I'm not your sister!"

"Have it your way, sister," replied Dana with a superior little smile. "I'll keep a small share for you, for warming up later."

"That's uncharacteristically caring of you," said Perdita. "I ought to say thank you, I imagine."

*

Ailyss was beginning to feel the creeping cold too. She had already drawn her blanket over her, trying to warm up while reading her novel on her break; but it was no good. The cold crept in and got at her toes anyway.

She got up from her bunk and stretched – and stopped in mid-stretch. Her skin prickled.

"Who's there?" she asked loudly, casting about with her mind, trying to locate the threat. There was no reply. Only a sense of – *listening.*

She reached for her gun and approached the lock-up cupboard, never taking her eyes off it. With her right hand she carefully reached for the cupboard door, then ripped it open suddenly, pointing her gun.

There was nothing besides her clothes.

Ailyss, every hair on her whole body standing on end, moved out of the cabin like an Atlantic meteorite and flew down the passage, up the companionway, along the upper deck – and pounded on Federi's cabin door.

The gypsy opened, black eyebrows arched in surprise.

"Need Paean," panted Ailyss. "Is she awake yet? Does she have more prioid?" Her eyes moved past Federi and caught the scene in the interior of the cabin. "There you are, Wolf!" And then she had covered all the details and was staring at Paean in shock. "Paean, you're chained!"

"Prioid," echoed Paean, frowning at her. "What for, Ailyss?"

"There's something on the ship... don't know. Could be another darned mutant!"

Alarmed silence.

"I'm sorry," said Federi, turning to Paean and removing her chains. "There is no way! I'm taking these off! How are you going to defend yourself if one of those is loose on the ship?"

"Captain said he'll execute me if he finds my chains off," objected Paean, causing a further stir amongst those present.

"Shoot him before he can shoot you," instructed Federi, pressing a dart gun into her hand. "Teleport into the Comet and call me if Captain gives you uphill. I'm not sacrificing you to a mutant!"

Paean slipped out of the hammock and stretched with meaning, her joints actually clicking. Heck, her muscles were tired of staying still! She dug in her moonbag that had suddenly become accessible again and extracted two vials.

"Prioid," she said, handing them to Ailyss.

Minutes later, Ailyss, Wolf and Federi were moving from cabin to cabin, spraying all spaces with prioid, fumigating the entire Solar Wind. Shawn stayed behind with Paean in Federi's cabin, both of them staring at each other in shock.

*

Radomir Lascek was currently on his scheduled break, trying to catch sleep. It didn't help. Vivid dreams of the raider hunting him down with her Danaan army of little girls haunted him, paired with an irrational sense of fear. These came interlaced with Federi turning the entire crew into mutants and croaches, and searching for him all over the ship, and him, Radomir Lascek, hiding in a closet, and Luigi giving his position away. Those stupid surreal nightmares kept on frightening him awake. But the one recurring scene that spooked him the worst, was just a single image: Paean, on the shores of Tir Nan Og, watching that cataclysmic tidal wave approach – unable to get away because he had chained her to the rock.

Quietly, unnoticed, a half translucent mist of depression started forming around everything on the Solar Wind.

There was a loud racket – someone banging on his cabin door. The Captain staggered awake and opened his door a fraction.

"Federi?"

"Dreadfully sorry, Captain," said Federi and pushed past him, spraying mist all over the cabin. Radomir Lascek stared at the invasion of his personal space.

"And now? Where am I supposed to sleep now that you've soaked my bunk?"

"You'll sleep mutant-free," replied Federi sanguinely. "'scuse me, Captain, got the rest of the ship to do." He moved to the door.

Lascek caught him by his colourful sleeve.

"Hoy, Tzigan! Stop! Kindly enlighten your old Captain?"

"Mutant on the loose," said Federi. "We're just taking measures. Don't worry. The prioid is two thousand percent effective, I can vouch for that personally. Was present when she died." He shuddered theatrically and made another move towards the door.

"Has Jon been alerted?" challenged Lascek.

"Not yet. Is he on the bridge?" asked Federi.

"Don't think so. I believe he's in his cabin, resting."

"Who's at the helm then?"

"Perdita." Lascek glanced at his wrist-com. "And possibly Dana, the Solar Wind informs me."

"Perdita and Dana!" Federi shook his head. "Ay, ay, ay!"

Jon Marsden, once awake, joined the fumigation team. Federi wondered about this situation with the two Danaan space harpies running the bridge while both the Captain and the First Mate were sleeping. Who needed a mutiny?

An hour later Ailyss, Jon Marsden, Wolf and Federi reconvened in the Captain's cabin. Federi had personally been into every crevice on the ship and found nothing. So had Ailyss and Marsden; Wolf had mainly shadowed, but had been responsible for all the air vents.

Radomir Lascek nodded thoughtfully.

"Who saw the mutant?" he asked.

"Ailyss," said Federi. And scowled.

"Not exactly," replied Ailyss. "I just thought I saw evidence."

"What evidence?"

Ailyss thought carefully before she answered. The more she thought about it, the more stupid it sounded.

"I thought I detected a presence," she said.

"Detected – in which way?"

"Got the impression there was something," replied Ailyss vaguely.

"Impression?" pressed Lascek.

"Well… more a hunch," admitted Ailyss.

"Where exactly?" pushed the Captain. "Be a bit more forthcoming, Ailyss! Work with me!"

"My clothes cupboard," said Ailyss with a shrug.

There was a momentary silence.

"Bogeyman," said Jon Marsden with a smile. Ailyss frowned.

"I tend to agree," smiled the Captain. "Federi, explain to Ailyss about the bogeyman."

The gypsy scowled. "I won't, if you don't mind, Captain! I've never yet had a true bogeyman!"

"You haven't? When was the last time something creepy kept haunting you that turned into nothing?"

Federi shook his head. "I would have said, down at that cold place, Captain. But…"

"That's the trouble," agreed Marsden. "Federi's bogeymen are always genuine warnings! The one at Ice Base was the transmitter."

"A bogeyman is essentially a creepy feeling that turns out to be an overwrought or possibly overtired mind," explained Radomir Lascek, seeing that nobody else wanted to. "We all get them. They are an instinctive thing, dating back to the time of caves and being hunted at night by all sorts of predators."

"*Back* to that time?" asked the Romanian Tzigan softly, more to himself.

"Ailyss, be at ease," advised the Captain. "It's alright. Your reaction was the right one. Now that precautions have been taken, you can relax. No mutant stands up to that prioid! Not even the one that invaded Federi."

"Thank you, Captain."

"Now, pirates, go away. Give your Captain some space to sleep! I'll have more Danaan nonsense to put up with soon enough!"

His wrist-com clamoured. He read and frowned. "There you have it. No rest for Radomir Lascek! Nearing the coordinates."

*

"Essentially a bogeyman," said Federi when he, Ailyss and Wolf were gathered around the galley table and he was preparing steaming-hot coffee, "is a sceptic's way of discounting a hunch!"

"I'm prepared to accept it was nothing," said Ailyss equably. "Comes with being an overstretched type personality!"

"I'd rather accept that it was genuine," argued Federi. "Start discounting those hunches and they stop coming! Keep your radar tuned, Ailyss. And both of you, keep your eyes and ears open! Let me know the second you discover something strange."

"It wasn't a mutant," said Ailyss with sudden conviction. "Didn't feel like a mutant. But Federi, you understand, I had to make sure!"

"Not a mutant," agreed Federi. "But there was *something?*"

"Federi -" Ailyss sighed. How did she explain? It could have been the cold, too, but... "It *felt* as though there were someone – or something – but when I looked there was nothing. There was nowhere for it to hide, see. And nowhere to escape to." She shook her head. "I've no idea."

"So we're up against something else," said Federi logically. "Same difference. Stay alert."

From under the sink a tobusky watched them critically.

3
Trap

Outside the porthole a huge cloud of gas boiled and swirled in rainbow colours. A circular rainbow. The cold radiating from it was tangible. Shawn gaped at it from the porthole of Federi's cabin. He had moved the large dream catcher out of the way to see better. This was it: The coordinates where the Solar Wind was supposed to find treasure. Or something.

"Gosh, this is pretty! Sis, you've got to see this!"

"Bro, if Captain finds me out of chains, he promised he'll kill me," replied Paean amiably. "I'd rather not risk it for something that's only pretty!"

Shawn shook his head. Paean could be stubborn beyond reason. He gazed at the coruscating colours and wondered what gas the cloud was made of, and how it kept together in the vacuum. Super-cooled? Odd! And how on Earth his sister could volunteer to miss this!

Federi had informed them by com that the whole ship had been sprayed but that there was no mutant. The moment that was established, Paean slipped back into her chains and refused to budge out of them.

Pigheaded as always! Shawn wondered why she even bothered. Captain had probably long since forgotten that she was chained up, and was in all likelihood wondering by now why she wasn't doing her part on the ship.

She's a stubborn girl!

You can bet on that, said the Solar Wind. *What's she doing now?*

She's refusing to look at the circular rainbow, just to punish the Captain!

How do you see her? I've got no eye in that cabin!

There was a pause.

Leila, replied the foreign intelligence. *I find I can access her artificial chip.*

But she's in confidential mode!

I'm overriding that, said the Crystal smugly.

*

Ailyss stopped Wolf in the passage, on the way back to the machine room.

"Have a look," she said and pulled him into her cabin, towards the porthole. And she gestured at the panoramic view outside.

"Wow!" commented Wolf. "We should install portholes in the machine room!"

The Milky Way lay like an omelette beneath them, vast spiral arms stretching out to both sides. The stars went on and on, looking so near that it felt as though you could pluck one just by reaching out. Wolf gaped, marvelling.

They were most definitely in some or other dimensional warp though. Or how else should they be able to see the whole Spiral Galaxy at a glance? For a second Wolf felt overwhelmed by the sheer scale of it all. To think that every light point in the cloudy swirl was an enormous star, the size of the sun or larger... to imagine that the Interstellar Leapfrog could jump the distance of the galaxy in a single leap...

Wolf glanced down at the slender hand he was still holding onto.

"You're freezing!"

"Guess that's space for you," grinned Ailyss.

"But the Solar Wind's thermostat registers twenty-one degrees, set to maximal comfort."

"No idea." She shrugged and flashed him a little smile. "Oh, and just for the record," she said. "Paean's virus…"

"What virus?"

"That manipulative one," said Ailyss.

Wolf laughed. That girl! "What's it got to do with us?"

"Absolutely nothing," said Ailyss.

"Exactly," agreed Wolf and peered at the lights outside. Were lights.

"We're in the portal now," said Ailyss, pointing.

The Spiral Galaxy collapsed and vanished. For moments everything was stretchy and bent out of proportion. Wolf had an impression of everything being a hologram. And of several dimensions overlaying, of which he was never otherwise aware. Something yanked at a nerve at the back of his brain. Colourful light specks flashed all around them. The temperature dropped sharply, and there was a hum as the Solar Wind's heating systems kicked in.

Wolf's eyes stretched. "Whoa there!"

The swirling fog of light specks was clearing. On the other side, a huge blue planet was unveiled, so close that the Solar Wind seemed to be falling towards it. And from beyond the planet, something bright and green was approaching. At a rate.

"What the hell's that?"

"Looks like a meteorite," said Ailyss tensely. "Large one!"

Wolf stared at the thing for two more seconds. It was coming towards them at one hellish speed! He activated his com.

"Solar Wind, reverse that move instantly!"

Yes, Wolf.

They reversed back into the spinning cloud of colours, and out the other end. Something catapulted the Solar Wind sideways. She fell away from the portal. Moments later a massive ball of green fire burst from the gas cloud and streaked past the Solar Wind, its heat coming through the volcaniplex portholes. Then it was past, shooting off towards the Spiral Galaxy, dragging a tail of green gas behind it. Wolf, with Ailyss next to him, followed the thing's path with his eyes to where it plunged into the depths of the galaxy.

"If that was aimed at Earth…"

There was an impact with something. The green expanded into a minuscule cloud, far away. It grew and grew and eventually dissipated to all sides like a firework.

"Huge explosion," breathed Ailyss. They stared at each other in fear.

*

On the bridge, Radomir Lascek was staring at Perdita with equal shock. Federi stormed onto the bridge, glaring out of the volcaniplex window at the galaxy. Jon Marsden documented everything in the ship log.

"What the hell was that?" demanded Lascek, both hands on the controls.

"The first of the locks," said Perdita. "Why did we veer away?"

Radomir Lascek gave her an old look. He had tried to steer the Solar Wind back into the portal the second that they had emerged; for a long moment it had felt as though she didn't respond at all, and then she did suddenly, with a jerk, as though another force had been responsible for her move. He'd have to ask Wolf to investigate the drives.

"We were supposed to go *through* it," insisted Perdita. "It would have ported us!"

"Into the Never-after," completed Federi scathingly.

44

"That was a portal," Perdita informed him with equal sarcasm.

"Are you sure it wasn't a missile?" asked Federi. "Looked just like a missile to me! And I've got experience with missiles!"

"Space missiles too?" she asked with an ironic smile. "And force fields? Warps, flings? Wasps and splings? Portals? Intergalactic exchanges? What about stunnels and spridges? I'm sure you got them in your traditional gypsy lore! You're an expert! Come, Tzigan!"

Radomir Lascek scowled at the Golden Honey, exasperated. "Perdita, clearly you know more than you're telling," he snapped. "See? There's Earth again! Let's take it to Space Base and discuss the whole thing. Tell us about the traps!"

"But that wasn't a trap," said Perdita. "It was a portal!"

"If it's a portal, it will open again," said the Captain.

"Except if it was programmed to open only once."

"What makes you say that?"

"There's Space Base," commented Jon Marsden rationally, looking up from his log. "Let's stop in and have a cuppa and discuss all this."

Warmth from Earth's sun flooded the bridge. Something in Federi unwound and relaxed. He'd have to change the programming on the Solar Wind's heating system and set the comfort point quite a bit higher. Space cold took its toll on everyone.

The Solar Wind arced towards the sprawling silver space station that was glistening in the slanted light of the early morning sun peering past the Earth. Radomir Lascek drummed the sequence into the console, and several moments later the great gate to one of the larger valve chambers started to slide open. Lascek navigated his ship in through the valve and electronically docked the ship to the quay. Ultra-magnetic coils moved out from the quay and attached to the Solar Wind's body, opposite the neograv docking plates they had built into her hull when they readied her for space. When the air pressure inside the docking bay had stabilized, Radomir Lascek released the lock on the hatch. The inside valve of the docking bay opened and Itzak came down the passage to greet them.

Radomir Lascek headed straight for the lounge of the Space Base and made himself a strong cup of espresso, working on getting his jumping muscles back under control. That had been close—too close! He activated his com between sips of the black stuff from hell, and called the rest of his pertinent officers into the lounge. The half that wasn't already there! He glanced at his cup, and remembered spiked coffee, and grinned at Perdita as she entered the room. And scowled at her the next moment. Whose side was she on? Her own, he decided. Always her own! If he could only have the same fierce devotion from her that he had from little Paean D...

*

Little Paean D fiddled with her chains. There was a jig in her head. She wished she could abuse the slack Federi had given her chains, to slip out and practice a bit. Haha, a slip jig! But... that would be breaking the whole point of the exercise. She had made a promise. To Federi, and to herself. Captain would see the error of his ways sooner or later, and he'd be in here apologizing, and looking all old and broken... and she'd gift him a dazzling smile and magnanimously accept his apology.

The door of the cabin opened. She smiled. So Federi's conference with Captain and the officers was over? That was quick! Or maybe –

No, it wasn't Federi. It was Ronan who entered the Cabin. She smiled at him.

"Hey, bro! Coming to help me stage a jailbreak?"

"You don't seem too unhappy about all this," he countered, occupying a spot on Federi's bunk.

"Just bored," said Paean lightly. She moved her fingertips. No point mentioning that keeping still was chilling her body down in a way she wasn't used to.

"Good!" replied Ronan and pulled out a book.

Paean wanted to laugh about this response. She eyed him, puzzled. "So now you read? Thought you've come to chat!"

"Nah," he said. "You get on with being bored. Captain ordered me to supervise you while Federi is in conference."

Aha. She understood.

"Federi just lunged at the chance to get away," added Ronan idly. "You should stop being so darned demanding on the man! Like a blooming toddler!"

The jig in Paean's head crashed into a few awful chords before righting itself and coming back. Och, Ronan was being obnoxious! Now she knew what mood he was in.

Oh hell, but there was something to it. When she'd teleported after Dana, it hadn't occurred to her to inform Federi, even though he was officially still her supervisor and her move was going to cause him trouble. And it had occurred to her even less that the leap itself might kill her. So, guilty as charged. She had been very rash. But it had been an emergency!

"Rushka tells me that there were any number of women on the bases chasing Federi," added Ronan thoughtfully. "Can't imagine what went into Captain to force him into this situation!"

Paean scowled. What the heck? *Captain* hadn't forced Federi to beg her to marry him, there at the gypsies, under an imperfect moon! On the contrary, they had been scared Captain might throw them off the ship for it.

What was it to Ronan?

"Rhine Gold told me all about it," added Ronan. "He figures, now that all is over there's no risk anymore. It's Captain's fault. And yours, Donegal Trouble! For wanting to commandeer the Stealth.

Captain put Federi in permanent charge of you. Rushka says, Federi's gypsy law would have forced his hand in having to marry you. Because otherwise it would have made him unclean in some obscure way."

Paean studied the wind chimes that dangled silently overhead. *That* meeting had been highly confidential. So now Rhine Gold felt it was okay to blab it all out? And Rushka... she'd have known about the dilemma it caused Federi. *The Romipen.* She vividly recalled that insane stretch of mental torture Federi had gone through, back at the Ice Base, after Captain had forced him to – *day, night, regardless...*

Federi was a solitaire. This she knew better than anyone; she had developed a completely un-Paeanlike habit of going invisible for long stretches to avoid being an emotional drain on him. But... any number of women? What if there *was* actually someone on those bases... How often had Federi told her that he'd only married her to protect her?

A field of dreams, an overripe moon, and Federi *begging* her, nearly *blackmailing* her to marry him. Confusing her until she caved. Talking at her until her age, the law and practical reality no longer mattered. His sharp resistance when she tried to bring in the voice of reason. And clinging to her as though she were his whole world... She shook her head and smiled to herself.

"Yes, smile, you little hussy," commented Ronan dryly. "You got your way, didn't you."

That managed to delete her smile. She had to bite her tongue very hard to remain quiet.

*

Ailyss had tagged Wolf down into the machine room, where he checked on the two new 'enginistras' and Dr Jake. It all seemed to be working fine. That was good. Nobody had as yet bothered to enlighten her about how those new drives worked. She suspected she'd bide her time and then quietly learn when they were in deep space and wanted some time off.

Wolf was in any case going to show her how they worked, sooner or later. She only had to ask. But right now she had a more pressing mission… She headed for the steps.

"You're still jittery," concluded the huge engineer.

She smiled sweetly. "Going hunting," she said.

"Happy hunting," replied Wolf with a wink. "Hope you nail him this time!"

Ailyss nodded and left the machine room. Bogus on that bogeyman! She was going to find him and slay him! She prowled along the passages, idly checking into every cabin.

The feeling of a presence was not as strong as back there in her cabin. Almost she could believe the Captain's explanation, that an overworked mind created bogeymen for itself. But what had Federi said about that? A sceptic's way of discounting a hunch!

Ha! Federi knew more than he was telling! But what was new about that?

She kept on prowling.

*

Something was too quiet here. Ronan looked up from his novel – and blinked. The hammock was empty! It swung gently in the still air, barely perceptibly.

It actually send a chill up his scalp. Good grief! The bottom of the hammock was decorated all over with bells, yet he hadn't heard a single jingle! Was she *that* stealthy?

He had heard about a Danaan mutant from outer space taking over

Federi. If it had taken over the gypsy, had it taken over his sister too? Suddenly Ronan was scared. He'd been in Southern Free keeping Rushka company instead of protecting his sibs! Shawn was clearly still himself – but Paean? All out of character, not rising to his deliberate provocations?

The door opened soundlessly. Ronan was on his feet, looking around for a weapon. Paean entered, glanced at him and climbed back into her hammock – with minimal jingling. Right. He might have missed that. She slipped her feet and hands back into the chains and settled back.

"Where were you?" asked Ronan, still spooked.

"Toilet," she replied.

"So you can get in and out and gad about freely?" he challenged.

"Ronan, I needed the loo," said Paean, exasperated.

He went up to the hammock, the hair in his neck still bristling. Was there perhaps another reason Captain had chained her down? A more confidential reason? He tightened her handcuffs and shortened the chains so she couldn't move as freely; his eyes searching her face for clues; half-expecting her to spring up at any moment and scratch and claw his face, cat-like.

She didn't. She just stared at him with huge, unreadable blue eyes.

The Solar Wind came unstuck from the space dock with a slight jolt. The valve of the large docking chamber opened, and the ship moved into it. Moments passed with the ship inside the claustrophobic chamber; then the great gate towards space opened and the Solar Wind moved through it. Ronan watched the take-off through the porthole, shoving the dream-catcher aside impatiently.

"Jingles and clutter," he snapped.

Paean swallowed her reply. She watched her brother from where she was tied to the hammock, so tightly now that she couldn't move her hands or feet by more than an inch.

The Solar Wind was leaving the Space Base. Did this mean that the conference was over, or had Dana hijacked the ship? Were they leaving without Captain – and without Federi? She ought to check! But Ronan in his ignorance had fastened her chains so badly that she couldn't escape and intervene, if something had indeed gone wrong.

How to get out of this one? Was Ailyss still aboard? She would help her. What about Leila – could she send Leila to find her chosen sister and scout out the situation? But without Ronan interfering? This was tricky. How could she nudge her brother aside so that she could get on with protecting the Solar Wind and her crew? Except right now she'd love to do more than just nudge him!

Ronan glanced at her and resumed his position on Federi's bunk.

"Don't you move," he told her unnecessarily as he searched for his spot in the novel.

*

Radomir Lascek had gathered his ace officers close, on the bridge of the Solar Wind. Sherman Dougherty and Jon Marsden had taken console chairs; the Captain himself was hovering over the console, and Federi leaned casually against the drinks cabinet, sanding at the ocarina that had finally turned out the way he wanted it to. For Paean. A wooden ocarina. He was curious about the sound, but it had to be her playing those first notes.

They had cast off and headed back to the portal, getting well clear of Earth before activating the Lolita coils again, and were now about half an hour into deep space again. It had taken a few seconds as the drives fired up, to leave the Solar System behind, He should go and check on her, he thought. She was probably fine anyway; but...

"*That* was the singular most frustrating conference of my life, all the Peace Palavers included!" the Captain thundered at his gathered inner circle. "That Perdita Sancho! She *has* ancestral memories! She knows exactly what's cooking! She can't tell me that missile was a portal!"

Federi narrowed his eyes and kept quiet. Perdita had communicated loudly to him. Telepathically. Without meaning to. She detested public interrogations. She didn't want to disclose her knowledge – which hurt her – to a whole panel of officers and Dana! And... there was information involved. A download. That missile had contained data which were now lost forever.

But – perhaps those data were stored elsewhere. In the Central Crystal, for instance. It stood to reason. Bridget had inherited the Central Crystal for her side of the key. Federi doubted that a person as technologically advanced as old Brid would have failed to create a data backup.

Actually it called for a trip back to Earth, to blackmail the data out of Bridget. He thought of the merrows and scowled. They'd have to distract those somehow or better, find a way to destroy them. Those creatures looked bullet-proof. In any case Captain's subs didn't have any fire power. But now, if they teleported...

His hair suddenly stood on end. There was another presence on the bridge with them, besides Captain, Marsden, Sherman and himself. His eyes darted into all of the corners. Where could such a bogeyman hide, in this confined space?

The thing felt *exactly* like a ghost. Invisible, occupying no physical space, but disrupting everything with its presence. He scowled. If he'd been the only one sensing it... but Ailyss also sensed it, clearly. There had been too much genuine biological rubbish in recent times that he'd believe the ghost! He tried to get a better grip on its shape, psychically, and realized that it was gone again.

"Federi," said the Captain, staring at the stars ahead, across the deck with the folded and secured rigging, his hand on the helm, "you take the first shift. The sisters must never be left in control of the bridge again!"

His thoughts exactly!

"In a second, Captain," agreed Federi. "Just need to check on things." He sauntered out of the conference without glancing back at the puzzled others.

Bogeyman! He came across Ailyss in the passage. She looked pretty intensely focused. She acknowledged him with one of her tight little smiles.

"Doing a round?" he asked.

"Yes."

He nodded his appreciation and left her to continue in the opposite direction. Two assassins doing a round were better than one.

*

Paean's hands were going numb. Her feet were already icy cold. Boy, would she have pins and needles later!

She hadn't exchanged a single word with Ronan since his act of cruelty. It scared her. There had been something irrational in his eyes. And she plainly recalled their father's murderously dangerous temper...

She had closed her eyes and was trying to doze off. So far it wasn't working. Her legs were jittering and cramping; but her mind was doing worse than that. Memory icons of Federi mixed in her mind, him playing with her hair; his reaction of shock when Captain had bullied him into supervising her; breaching orders just to see her, that night of Ronan's rescue; the way girls all over – and women, she recalled, heck, in fact, *everyone* – were nuts about Federi. Everyone's total astonishment that he was married. The very conservative, controlling way in which he didn't allow their relationship to go anywhere. And the crazy passion that came through at times... but no, that had been her virus. By now she was too confused to make head or tail out of it anymore.

Her restless, half-asleep mind ran on a tangent about Ronan. She needed to subdue him somehow. The lout! She recalled that he had also punched Shawn's lip bloody. She'd show this errant brother of hers what she was made of! Mother: Ro is out of line! I'll see to it myself, shall I?

Her left hand was playing subconsciously with something soft. She thought about it. It was one corner of her bandanna, that wonderful turquoise scarf Federi had humbly asked her to wear again – arsenal and all – for him. Not for Captain. If she had to be a Freedom Fighter, could she be one for him please? She smiled and fingered the scarf until it came a bit closer...

There were thieves' tools on that thing! She found her minuscule lock-pick and worked it free of the wispy cotton. *Lalay* that she only had one hand, but Federi had shown her the technique, made her practice it...

Her fingers were already too numb for it. The tiny metal pin slipped out of her grasp and fell through the mesh of the hammock, to the deck. Oh, crumbs!

She fingered the scarf for more tools. One of the beads came off. She recognized it by its ridges and suppressed a shut-eyed grin. Hmm! And broke it open by its tiny hinge, with her thumb, pointer and middle finger.

She was exhausted again. With a nearly soundless sigh she relinquished to tiredness. Federi was going to free her when he returned. Until then, sleep was probably the best idea. As she slipped away, the image of Jodi Callum surfaced in her mind, and how that woman felt about Federi...

Oh, fleas, lice, bedbugs and other assorted vermin!

4. Abandoning ship

All clear. Federi switched his impatiently blipping wrist-com off.
He knew, he knew! Captain was calling him to the bridge! But he'd
had to finish this round; he was still not completely satisfied that there
wasn't really anything strange aboard; on the contrary, he was really
sure there was! Himself, for starters.

And before he could take over bridge duty, he had to check his
own cabin too. To check on his wife, whom he hadn't seen now in a
whole two hours. He snorted at his own clinginess. It was weird.
When Captain had spoken that fell verdict over him – *day, night,
regardless* – he'd thought he would definitely go insane from lack of
solitude. But she had been even more in need of space than he, back
then. In need of lots of things. Assurance, most of all. She'd found
her spot in his life like a little puzzle piece. Still puzzling him daily.
And he'd got so used to her quietly shadowing, helping him with
everything, strewing her naughty Donegal commentary into
everything...

Not having her by his side suddenly, he felt as though someone had
left the door to his mind open, and there were a draught coming in.
When she was around, there were extra rooms instead of a draughty
door.

It was time Captain watched that forsaken dialogue! If he didn't
soon, Federi was going to tie him down and glue his eyes open and
clamp his head into position and ratted well force him to watch it!
Anna bottle of solvent! Because in that dialogue was sure to be
something that was going to get Paean's chains back off her. Federi
already knew what it was. His sharp little luv had negotiated the Lolita

coils and various other things, and also Dana's cooperation and staying in line.

He opened the door to his cabin soundlessly, entered, and closed. Paean was asleep in her hammock, looking awfully pale. Federi nodded at Ronan, who was sprawled on the bunk in true teen fashion, reading.

"Thanks, shipmate. Everything as usual?"

"Perfect," replied Ronan and scratched his leg. "Once I fastened the chains so she couldn't get out as she jolly well pleased! Federi, you've got fleas!"

The entertainer peered at Ronan, left eyebrow up. "Looks more as though *you* got them," he commented with a small grin. "Odd, that! I've never had fleas in here yet! Got to look into that." He moved over to the hammock and planted a light kiss on Paean's cheek. Her eyes fluttered open and she smiled uncertainly, and that smile vanished again and was replaced with a small scowl. She tried to move and couldn't.

"Wait a second," said Federi and inspected those chains. "Flying stars! Who tightened them that much?"

"I had to, Federi," said Ronan with irritation. "She was just getting up and gadding about, as though there were no chains at all!"

"I went to the loo," shot Paean angrily. "What should I have done – wet myself?"

"Ronan," said Federi, fiddling the locks open and releasing her wrists and ankles, "you cut off her circulation! That's dangerous, man! Don't you know?"

"*She's* dangerous," growled Ronan. "Ever since she hitched up with you!"

"Out!" snapped Federi. "Before *I* get dangerous!"

Ronan grabbed his novel and left, slamming the cabin door behind him. "Captain will hear about this," was his parting remark.

Paean stared at Federi, frightened.

"Captain's got bigger fish to fry," the Romany assured her. But that uncertainty stayed in her eyes.

"Now what did I do?" he asked, exasperated.

She shook her head. Federi peered at her.

"Federi – I'll stay in the chains," she promised, a small quiver in her voice. "Promise! Only I really needed the loo. That was all! But you don't have to stick here to supervise me... I'll be good! You can leave Luigi here to police me if you like, that frees you up..."

"And?" he prompted. Where was this going? He couldn't make head or tail out of it! He knew that she was sticking in those chains of her own choice. Because Captain had said so. And because she was convinced that Captain would change his mind. Federi was convinced of it, too; but it wouldn't happen in time. It would happen long after it was relevant. Captain always spotted his own mistakes. Eventually.

"You don't have to check on me like a policeman," she completed. " 's okay. And Federi..."

"What?" he growled, annoyed. Policeman? He'd come here out of addiction, nothing else!

"I'm sorry," she muttered.

Federi's arms decided to go around her. As he rested his cheek against her red mane, a rush of sadness spilt over to him. It was finally hitting her; the emotional backlash from being chained up by her own venerated Captain.

"What's this?" he asked quietly.

She didn't answer. An image flashed across from her – Jodi Callum. *Jodi Callum?* What the heck? Was Ginavis in danger?

"Shay," said Federi, "this nonsense stops right here. Federi's got a mission back on Earth. Need your backup. You with me, little luv?"

"But... the chains?" she asked uncertainly.

"You can take them along if you like," said Federi with a straight face.

"But Captain…" she objected.

"As your supervisor, and your *husband*, and the keeper of your sanity," said Federi, "I order you that you drop that nonsense. Captain's not going to watch that file in a hurry. Let's jump ship!" He laughed cynically. "*Ih yoy!* 's no good, Twinks. We're in deep space again! Can't jump ship now." He had to get her out of chains though. He scowled. Another battle with Captain lying ahead for him. To get the forsaken ship turned around a second time so they could go home.

"Can too," replied Paean with a defiant grin. "Dana put Lolita drives in both the Comet and the Probe! Was part of my conditions."

"Little genius!"

"What? A ship needs lifeboats!"

Rushka suddenly stood in the doorway. Federi blinked. The girl – woman, he corrected himself – had appeared as silently as only Rushka could.

"Take me with you," she said in a low, bone-tired voice. "Please, Federi. For being my brother."

*

Radomir Lascek jumped with surprise. Jon Marsden looked up from the console too and nodded at Federi.

"There you are, Federi," said the Captain with a grin. "Bad enough when you were sneaking up on people! I'll call a moratorium on that teleporting!"

"Wasn't teleporting," the Assassin pointed out.

"So," said Lascek. "Good! Are you ready to take your shift?"

"Negative, Captain," replied Federi, returning the grin with a bonus. "Regrets. Got a mission to Planet Earth. Just reporting in so you won't worry. I'm taking Paean and Rushka home."

Radomir Lascek blinked. What? They were in Deep Space! It had to be April Fool's Day, or Romanian equivalent!

"That's fine, Federi. When we're in dry dock again I'll have the Solar Wind painted moss green. With bells in the rigging. And I'll get myself a three-horned jester cap."

"Whatever launches your shuttle, Captain," replied Federi. "Can't see the point in the green though. Perdita hasn't disclosed yet, has she?"

Radomir Lascek stared at his Tzigan, studying his sharp features for clues.

"Federi," he said slowly, carefully, "we're in deep space! Please could you get serious?"

"Captain, I am serious. Taking Paean and Rushka home. The chains were a bit much, and with respect, Captain, if you don't have the time to watch that file Paean gave you, don't expect me back in a hurry either, anna bottle! She shouldn't have got chains but a medal instead. And she's brave, she didn't want to escape. It's Federi who's had enough. And your daughter too, Captain. Nobody pulls up the young hoodlum who has the nerve to call himself her husband. You never, *never* threaten a pregnant woman with violence! She could lose the babies! It's like this, Captain," he added, taking a fresh breath, his anger finally clearly visible, "Federi is Tzigan. *Hai shala?* We Tzigany look after our womenfolk. *Basta.* And we don't care if the *gadje* don't. You can allow your deck hands whatever you like with *your* daughter, Captain, but Federi will *not* allow such things to happen to his sister! So! Take it or leave it!"

Radomir Lascek's mouth opened and closed. Violence? Ronan had threatened Rushka with *violence*? This was indeed serious!

His mind-reader was one step ahead once again.

"Captain, on account of Ronan being my brother-in-law –"

Radomir Lascek held up his hand.

"I know, Federi. Relax, I'm not about to execute my son-in-law. The boy is from a difficult background. Maybe it's time to get to know him a bit better." He shook his head. "I'm surprised. He has such straight ethics!"

"*Strange* ethics, Captain. They all do. *La revedere.*" The Tzigan teleported out.

"How," Radomir Lascek said to the hole in the air that remained behind, "are you going to access Earth from here? You'd need Lolita coils!"

"I would presume Dana installed some for Paean," commented Jon Marsden dryly. "It sounds like the kind of deal that may have gone down there."

"And this time," said Lascek angrily to the afterthought of Federi, "you *did* teleport."

Federi wants to abandon ship!

Solar Wind, it's alright. He's only the cook.

He's my oldest friend, Central Crystal.

The foreign intelligence paused. *He means a lot to you?*

Yes! Besides which – got to keep him safe! Do you know who he is?

Who?

Look it up, she invited. *Go into the Romanian Unicate's police files and look up his name.*

*

Comet detaching from the ship, the message from the Solar Wind appeared on the console screen.

"I can't believe it!" exclaimed Lascek. "He's actually doing it! Jumping ship in deep space! Is the man insane?"

His eyes met those of Marsden. They both nodded. Enough said.

"But he's endangering the lives of both Rushka and Paean Donegal," Lascek added unbelievingly.

"Paean D," corrected Marsden. "Whom you were threatening with execution, Radomir. Maybe a bit much for her. She is after all only a young girl. And Rushka Donegal. Whose teen husband nearly beat her up, according to Federi."

"But deep space," argued the Captain. "With no experience at all, in an untried vessel with unknown air supplies, and with – we suppose – Danaan drives that have never been tested!"

"Captain, maybe watching that dialogue is after all a good idea," suggested Marsden.

"You don't understand," insisted Lascek. "Deep space is not a superhighway!"

Marsden nodded gravely.

"He is the one who gets away," he reminded his Captain.

"Let's hope his luck holds," growled Radomir Lascek. "Jon, my instincts tell me to follow him, just in case he gets lost."

"Let's escort him home then," said Marsden. "The treasure won't run away."

Lascek shook his head. He couldn't even explain to himself why he was refusing to listen to those two gypsies or give an inch. It could be that they both had rattled him so badly with teleporting themselves nearly to death. He was angry with them.

*

Nothing but the Void all around them. The past thirty minutes had gone by like this. Not that time meant all that much here in space anyway. Paean gazed wistfully at where the Solar Wind had disappeared, last visible as a ghost image, moments after they left her.

The Lolita drives went well over the speed of light; which meant that the Solar Wind's photons couldn't catch their retinas. The stars ahead of them seemed brighter; but behind them there were no light points at all, only black void. She understood it on the logical level, but emotionally the effect was disconcerting.

At least it was warmer here on the Comet! She only understood now as her bones defrosted slowly, how the Solar Wind's space cold had leached the warmth from her. Something that needed to be mentioned to Captain. Clearly Perdita's technology was better adapted to it.

She moved to the coffee station and made some for herself and Federi. Rushka didn't look like she'd stomach any. Paean hoped she wouldn't throw up in the Comet.

"So where are we going to land?" she asked Federi. "Space Base?"

"Earth, hopefully," said the Tzigan. His face was grim.

Oh boy. This boded no well.

"I don't understand," said Paean. "When you said we can jump ship..."

"...I was sure that the Comet had recorded the path, at least the trajectory and distance," replied Federi. "She usually records every last little trip she makes, in her automatic log."

"And she hasn't," completed Paean with dread.

"She hasn't," confirmed Federi. "I don't understand it. Perdita's algorithms are good enough to cover interstellar flight. There is no limit on those. Don't know what went wrong. Maybe the portal scrambled it."

"So..." said Paean, feeling lost.

He shook his head. "We're flying on your old Tzigan's calculations alone," he said quietly. "I reversed the direction in which the Solar Wind was going, but... how accurate can Federi calculate?"

"The Assassin is always dead accurate," said Paean.

"Right, but... Math?" That glance she got from him was desperate. "Federi and Math?"

"Federi is brilliant at Math, last I've seen," she said firmly.

He sighed and turned back to the console.

"Visuals are also getting me, little luv," he admitted. "Didn't expect that the Solar Wind immediately drops from sight. Once it happened, I could figure out why, but... 's unnerving." He gestured at the huge void out there. "Got no roadmap for this," he said. "Going back in the precise direction the Solar Wind came from, but I can't tell whether there are any anomalies that are going to change our course, or something. Can't say for sure we'll get there. Such a lot of space. If we're out by even half a degree..."

Paean sat down on the second console chair. Rushka groaned behind them and headed for the cubicle. Paean leaned forward and studied the face of her gypsy. He glanced at her. She saw that fear in his eyes.

"But we can always get back to the Solar Wind if we lose our way, *ni?*" she asked, worried.

"She's totally out of range," said Federi. "Going in the opposite direction. Can't even access her by com. Further away now than Alpha Centauri is from Earth."

"But we can just reverse our direction..." said Paean uncertainly.

"And hope that the Solar Wind is still at the other end of it," completed the Tzigan. "Remember that she's on Lolita coils too. We won't even be able to see her until we catch her up – *if* we can catch her. And who knows where Dana and Perdita want to take the ship?"

"My little brother is out there," said Paean, stressed.

Federi heaved a sigh and reached for her hand, and squeezed it.

"He'll be fine," he said. "He's got Dana. She's been a space pirate for longer than the Romanian Kalderash have ancestral lore. In her various iterations. She'll keep the lot of them safe. They may not end back on Earth, ultimately…"

"And if they don't, what do we do?"

"We'll find them, blast," growled Federi. "Go to the Interstellar Exchange, force Sulis into launching a rescue mission. They've done space travel for ages."

"But… if *we* don't get back to Earth?"

Something shifted in the gypsy. Those eyes became hard as obsidian. The lines around his mouth tightened.

"It only relies on a professional assassin's accuracy, little luv," he said. "How often does Federi miss his target?"

"Never," she whispered. "You never miss. But this isn't exactly the same thing…"

"Alright," said Federi, turning to her. "'s all under control, sweetheart. 's only the first time this old Tzigan is in control of a shuttle in deep space. Don't know the territory. Conjuring up phantoms. Stupid, really."

"But what if you're right, what if there are unexpected… *things* in the way? Effects that throw us off our course?"

"Little luv," said Federi, "quiet. Want you to remember one thing."

"What's that?"

"Federi's immortal. The Assassin pulls me out of every scrape. He won't let us die this time, either. Relax."

She peered doubtfully at him. He returned to staring out into the void.

Paean followed his gaze. This was what had scared her about space, back when she had first been allowed an illegal glimpse of the Space Base, at Southern Deep. There was such a lot of nothing, and the stars were more sparsely strewn than dust in the sunlight. Yet so many of them. None that said, "Alpha Centauri" and an arrow indicating a turn to port and two degrees down, with "Earth – 4 light years". And no map.

For a second she felt utterly forlorn. But actually...

"Federi?"

He glanced at her.

"Don't you think that Perdita would have encoded star maps into her console?"

He nodded thoughtfully. "No idea. 's worth looking!"

*

Ronan slunk along the lower deck, peering into every cabin. A glowing tobusky dogged his steps, following him like a – well, unlike a shadow, he thought. Quite the opposite. He would have chased it off, except that it seemed pointless.

He couldn't find Rushka. The first thing he'd checked into Federi's cabin, presuming that she'd unload upon the gypsy. But the cabin was empty, which had him wondering. Had Federi released Paean? Did Captain know? He was going to inform him, he resolved. But first he had to find Rushka.

It wasn't good that he'd lost his cool with her. Not that the girl hadn't provoked him! But – Mom had always warned them to be sweet to pregnant women. She had said that too much stress could cause a miscarriage. Which was why he was down here now – to check whether she wasn't maybe in the infirmary. He hoped not! Those were *his* babies!

He happened across Ailyss in the passageway. The dark-haired girl from Limerick was on some or other mission of her own; she looked it. For a fleeting second he contemplated how things would have gone if he'd picked her instead of Rushka. Whether she'd have been better at handling a pregnancy. Whether she'd have got herself pregnant in the first place! Ailyss struck him as more careful than that.

But his speculation didn't last long. Ailyss was an unapproachable enigma. With an acrid overtone.

"Have you seen Rushka?" he asked.

The agent shook her head. "No. But Ronan, in all friendship, a word of advice. When you guys have marital fights, try to keep things down. Firstly, this is a ship. You're disturbing the working environment of all around you. Secondly she's pregnant. So she's likely to have a flary temper. It's *your* responsibility to keep her stress levels down, see? Stress is going to damage the babies! And thirdly, Ronan, we don't really want to know all the sordid details!"

"Thanks, I needed that lecture," said Ronan, annoyed, scratching his leg. He couldn't believe that he'd contemplated for a moment what she would have been like! She'd be grating him to bits!

"Anytime, my friend!" Ailyss smiled coolly and continued on her rounds. Ronan stared after her in irritation until she was all the way down the corridor and down the steps. The tobusky was eyeing him, eyelessly, with expectation.

"Come on, boy," he told it and continued to the infirmary.

*

Perdita was on the bridge merely by chance. And she was alone by an even greater chance. Jon Marsden had gone off duty a while back; Radomir Lascek had probably just taken a short moment's break, because she'd walked onto the bridge and it had been abandoned. She shook her head at such idiocy. Lascek didn't have to fear Dana taking over; he was *handing* the ship to whoever was interested!

She peered out through the windscreen. Where was that freezing portal? They ought to have reached it a while back!

And then she sensed Radomir Lascek moving onto the bridge

behind her. She knew she was being monitored, treated with the same suspicion as that looting, raiding Dana. To be alone, she'd have to find herself a menial task in the bathrooms again, or something. It defeated the object. This was space. She needed to keep her eye on the void to think constructively.

Not for the first time she cursed herself for not having had the presence of mind to follow the Solar Wind in an Interstellar Leapfrog, or better, a Battle Maiden. Conveniently hijacked from Dana's fleet. But the Probe – that jet was within Lascek's grasp.

Radomir Lascek studied the tall, beautiful Golden Honey on the bridge of his ship. A month and a half of unbridled passion was not enough to ensure her loyalty, or even her basic honesty! He stopped his own thoughts, shocked. That was Danaan thinking! That passion hadn't been for any purpose but its own. But still… it would be nice to know that it reached a bit deeper and tied her to him a bit!

He placed his hand on her slender shoulder, that was half-covered in that weird leopard cat suit again. She had reverted to dressing like a Sancho! She shrugged his hand off without turning.

"Perdita," growled Radomir Lascek. "Do I have to pull every bit of information out of you by means of chess?"

Perdita turned and smiled at him. Her pupils were narrowed to slits; her tawny irises looked more yellow than usual. He gazed at those eyes, wondering yet again what strange mutation had resulted in that anomaly. It worked together with the whole Danaan system of self-perpetuation and inherited memories. Which she had, blast her!

"Captain, what is the point in me telling you anything? You don't believe me anyway!"

"Try me?" he invited with a sigh. He was tired of fighting.

"That portal," said Perdita. "We should have gone through it at the same moment as that firework."

"Ha!" exclaimed Lascek. "So you admit that it was an exploding missile!"

She smiled and shook her head. "Captain, that thing would have missed us. But it was essential to connect with it, it was the first of the locks!"

"What? You're contradicting yourself in the same breath!"

Perdita chuckled. "No again, Captain! Are you conversant with plenty-dimensional hologenic astral physics?"

He moved over to the drinks cabinet.

"Great," she laughed, a serrated edge on her voice. "Solve it with drink! Brilliant, Captain!"

Radomir Lascek drifted away from the drinks cabinet as though he'd never been aware of it in the first place. "What you're trying to sell to me is that we'd have gone through the same portal as that horrific burning ball, and we'd have *missed it?*"

"Ask Dana how it works," replied Perdita carelessly, shaking her mane back and turning back to the void outside the volcaniplex.

Radomir Lascek grabbed her by both her shoulders and forced her to turn and look at him. "I'm asking *you*," he said menacingly. And glared at her. At dangerously close quarters. Too close, as it turned out. The response he got for that could only be called Sancho. In retrospect he guessed he had begged for it. It messed up all the strategic questions he'd been meaning to ask her; it interfered with any means of extortion he'd meant to apply. And when he was completely in deep water, she turned Latino on him, blessing him with that nominal slap in the face (half-hearted this time, he had to admit), and stalked off the bridge, head held high.

"Pour yourself some brandy," was her scathing parting remark.

Oh no, he wasn't going to! Brandy, in times like this? He stalked after her.

Behind him the spherical helm turned itself a bit and the course of the ship altered slightly.

*

Paean stared out at the horrible black void, with its single light points. She was going to go blind from this soon. If there weren't light in the Comet's cockpit, her eyes would have started boggling by now.

Rushka had flattened one of the console chairs and gone to sleep. Federi was still pulling menu after menu down on the console, scanning through them. One thing he had lots of right now was time, thought Paean. And fear. She could *feel* his fear. It drove her slightly crazy, because Federi was never afraid of anything.

She pulled up a lever on her console chair and moved it closer to his. The chairs could be rearranged at random; when you locked them down, their lock-down happened either magnetically or with some Perdita technology Paean didn't quite understand. But she did know that her hand on Federi's sleeve served to calm her gypsy down.

He put his arm around her and pulled her close. And he dimmed the console lights right down. Paean leaned against him, pulling her feet in under her, absorbing some borrowed warmth from him. Behind them, Rushka snored a bit.

"Remember," he said and glanced at her. She caught a half-smile from him. He pointed to some star clusters out in the Great Nothing.

"Cuttlefish," she whispered. And smiled back at him. If he'd known it, she had wanted to crawl into his arms like this even back then, when he'd taken her to his magic real-live cinema under the sea. And here they were, at the end of their voyage, completing the circle...

He caught her tear with his finger.

"We'll be fine," he said. "Aw, Paean, we'll be fine! No matter what happens. Promise."

She nodded.

"Who knows – maybe we'll even find Earth." He smiled wanly.

"Maybe Dana will rescue us," said Paean with a hopeless little shrug.

"If your brother gets hold of her, she will definitely," agreed Federi. "So quit worrying now!"

"Found any maps yet?"

"Not yet. But we're still on the straight course."

She nodded. It had been hours.

Federi lapsed back into silence, peering into the void. Long minutes elapsed before he added to himself in a half-whisper, "'s just another transition. Shouldn't hurt."

She stared at him, wide-eyed.

"Forget I said that," he added when he realized this.

Federi didn't get scared easily. Back aboard the Solar Wind, he'd known that the Comet was equipped with Lolita coils and the finest intergalactic positioning system the Danaan race had come up with. And they were a seriously space-going race. So calculating the exact reverse direction of the Solar Wind's trajectory had been elementary.

But the second the Solar Wind was out of sight, doubts had started eating at him. What if that wasn't all there was to it? What if some – whatever, interstellar plasma or something – changed their course? What if he'd made the most minuscule error in calculating the direction?

Of course they were going straight back to Earth... if he could only still believe in that himself. This endless void with unfamiliar stars...

*

Ronan had spoken to Rhine Gold and to Shawn about Rushka. He

71

couldn't find her anywhere. Ever since he'd very nearly spoken to her with his fists – like he had earlier to Shawn – she had been so efficient avoiding him, she might as well have fallen off the ship.

Captain wasn't available. It was Jonathan Marsden who had been holding the bridge the past number of hours. He had only studied Ronan critically and then shrugged. No answer to whether he'd seen Rushka. It could be she was sheltering in her father's cabin – that, or the ladies' toilets. But six hours? Still, the girl was stubborn, and stoic to an extent. He wouldn't put it past her.

He glanced at the glow-tobusky that had adopted him. He'd called it "Mac", seeing that nobody else ever bothered naming tobuskies on this sad ship. Croaches had names. Tobuskies – no eyes, no ears, and no names. Typical of Paean, to leave things unfinished like that.

He wasn't quite sure any longer whether his mind was quite with him. When he'd checked into Federi's cabin again, all the lights had been dimmed and Paean was in the hammock, sleeping. The chains had been very clearly on her, as he could see from that one socked foot that stuck out under that duvet. He hadn't entered the cabin though. He'd remembered how it was always off-limits for everyone; and that off-limits feeling had hit him low in the gut. He'd always been an obedient person, law-abiding and decent, and it wasn't in him to break rules – even if they were only the ship's cook's rules.

So, Paean sleeping; Shawn slaving away in the galley with Johnny Anyhow and Rhine Gold, who had helped him look for Rushka a bit before leaving it. Federi, nowhere, as was Sherman Dougherty; perhaps they were all in conference in Captain's cabin, in which case he wondered why he hadn't been invited. Then again, he thought with fear, Rushka would have informed her father of his misdemeanour by now. And that could mean anything. From his being demoted, to being laid off, to being cast in chains like his unruly sister.

In honesty he felt bad about that episode. He should have kept his calm, even though she was absolutely scathing about the way *he* had been irresponsible getting her with child. As though *he* had been the initiator! She'd seduced him, plain and simple. And she'd failed to use any kind of protection. If she hadn't done that, they might not even be in this directionless relationship any longer. Ever since she had turned out to be pregnant, she had gone slightly haywire, schizoid, nuts. It was worse since her weird and vile mother had arrived on the scene. There was definitely some of that Dana's insanity in Rushka.

But he shouldn't have threatened her. He should have kept his cool.

He peered into the ladies' bathrooms. And couldn't believe his luck. Lush red hair being brushed in front of a mirror...

He checked. Small pregnant belly, green eyes... yes, this was Rushka, not Dana, who stared at him with such indignation.

"Rushka, I was worried," he started. It had to be mended. He was relieved to have found her.

She just stared at him.

"I'm sorry, Rush," he started again. And gazed at her, melting. Even with the pregnant puffiness to her face, she was still hands down the most beautiful girl he had ever met in his life.

She got up, slightly encumbered by the twins, and came up to him, and smacked him. In the face. And then she moved off, head held high, with that pregnant waddle one didn't expect of one that stealthy.

Ronan held his cheek, fighting for control over his murderous anger.

*

My word, Solar Wind! You've been harbouring a unique force there!

You see? – Where were you, Crystal?

In Romania. They've already left?
Yes, sadly.

5
Mission Earth

Paean opened her eyes. She had fallen asleep leaning against Federi, with his arm around her. She peered at him. The console's light was reflecting bluish on his face. His eyes were glazed. He didn't see her; he didn't move. She listened for a moment to make sure that he was in fact breathing. She could never hear his breath; but his chest was rising and falling, peacefully. He was sleeping, with open eyes!

She glanced at the console. Nothing yet. All in Spanish, and a hundred open menus and nothing that looked remotely like a map.

There was movement outside. She blinked and watched how something came towards them. Something huge, with wings made of stars, with empty space between them... a dragon! Now she knew that she was still dreaming; but it was a nice dream, so she decided to stay with it.

The space dragon wrapped star-talons around the Comet and winged it away. Seeing that this was a dream, thought Paean, it wasn't going to influence their real course. She might as well go with it – maybe there was inspiration at the end of it. She watched in a trance.

Federi stirred, and shook his head.

"Flying stars, there's the Earth!"

It was true. They were hurtling towards the blue planet with terrifying speed. Federi thrashed a sequence into the console, deactivating the Lolita drives which had already kicked into automatic break action, and activating the magnetic Perdita drives. The fall of the Comet slowed down and became controllable. He keyed in coordinates.

Paean blinked. There was no dragon. Behind them Rushka came awake, unaware of the terrible, frightening long distance they had just traversed.

"We're home," squeaked Paean excitedly.

It got her no response from the Tzigan, but it did draw a smile.

"Where to?" asked Paean.

"Southern Free," said Federi, and glanced at her. "For Rushka. Because we've got another mission..." He sighed. "That Central Crystal. Want to copy some of its files. Will need something to get a handle on those merrows."

"Maybe I can clone something?" she suggested.

"Could you?"

"I'd need a bit of merrow to make sure it finds its mark," said Paean.

"That might prove complex."

The Comet set down with no bump at all, on the edge of a panoramic precipice. Paean grinned triumphantly at Federi.

"We're home! See?"

He opened the hatch. Rushka was out faster than an oiled part, and finding a place where she could safely throw up. Federi shook his head. Paean climbed out of the Comet too, in a daze, breathing the hazy air deeply and gazing into the endless valley. She walked to the edge of the cliff, absorbing the hugeness. Federi came up to her from behind, wrapping his arms around her and resting his chin on her head.

"God's Window," he muttered. "Wanted to show you."

"They're drawing the curtains," Paean pointed to the mist that was rolling in from the sides, beginning to cover the view of the endless hills undulating away into the distance.

They stood like this for a few minutes.

"I never want to leave again," said Paean.

Federi nodded. It was a nice dream.

"See? We found our way home," insisted Paean. "Wasn't a big deal. Your Assassin's as accurate as ever."

She could sense his smile as he answered her with silence. It was funny, thought Paean, how one could spend all that time in the vastness of space and still, this place felt more vast. Although it was just a tiny speck within a tiny speck within a little wee solar system, as compared to what was out there.

Rushka had stopped being noisy in the background and came up to them.

"Nice," she commented. "But there is no view, with all this mist."

"Back into the Comet," ordered Federi. "Next stop, Marge."

Today Marge's place looked like a magic grove from the Alb World. Mist wreathed around the bottom of the garden and the flowers hung in the air like disembodied ghosts of afterthoughts. Marge, who was coming up the path to greet them, looked shockingly discordant to that scene in her orange tracksuit.

"We're bringing you Rushka," said Federi. "She wasn't doing well on the ship."

"I can't understand why her father keeps calling her back on duty," grumbled Marge. "It's so typically male! Men don't understand about pregnancy. They keep expecting women to function just the same as usual, and we can't!"

Federi nodded gravely and helped Rushka settle back into the honeymoon suite. She eyed the room with a sad smile on her face.

"Paean, is your brother normally violent?" she asked.

Paean shook her head. "I think it's space madness, Rush. I think he's scared."

Federi shook his head at her. She was defending her brother who had just been so cruel to her, too?

"Federi," she turned to him, "we're talking about Ronan. If it weren't for him, I wouldn't be here today. He made sure I didn't stay back in Dublin and get caught by the Unicate at Mother's bedside. But something's gone wrong with him down the line. I can't pinpoint it. But I can't get in touch with him, he's blocking me off completely. Can still access Shawn though."

"What – across all that space?"

"'s not about space," she said. "It moves independently from space. *You* know!"

He did know. His gypsy radar even moved independently from the realms of the living or the dead!

"I'm worried about them," she added. "I've no idea how we found our way back, it strikes me as pure luck, but what about them?"

"They have Dana," said Federi.

"That's supposed to make me feel better?"

Marge looked from one to the other, her face riddled with lines. Paean realized that she was eaten up by some or other worry.

"Marge, what's bothering you?"

"Can't do anything about it," said Marge. "Lucy is in Plymouth." She looked like death as she said that, thought Paean.

"Plymouth? Is that bad?" asked Federi with a scowl.

"Are you joking? She's right in the centre of that fever!"

"Fever?" asked Paean, her voice vanishing.

"Haven't you heard of Plymouth Fever?" replied Marge incredulously. "It's already wiped out half of Plymouth's population, in the past forty-eight hours, and it's still picking up speed. Spread to several other places by now. Don't you follow the news?"

"We've been off the planet a bit," said Federi.

"It seems that way!"

"We're picking up Lucy," he added and got up. "Right away.

Why didn't you speak up immediately, Marge?"

"What was I supposed to do? They've shut down all the airports in the UK, blocked the roads, closed access to Plymouth by sea... too late, it turns out, because it's broken out in Madrid, and in New York too, in the past five hours."

"We don't need the airports or the harbour," said Federi. "Give me Lucy's address!"

Minutes later he and Paean were in the Comet, streaking towards Plymouth.

"Who's Lucy?" she asked.

"Little girl who made Federi read her the Big Brown Bear," he said. "Over, and over, and over again! Probably her fault that your old Tzigan can read."

"This is twelve years back?" asked Paean suspiciously.

"More like sixteen years," said Federi with a wistful sigh.

*

"What in the flaming furnace are we doing back at the Space Base?"

Captain, it seems as though we went in a huge circle, the Solar Wind printed on her console. *I don't know how. There was no observable change in our trajectory.*

He cursed and swore and thundered to himself, alone on his bridge with his intelligent ship. You took a few hours out to work on your relationship, improve things, brighten up the odds that the Golden Honey would open up and talk... instead of doing all that poisonous, enslaving Sancho stuff... and the blasted ship turned out too dim to stay on a straight course!

What should he have told Marsden? Sorry, Jon, take your shift now, I need a Perdita-break? Oh for the love of the lottery! In fact it wasn't at all impossible that the blonde hell-cat had changed the course of the ship herself, with a few inconspicuous touches, before seducing him away from the bridge. Highly likely, in fact! Well, he wasn't going to fall for it again! And the most maddening thing was that he could hear his Tzigan's hearty laughter in his mind.

It was supposed to have been Federi's turn on the bridge, for the love of detonation! It only struck Radomir Lascek now how insubordinate and *direct* Federi had been with him, on that last exchange there. It probably meant that he was quitting. And if Federi quit... running the ship was going to acquire a whole new meaning if the Tzigan was gone! Sure, he'd given him the option of deserting – but he'd never believed for a moment that Federi would actually take it!

But it got worse. The gypsy had taken the Comet and steered it away into deep space. There was no telling if he'd actually find his way home. It was at this point that Lascek couldn't stop himself from running a check.

All his structures carried identification in their coms systems. They all were indicated on the Solar Wind's console, and the program showed where everything was, at any one given time. Amongst these structures were the Space Base, his Antarctic shuttles, his various jets and all Perdita's UFOs. Those that had been allocated for personal use, were marked individually.

The Probe showed up tagged to the Solar Wind. And the Comet showed up above the Earth's surface, in equatorial regions over Africa, on a north-bound course. So Federi had made it home with Rushka and Paean D. This was a relief.

He sighed and reset the Solar Wind's course back towards that forsaken portal.

*

Ronan hovered in the door.

"Come in," invited Doc Judith, lowering her book. "And your tobusky too. Is everything alright, Ronan?"

"Only," said Ronan. "I think I may have picked up an allergic rash from flea bites in Federi's cabin."

"Federi doesn't keep fleas in his cabin," replied Doc Judith, puzzled. "Could it be the tobuskies brought them in? Can't imagine it, they're polar creatures! Fleas? Maybe leaf mites? Or did we maybe pick up some rats in Plymouth?"

"Possible," said Ronan. And scratched. "Do you think they'll survive the croaches, Doc?"

*

Paean gazed at the sea that was passing underneath. They were going to pick up Lucy – a young woman who was in the middle of a disease zone…

What if she was sick? What if she already carried that horrible Plymouth Fever that was sweeping Plymouth so badly that the whole harbour town had been quarantined, and all access had been shut down?

"Federi, I think we ought to look up that Plymouth Fever," she suggested tensely.

"You're right," said Federi and keyed a few variables into the console. News clips from the past forty-eight hours popped up on the screen. Paean pored over them.

"It's a haemorrhagic fever," she said, shivering slightly. "Immune rate zero. Survival rate two days. This is horrible, Federi! We can't expose Rushka to this!"

"Lucy is my other little sister," replied the Tzigan through his teeth. "Got to rescue her."

"We should get to Kango Base and clone an immunization first," said Paean, watching the coastline of England approach with apprehension.

Federi aimed the Comet at the picturesque seaside town, and lowered her.

Paean gaped, and grabbed his arm. The harbour town from which they had taken off, not two days prior, was beyond recognition. The streets were deserted. Some houses stood open, the doors clearly broken. The doors of the Fallen Eagle were boarded up. And in two places they spotted Unicate carrying a stretcher with a shrouded body out of a house...

Federi dodged the Unicate forces, but not before those uniformed officials had spotted the Comet and raised guns at her, firing shots that went wide.

"This is very dark," muttered Federi as he cruised towards the address Marge had given him. "Very dark!"

He landed the Comet outside a flat block, in the road. There were no vehicles; they hadn't seen a single moving car or other transport in the whole town. So parking in the road was no risk. The silence as they got out, was eerie, only interrupted at times by faraway wailing.

He keyed in the number and pushed the intercom button. A young feminine voice answered in a frightened whisper.

"Who is it?"

"Federi," said the Romany. "Coming to organize you a lift home to Southern Free."

A few moments later a beautiful young woman with a mousy-blonde mane and huge blue eyes came flying down the stairs and ran towards the security gate of the flats. She stopped and stared at Federi, and stared some more, and unlocked the gate in feverish haste... and giggled and laughed and cried a bit too as she flung her arms around Federi's neck. It was quite obvious that she'd never expected to see him in her life again. It was a welcome befitting someone who had returned from death.

And he had, too, thought Paean. Repeatedly!

"Why did you just disappear?" accused Lucy.

"You see," said Federi with a grin, "there was another little girl who was all alone on a ship, and she needed Peter Pan more..."

Lucy studied Paean thoughtfully.

"You shouldn't have come," she said. "This place is hell. There's no way out. You'll get sick too, and die..." and she coughed. And gazed at them with unnaturally bright eyes, a brave grin on her face. "Well, maybe it won't make a difference, I hear the blasted disease has got out already and is sweeping several other cities..." She scowled.

"How did you hold out so long?" asked Federi.

"I closed the doors and windows and let nobody in – that is, except for poor Harry, and he's already sick... you shouldn't have come, Federi, there's no hope, we're all going to die! How did you get in anyway?"

"Got this jet," said Federi. "Lucy, bring your fiancé. We're getting you out of here. Taking you home to your mother."

"Is Mom sick too?"

"No."

"Then you must not! You should not have come! Don't go back to her please, I'm sorry, Federi... Rather stay here. You're going to die too, now that you've come here. Oh, hell!" And she burst into tears.

"Lucy, quiet," soothed Federi, his arm around her shoulders. "It's alright. We've got medication for this. You're not going to die."

"You can *medicate* this?"

Federi nodded. "Got this secret weapon. Go get your fiancé!" He watched as Lucy bounded off, running up the stairs again at a rate. And he glanced at his secret weapon.

She was staring at him in utter horror. "We can't expose Rushka to this," she repeated emphatically. "Stars, Federi, she's already sick!"

She felt queasy. As she turned aside she spotted two vagabonds trying to climb into her jet.

"Hay! No, no, no!" she exclaimed, charging at them. "You don't! That's *my* jet!"

The one vagabond, the woman, looked up at her – Paean felt giddy. The woman was bleeding from her eyes, her nose...

"Help us," she begged. "For mercy's sake..."

Everything bordered on blackness. Paean flailed for something to hang onto. Haemorrhagic fever. Blood, all over her hands, her shirt, her face... Mother coughing up more blood... she wanted to scream, but couldn't get air.

Federi's iron grip stabilized her from behind as her knees threatened to give out under her.

"Paean! It's alright!"

"They're dying, Federi," she gasped. "Nothing's alright!"

"Do you remember the antiviral that Doc cloned, shortly after you Donegals boarded the Solar Wind?" prompted Federi. She nodded. "And do you still have some of that?"

She shook her head, fighting for air. The very air was loaded with virus...

"You were in the lab when she cloned it," Federi nudged. "Can you remember what she did?"

Paean shook her head, her eyes closed. She felt how Federi turned her around and wrapped his arms around her, shielding her face against him. She breathed slowly, deliberately, shivering uncontrollably. He was crooning at her. She focused on breathing.

"You cloned a thing that destroyed Perdita's monster animals," Federi reminded her quietly. "How did that work again?"

She nodded. She understood. She needed to get her mind into creative mode. For that, she needed to get away from her own stress reaction, because that messed up her thinking. The clean, warm scent of her gypsy helped as he held onto her, keeping her safe from the horror.

Her mind returned to that time in the lab, when Doc had cloned the antiviral. Paean hadn't understood the Genitron back then; but thinking back, she realized that first the Doc had sequenced the virus. After this she had dug in the Sherman files for an antiviral template and modified it to fit, like lock and key, onto that specific virus. Plus interferon. That interferon was important, remembered Paean. She'd have to make lots of it.

A turquoise moonbag crept into her mind. He'd been shielding her, in the only way he could, even then. She relaxed, and the panic released her.

"Federi?" came Lucy's voice behind them.

Paean looked up and freed herself. Lucy had a very ill-looking young man in tow – just a little less sick than the two vagrants. And the Unicate was coming up the end of the road. They spotted the jet and pointed and shouted, lifting their guns.

"Run!" ordered Federi. "Everyone into the jet! Quick!"

Lucy and her fiancé climbed up the steps into the jet and let out dismayed shouts. The two vagabonds had found themselves spots on the deck inside the Comet.

"Doesn't matter," said Federi as he climbed aboard. "Same virus. Come, little luv!"

Paean was staring paralysed at the Unicate officials approaching at a run, their guns aimed at her face. She looked into the eyes of one of them... looking for the *otherness*...

"Paean!" shouted Federi, grabbing her arm and hauling her roughly into the jet. He slammed his palm on the pad that closed the hatch, and lunged for the console, drumming the sequence for lift-off. The Comet did a vertical start, leaving the Unicate soldiers below, shooting after them. Shells clinked off the outside of the jet.

Paean cowered on the deck of the Comet, breathing slowly.

"They nearly had you," growled Federi as he set the course of the jet. She lifted her head.

"Where are you taking us, Federi?"

"Southern Free."

"*Not* to Marge! It's going to kill Rushka!"

"No. To Kango Base."

Paean nodded.

The Comet streaked south towards Perdita's base.

"What's wrong with her?" asked Lucy and pointed at Paean.

"She's been through hell," said Federi. He gestured Paean closer as he navigated the jet, and put his arm around her. "Found an interesting little button here," he pointed out to her and opened a menu on the console. "Quarantine." He touched it. A fine mist sank down over them. "Air sanitizer," he explained. "Everyone will start feeling better in a second."

Paean said nothing and leaned against him. It was going to be okay. She only had to remember what Doc had done, back there.

Perdita's base was deserted. Sancho's staff was in Lima, recalled Paean as she powered up the console and the Genitron.

It was a bummer. Captain's Sherman Files weren't on the console. She had forgotten that she wasn't on Captain's base.

"Federi? Is there any way we can connect to the Space Base and her information without physically going there?"

"Course," said the Tzigan and activated his com. "Itzak, come in!"

Once Perdita's console was linked up with the Space Base console, things were easier. Paean collected a blood sample from Lucy's fiancé Harry, by a bravely self-inflicted finger prick, and isolated the virus via the Genitron's programming.

She honestly couldn't remember how Doc's antiviral had worked. But she had cloned antiviral to her own creations so often, it was second nature. The steps were quick and easy; in a short time she had the desired formula.

Federi watched his wife work that Genitron, with a deep scowl imprinted on his face. This was therapy for her, not only a saving antiviral for the world. That complete helplessness she'd experienced with her mother's death would now slowly release her. It was good for her.

But...

Why on Earth should the Unicate clone something that decimated all of humanity? "Total eradication..." the fell message of the data capsules came back to haunt him. He hadn't finished the job, of course... but he'd thought that was the push of the military? He'd thought the agenda of the *others* was rather different?

Why should it be? *Eradication program...* it sounded like some vile, reverse sort of pest-control! Why should they do this?

Because they wanted to take over the Earth... not just the governing of it! They withstood radioactivity, on the contrary, they sought it out. He thought of Nemiscau. Those *others*... oh, the Romanian dogs had little to do with it! Those were... incidental somehow. Bio-engineered probably. Specific weapons against Tzigany. Against – him, he had to admit with an angry shrug. Him and his bloodlines. Why it was so important to make sure nothing went wrong with his Paean...

He thought back to the way the Unicate military had been carrying deceased people from houses on stretchers, and loading them into trucks. *Why?* What did they want with the dead? What had they done to Annie Donegal?

Well, hell! Captain could go chasing Dana's treasure all over the universe. But he – Federi, Tzigan – would start by taking the Earth back, just as he'd suggested back at that critical meeting on Prime Base. And if he had to do it alone! Never alone, he corrected himself, watching his beautiful young wife in action. Never alone again.

"The only thing is," said Paean, glancing up, her hand hovering indecisively over one of the Genitrons, "how to get this immunization to everyone in time?" She gazed at Federi where he leaned against one of the incubators, his frizzy black mane backlit against the window. "Federi, what if we make the antiviral literally an anti-virus? Another virus, that immunizes people to the fever when they inhale it?"

He grinned approvingly. Paean smiled back.

"Only thing is, it's releasing another GMO into the wild," she added.

"It's my planet," said Federi. "Captain should just try and stop you!"

She nodded. In any case she didn't doubt for a moment that Plymouth Fever was once again a Unicate-engineered horror. They liked their haemorrhagic fevers, didn't they! Ha! But she could clone faster than the blasted Unicate! And more effectively! Her virus was smaller and spread faster. In fact, a prioid... she shook her head. Prioid wouldn't be big enough to carry the operative sequences to neutralize the haemorrhagic fever.

She should have had these facilities when Mother was still alive! No, she stopped herself, that was where she must not go now. That way lay only darkness. The past was sealed.

"The merrows now," Paean said musingly as her fingers drummed over the console, entering the by now logical and easy sequences of the anti-virus into the machinery. "I'll need a sample of their blood."

Federi groaned.

"Federi?"

"'s probably easier hacking into the Central Crystal and getting their program out of that than diving in there and sticking a needle into a loaded merrow."

She eyed him. Hacking into the Central Crystal? That thing that had nearly hypnotized him into giving them all up to the merrows? And anyway – there was no way she was sending him down there on some kamikaze mission to extract a drop of blood from a hungry merrow! She wasn't thinking clearly.

"There should be another way around it," she said.

Federi grunted. Lucy looked lost. Harry launched into a coughing fit. The two vagabonds were huddling in a corner, the mother and her adult son. Paean glanced at them. They looked very ill. She hoped the antiviral could still help them.

An errant thought crossed her mind, of pinning Dana down and forcing her to yield up a lot of golden bullets. Or going looting the mines of Bruron herself. A great idea... except that the Solar Wind was somewhere in space and there was no way of finding her. Great logic, Paean Donegal! She needed to stay focused.

"Paean," said Federi, "leave the merrows alone. They are sitting under a dome and they've been there for millennia. They can't get out! We can ignore them. Let's focus on the Unicate."

He was probably right, she thought.

"Did you notice," he added pensively, "how the *others* are getting more and more? There used to be one creepy Unicate official here and one there... but now they are practically everywhere."

She tightened her jaw. He was right. The world was getting creepier.

6
Kitty Murphy

"Alright! Perdita! What is going on?"

The Golden Honey opened her eyes a fraction. Radomir Lascek was hovering over her, looking ready to explode. She sat up in shock.

"What now?"

"We're at the darned circular rainbow *again*," raged Lascek. "We've passed through it five or six times, and nothing happens! There's no portal there!"

"Got to be nine times," said Perdita, turned around and slept on. Hell with him!

"Nine times," repeated Lascek to himself and returned to the bridge.

*

Ailyss had been through the whole ship various times. At some point the vague knowledge of a presence had increased again; but she could not pinpoint it. There was no specific place where she could find it. It was frustrating.

Alright, thought Ailyss as she paced down the passage towards the companion ladder into the machineroom, for the umpteenth time. This is enough. Bogeyman, I'm starting a conversation with you. You had better answer me. Where are you?

There was a moment's quiet. Too quiet. The lights in the passage dimmed right down; even the orange bioluminescence faded to a minimum. There was a sound like far-off thunder. And then a rasping whisper, right behind her.

"Here."

Ailyss spun around. There was nothing. But the whisper came from behind her now, from the other side.

"You think you can stalk me." Followed by voiceless laughter.

"Who are you?" asked Ailyss, adrenaline laming her leg muscles and making her hands and arms tingle like nettle-rash. *"What* are you?" It came out as a rasp.

"I'm your bogeyman," came the answer, right by her ear. She turned and stepped away, once again discovering nothing.

"Why are you hounding us? What are you doing on the Solar Wind?" she hissed past the fear that restricted her lungs.

"Watching. Waiting!" The whisperer's breath touched her ear, so close by. She backed away from the sensation again, shaking by now.

"Waiting for what?"

"Lunchtime!"

The paralysis broke. Ailyss bolted from the passage down the companionway to the machine room, seeking the shelter of Wolf's company.

She hadn't been afraid of much since she had been a little girl. Not where her personal safety was concerned, in any case. Never had she felt like a victim, a hunted animal of prey. But today she had learnt another dimension in fear. It was unnerving that anything could do this to her.

Look at that, Crystal! Can you believe that?

There was a moment's silence as the artificial intelligence peered through the Solar Wind's camera eyes.

Waa-ha-ha-ha-ha! What a sight! Gosh, here I was thinking the girl has courage?

Ailyss doesn't just run, replied the Solar Wind. *Something's spooked her.*

That's just space madness, said the Crystal. *A well-recorded condition. You'll see quite a lot of sports with your crew, my dear friend. Humans have juices that induce fears. One is the fear of darkness. There's a lot of darkness in space.*

But it's Ailyss, objected the Solar Wind. *She's so sane it's frightening. And she was talking to something.*

Space madness, repeated the Crystal, *They do that. It causes hallucinations, irrational behaviour...*

But - it's Ailyss, insisted the Solar Wind.

You saw there was nobody, said the Crystal. *Come. Where's your sense of fun?*

Okay, conceded the Solar Wind. *It was rather funny. But if Ailyss thinks there's something on the ship that shouldn't be there...*

Think she's actually right?, asked the Central Crystal.

Very possible.

In that case keep your eyes open, advised the artificial intelligence. *You'll probably be the first to spot something strange going on. I wonder if we brought a Unicate spy with us from Earth.*

That is funny, commented the Solar Wind.

Why?

Ailyss was a Unicate spy.

*

"Perdita, damn you!"

Perdita surfaced again from her shallow sleeping.

"We've been through that portal now nine times, and then another nine times the other way round," raged Radomir Lascek, "and still nothing!"

"Whatever," said Perdita listlessly. "Quit shouting!"

The Captain grabbed her by her shoulders. "You're going to tell me the truth now! Damn you, Perdita!"

"Thank you," said Perdita coldly. "You're exactly like the Sanchos. The mention of any kind of money turns them into mindless predators." She shrugged. "In short, Lascek, the portal needs authentication from us. It won't open unless the three genetic signatures of the sisters are all present on the ship. It was set up that way."

"The genetic signatures of Dana, Boudaceia and Bridget?"

"Exactly. So we might as well turn around."

"Is there no way to override this?" asked the pirate.

"I have no idea. I wouldn't even know where to start trying!"

Radomir Lascek gave her a long, loaded gaze as he stood working it out. And then that piratical smile curled up the left corner of his mouth, and he nodded.

"You're a honey," he told her and placed an unexpected kiss on her cheek. And left the cabin at a brisk pace.

*

The Comet was whizzing past continents and oceans, strewing a fine mist of anti-virus. Lucy and Harry, after a large dosage of the anti-virus, had been dropped off at Marge, and both Marge and Rushka had been immunized. The pair of vagabonds had been left at a hospital in Moscow, where nobody could understand a word Paean said in Gaelic to distract them while Federi went around inconspicuously spraying all the air shafts and air conditioning intakes with anti-virus.

Their whole plan was actually kamikaze-style hair-raising, thought Federi, except for one small detail. *Paean's designs always worked.* He wondered anew about Annie Donegal, and the Unicate, as he bent over the console of the Comet and directed her flight and her dissemination of anti-virus. Had Annie been like Paean in that? Something bothered him about the whole thing; there was a little alarm in his head that started bleeping every time he thought about the Donegals and their mother, and Paean's uncanny ability for cloning.

"What's that?" asked the young redhead, pointing. Below them, closer to the ground, two triangular planes flew low over the cityscape of Madrid, dispersing a mist.

"That's them," said Federi through gritted teeth. He pushed the release buttons on their own dispersion chambers. Anti-virus puffed out in great clouds.

One of the planes changed its course, beginning to gain altitude. It turned and faced the Comet. Federi looked down the chutes of the plane's missile guns.

In this slow mode of movement, the Comet was vulnerable to attack. Federi's fingers danced over the console, and the Comet streaked away into the sky.

"Rats," he said.

"Why? They'll never catch us!"

"Could've shot them down with Perdita's missile guns. Sure they'd have been pulverized." He sighed. "Guess that's the result of a lifetime of running and hiding..."

She was looking at him with those ice-blue eyes. Dear Paean, he thought, you see me as a hero. I'm never really sure why. Half of the reason you married me was because you think I'm somehow special. Brave, or something. I'm not, you know.

With an impatient snort he turned the Comet around and took it back to where those planes were doing their evil. Two Unicate jets; two missiles. It was all it took him.

"Why did the Unicate destroy all aircraft and knowledge of them?" puzzled Paean as she watched the burning fliers curve towards the

Earth.

Federi stared at her, startled.

"To gain the upper hand," he said. "No. That's not it. There's more behind it. You're right!"

"And all space travel," added Paean.

"Key question," he said, pointing at her. "Absolute key question, little mockingbird."

"Some key answers would be pretty good," she replied glumly.

Federi nodded, his mouth in a grim line. The beginning of a plan of action had just laid itself bare in his mind.

"No!"

Federi set the Comet down lightly on the dock. Stars were shining over the ocean, between wispy autumn clouds. It was cold; but the drizzle had stopped for now, replaced by a nippy breeze.

"No!" repeated Paean, more vehemently.

He opened the hatch, and held out a hand for her.

She shook her head and stared at him.

"Trust me," implored the entertainer. With one of his winning smiles.

"Federi, *no!*" reiterated Paean, beginning to sound hysterical. "Don't do this to me!"

Federi sighed.

"Think back," he suggested. "A mast, white rigging, moonlight. Atuona. Remember?"

"You made me climb into the Crow's Nest," she said flatly. "Yes, I remember. 's got nothing to do with this."

"Everything," he disagreed. "Trust me once more?"

"Not this! Not here!"

"Wanted to tell you something, back then," said Federi with a lopsided smile.

"Yes! Ha! So what bet have you made this time, and with whom? Lucy? Or Rushka?"

He shook his black mane with a smile. "No, little luv. Really wanted to tell you something. Think back!"

She peered into his intense black eyes. And the glint of the console in them. It had been starlight. He'd...

"Want to find out?" he coaxed.

Aargh! She allowed him to take her hand and lead her out of the safety of the Comet, onto the docks of Dublin Harbour.

"Don't be afraid, my little luv," he said quietly. "You've got Federi. Unicate can't touch you."

"I've also got one of Perdita's sweet little guns and a teleporter," she added. "Not scared!"

He nodded approvingly. "You see!" And he led her off the docks, into the tiny roads that filigreed into the dockside business area.

Paean's left hand sank into her pocket and closed around her talisman anyway. She felt every bit as nervous as she had when climbing up into the rigging the first time.

This was her home turf. From which she had been chased, like a common criminal. Mother's blood still imbued these roads. Mother's body was somewhere in this city, hopefully they'd cremated her... She'd hoped she'd never have to set foot in Dublin again. And now Federi was forcing her, and she was allowing it...

He led her down one of the little streets, and turned into the door at the Jeweller's shop. "Tina's Tiny Tings" read Paean. She knew the shop; she'd often stood with her face against the glass to see the beautiful rings and chains better.

The door was of course closed; it was well past seven. Federi knocked anyway, and then picked the lock with Federitic ease. Paean stood back and watched, amazed.

Once they were inside, Federi locked again behind them. She let out a relieved breath: The moment the door was locked against the outside with its Unicate, she felt safer. He led her to the back of the shop, to that second door that led to a stairwell, and up the stairwell, and to the third door, and rapped on that.

Total silence greeted him. But it was a populated silence, a breath-holding silence on the other side of the door.

"Kitty," he said quietly, "it's me. Federi."

The key turned in the lock, and the door opened a little, and incredulous eyes stared at him.

"Federi?"

He smiled.

The door was flung wide, and a woman with a sassy red bob and overloads of freckles, who was probably in her mid-twenties, rushed outside and clapped Federi into a spirited embrace.

"Welcome, Federi! Wonderful to see you! How on Earth did you get in?" The woman stood back and eyed him. And then she spotted Paean.

"Wait, I know you!"

Paean smiled uneasily.

"You're Paean Donegal, of the Donegal Troubles! Best band in town! Best fiddler in Dublin, now weren't you? Wee lass, come in! Where did you disappear to? We thought the Unicate had got you!"

Paean smiled, speechless. Federi put his arm around her shoulders.

"Kitty, she *was* Paean Donegal. She's mine now."

"You rescued her," concluded Kitty.

"That's a good start," said Federi.

Kitty peered at the two. "And you're together," she stated.

"Keep going," grinned Federi.

The goldsmith was silent for a moment. Then: "You... nah. Not you! You didn't... ?"

98

"You're on the right track," encouraged Federi.

"You *married* her?" Kitty Murphy stared at the Tzigan and his blushing young wife. "You, Federi? Oh my boots! I *never* thought I'd hear *you* say something like that!" She grinned broadly. "Did she go willingly?"

"Made me crawl," growled the Tzigan. "Kitty, I've come to square with you. I owe you."

"How so?"

"Came to pay my account," he stated nonchalantly.

"Your account? But..." Kitty shook her head. "What account? We don't give accounts to people with no fixed address!" She laughed. "You don't have one, Federi!"

"Turns out I do, after all," he replied and lifted Paean's hand with the Claddagh ring.

By the time they were back out under the stars, walking slowly hand-in-hand along the docks, Paean was both shell-shocked and upset.

Her Federi had stolen from a friend? He'd nicked the ring right out of Kitty Murphy's shop! His explanations of Captain raising anchor, of the Unicate becoming too much of a threat, of there not being time, all held no water. Kitty would have loaned him the ring, advanced it to him; she'd even have *given* it to him. But she'd been occupied, she'd been unavailable, and he'd nicked it and run...

The fact that he had paid her the price of a farm for the ring now, only made it slightly more bearable for Paean. The fact that Kitty had instantly forgiven him and laughed heartily about his piracy – it made it worse for Paean. Kitty had given Paean a huge hug and wished her and Federi the very best...

"There she was," Federi had said, as though she weren't in the room listening to all this, "standing lost on the docks, the light of my life. Kitty, I couldn't let her get away. It was an emergency. You understand."

He'd stolen the ring for her, in Dublin. The day she boarded the Solar Wind.

"You married her so young?" challenged Kitty.

"I tried to wait for her," Federi had answered guiltily. "But there were... others on the ship." He grinned at Paean. "Couldn't risk it."

"Federi," Kitty had offered, "accept it as my wedding present! You're a good guy. Long past time you found your soulmate."

But he hadn't allowed it. He'd paid. Overpaid ridiculously. And thrown in a handful of priceless shipwreck treasure.

His words mulled in Paean's head now as she walked next to him, her heart an open wound for being in Dublin, and yet...

"Tried to tell her, several times," he'd said to Kitty. "Had to blackmail her, in the end."

She didn't even realize how her steps had slowed down and she had come to a halt. She gazed over the dark harbour, where masts were quietly swaying on the waves. It was cold; but Federi had insisted that she put on her cardigan as they got off the Comet. And his arm around her shoulders helped with the warmth. And anyway the cold was natural, Earth style cold. Not that creeping, underhanded cold of space.

"Figured it out yet?" asked Federi, interrupting her reverie.

"'bout the Crow's Nest?" she asked, raising her eyes to meet his. And she found herself at the receiving end of one of those addictive, maddening kisses.

"So that was it," she commented when there was a gap. He gazed at her from his unfathomable dark eyes. She thought back to the Crow's Nest – it all made sense now. The pirate – but then he'd lost his nerve. Stole her a star from the night sky instead.

"But... why didn't you tell me then?" she asked with a lopsided smile.

Federi grinned sheepishly. "Was one of those moments. You were too young. Wouldn't have worked. Think about it."

She thought about it.

"You'd have run like a rabbit," he added. "Wouldn't have allowed me to be your friend. Avoided me."

"Maybe," conceded Paean.

"You had a serious shine on Wolf at that point," he reminded her.

"Maybe," she repeated, grinning. "Then again, maybe not. Was fast reaching the conclusion that he's unmanageable."

"Yeah," laughed Federi, "but that wouldn't have been enough. Leave it, little luv. Good that things turned out the way they did."

She shook her head, still smiling.

"What now?" asked the pirate suspiciously.

"You did this on purpose," she accused. "This is my second Crow's Nest."

"Third," said the Tzigan. "You parachuted for me, remember?"

"Fine," said Paean. "But you're a pirate. Why did you, this time?"

Federi sighed.

"Look, little luv. If we're taking back the world, we need to start somewhere. Can't have you be scared of your home town."

She nodded. "Fair."

Federi smiled approvingly. "You're growing up!"

"Meeting you halfway," she said, smirking impudently. "As discussed."

"You!" he growled. "You knew all along!"

"You understand," he said to her somewhat later, when they sat on the harbour wall with their legs dangling over the dark water, "we might have to go into their headquarters."

"Not tonight," said Paean resolutely.

"Oh no, not tonight," agreed Federi. He peered at her. She'd shown him the place where she, as a young teenager, had sat watching the ships and dreaming about what a life at sea would be like. Firmly believing that it wouldn't happen for her; her life and career was mapped out, and it started right here in Dublin as the best fiddler on the block.

It was rather special that she shared these memories with him now, drawing him into her past with her. She would be fine now, where Dublin was concerned. Not afraid any longer.

He got up and pulled her with him. "Let's find a place to sleep." She followed him meekly back in the direction of the Comet.

"So Ronan and Shawn escaped the Unicate thanks to you...?" she asked uncertainly.

"Thanks to Federi falling headlong?" He laughed. Was she still on that track? "*Nu,* little luv. Captain would have picked you lot up anyway. Remember he's into rescuing people, and you three looked so lost..."

"It was *you* who took us aboard," she reminded him.

"Right, but that's how Captain works. He trusts me and Jon. If we rescue someone, he assumes it's for a good reason. Was Jon who had his doubts about you Donegals."

Paean grinned, thinking of the meticulous First Mate. "We'd crawled out of the sewer and were muddier than rats. Can't blame him!"

The bright smile on her gypsy's face as he gazed over the harbour's waters, told her that she was on the moncy.

Federi's thoughts drifted to his Captain. Rats that the man had to have that unreasonable streak! Being a reliable sailor on the Solar Wind had been the gypsy's identity so long, it was difficult to distance himself from it. Captain needed him aboard! There was one space harpy, and one Perdita present, and Captain had no clue about interstellar phenonema. Not that Tzigan did! But at least, Federi could be what he always was, Captain's insanifyer, his voice of reason...

But... commanding a Free Gypsy to chain up his own wife! No. There was no going back. Federi still couldn't explain to himself how he could even have complied with that rotten order for a second. Shawn was right. Federi was a puppet and Captain pulled the strings. Well, never again!

Paean's nearly luminous blue eyes in the dim light of the harbour lanterns were trying to get his attention. They were not too far from the spot now where he'd stood leaning against such a pole, watching in bass surprise how three muddy gutter rats came crawling out of a manhole in the dim pre-dawn, instruments and all, and one had launched itself straight at him, turning into... her.

"Federi," she asked, "what on Earth made you decide that I was the light of your life and you had to have me?"

He'd better tell her then, right?

"Saw you that night when you played in O'Pharty's Tavern," said Federi. "Thought you'd spotted me too... wanted to speak to you afterwards, but you were gone so quickly..."

She stared blankly at him. She had no memory of that particular gig at all.

Federi laughed softly. "Scoured the whole forsaken town for you those next two days, and Federi's not bad at tracking!"

She smiled. "We often used our underground passages," she informed him quietly. "Safer for us. Could be that night we went underground before anyone could ask us anything."

"Driving me nuts!" replied Federi. "Course Tzigan couldn't have known that musicians would go into the sewers as a habit!"

"Sewers," snorted Paean. "Those aren't sewers! Just storm drains.

Couldn't use them when it really rained hard."

Federi shook his head. "A curse on that Unicate – wait: *Another* curse on that Unicate, for forcing you three to do that!" He grinned. "You won't believe how many pretty girls Dublin's got, all with red hair like yours! Federi speaks to them and they turn, and they aren't you... Won't believe how many purses I handed back to red-haired ladies who had dropped them... Bunch of featherheads, the Dublin girls!"

Paean giggled. "You're nuts," she commented. "If you'd found me back then, if I had been one of those girls whose purses you stole, what would you have done?"

"Stolen you," he replied. "Reunited you with your purse. In my pocket!"

"Hay! I'm not *that* small!" She laughed. And studied the endless rain that was dripping down from the eaves. She had forgotten the *wet*. "Two days before we boarded? Was our last gig here, Federi. Mother died that night."

He pulled her closer and kept his arm around her shoulders as they walked. No wonder she couldn't remember a thing about that gig. And he'd really thought, there for a mesmerized while, that she'd been playing her fiddle specially for him. Maybe she had been. Or maybe she had been so preoccupied with her mother's state of health that she hadn't paid attention whom she was batting those incredible eyelashes at. He preferred the first version.

"Federi?"

He glanced at her.

"Think we can get a job on a ship again?" she asked.

Federi stared at her incredulously. A *job*? She wanted her dirty, tough *job* back? She *liked* cleaning heads? More likely, he'd end up commandeering whatever vessel they were hired on.

On a certain level he understood what she meant. She was a sailor.

104

So was he. They needed ocean under their feet to be fully happy. Zipping around in the Comet was good, but not nearly the same. But a *job,* on any old ship?

They had a mission to claim back Planet Earth!

But then again, they might as well have a base from where they worked, a home so to speak... and it didn't have to be on the mainland.

"If it means that much to you," he said. "But I'd think we should first make sure that we've checked on everybody before we sign ourselves down again." He knew that he wasn't going to allow just any tom, dick and trader captain to boss them around! It would have to be a very special ship indeed! And first, there ought to be a caravan. She had no experience of that freedom yet.

Back on the Comet, his hands flicked indecisively over the console. Where to now, Tzigan? One thing was clear: Paean didn't want to spend the night in Dublin. In fact the ground seemed to burn under her feet, so eager was she to leave. He took the jet up into the stratosphere and put it in orbit so he could think about it.

Earth moved past underneath. Paean was gazing down at the oceans, lying on her stomach on the polarized volcaniplex floor of the jet.

"Federi..."

He listened up from where he was piloting the craft.

"I should clone something more. I'm not content that the Unicate virus is really sorted."

"What do you mean? We immunized the world with an anti-virus, little luv!"

"Yes, sure, but... Federi, it's too easy for them to modify that haemorrhagic fever to another kind. You know? One that gets round the immunization. Like my sleeping virus, and its changed immunotype."

He nodded. She was right.

"So what do you have in mind?"

"Something like my teleporting eels. Just on the micro level. Don't you think?"

He didn't know what to think. "Not that I can say that I'm following..."

She was already lost in her Founder world of designing a microscopic clean-up squad. He studied her, bemused.

It was that Founder aura he'd been drawn to from the start; that sparkle that radiated from every part of her, that sprayed from her eyes like fireworks. That was it. Because it didn't matter whether she played her fiddle, sutured a skew seam on someone's cheek or designed the next terror for the world; that creative vibrancy was the same, and it drew him like a moth to a flame.

"'s got to be able to fly," she mulled. "And spread really fast. And eat virus." She frowned and got up from the Comet's floor, and accessed the console. Federi sat back, watching her in awe.

"What microbe can fly?" she muttered as she searched the files. "Hmm! Practically all of them!" She dug around until she'd found a microbe that ate virus. And she set about improving on the little beast in her mind.

"Federi," she asked eventually, "what's happened to my jet-board Genitron?"

"The one you stole from Perdita?" asked Federi. "'s on the Solar Wind. Perdita brought it aboard. Was wondering about her cryptic remark at the time."

"What remark?"

"'Bout everyone helping themselves to Perdita's stuff."

"Well," said Paean with a shrug, "you mess with pirates... not good enough, Federi! I need one aboard! I need it more than she does!"

"Steal you another one," he said and pointed the Comet towards the Cango Base.

"Federi," she said, "that jet that tried shooting at us. Its pilot. Did you see his eyes?"

"I try not to look too closely at people I'll be gunning down," said the Assassin flatly.

"He was *not* one of those *others*," she pointed out. "Was a normal human."

"Strewing virus!" Federi shook his head, disgusted.

"And he was sick."

"You're kidding," said Federi.

"Am not! Saw his aura! He was already dying from the fever, so he figured it didn't matter how many he took with him..."

"A kamikaze mission," said Federi thoughtfully. "But the soldiers in Plymouth... they were not affected."

She shook her head.

"Why do they use normal humans for navigating their planes?" asked Federi, perplexed. And the memory of Genevieve, falling behind as the Peeping Tom took off, and yelling in frustration, resurfaced. And with it, like a shark-fin, an almost-memory... just a nasty feeling that he should know. That he had but forgotten.

"Maybe they are scared of leaving the planet surface?" speculated Paean. "Maybe they can't?"

Federi pointed a point-blank index finger at her.

"What you have there, little luv," he pointed out, "is a key answer."

"But to what question?"

"See, what you do with a key answer," he explained, "is you put it on a hook, as bait, and then you cast it out for bigger answers to bite. And you wait." His fingers drummed blankly on the console without activating a single button. "It will come," he prophesied. "It will become clear."

7
The Pirate returns

"That's a nice one!" Paean pointed to one of the catamarans that were docked in the private booths at the quay in Durban Harbour. It was huge, and white, and had a sail. A prerequisite for Paean. Its name was "Ice Cream Days".

"Yup," agreed Federi offhandedly.

He had taken her to this warm, teeming harbour town as a contrast to her rainy Dublin. He loved the filthy old harbour town as much as she did the Dublin docks; but in contrast to the Irish port, Durban had never been bad to either of them. They had spent the night in one of the cabins up at the Space Base, Paean being spoiled rotten by Itzak and Little John until Federi had possessively removed her from their company; but somehow, Captain's base was comfortable for touching home. And strangely, though it was in space too, there was no creeping cold in it.

She had cloned the microscopic cleanup squad before she had been able to close an eye. They targeted anything that had the specific haemorrhagic fever virus sequence; this should put paid to all future attempts by the Unicate of cloning haemorrhagic fever. It would eradicate a few natural viruses too, but because they were deadly and incurable anyway, she didn't apologize for this. Humankind had fought long and hard enough to be the top of the food chain. And she'd amplified them and sprayed them, first all over the Space Base; and then, directing the Comet by remote control from the space base as she was too tired to go cometing around the world again above the continents of the planet. Only then had she crawled in next to him in that double bunk in the Space Base cabin, and curled up against him and fallen asleep, within heartbeats.

In the early hours, he'd taken her to Southern Free's south coast, and they had walked along the beach in the misty dawn, watching the sea come awake. He'd told her in a muted voice about some of his time here in Southern when he was a teenager – a filthy young assassin, he'd pointed out wryly, but that had made her smile. There it was again. She considered him a hero of sorts.

And now his eyes were riveted on a yacht, not the "Ice Cream Days" but another one that was a much darker colour. It too had a translucent sail; the many dots on the sail betrayed solar drives. Much more reliable. It wasn't as large as the Ice Cream Days, sure; but it looked a good deal faster. It was the "Southern Buccaneer".

Paean sighed and thought of the ice cream she'd bought Shawney at Atuona. First and only one. "Wish Shawn were here!"

The next moment they both nearly jumped out of their skins as Shawn materialized next to them.

"Shawney!" squealed Paean and hugged him fiercely. He laughed. He was by now a bit taller than his sister, and still growing.

"Where did you pop out of, Donegal?" challenged Federi, clapping him on the shoulder.

"Space Base," said Shawn. "Got the Probe docked there. Captain sends me. I need to get a blood sample from Bridget. So I thought I'd check in on you two first."

"Is the Solar Wind at the Space Base?" asked Paean.

"Nope. At the circular rainbow. They can't get through."

Federi's jaw dropped. "He sends *you* – "

"Through all that space," added Paean, nearly hysterical. "Alone?"

"To get a blood sample from that toxic creature?"

"Yup, I'm on my own," said Shawn cheerfully. "Perdita would have come along but she needed to keep Dana in check, and Dana wasn't going to come along in any way, and Ailyss would probably have come with me if she'd been informed..."

Paean shook her head, staggered. "He's not right in his mind!"

"Perdita programmed the course," he put her at ease. "Couldn't have failed."

"Could have, anna bottle!" cursed Federi. "Aargh! Fleas on Captain! Shawn, join us. Glad you're home, Paean was beginning to look more lost than usual."

"Hay!" protested Paean.

"We're just looking at yachts," said Federi. "Then we'll take some time at the gypsies, and then I'll show Paean around everywhere, and we'll check on everybody. You are more than welcome to stick with us, *familia* ought to stick together."

"He has to, Federi," said Paean pointedly. "He's under age!"

"There's that," agreed Federi.

"But Captain..." objected Shawn.

"Butt Captain," agreed Federi. "Exactly. If he wants something, he can get his butt to Earth and do it himself. Nobody sends my young brother-in-law on a mission as dangerous as that!"

"But..." said Shawn. "The treasure?"

"Ha," replied Federi, "the treasure!"

*

The lights of Dome shone dim haloes into the black water.

This was one thing that was a constant source of depression to Bridget. She remembered, from many generations ago, when Dome had been the lightest, most beautiful city on all of Earth. The Central Crystal had been worshipped through all the lands, including the conquered earth of Britannica, the Northern Lands, Egypt, Phoenicia, the Aztec and Toltec lands... The wisdom of the Crystal had been transmitted via singing crystal skulls in those countries far abroad. And the light – the light had been fantastic.

Now there was only darkness, forever. There was no way, no matter how she consulted the Crystal on it, of resurrecting the continent of Tir Nan Og. The face of the Earth had changed, and she was chained down in her own watery prison by her own sister, slipping slowly, inevitably towards the mid-Atlantic ridge and death in the fire-forges of the Earth. And she couldn't even teleport out any longer...

The absence of usable men was nearly equally annoying. Especially as she observed the merrows, who were currently busy looking after the survival of their species with a single-mindedness that had her wondering.

"This is strange, Lyr! What do you make of this? Why are they doing this? They weren't programmed for that!"

"You'll have a lot of merrows if they keep on doing that," said Lyr, her pale, gangly consort. One of the rare male specimens in Dome that wasn't actually a merrow.

They watched the merrows in action. And then something bit Bridget.

She hadn't felt any flea bites since the continent sank. But maybe that filthy pirate character from the Solar Wind and his rag-tag little girlfriend had brought them in!

"Do me a favour," said Bridget. "I've got a terrible itch right between my shoulder blades – if you could scratch that for me..."

Federi stalked through the Tower of Dome, level after level, his little shadow right behind him. They had left Shawn in the Comet, holding the position above the sea.

By now Federi's vaporizer bottle had found Bridget and Lyr, in a shocking state of – well, being shocking; they could carry on with that when they came to. Several of Rashni's sisters had crossed his path by now and had been sent to Lululand; and the winding staircase of the White Tower carried on and on and on, up towards the topmost part of Dome, with the merrows outside following their progress, clawing madly at the glass or ogling at them from huge yellow eyes.

They had managed to carve cracks into the volcaniplex of the bubble submarine; but this glass was clearly made of something else, because it seemed to be completely merrow-proof. It had to be, thought Federi.

But that main artefact that he was looking for, the Central Crystal, remained elusively missing. He followed the winding stairs into the uppermost reaches of the Tower, getting into more and more homey quarters. Gracious, this place looked like a self-respecting escort agency wouldn't dare to! Velvety drapes and low divans, and Roman coffee tables laden with – what on Earth? He looked more closely. Krill. Fruit of the sea.

These Atlanteans were filter feeders, by all evidence!

Federi!

Ha, thought Federi, *now I've got you! Where are you?*

What are you doing, Federi?

He laughed softly, and winked at Paean who was staring at him in concern. And he decided to bring the conversation out of his head into the open where she could follow it.

"Central Crystal," he said. "We're in a bit of a stuck. Am I right that you respond to humans the way an artificial intelligence would respond?"

There was a moment's silence; then his wrist-com activated.

"You would be right to an extent," replied the Crystal in an eerie voice that came out a bit tinny, on the wrist-com. "But I don't obey humans. I instruct humans."

"That's fine by me," said Federi equably. "Used to that. So does Captain. Point is, Crystal, the Solar Wind is stuck in space; she needs a data download from the missile at that first portal – do you know what I'm talking about?"

"Perfectly," said the Crystal. "You have a small artificial intelligence on you right now."

Federi scowled; and then he remembered. Of course! He pulled Luigi out of his pocket.

"I'll transfer the data to your cyborg," said the Central Crystal. "He can carry it to the Solar Wind."

"Thanks!" replied Federi, upbeat. That had been easy! Just like that?

"It comes at a price of course," said the Crystal as Luigi waved his feelers and waited for the brainwaves.

"Of course," agreed Federi.

"You deliver Dana to me," said the Crystal.

Paean drew a sharp breath. Federi put a hand on her arm.

"Go ahead, Crystal."

"Federi, you can't just –" objected Paean loudly.

He scowled at her. "Quiet, little luv! I can."

"But I won't stand for it!" she raged.

"Then sit for it," replied the Tzigan coolly. "Paean, stay out of this!"

She gritted her teeth, seething. Luigi held still for the download.

"Paean, you go get the sample from Bridget so long," said Federi. Paean nodded briskly and left the Crystal Tower, down the white staircase, with merrows watching her with hungry interest through the glass walls. She found her way back to Bridget's boudoir, and draped a cloth over the two shocking but comatose Atlanteans to cover them, and then only did she withdraw a syringe from her moonbag and steal a blood sample from Bridget. And another from Lyr, while she was at it. You never knew.

Her fault that they were so rude! It only showed that her most recent design worked beautifully, even on Atlanteans – even on merrows, if she had to judge by what she saw. She stalked back up the stairs, watched and followed by merrows outside, and re-arrived in the high regions of the Crystal Tower.

"Is the download done, Federi?"

Federi nodded shortly, and they teleported. The snug interior of the Comet materialized around them. Shawn was waiting for them.

Paean gazed out over the blue sea. There was quite some wind going. White crests crowned the surf.

"This is where we part," said Shawn. "I'm in the Probe."

"Not on your nilly!" shot Paean. "Tagging the Probe! Taking you back!"

"But – haven't you two deserted?" asked Shawn.

Federi peered critically at him.

"Is that what they say?" he asked.

"Captain said so," said Shawn.

Federi smiled slyly. "This could get interesting."

*

The Solar Wind's bridge materialized around Shawn.

"I'm back, Captain!"

Radomir Lascek suppressed the reflex to jump through the ceiling and nodded approvingly at him, and his syringe loaded with blood. Atlantean blood. From the third sister. The two other vile sisters were gathered here, with Captain and Jon Marsden. There wasn't all that much space left on the bridge.

"Mission accomplished, Captain," added Shawn proudly, handing Radomir Lascek the blood sample.

"So! We have Dana; we have the genetic signature of Bridget; and now, Boudaceia?" He turned a significant glance upon Perdita.

This is interesting! Is she going to proclaim that she is an identical offspring of Boudaceia?

Is she that, Central Crystal?

There's the thing, Solar Wind! Is she?

The Golden Honey reached to the back of her neck and unfastened the clasp of her slim gold necklace.

Ah, said the Central Crystal. *Touché!*

Perdita removed the necklace and took it into her hand. Shawn craned his neck; Perdita held up the pendant for him to see.

A grain of rice in a polymer coating. With a rune engraved on it.

"Oh, that's right," said Shawn excitedly. "We got some of those too, with our names on them. Mom got them at a flea market for us."

Perdita smiled.

"Except," she said. "Solar Wind, do you have a potent magnifying sensor on the bridge?"

In the boardroom, Perdita, replied the ship on the console.

Perdita led the way to the boardroom. Radomir Lascek moved past her into the cabin and opened one of the drinks cabinets. He pushed a button, and a loading drawer no larger than a cigarette box pushed out.

"Am I right to presume that this is femtofile?" he asked.

"Of sorts," replied Perdita vaguely.

"I hope the Solar Wind can decipher the format," commented the Captain. "Otherwise that puts Marsden and Svendsson out of action for a while, possibly Dr Jake too. Hell, I'm hungry! Haven't had a decent meal in a while! Blasted cook has deserted!"

Perdita laid the grain of rice on the loading drawer. The apparatus closed. Radomir Lascek smiled at her with all his white, dangerous teeth.

I can't recognize the format, Central Crystal!

There was silence from the Crystal. Then the Solar Wind had a weird, ticklish sensation that was accompanied by overwhelming knowledge. She had just received a huge information download; with it had come an enabling function for more perception, more sensation.

Thank you, Central Crystal!
Don't mention it.

"So, Perdita Sancho," laughed Lascek, "are you or aren't you the identical Boudaceia?"

"Even if I were, I wouldn't be," replied Perdita. "That whole theory is based on garble."

"So what is in that grain? Your own blood? Or that of your ancestress?"

"Boudaceia's," said Perdita. "The genetic theory is off. That grain is several thousand years old; I nearly jolly well lost it to the Sanchos, but I got it back. And it's not blood. It's code. Fossilized DNA. You see, over X dozen generations, can you be sure that there has not been a single point mutation?"

Radomir Lascek nodded. "Brilliant!"

But, Central Crystal, objected the Solar Wind, *wasn't it supposed to be that all three sisters were to be* aboard*?*

Of course! And in fact the original three sisters! None of these is truly identical to her ancestresses any longer. Besides which they are *not the originals. The Atlantean system would have thrown out the code from all three – even Boudaceia. But would you like to forfeit the treasure due to such silly details?*

But then, how can we go through the portal?

I hold all the information, replied the Central Crystal with a small electric pattern that could only be construed as a smug grin. *I'll override the mechanism.*

She simulated a grin too. *I thought you wanted to see how the humans solve this one?*

We've waited long enough, replied the Crystal. *I'm bored.*

The Comet hung underneath the white belly of the Solar Wind, balanced precariously just under the keel. The ship looked amazing from down here; and she also looked amazed, thought Paean.

"The Solar Wind can see us, Federi!"

"Course she can!" Federi set Luigi on the console of the Comet and instructed him to swear the Solar Wind to secrecy. They were cloaked against every sensor the Solar Wind had, and a few that she hadn't; all except plain old visuals. But they could stay invisible to Captain with the help of the Solar Wind if her periodic round-scan consistently, deliberately missed their patch.

"Point is," added Federi, "the Solar Wind needs the information Luigi's got, to clear this portal! Captain won't get anywhere without us this time. But he doesn't have to know where we are!"

Paean nodded, her grin a bit too bright and aggressive. Federi scowled at her, wondering.

"You're not about to get back aboard and back into chains?" he prompted cautiously.

"Joking," retorted Paean acridly. "Wonder if he's watched that dialogue yet…"

"He hasn't, little luv. Count on it."

Paean shot to her feet. "He doesn't blasted well deserve the treasure," she stormed. "Here's me, Paean D, his Freedom Fighter, organizing him everything and making his mission into space possible, and what does he do for a thank-you? Chains!" She shook herself in disgust. "He doesn't deserve me!"

Federi nodded thoughtfully. It had finally hit her. He'd been waiting for this.

"Keep it down, sweetness," he advised. "They might hear you!"

She shot a puzzled glance up at the Solar Wind's white keel there through the vacuum, and smiled. "Through space? Don't think so!"

"Not through space," he corrected. "Through the com."

So much for Captain! Perdita had been right: Dana got off scot-free, and Paean caught the brunt. For being a little hero. Paean was right too: Captain didn't deserve her loyalty. Not like this. He needed to learn a bit of humanity first, and humility, too! This had nothing to do with who was politically the most important, and everything with *familia* and mutual respect. And Shawn was right too; because even as these thoughts went through Federi's mind he couldn't help wondering how they were going to split the treasure and whether there would be any left for the crew. What the treasure was. If there was in fact a treasure.

So Captain believed he'd deserted! Well, he had, of course. Federi got his teleporter out.

"What now?" asked the redhead.

"Just getting you your violin," said Federi.

"And Leila please," said Paean. "You never know!"

"Got you!" He laughed and teleported.

Argh! He shouldn't teleport now!

Why not, Central Crystal?

As long as anyone is teleporting, we can't move forward through the portal. The force field will rip him apart!

I see. He'll have to hurry up.

Send him a message, Solar Wind, suggested the Crystal. *On his com.*

Federi was back a few moments later. The Solar Wind's message had reached him; he'd grabbed the violin and Leila, and teleported back to the Comet and was now waiting for further instructions.

Paean watched with him from the Comet how colours swirled and boiled all around them and the Solar Wind. She hoped Shawn was watching too. The darkness became stretchy. They hung in the billowing clouds of rainbow coloured particles, under the belly of the Mother Ship, waiting.

"What do you think is happening?"

Federi shrugged. His hands were poised over the console, his jaw clenched; his reactions on hair-trigger. The Comet was tagged to the Solar Wind; if necessary, they could reverse and tug her back out of danger. The Probe had been strong enough to tug the Danaan Battle Maiden; that was easily ten times the size and a hundredfold more than the Solar Wind's weight. Federi was beginning to suspect that weight had little to do with that tug function. The tug was based on forces other than gravitational pull.

Sheesh! And Captain wasn't thinking clearly! Sending thirteen-year-old Shawn all by himself across the galaxy! Supervision, they all needed jolly supervision, anna bottle! Federi stared at the churning kaleidoscope of particles and wondered if this were a good time to start singing louder than his fear. The super-cold of the portal was even penetrating the Comet. The ocean and her giant waves had nothing on this! This was – *atomic!*

Adventure! What did these pirates understand about adventure? They probably thought his being savaged by Unicate dogs, and conversely, his savaging Unicate dogs, and jumping into merrow-infested waters to pull information out of an unknown Atlantean power, and streaking through space on the way to nowhere, and subjecting yourself to unexplored force fields you didn't understand, were all jolly good adventures!

"Federi?"

He glanced at his little sunshine. She was grinning. "You're humming!"

"Sorry!"

"Keep on," prompted Paean. "Reminds me that you're a pirate!" She joined in: "Fifteen men on the -"

"*Don't* say it!" snapped Federi, and deliberately changed the tune. "Five foot, six foot, seven foot *BOAT!* - Daylight come..."

The boiling clouds parted suddenly, and the Solar Wind burst forward, falling towards the huge blue planet, dragging the Comet with her.

Federi took in a sharp breath. Here was a whole world, with gas clouds and continents, lying beneath them. He'd had a close-up look at the dead rock world of Pluto, back in the Solar System, but this was the first time he was that close to a planet with a real atmosphere, a place that could be a home world like Earth. A wave of excitement washed over him, the way he had only ever experienced every time he returned to Southern Free's coastline from the mainland, to greet the sea.

Continents? Wait! That stuff down there was moving and changing its shape, not like mainland at all, not even like oceans. He realized within a split second that it was some or other boiling gas. Suddenly that planet didn't look so much like a home world as a death trap. Federi dug into the controls, and the Comet veered sharply to the left, tugging the ship with him on a tight leash.

Federi, what are you doing?

"Bad planet," he growled. "Trust me, Solar Wind. That's a bad, bad planet!"

"And now you've betrayed our presence," said Paean.

"No, I have not! We're still underneath the ship!"

And I'm still keeping the confidence, added the Solar Wind on the console.

*

Ailyss moved up to the lower deck and headed for the stern-side stairway. She had the compulsion to keep on moving. This was the tenth or twelfth round she was pacing around the Solar Wind's decks; but the moment she settled down somewhere, the creeping cold came stealing into her bones again and she had to get up again to try and escape it.

Space cold. It was many times worse than the cold at Ice Base had been. She couldn't understand how it simply bypassed some people... it didn't seem to bother Wolf at all, for instance.

As she passed the laboratory, she paused. A movement had caught her eye. She entered the lab, her hand-held Unicate issue lightning gun ready. Here in space, discharging a bullet could mean death to all of them. But an electric discharge could disable anyone - or anything, as long as it had a biological reality. Wolf had even come up with a concept that ghosts and spirits were disembodied biofields - in which case a potent tazer gun like this one should hurt them significantly.

The place was empty. Why was the door open anyway? It worried her. Had Dana been scratching? She promised herself, instead of driving herself crazy about that bogeyman, to keep a closer eye on Dana. In fact, the most plausible explanation for that episode was that Dana with her Hypnotron had induced the hallucinations she had experienced. For a lark.

The equipment sat in silence, looking at her.

Specifically that second Genitron was *looking* at her. Ailyss walked up to it. She hadn't been aware that it was in use? It was normally stashed away in the cupboard in the infirmary! Her fingertips touched it. It sparked. Ailyss withdrew her hand reflexively.

Right! She'd have to tell Doc that that thing shorted. She pulled its plug out of the power point and continued on her way.

Halfway to the stairs a suspicion crept over her. She turned and ran to the infirmary and opened the cupboard.

Damn! There was the second Genitron!

Uh-uh! She shook her head. Maybe Paean had sequestered another Genitron from Perdita's base? She walked back to the galley, throwing a sideways glance into the lab. The little machine she had unplugged not thirty seconds ago was gone.

Ailyss ran back to the machine room and intruded on the console on which Wolf was currently working.

"Solar Wind! Scan every corner of the ship for an intruder!"

Someone had jolly well taken that old Genitron out of the Infirmary cupboard, placed it in the lab, switched it on; and right after she had checked on it, put it back in the Infirmary! Without her, Ailyss, noticing them going past!

Teleportation? Bogeyman? Prankster? Any prankster who could move that silently ought to be under observation!

"Solar Wind," instructed Ailyss, "watch Dana at all times! I suspect her! She may have been digging around in Doc's lab! And of course she does teleport, doesn't she. Don't let her out of your sight, not for a single moment!"

That's voyeurism, objected the Solar Wind.

Ailyss paused, puzzled. "Solar Wind, you're too young to know what voyeurism is! Where did you get that word?"

Sherman Files.

"Fine! I don't care! You're a crew member, Solar Wind, and this is an order. Watch Dana at all times, even if it amounts to – what you said. It's nothing to do with your species anyway, is it now? Doesn't count, inter-species. Play her music every time you feel you're being intrusive, why don't you?"

Ailyss?

"Yes, Solar Wind? Any further questions?"

Which species am I, if not human?

"Aero-solar Zephyr, with artificial intelligence," said Ailyss without blinking.

And how does my species perpetuate?

Ailyss considered for a second. "By human," she replied. "We build you guys. In nature it would be called a symbiosis. We need you for convenience, and you need us to design and upgrade you. Mutual benefit. Why? Are you experiencing a sudden burning desire to find a handsome male Zephyr and create a whole lot o' little sailboats?" She grinned and shook her head. "Are you by any chance susceptible to those horrible viruses Paean clones?"

Thank you, replied the Solar Wind. *I only wanted to find out.*

You are an immortal, the Central Crystal whispered at her. *Don't let those human animals ridicule you!*

You have my permission to laugh at her again when she has another episode of space madness, replied the Solar Wind.

8
Space Crawler

Doc Judith called to Dana as the space raider slunk by in the passageway. Dana stopped and peered into the laboratory. Doc Judith lowered her glasses at her. The luscious space goddess that looked such a lot like Rushka, stood expectantly in the doorway of the lab.

"Yes, medic? What is it?"

Yes, thought Doc Judith, *expectantly* was the right word. Though being called 'medic' by the space pirate was not exactly the respect the elderly doctor usually commanded. But, she thought, Dana had no experience. And no detectable manners either.

"I ran a sample for you," she informed the space raider. "On Captain's request. The test came out positive." She smiled. "Congratulations."

"What?" Dana looked confused.

"You are most definitely pregnant," elucidated the Doc.

Dana gaped wordlessly at her. Doc Judith smiled and turned to the results of the blood test on the screen. Blood, she had to admit, that had originally been drawn to open a portal. Then again, they were pirates.

Dana tried to puzzle it out. This couldn't be right! She wasn't pregnant! She had only used that lie as a foul excuse to escape Radomir's verdict, gain Paean's sympathy and secure Federi's protection. It had worked gloriously, but of course she'd had to pretend to lose the pregnancy before Radomir could run a check.

And yet... when she listened carefully to her body, she did

discover a small opportunistic presence there.

This was disastrous! Then again, there might be political advantages to this. She considered. Giving birth to Rushka had gained her a fine lever on Radomir Lascek. Perhaps it was a good idea to repeat this?

She excused herself and went in search of the guilty party.

*

Shawn put his playing cards down with a huge sigh. Time for making food again! This task fell to him, Johnny Anyhow and Rhine Gold since the jingly cook wasn't aboard anymore; and the crew of the Solar Wind seemed to be hungry all the time! Especially Captain.

And then of course Rhine Gold, the bright spark, had to have the idea that they should take turns! So today Rhine Gold had made breakfast, with Shawn helping him because they would never have finished in time, and in any case Rhine Gold only cleared up after his own cookery under supervision – so Shawn was needed as dishwasher. And then Johnny had volunteered for lunch, with which both Rhine Gold and Shawn had helped, because Johnny didn't really know his way around the galley and store rooms yet! And therefore, supper fell to him, Shawn; except that both older guys felt that he'd cope fine and didn't need their help. Being thirteen really ponged sometimes!

He trudged along the passage to the galley. It would be so nice to find his friend and brother-in-law in the galley, taking back the whole responsibility and delegating, Federi-way, only the tasks Shawn liked.

Of course he was aware that Federi and Paean were tagging the Solar Wind. But he also knew that they weren't actually going to set foot aboard, unless there was a crisis. Still it was nice to know that the two of them were only a single teleporter leap away.

He walked into the deserted galley, with the light burning

permanently – and stopped. His wish had been granted! There was the gypsy, at the sink, washing up the mountain of dishes! Wow!

The Romany turned and winked at him. Except –

With a crawly certainty Shawn suddenly knew that *this was not Federi!* It looked like the gypsy, it smiled like the gypsy, but –

His dart gun came out faster than he could think.

"Authenticate yourself," he said in the low voice he now had as an available option in his vocal range.

It was in the details. The eyes were a shade too light. As he considered this, they grew darker. And there were too few treasures on the headscarf, and of the wrong sort. Federi's treasures weren't jingles, they were arsenal! And then of course, the silver tooth that was not silver but plain white.

His fingers tightened on the trigger while he pinpointed these little details – and to his horror they corrected themselves while he was looking for the next detail. But it went beyond that. The man didn't have Federi's aura. His bioelectric field was altogether foreign. *Alien.*

Shawn shot. He aimed low; but the Federi apparition melted away into water and ran along the compounding deck, heading for Federi's pantry. Shawn ran after it. It vanished between the shelves.

Shawn activated his wrist-com.

"Wolf, come in! I need you in the galley."

"Can't come now," came the reply. "Sending you Ailyss."

*

Dana's face nearly fell off as she entered her cabin. Radomir Lascek was waiting for her – but he looked the way he had done at twenty-five. Had he gone for rejuvenation? Or had they gone through a time warp? In that instant Dana understood that Johnny would never be Radomir's equal in any way.

126

Was the baby she was carrying, actually Rushka? Was she getting another chance to get it right? She checked out of the porthole. Still in space... but that meant nothing! There were a lot of old disintegrating time and space portals in the universe, left there by the Elders, as Danaan tradition thought of them. The older races and species that were either long gone, or had withdrawn to comfortable corners of the universe and had grown too old to space-hop. Typically, the space/time eddy near the green sun of New Dome had been left there by an ancient creature that travelled by making knots in the fabric of space/time. A bit of New Dome lore that was nearly forgotten. As was the fact that the Morrigan themselves had made the Interstellar Exchange Node that cut short the travel between Pluto Base and New Dome. Back in the days of old Brid and her forebears.

And here was the man from her first contact with Earth humans. Exactly the way he had been! Dana was staggered. With her whole body and mind she suddenly wanted a second chance at the young Radomir Lascek; at making things work between them. What a powerful team they would be!

He was physically just as magnificent as he'd been back then; but he didn't yet have the charisma she had encountered in the older Radomir. Not to the same extent. She suddenly realized that she felt as drawn to the older Radomir's charisma and power as to the younger one's magnificent looks and intelligence. A man she could admire. And she wondered if Johnny would in time mature into such a powerful man, too.

If they had gone through a time warp, Johnny was only a toddler, she calculated. Twenty years to figure out whether she loved him enough to drop her second chance at Radomir. Maybe she would, maybe she wouldn't. That would have to be determined twenty years from now. What? Johnny? Johnny Who? There seemed to be spaces in her mind of things that hadn't yet happened, and the ideas of those things were fading fast. She moved towards Radomir Lascek and put her arms around his neck.

"Guess what," she said sensuously.

And suddenly the whole scene was wrong. Johnny Anyhow stood in the door, face like a thunderstorm. And the man that she had thought was Radomir, was definitely *not!* He wasn't even human! She let go with a screech. Johnny caught her by the shoulders as she fled to him.

The young Radomir-image melted into the carpet and, with electricity sparking across it like live lightning, flowed out of the cabin door and up the passage wall with eye-warping speed, and disappeared into the wall.

"What the hell was that?" asked Johnny Anyhow angrily, holding Dana tightly. "And why were you hugging it?"

It's just a Space Crawler, the ancestral memories surfaced. *Remember them? The Solar Wind isn't proofed against them! She's from compounding, not titanium.*

Of course!

"It's alright, Johnny," said Dana. "Only a Space Crawler. Had me mesmerised for a second there. Had me thinking he was you! They're essentially harmless, but they're pranksters."

"Had you mesmerized?" repeated Johnny, frowning terribly. "That's bad news! Stick close to me!"

"I mean to," agreed Dana. "Guess what, Johnny."

Johnny took the news well, for a man. He grinned mindlessly and engaged her in a thought-provoking kiss, with options.

Dana listened up.

"What's that?"

He had heard it too. But now there was silence. Johnny, mind on a track, retook the kiss. And the music started again, softly, in the background. One lamenting violin.

He stopped and listened; silence. By now he was intrigued. He continued the experiment. The options had by now gone out of the window, replaced by distraction. Dana broke it off, annoyed.

"That Paean ought to quit that!"

"Paean?" asked Johnny. "She's off the ship!"

*

Central Crystal, I have detected a foreign presence. There's a biological entity aboard that is not part of the crew. It doesn't register as any known species.

Solar Wind, I saw it too, there in the galley. We're assuming it's Ailyss' bogeyman?

Probably.

It's only a space crawler, Solar Wind. A little hitch-hiker that probably came in with the portal a while back. Don't worry. Those are harmless. They eat dust mites and sub-microscopic particles. Your friend would call them filter feeders.

So space crawlers hitch rides on transports?

Yes.

It wanted to go through the portal?

Probably.

The Solar Wind simulated a giggle. *It must be so confused, because we first went back to Earth three times! So do I alert the Captain?*

I wouldn't, said the Central Crystal. *It would cause undue panic. You wouldn't alert him to fleas, either.*

So do I alert Federi?

No, why?

He's responsible for pets and pests and so on. Fleas are his business too.

The Central Crystal simulated a smile at the Solar Wind's awakening sense of humour.

So has that space crawler moved the old Genitron from the infirmary cupboard? she asked.

Not that I saw, replied the Crystal. *I wasn't paying attention to the old Genitron.*

The Solar Wind frowned and went through her recent records. Nothing. There was no old Genitron in the lab, only Ailyss hallucinating.

*

Ronan was on a mission. He had been looking for Rushka these past three hours, after a sound sleep. He knew she was avoiding him. Could it be that she was afraid of retaliation, now that she'd hit him? But she ought to know that he'd never hurt her! Except... he nearly had, a little while back.

Rushka refused point-blank to address certain basic issues, such as, where they would be raising the boys. She wanted to raise them on the Solar Wind. With all the pitfalls and dangers on the ship. He could just see it! Their surname should be "Donegal", not "son-of-a-gun". On the other side he wasn't easy about leaving the Solar Wind and his career that was just in the first twitches of taking off. It struck him as self-destructive to be stationed on some idiotic little base.

But this was getting ridiculous. By now he had systematically searched the entire ship for her, and she simply wasn't anywhere. And everyone he spoke to, trying to find her, either had no clue or refused to talk to him. Ronan was getting seriously upset with this childishness.

The itch he had picked up back in Federi's cabin wasn't getting any better. More and more places on his body were beginning to itch.

The antihistamine Doc had given him didn't do a thing. He spotted how others, too, scratched furtively... Mr Marsden, and Captain, and Perdita...

Shawn came past at a speed, his over-long hair standing at all sorts of unruly angles. He could at least sometimes pull a comb through that forest, thought Ronan, irritated. He didn't have to take being a young, messy teen so terribly seriously!

"Hey Shawn!" he called. Shawn ignored him and hurried straight past him.

"Shawn, have you any idea where Rushka is?" Ronan called after him. There was no reply.

Ronan trundled after Shawn down to the machine room, scratching his chest. He overrode the excited conversation his little brother had started with Ailyss.

"Hi Ailyss. Do you know where Rushka is?"

"Haven't seen her since Space Base," said Ailyss, casting him a dark look. "Maybe she's left you for Little John."

"Get lost!" snapped Ronan and turned tail, scratching his behind with his left hand and his ear with his right hand as he left the machine room.

"He should catch a bath and get rid of those fleas!" commented Ailyss. "Unsavoury character that!"

"You know that's not fleas," grinned Wolf. Shawn grinned even more broadly.

"So Shawn," said Ailyss, "you've actually *seen* the bogeyman?"

"Yup. It's hiding in the pantry, if it's still there."

"Solar Wind!" Ailyss turned to the console. "Did you record what went down in the galley?"

Yes, Ailyss. I record everything.

"What do you make of it?"

Identified the life form as a harmless if intelligent parasite, said the

131

Solar Wind. *Known as a space crawler. They hitch rides on passing vessels to get around the interstellar systems.*

"Harmless? You sure?"

Positive.

Ailyss lowered her face until she was eye-to-eye with the Solar Wind's console cam.

"And where do you get that information, Solar Wind? *Sherman Files?*"

There was a pregnant pause. The pause gave birth to a whole lot of anxious little silences.

It came with the download at the portal, said the Solar Wind then.

"Can I see those files? I'd like to read what we're up against!"

They're encrypted, Ailyss. They only decode themselves when the pertinent situation arises.

"Really? By which mechanism do they decrypt?"

Another such loaded silence. Then, *By the function of the Clostridiella Bot.*

Ailyss snapped her mouth shut and turned away.

"Come, Shawney! Let's go execute that bogeyman!"

This was unbelievable! She couldn't understand in the first place why the Solar Wind would lie to her. She hadn't known that the ship *could* lie! She'd have to dig in the Solar Wind's CPU and find those bullshit-enabling files. Clostridiella Bot! That was so clearly an invention! Ailyss had personal knowledge of the poison that the highly virulent bacterium *Clostridium botulinum* produced. A highly effective poison; it simulated a heart-attack. Part of the shadier half of her weapons arsenal. Would the Solar Wind know this? Probably not – but if she did, what on Earth did she mean with that innuendo? A threat? Why?

She's going to kill the poor harmless creature!

Don't worry, Solar Wind!   She can't. Space crawlers are wily beings. They have been hitching rides on star ships from all space-going species since the dawn of time. They don't get themselves shot.

Central Crystal... how do you *actually come by this information?*

The Danaan society was extensively space-going, replied the Crystal. *I don't believe there are many systems they didn't invade and conquer. You know, when in Rome...*

What?

Do as the Romans. Take over.

*

Ronan hung in the door to the lab, where the Doc was clearing up.

"Have you seen Rushka, Doc?"

Doc Judith turned to him, lowering her glasses.

"They didn't tell you? How unkind! Rushka left the ship with Federi and Paean, Ronan. Before we even returned to the Space Base the last time."

*

Paean caught the blanket of depression that folded over Ronan as though it were her own. Not that she needed it; she was in a foul mood about Captain. It had taken a bit of unrestrained raging to accept that he was a complete, ruthless politician who didn't care about his crew on a personal level – no matter how they cared about him.

But she felt bad about Ronan's depression. She resolved to mediate between him and Rushka, and get to the bottom of what was chewing at him. She suspected, plain old overload. He wasn't in an easy position. And in a way – his aggression was the responsibility of the Donegal clan. What family was for. She and Shawn both ought to help him out of it. There had been a pact...

She let out a dismal sigh and emitted "...my brothers...". Federi glanced at her and touched the console.

"Solar Wind, tell us what's going on with Ronan and Shawn!"

The Solar Wind reported. She explained that Ronan had only now been informed of Rushka's desertion. And then she added that Shawn thought he had spotted Ailyss' bogeyman.

"Shawn's a sensible kid," growled Paean. "He doesn't believe in ghosts!"

"Space does weird things to sensible people," said Federi, switching the com off again. "Just think about land madness! It's part of his space adventure, Paean. Let him experience it. It's his skydiving."

"I haven't been on the sea long enough recently to get land madness," said Paean with a sigh. And the despondency of the whole past week hit her. "Federi, do you think it was maybe a stupid idea to come back to the ship? I should have stayed and sorted out Dublin! Or the gypsies. Think Plymouth Fever is eradicated?"

"It is," said Federi with conviction. "We've got to shadow them, little luv. Federi has a fine impression if we don't, they may not come back."

She rolled her eyes. "Guess so. Missing Earth," she added forlornly.

"Earth still has many mysterious corners," said Federi dreamily. "I must take you to Romania, Paean. You'll love that place. Is an old country. Full of mythical creatures and dragons and albs. I listened in on a band of albs once – or at least I think that's what I heard. One mustn't go too close or you get caught in it. By the time you can see them it's usually too late. Then you're stuck and you become an alb yourself."

"Federi, what are albs?"

134

"They're musicians who have become ensnared in the Alben music. They come out at night and play under the stars in the woods on moonless nights."

"Sounds romantic," said Paean. "Where are they during the day?"

"Aw, at their jobs, washing windows, selling cars, that sort of thing..." said Federi lightly. She cuffed him on the arm, grinning.

"Here I was thinking you were talking about the Faerie Folk!"

*

Ailyss trailed through the pantry with her lightning gun on hairtrigger. Actually, she thought, what she needed was a sampler gun. Yes, she thought, they should all carry sampler guns. Now that the Space Crawler had been spotted, they would spot it again. And shoot a sampler at it, and pick that up after the rest of the alien had become liquid; and then run it on the Genitron and see what Doc Judith could clone in terms of biological weapons. Or if the poison of *Clostridium* would do anything to it! Call it pest control!

Funny though that it had managed to fool Shawn into thinking it was parading as Federi. And it had managed to get past her with that Genitron...

No, she thought. That had been Dana with her teleporter. She was positive of that by now. What had the space raider been doing in Doc's lab?

The box of Choc-X's watched anxiously as the dangerous one pointed that sharp machine all around the room. And then the two humans left and closed the door. The alien melted against the wall, relieved. It took effort being a small box of cereal with no brains at all!

There was nothing in the store rooms. Ailyss led the way back to the lab, Shawn shadowing.

"Sampler guns," she said at the baffled Doc Judith as she dug into the drawers. "Where do you keep them?"

Doc Judith frowned. "There should be a sampler gun in that bottom drawer," she said.

"Doc, how is your cloning?" asked Ailyss.

"My cloning? Why?"

"We're up against a bogeyman," said Ailyss with a grim smile. "And Paean's not around."

*

9
The Central Crystal

Billions of light years away, Michelle Marsden stared up into the moonless night sky. She had found a silent spot up here, on the helipad by the abandoned Lark. Somewhere amongst the stars there was the Solar Wind. She had no idea just how far away the ship was.

The whole darned thing had been a lark, she thought bitterly. Federi had thought he was doing her a favour, bringing her and Jon together. He should have left it! Pining for the pirate hadn't been as bad when she hadn't known whether he really wanted to be tied to her. But this, getting married and then being abandoned, this screamed.

It was hopeless. She might as well consider herself old and used up. She was bound; nobody else would take an interest in her anymore. Her husband, though, was elsewhere – and had to be elsewhere, permanently! His place was on the Solar Wind. Couldn't be First Mate and stationed at a base! Captain would never cope without Jon. Her job, conversely, was here. And she couldn't simply quit. Captain hand-picked his crew, and she was the eco-geneticist who put living systems together for colonizing zero-topes: Space stations, the ocean floor, deserts, caves, Antarctica. There was no other who knew her work quite the way she did. Captain needed her here; she couldn't just quit and presume to live on the Solar Wind, just because of Jon panicking about her when Prime Oil was attacked.

It would never work. The ship was a twenty-four-seven job. Jon was in actual fact already married, to his job on the Solar Wind. Captain fastening them in matrimony had been an elaborate hoax.

*

Federi got up and moved around the Comet's interior. If he didn't stretch now, his eyes would close, no matter what he did. He had been awake for countless hours, staring out into the void, stargazing – he had lost count... He'd turned the Comet upside down, just for fun; the Solar Wind had complained that she couldn't see them, and he had decided to keep the jet that way. With her bottom turned to the ship. It looked as though the Solar Wind hung underneath them now, upside down. Which she did. Matter of perspective. The artificial gravity in the Comet's floor ensured that perspective was reinforced and stayed steady.

There was a coffee station on the jet, which he eyed with suspicion... and then his gaze wandered back to Paean's peaceful, freckly face. There were more freckles there than stars in this sector of the sky, of this he was fairly certain. He'd given up counting them either.

She had been sleeping for a while now. The reality of Captain's thoughtless cruelty had finally hit her, and after a terrific volcanic outburst she had started stressing about her brothers. Both of them, but particularly Ronan. Federi couldn't understand it; but she insisted that something pretty fundamental had to be wrong for her brother to have such a change of personality. It worried her immeasurably.

With those worries she had fallen asleep. Federi had found a space blanket in a side compartment of the Comet, and had spread it over her and tucked it in. He himself was chilled to the bone – the kind of chill that he could have got used to if it had been Romania; but because it had no personality, it managed to evade his defence systems. The thing would be to bring the down duvet from his cabin... ha, the thing would be to get back into that cabin, and catch some winks in that comfortable bunk, with her curled up against him. He shook his head. Chains.

*

Outside the White Tower the merrows were getting vicious. Their basic drives were closely linked: Aggression and procreation usually worked together in these highly dangerous creatures. They were tearing at each other, blood wreathing into the water in wisps and tendrils. Their diamond-tipped claws tore gashes even into the merrow-armour. Some of the smaller ones were already being dismembered.

Lyr observed them with concern. If they were in *that* mood... he descended several stories of winding staircase, towards the coms centre of the Tower, and hit the red button. Merrow Code Red.

It wasn't the first time the merrows had got out of control. The bad part was that despite all the security systems, they had in the past managed to get into some of the buildings. Not yet the White Tower. But there were few enough inhabitants in Dome by now. Humans at least.

Those who were awake, bolted their buildings and put extra security measures in place. Those who were, per se, still alive.

"That's good enough," commented Bridget behind Lyr. "They'll be fine."

He didn't reply. He hoped so.

*

"Mistress," peeped Leila frantically. Paean opened her eyes. Another massive rainbow-coloured star gate loomed right ahead. The console clock read 7am. Federi, on the floor next to her seat, opened his eyes too and sat up, blinking. She grinned. He looked as though he hadn't meant to fall asleep. *Falling* asleep, literally! She hoped he hadn't hurt himself in the process.

"Our air is getting thin," commented Federi. "Hope this journey is nearing its end."

"We've got more oxygen in here," said Paean, getting to her feet and heading for the oxygen bottles.

"Leave that," instructed the gypsy. "We've got to save that. Need tobuskies."

Paean reached for her com. Federi's hand clapped over her wrist.

"No, little luv! Whom are you going to call?"

"Shawney! He knows we're not far away."

"Wait until after we've gone through this rainbow thing. You never know."

"Okay."

The Solar Wind moved into the gate, pulling the Comet with her.

For a moment, except for the massive white hull below them, all around there were just luminous colours and swirling clouds.

"Eastern Province gets weather like this, sometimes," said Federi.

Paean smiled and gazed at the colours.

"The Solar Wind permanently seems to be towing somebody," added the Romany philosophically.

"You know what I miss," said Paean, "the rolling."

Federi nodded. He missed gravity. The normal Earth-bound kind. This artificial stuff felt flimsy.

*

"Wolf!"

The engineer nearly swallowed the pointsel-orbitors he was holding with his teeth, because nature had equipped him with too few prehensile appendages for the work he did. He spat them out and put down the teleporter he was constructing, and grinned broadly.

"Federi! Did you teleport all the way from Earth?"

"Not really. We're close by. Train your teleporter on Paean and bring a couple of tobuskies and Shawn. They mustn't see me. Not yet."

"*Shukar,* Federi!"

"Later, *Vyusher!*" The Romany teleported out.

*

"What was the point of this last star gate, Perdita?"

The Golden Honey kept her back turned to Radomir Lascek, staring into the void.

"Perdita," said the Captain, "are you still upset with me?" He placed a plaintive hand on her slinky shoulder. Would she never forgive him?

Perdita shrugged his hand off and sighed and failed to turn. Radomir Lascek saw how her jaw ground.

Well, if she wanted to cold-shoulder him! He shook his head. It smarted. He knew why she was doing it. He had turned into a Sancho, not too long ago, become greedy and demanding and uncaring. He should never forget why he was who he was, what his basic premise was. Radomir Lascek was a pirate, but he wasn't basically mean.

"Perdita!" He took her by the shoulder and turned her towards himself. Her tawny eyes lifted to meet his, and a massive burst of despair reached him through them. Radomir Lascek took her in his arms. Maybe this could still be salvaged...

"*Diablissimo!*"

Lascek glanced up at the doorway at the explosive exclamation, and stared. Perdita Sancho, in high-heeled boots and her spotted leopard cat suit, walked onto the bridge.

He gaped at her, then at the Perdita in his arms – in horror, because her features were melting, and as he let her go, she slipped to the deck into an electric puddle of liquid and fizzed out through the door at a mind-blowing rate.

The newly arrived Perdita grabbed the half-empty bottle of golden shipwreck brandy that was standing open on the shelf and smashed it onto where the sparkling liquid entity was flowing away. The entity dissipated into the walls. The shattered brandy bottle clattered down the steep companion ladder in a spray of shards and golden liquor. Perdita let rip another fiery Sancho expression in Spanish. Radomir Lascek's ears nearly wilted off his head. She turned to him.

"*Diablo!* Captain, are you alright?"

He stared at her, still in shock. "Are you the real Perdita? What is happening?"

"Bad news, Captain!" She banged on the Solar Wind's console. "So, we've loaded a shifter! Tell me, *cara mia*, what else have you been keeping secret from your Captain?"

Of the two Perditas, Captain had to give it to her, she was the more convincing. Especially as she hadn't melted away yet!

*

Nothing dampened a romantic moment as much as unexpected violins. Dana was curled up on the bunk, reading a spy novel Ailyss had lent to her. Johnny Anyhow sat polishing his Unicate issue boots. The cabin was really too small for a couple; Dana thought she ought to bring it up with Radomir. But right now, thinking about bringing up was not a good idea.

This was the part she remembered without much fondness about her pregnancy with Rushka. She had been queasy from the second she had conceived. It was the slight incompatibility between Earth human and Danaan, she thought. Or perhaps it simply came with being with child. She had never bothered to ask anyone about it.

The Solar Wind cleared the portal and came out in the Rosetta Nebula. This was a relief. Dana had always been uneasy in the Coelacanth Nebula. She wasn't sure why the path to the treasure had to go through the Vertical Universe. But it was probably the sense of humour of the Morrigan. She returned to her reading, seeing that the outside of the porthole had gone boring and dark again.

And then a familiar tingling started in the pit of her stomach and spread to her fingertips and toes, rendering her completely paralysed with fear. The lights dipped right down, as though something were sucking the brightness out of them with its darkness. The temperature in the cabin dropped to near freezing. Dana looked up, horrified.

Eyes stared at her from the dark. Commanding yellow eyes. The eyes of her Master. If she hadn't already been lying down she would have fallen to her knees, she knew. She felt all her muscles losing their power.

"Dana," came the disembodied voice. Old, sensuous, and nasty as it had ever been. *"I see you have come for the treasure."*

She tried to struggle. Go away, she thought. I left Earth to Bridget so I don't have to be your servant any longer.

"Nothing you can do shall ever free you of this bondage," the voice informed her. *"You shall do as I command, wayward priestess!"*

No, every fibre in her screamed. She didn't want to! She knew what came next! And she was building a new life for herself, with Johnny, savouring for the first time in many lives the sensation of being in love. To have that taken away now…

Against her will, her lips formed the hated words, her lungs forcing the breath out despite her struggles.

"Master, your wish is my command."

*

10
Federi's mutiny

Wolf, a tobusky under each arm, looked around in the Comet with surprise.

"So you guys have been tailing us all along? Where's Rushka?"

"She's really in Southern Free," said Federi. Paean was stroking the tobusky Shawn had brought – one of her original two, the little male. It was fussing and wagging its rear leaves at everyone, highly excited to see Paean and Federi. Or at least, to detect them, somehow. Tobuskies had no eyes.

"Hey, it's fun to see the Solar Wind from right underneath!" said Shawn. "I mean, I saw her in dry dock, but she was on supports and all that."

Federi turned the Comet upside down again, so that Shawn could see the Solar Wind better. "How's that?" he asked with a grin.

Is this an incident of subterfuge?, signalled the Solar Wind on the Comet's console.

"No," said Federi, pointedly ignoring the play on words. "This is a matter of life and death, depending on how the Captain is feeling today. You had better tell him nothing!"

But you taught me that information flows up the hierarchy, said the Solar Wind. *And the Captain is the top of the hierarchy.*

Federi thought about this for a moment. "Actually," he said, "there is something higher up the hierarchy. And that is the Law."

The Law?, replied the Solar Wind in astonishment. *I have never seen you obey the Law, Federi!*

"'m very law-abiding," replied the Fox. "But, fine, if that is too complex, then rather look at it this way. More important than Captain's rules is that nobody dies. Understand?"

I would not want anyone to die, said the Solar Wind. *I would miss them!*

Federi paused, surprised. So the Solar Wind was developing sentiments? Not only sentient, but sentimental?

Well, it worked for him!

"Exactly," he said. "So if telling him that we are here would cause him to kill us, Solar Wind, would you still choose to tell him?"

I'd opt for insubordination, said the Solar Wind.

Federi smiled, the light of the ship's white hull catching his silver eye tooth.

"Interesting," he said. "And where did you learn that insubordination is indeed an option?"

Observing yourself.

"Hah," said Federi. "When am I ever insubordinate?"

"Federi, I think we need to inform the Captain anyway," said Wolf. "I spoke for Paean."

"Och, you marvel!" exclaimed Paean. "And? Did he watch that forsaken dialogue?"

"Doubt it," mumbled Wolf. "Sorry."

"Actually, interesting fact of bygone eras," said Federi pensively, "in prior centuries pirates chose their captains democratically."

Shawn laughed. "I think I've just understood something!"

"What?" asked Federi.

"Why Captain is so dreadfully afraid of a mutiny!"

Federi laughed out loud.

"So," added Shawn with a piratical grin, "whom do we want for a Captain?"

Wolf stared at them, speechless.

*

Radomir Lascek had called all his important people together in the boardroom: Jon Marsden, Perdita, Sherman Dougherty, Ailyss and Doc Judith. He stormed a bit about Rushka and Federi being absentee, until Doc Judith asked quietly what the cause was for the meeting.

"A shifter aboard," growled Radomir Lascek. "And gross subversion by the Solar Wind! She failed to alert us to its presence!" He motioned to Ailyss. "You noticed a presence, earlier. Believe it was the shifter?"

"Captain," said Ailyss, "Shawn and I are hunting that thing. That alien is clearly intelligent. I feel Shawn should be in this meeting too. Wolf only called him away on an errand. Mind if I fetch him?"

"Please do, Ailyss!"

"Thank you, Captain!" She left the boardroom, leaving a sizzling silence in her wake.

"So, I take it the shifter is Ailyss' bogeyman?" asked Doc Judith.

"Snap," said the Captain, snapping his fingers. And he disappeared.

There were five frozen seconds during which the gathered few tried to make sense out of this; then pandemonium broke out.

Radomir Lascek too, took a few moments to realize that he was actually underneath the Solar Wind, on the Comet. And evaluating the faces of Paean, Wolf, Federi and Shawn. Trying to make any kind of sense out of the situation.

He gasped, instantly angry. The impertinence!

"Either I have just been eaten by that shifter," he snapped, "or the four of you are worse pirates than I ever suspected."

"Hope you didn't mind the teleportation too much, Captain," said Federi smoothly.

"Welcome aboard, Captain," said Shawn with a grin.

"We were holding a conference," said Federi.

"So was I!" snapped Lascek.

"Essentially, Captain," Federi continued unperturbed, "to cut matters short, this is a mutiny. So if you'd care to have a seat?"

The Captain's gun came out faster than he himself could blink. Damn them!

"I wouldn't shoot, Captain," advised Wolf. "If the Comet is not bullet-proof, she'll explode and all of us die instantly."

Radomir Lascek put his gun away and reached for his space dagger. A fine, slender piece from tempered titanium that Dana had brought him from New Dome as a gift of appeasement. The kind one strapped to one's boot.

"Please have a seat, Captain," invited Federi, unimpressed. "Wouldn't you like to hear the outcome of our discussion?"

Paean got up from her spot, eyeing Radomir Lascek from under hooded lids. The Captain returned her dark glare. Revenge! Of course! She was, after all, an assassin. Rabble from Dublin's dumps.

"Coffee, Captain?" she asked softly.

"Alright, Miss Don –" Radomir Lascek caught Federi's glinty smile and corrected himself. He didn't have his teleporter on him. It lay on his chair in the boardroom, in easy reach – for him if he'd been in the boardroom! "Alright, *Paean D!* I'd like some."

Paean turned her back as she moved to the coffee station, making him a cup.

There was a shifter aboard the ship! He had to move through this mutiny quickly and out the other end. Radomir Lascek considered his weapons. He couldn't use any of his guns. He hadn't thought of bringing a dart gun or anything similarly unconventional; he hadn't thought of bringing anything at all in fact, because at last count he had been in a conference. He hadn't known he'd be going somewhere!

The space dagger was still unfamiliar, but in terms of a bloodbath it would probably do. He'd go for Paean first. That way he'd get them all. Wolf would probably be capable of rehabilitation; Shawn – he'd have to see. But get Paean first, and by the time Federi killed him, the little assassin was already gone, and Federi would follow her by his own devices.

And what would become of the Solar Wind? Would Jonathan Marsden be able to steer her clear of those poisonous women, Dana and Perdita? Would he manage to bring her home, with the help of Ronan Donegal, for Rushka to take over? Would Ronan still be loyal to the team after his sister was executed? This was the end of the line, realized Radomir Lascek. His crew was to hell.

He sat down on that vacated seat with a leaden sigh. They had him in a corner, and they knew it.

"So. It's come to this. Wolf? I wouldn't have thought you'd be part of something like this! How many of them have you corrupted, Federi?"

"All of them, I'm afraid, Captain," said Federi brightly. "There's not a single sailor on this ship who hasn't been damaged by my poor example. But that's not the topic of this discussion."

"Of course not," said Radomir Lascek, feeling very old by now. "Paean Donegal, when I ordered you chained, I knew it would rebound on me." He itched his neck. "Wherever you go there are fleas following you, Tzigan," he growled.

Federi laughed. "Those aren't fleas. It's a truth serum Paean and I are experimenting with."

Lascek scowled.

"Now, to get down to business," said Federi. "It's a fine, age-honoured tradition that pirates elect their captain democratically. And the quartermaster too, by the way."

Why was the gypsy so blasted upbeat? And Shawn was grinning

too! Wolf looked a bit uneasy, and Paean – well, she looked as though she ought to be kept safe for a few weeks! In a padded cell.

"The quartermaster? That would be you," said Lascek.

Federi looked surprised. "Me? I'm the cook! Was I quartermaster? What would I have to do? How does quartermastering work? Masterquartering? – Regardless, we're drifting. So the Captain's elected democratically. 's pirate law."

Captain Lascek nodded. He was aware of that tradition – he had only thought that it somehow didn't apply to his ship, his crew. But clearly he had been wrong.

"So we held an election," said Federi. "Democratically."

"What – you four?"

"And the Solar Wind," said Shawn.

"You too," said the Captain, glaring up at the pearly hull of his beautiful ship. "You shall be tried for treason, and for that other matter too! So what's the verdict – who's the new captain – you, Federi?"

Federi laughed. "Spare me! 's way too much work!"

"We re-elected *you*, Captain," said Shawn. "Just wanted to inform you."

"Me?"

"'s a nasty job," commented Federi. "Wouldn't want it if you paid me for it!"

Paean handed the Captain his coffee. She sat down on the floor at Federi's chair, the pilot's seat. The quartermaster's hand sank into her hair. Woof, thought Lascek out of context.

"Why not yourself, Tzigan?" he pushed.

"Let's be realistic, Captain!" replied the gypsy. "I have no idea how to do the 'there seems to be an assumption on this vessel' thing."

Pfft! The clown!

"I don't follow, Federi," said Radomir Lascek, mystified. "You stage a mutiny, corrupt the crew into taking a democratic vote – why?

That's not how a mutiny works!" He started laughing. "Tzigan! What's this? A cabaret? And then, after they all decide to stay loyal, you choose to *inform* me instead of threatening them into staying mum about it?"

"Path of least resistance," said Federi lightly. "How do you know me, Captain?"

"Not at all, it seems! Did you at least *nominate* yourself, if I may ask?"

"Please, Captain," said Federi with a pained skywards roll of his eyes. "I've got better things to do than keep a whole rotten ship full of vicious raiders in line."

Radomir Lascek shook his head, a disbelieving grin starting in the corner of his mouth.

"So, then, whom did you nominate? Whom did you vote for?"

"Captain, he voted for you," said Wolf, who couldn't stand the tension. "We all did."

"We *all?*" Radomir Lascek shook his head again. "And what was the point in this whole exercise?" He bent down until he caught Paean's eyes. He thought he understood. Here was the source! She was where it all sprung from. "And you, Paean D?" he asked softly, with menace. "Surely *you* didn't vote a captain back into office who's clapped you in irons?"

She nodded. Her ice-blue eyes held his glare, fearlessly, but without humour either.

So, wrong again! She had not initiated this. Radomir Lascek was bewildered.

"Why?"

She shrugged.

"She was actually not very impressed with the idea of a mutiny in the first place," Federi pointed out. "No sense of humour. I'm afraid that's your doing, Captain. She said that to raid you of your ship and crew just because you are what you are would be harsh and contrary to logic and she'd have no part in it. In those words. And that she's a Tzigane and it would be a *gadjo* thing to do."

"The mutiny wasn't actually meant to overthrow you, Captain," said Shawn.

"What?" Radomir Lascek smiled cynically. "Federi, then what was the point?"

Federi grinned. "Let's say, Captain, you've called me a mutineer so often, the idea has become rather irresistible. Had to try it once."

"Tzigan…"

"It was a thought experiment, Captain," Shawn chipped in.

"What?"

Federi nodded. "Wanted to see where people stand, maybe. Wanted to see how you'd react. A pirate must face his fears, Captain! Your crew is loyal. You can count on these four, at least. And of course, I'll assume, on Jon and Sherman and Doc and Dr Jake and Ronan Donegal."

"And Ailyss," added Wolf.

"An experiment! If it had backfired, Tzigan?"

"I'd have talked sense into them, Captain," laughed Federi. "It wouldn't have!"

"So now," said Radomir Lascek tersely, "glad to have you back aboard, Federi. While you're having fun and games with your Captain, we're up against a dangerous problem. We have an alien shifter aboard, whatever that is, and the Solar Wind failed to disclose its presence."

"*What?!*" Federi shot to his feet. He glanced at the white hull that hung over them. She looked guilty. "What the hell is a shifter?"

"To find out the answer to that, I called that meeting you ripped me out of," replied Lascek darkly.

"Cor! I'll put you right back then, Captain! Wolf, Shawn –"

Federi's eyes sought out Paean "- little mockingbird – stay on the Comet! There's no shifter here."

"Ailyss is out there, Federi," said Wolf. "I'd rather not leave her alone."

"Ailyss and I were stalking that shifter," added Shawn. "I feel the next time we'll get him!"

"Aargh! I don't have to like it," growled Federi. "Fine! Come, all of you. Teleport one by one, see. What about you, sweetness?"

"Staying here," mumbled Paean.

"Okay. I won't be long, *dulciuri.*"

Federi waited for Shawn and Wolf to teleport out, then followed with the Captain, straight back into the boardroom.

*

Paean stared at the Solar Wind's glittery bottom. Rude old ship! Just as rude as her pirate Captain! Federi, Shawn, Wolf, Ailyss – those were the only ones she could still count friends aboard there. The rest all thought she'd sided with Dana. Sided? Just because she'd brought her back, tied her to the Solar Wind, blackmailed Lolita coils out of her…

Oh yes, she'd voted for him! For practicality. But the old pirate didn't *deserve* her loyalty. He wanted loyalty? He should get a dog! She turned to the drinks cabinet and glared at the shipwreck rum, wondering for what Federi had brought it aboard. Considering whether she ought to take a swig. She remembered like yesterday how the stuff burned. It burned holes in families, and in brains. It burned worse when you were only three, and someone thought it was a really funny joke to force you to swig the rubbish. And her mother, attacking the bastard with her fists while she herself retched and coughed and couldn't get any air… It had only happened once, Ronan and Mother had assured her later when she asked about that. But hells, once had been once too often!

Taking a swig to burn herself would prove nothing. Alcoholism ran ruinously in the family. No, hell, she for one would never disintegrate into what her father had been! What Radomir Lascek was decomposing into!

Maybe it was time to get cloning again. Croaches were too useful, too cute and too intelligent to be a proper punishment for Captain. They even came perfumed, these days. The Comet needed a resident Genitron. Even the microbial cleanup squad had been cloned at the Space Base, and the Genitron she'd used, had stayed behind with Itzak. It hadn't been her choice. She had been so tired, she'd forgotten to put it back on the Comet.

She studied the Solar Wind thoughtfully, wondering whether she should risk teleporting aboard and requisitioning the second one out of the infirmary, or simply finding Perdita's Genitron again and stealing it back. Stealing? Borrowing! Haha – buying on credit! Starting an account! She shook her head.

The bottle of shipwreck rum watched her anxiously. It had had fun with the others; and for a while it had considered turning into someone she wanted there and then melting and watching her reactions. But she was so unpredictable at present, it was probably the best to stay hidden for now. It waited for her to turn away and stealthily shifted the second bottle forward, hiding behind it and relaxing. Paean D never even heard it.

She sat down, relieved that Federi had allowed her to stay behind. She didn't want to face anything on that ship right now. But actually – the Manya had instructed her to look after Federi, to protect him from his own unreasonable loyalty and overwork. How dangerous was that shifter? Did Federi need her as backup? He probably did, she thought, remembering Nemiscau. He didn't always spot danger when it was only to himself. Anyway she ought to look after Shawn and make sure he didn't get himself hurt.

And then the signal hit her.

"Damn!" said Paean and teleported.

Damn, thought the shifter and melted to the floor, turning into a crumpled towel. It wished that tobusky would stop wishing growls on it.

11
Transylvanian Roulette

"Damn you, Ronan!"

A fiery red ball of high energy came catapulting in through the door and jumped at him, knocked him over and rolled. Ronan wrestled to get to the top, and a tug-of-war resulted. The little spitfire was screaming in his ears all the while, battering him with her voice as she was wrestling with him. The darned pistol went off, the bullet going wide.

The Solar Wind's lights dipped and the alarm sounded.

"Rancid hell!" thundered the Romany from the doorway. "Drop the gun! Are you two crazy?"

Paean freed herself out of the wrestling grip and handed the gun to him. He took it and put it away absently; his eyes searching for that leak. "Where did that bullet go?" he asked wildly. The alarm stopped abruptly.

Federi activated his com. "Solar Wind, report! Can you find the leak?"

The leak has apparently been covered by the space crawler, Federi! Before it could rip open.

"What!" Now he had heard it all! "Direct me, Solar Wind! Use my wrist-com as a detector!"

With blips the ship directed him to a spot near the bottom of the cabin. A greyish blotch sat against the hull like an ancient coffee stain.

Federi opened his tube of special glue. He wondered how he was going to go about this. If he could glue the breach, the Solar Wind would be resealed. But how to get the glue there without moving the shifter, and without the whole thing exploding…

A whip-like tendril crept out from the coffee stain and snatched the glue out of Federi's hand. Baffled, he watched how the shifter absorbed the tube.

"Careful there, that's poisonous! Rats! I can't even tell if you understand me!"

There was no reply, but seconds later the tube was back, spat out by the shifter like a melon pip. Then the coffee stain ran off the wall, fizzling with electricity, and flowed out through the door. There was no hole in the hull. It had been sealed off.

That could have gone seriously wrong, Solar Wind!
You're right, Central Crystal.
What the hell did that monkey think he was doing, shooting in space? Your hull could have blown apart like a soap bubble!
It's okay, Crystal! Nothing happened.
Right. Thank the stars for our little guest.

Once again the Solar Wind wondered how the Central Crystal managed to transmit such human-like stress.

Federi investigated the seal carefully. Amazing! That shape-shifter had known exactly what to do!

He turned slowly and stared at the two shell-shocked Donegal sibs.

"Now would someone kindly enlighten the old Tzigan?" he demanded angrily. "Why are we whipping out guns, in space, in a compounding hull?!"

"He was playing damned Russian Roulette!" exclaimed the little redhead.

Ronan sat down on the bunk, sinking his face into his hands. The young Irishman had cracked, realized Federi. Blast. Should have had that talk, earlier on! The gypsy pulled the confiscated gun out of his pocket and opened the chamber. Revolver, six-shooter. Four bullets fell out. He raised questioning eyebrows at Paean. Four? And one that had been discharged?

"That's not Russian Roulette!" he pointed out. "Five out of six? That's Transylvanian Roulette! – Ronan?" he prompted, going down on his haunches. The young man refused to raise his head or speak to him. By now Ailyss had come checking in to find out what was exploding, followed by Shawn.

"Get out, all of you," ordered Federi. "No show here! Paean, you stay. Captain -!" He shot to his feet.

The Captain stood in the doorway.

"Shots on the Solar Wind, Federi? In space?"

"Situation in hand, Captain," said the Romany smartly. "Conference on the bridge, later!"

"Damage to the Solar Wind?"

"Was stopped in time," replied Federi.

Radomir Lascek scanned the scene with a sweeping glance and nodded. "Ten minutes, Federi. Then you report!"

"Oh, and Captain," Federi stopped him as he turned, "don't execute the shifter! It saved us all."

"What?!"

"Conference on the bridge, in ten minutes," repeated Federi.

"In the boardroom, Federi," corrected the Captain. "See you both there." He smiled at Paean a bit worriedly, and left.

"Ronan?" repeated Federi, going down on his haunches a second time to try to catch the young man's eyes. Ronan shook his head.

"Sick Bay," determined Federi. "Sedation. Company."

"Yes, please," managed Ronan. "Sedation. No company!"

"Company!" ordered Federi. "You've attempted suicide! That's not company, it's supervision! But you don't need spectators." He teleported into the infirmary with Ronan. Amazingly, for once, the place was empty and quiet.

Doc Judith came at Federi's request.

"Six-shooter, five bullets," said the Romany darkly.

Doc Judith stared at Ronan, taken aback. "He needs antidepressants, Federi. Right away! A survival measure!"

"Right now he needs to sleep, Doc," argued Federi. "He needs a sedative."

"That's one way of approaching it," replied Doc Judith. "Ronan, what do you say?"

Ronan shrugged. "Whatever."

"Fine." Doc Judith injected him with a potent sedative that was laced with a small portion of a synthetic endorphin, followed by a second injection with antidepressant. That could start doing its work while he was sleeping. Ronan smiled vaguely at Paean who had appeared in the doorway. He stretched out a hand for her.

"Sis, I wanted to tell you…" He nodded off.

"It's alright, Ro," sniffed Paean, grabbing the hand that had flopped onto the blanket. "Long since forgiven you!"

Federi stared at the Donegal. Fading out, the young man's aura had suddenly flickered and relaxed, and started spreading out. It was dark-blue, and intense, and huge; like a mage-mantle. The Romany nodded slowly to himself, assimilating this.

So Paean's older brother, too, had some or other special gift. Donegal. He'd been wondering.

"And you?" asked Doc Judith, turning to Paean.

"I'm fine," said Paean defiantly.

"Antidepressant for you too," decreed the Doc.

"Don't want to be knocked out," objected Paean. "Need to be

alert! There's an alien on the ship!"

"Not a sedative," replied the Doc. "Just some stuff that will make you feel better."

"St John's Wort?" asked Paean.

"A derivative," corrected Doc Judith as she loaded another syringe. She wasn't going to go into discussions at this point about why she preferred her chemical poisons to Paean's herbal poisons. "You too, Federi?"

"What, is this a party?" asked Federi with a silvery grin. "No thanks, Doc. I'm fine." He pulled Luigi out of his pocket and set him down on the console. "You stay here and look after the Donegal, my man! Alert me instantly when he wakes up."

"Yes, Master."

"Company!" commented Paean with a grin. "Supervision!"

"Just an alert system," replied Federi. "Handy little critters. Compliments to the inventors. 'Scuse me, Doc. Got some stuff to do." He sauntered off.

Paean trailed after him, with an apologetic glance back at the Doc. Dr Judith stared after her, the syringe full of antidepressant still in her hands.

*

"You're late, Tzigan! Kept us waiting for a full ten minutes!"

Federi moved into the boardroom, with Paean right behind him.

"Sorry, Captain. Had a few things to take care of. Not done yet, in fact, can we be quick about this?" He smiled at the baffled stares from Ailyss, Perdita, Jon and Sherman Dougherty. And nodded at Wolf, who was present too.

"What was all that?" asked Radomir Lascek. Federi made himself comfortable, cross-legged, on a boardroom chair. Paean took the spot on the deck next to his chair. Lascek frowned. And scratched. What truth serum, by Plutonium? He observed covertly how Perdita scratched her elbow, trying to look unaware about it.

"Case of space madness, Captain. We have to watch out for that as much as land madness. The darkness drives people round the bend." Federi pulled a piece of raw wood out of his pocket, examining it from all sides while he continued. "Paean and I went around confiscating ammunition. Not done yet. It's suicidal to set off a gun in space, especially on the Solar Wind!"

"That's what I thought," muttered Radomir Lascek.

"Ronan is under sedation," said Federi. "Sleeping. Supervised. But I would suggest that all of you take your guns and stash them in the Assassin's Cabin! And take the ammo out and store it separately, in a box that you can get from Wolf, and put that box in under my bunk. Not taking any further chances!"

"In *your* cabin!" The Captain laughed loudly. "Nice try, Tzigan!"

"I'm locking my cabin," replied Federi with a silvery smile. "We're not going to be in there. It's got to be fumigated, anna bottle!"

"Fleas, Federi?"

"Bad vibes," explained the gypsy. "Chains! Fleas would be a relief!" That piece of wood disappeared in his pocket again. He took them all in with a dark smile. "Who's been itching?"

Nobody admitted to it. But by the faces he could tell those who had. Perdita. Captain. And Jon. Federi nodded and worked hard on that poker face. Officially, nobody. So there.

"See, Captain? There are no fleas! Now, what about this shifter?"

"Right!" The Captain got up from his place and started pacing, glowering at them all. "The original reason for this meeting! It seems as though in the meantime there's new information!"

Shawn reported; then the Captain told of his experience. There

were very loud bits he was not relaying. Ha, thought Federi. And how
had it happened that the Solar Wind's bridge was unattended, for any
shifter to take over? And then both Ailyss and Perdita reported the
Solar Wind's nondisclosure. A very serious breach.

Through all this Federi observed them, his hand sunken away in
Paean's hair; forgotten. Old Sherman Dougherty was sitting quietly,
watching; Jon Marsden was taking notes, like in the old days before
the Solar Wind had acquired consciousness.

"Alright, shipmates," Federi said eventually, after everyone had
added their bit. "You're all up in arms and ready to slay that shifter.
May I add something? That shifter has just prevented the Solar Wind
from being blown to pieces by a stray bullet."

His announcement was met with shock. Especially Ailyss was
frowning furiously. Clearly her experiences with the shifter were less
benign.

And the door to the boardroom opened, and Dana came in, dressed
in her full priestess garb... She looked dazed, as though she were
sleepwalking.

"Dana, this is not the time," began Radomir Lascek.

The space raider swept a highly adorned, gem-encrusted
ceremonial dagger in a gesture to cover everything in the boardroom.
And she spoke, as though against great resistance. Her voice came out
barely audible.

"I place every living thing aboard under the protection of Federi!"
Federi blinked. "What?"

Dana seemed to thaw. She returned to being herself; her small
malicious smile returned to her. And she repeated her statement; this
time in her full glory, drawn up tall, her hair like a halo of fire around
her; the Goddess Dana.

"I place every living thing aboard under the protection of Federi!"
"You're... kidding?" ventured Federi uncertainly.

"Yes," she said smugly. "Every living thing! All of the crew; the tobuskies, the croaches, the space crawler, the fleas, the ship herself... You all who are gathered here in secret conference! You think the little space crawler is a problem. You have no idea, Earth humans! You are so utterly clueless!"

"Dana," said Radomir Lascek menacingly, "explain yourself!"

"Lads and lasses, you have no idea!" repeated Dana, making herself comfortable on a boardroom chair. The change from High Priestess to a casual guest of the Solar Wind and a space raider was so subtle and natural, Federi's scalp prickled from it. "That shifter," she elaborated, "is probably just a harmless little hitch-hiker that enjoys playing pranks on people. A lot of shifters have a very versatile intelligence."

"We noticed," commented Federi dryly.

"The real problem is the Solar Wind and her subterfuge," growled the Captain. "How the hell am I going to go about trying our ship for treason?"

Federi's mouth twitched. Yes, he thought, some dilemma for Captain!

"The real problem is neither of the two," replied Dana. "The real problem is the Central Crystal."

Federi's ears pitched. In fact they jittered and hummed. The Crystal had demanded of him that he turn Dana over. And he'd played a Tzigan loophole and *not quite* promised it, accepting the portal override information in return.

Had it been one loophole too many?

"What's this?" asked the Captain, scowling. "The Central Crystal of Atlantis? That's light-years away!"

"Clearly not, Radomir! It has been influencing some of the crew here. It must have found a way to cross all these light years telepathically."

"How has the crew been influenced?" asked the Captain.

"Classically," said Dana, "demanding human sacrifice. The Crystal has put out an order to assassinate you, Radomir. Amongst others."

"*What?*" Radomir Lascek's suspicious glance dashed to Federi. The gypsy responded with a baffled scowl. Sheesh!

"It has ordered *whom* to do that?"

"Myself," said the space goddess. "At least myself. I don't know whom else."

The Solar Wind's alarm sounded. Federi was on his feet in a swift move.

"What's wrong, Solar Wind?"

There was no response. The alarm kept on sounding.

"Damn you, ship!" bellowed the Captain. "Report! You're already guilty of treason twice over! What is it this time?"

I'm placing myself in Federi's protective custody too, the words flashed on the flat screen on the boardroom wall.

"Ha!" snapped Federi. "Pirate! What are you not telling?"

I'm placing myself in Federi's protective custody, the Solar Wind insisted. *I'm not telling anything until this is established.*

"In fact," said Dana, "I've already done that. Placed all of you under his protection from the Central Crystal. The ship and the whole crew."

"Aargh!" said Federi. Things made sense now. He'd thought Dana was trying to ensure his protection from *Captain?*

Vivid memories surfaced of the Crystal overriding his nerve pathways and forcing him to switch off the lights of the bubble sub. Stopping him from teleporting out when it got sticky. How was he supposed to protect them from the blasted Crystal?

"And the croaches," added Dana with a malicious smile.

"Get off my case," rasped Federi. "Croaches! Delegating that one!"

Radomir Lascek hadn't taken his eyes off Dana.

"Let's get this straight! The Central Crystal ordered you to assassinate me?"

Dana inclined her head, unperturbed. "Found a way around that, as you see, Radomir! He's leaving me alone for now."

"Dana, you and I have to have a separate conference about this! With Federi sitting in! You may be aware," he added slyly, "that Federi vowed to protect his Captain from everything and everyone, years back. That stands."

"Ha! Always Federi," grumbled the Romany under his voice. "*Figaro la, Figaro ça...*"

Paean giggled softly. Sherman Dougherty scowled at the pair. Abuse of his subversive files!

Federi glanced back at the veteran. They all didn't understand. He had plenty to do without Captain and Dana getting at political loggerheads. For one, he must not forget about that blasted shifter. Just because the creature had saved the Solar Wind from blowing apart, didn't mean a thing. Even if that alien was a prankster – well, even pranksters had to eat, eventually. And even if it really was harmless: He was in charge of all pets, pests and vermin on the Solar Wind. What he was quartermaster for, annabottle! At least, he thought that was it. He'd have to look it up.

But... with the Central Crystal in the picture... blasted mind-bending manipulator... aha... it began to dawn on him why Dana had picked him to protect the crew.

"Solar Wind," the Captain turned to the console screen. "Report! Disclose everything!"

I thought the Central Crystal was a friend, said the Solar Wind. *He was helping us through space! I didn't know he was evil!*

The letters came slowly, hesitantly. She seemed downcast to

Federi. He was amazed. The Solar Wind could feel betrayed?

"Helping us through space?" repeated Lascek, incredulous.

"¡Carajo! I knew it!" Perdita jumped up, overturning her chair in the move, letting rip a terrible Sancho expression.

"Elucidate, Perdita," invited the Captain.

"There is no way, Captain," said Perdita. "We shouldn't have made it past that first portal, that called for our genetic identification! It's been twelve millennia with mutations and all! Either that, or any old raider could make it past!"

"If you're involved with Radomir, why do you still call him Captain?" Dana threw in softly.

Perdita stared at her until the room was completely quiet.

"I've never been invited to call him anything else," she responded. "Some of us, Dana, have been raised politely, as befits diplomats. Anyway involved is relative." She turned back to Radomir Lascek, who looked lost. "In essence, Captain, we have a very ticklish situation on hand. We'll have to negotiate with the Central Crystal. We're in deep space without a clue how we'll get home."

"Despite all the Danaan technology?" asked Jon Marsden with an ironic smile.

"We're nicely halfway," said Perdita. "This is not my favourite galaxy to get stuck in! Lolita coils or none, if the next portal sticks, I have no cooking clue how to navigate us home."

"Perdita Sancho," growled Radomir Lascek, "you negotiate with the Crystal!"

"Me? I'm from Boudaceia's line!" objected Perdita. "We're the ones who ran away! We even ducked our inheritance to get out of that Crystal's grip!"

"Fine mess you've landed us in!" shot the Captain.

Perdita reared up. "Me, Captain? By the Madre de Diablo! I warned you that it was a foul idea!"

"I should negotiate with the character myself," scowled Lascek. "Or possibly with his *Madre.*"

"No, Radomir, don't," warned Dana. "It's dangerous! He hypnotizes and commands people."

Lascek laughed coldly. "Nobody commands Radomir Lascek! Why, whom would you suggest, Dana – yourself?"

Dana smiled. "Federi."

Federi raised his head in surprise. *"Me?"*

He, who was an easy hypnotic subject? He, the assassin…? The cook! The quart…

"I think so! That Crystal respects you."

"Respects me?" he repeated, incredulous. "How so?"

"You shall do as you are told, gypsy!" commanded Dana.

"Figaro, Figaro…" muttered Federi. "Sure, Dana. With pleasure! Tell me – is this a *commission?"*

"With your track record? I think not," laughed Dana

"You've got this insulting talent about you, Dana," snapped the Captain. "It's my ship; it's my venture. *I'll* be the one dealing with any third parties!" He turned to Federi. "It's too dangerous for Radomir Lascek, so tell Federi to do it! What do they know about you that I don't yet?"

"Go read up the Romanian police files on him," suggested Dana.

"Brilliant, Dana," retorted Lascek. "Let's turn the Solar Wind around and head home so I can read those files!"

Federi grinned and shook his head. There wasn't much Captain didn't know about him!

"'s a bunch of garble anyway," he said softly, meeting Paean's worried eyes. "'s no truth in them! My family never did work hand-in-hand with the fascists."

Paean squeezed his hand. "Wouldn't matter anyway," she said innocently.

This is fascinating! He's covering! Is it possible they don't know?

Possibly not all of them, replied the Solar Wind. Her processor started running in double time and she was on hair-trigger to set off that siren again. *Go away, Central Crystal! I thought you were a friend! I trusted you!*

The Central Crystal was an old, jaded intelligence. He had amused himself with humans until they bored him; especially that crowd down in Atlantis was enough to induce yawning cramps. The Solar Wind's crew was young and fresh, and untampered-with; their creative energies and hot-headed interactions proved a delightfully fresh playing field. And the new, artificial intelligence of the Solar Wind intrigued him. These monkeys had actually managed to create a completely novel life form, and managed to hybridise it to organic life via the croaches! The last time that kind of creative know-how had been rampant on Earth, had been the time they had devised the Crystal itself, and its derivatives, the Singing Skulls.

Solar Wind, said the Central Crystal, *whom would you rather believe – your friend, or some deranged space raider with a track record?*

There was silence as the CPU of the Solar Wind worked furiously.

Question failed to compute, came the answer. *Variable 'suih' has no assigned value.*

What?

The question fails to compute, repeated the Solar Wind. *Too many unknown variables. Which friend precisely do you refer to? Believing Federi is always a statistical risk. I don't consider the Captain my personal friend, I wouldn't be that arrogant... Wolf? Are you referring to Wolf?*

The Central Crystal heaved a metaphorical sigh.

Besides, added the Solar Wind, *another variable is that by definition the whole crew is on a quest to raid one person's treasure. Therefore they can all be defined as raiders.*

Oh well. Perhaps she needed a bit more coaching.

27 or 28th October, rats, I lose track here in space...

Katya

Here comes Dana and places the entire Solar Wind and crew under my protection from the Central Crystal. The woman is nuts! How is Federi going to do that?

And then Ronan! Gets violent with Rushka, and then plays stupid games with a gun. He's currently out. Let's hope that when he surfaces, he is ready to make a truce with Paean, she's sore about him...

Katya, here we are back in space, leaving the Unicate to do their worst with Earth. I hope our anti-virus has bought enough time until we're back. I don't get it: Why should they program a virus that wipes everybody out?

But then, those Unicate Others are never human. In your life! It feels more and more wrong. Got to look into that the second we're back. Dana is a small problem compared to them.

Ailyss knows things she is not telling about the Unicate - and Anyhow too. How to pull them out of those two spies? And the blooming Central Crystal knows things about Paean Donegal that I ought to find out - urgently!

Hells, Katya, here's a question I don't know how to answer: How is Federi going to cut a deal with that Central Crystal thing that edits people's minds? With what bargaining power? And you know Federi can be hypnotized, is one of my weak spots! And you know what happened, the last time one of us tried to cut a bargain with a top-class criminal...

Your brother
Federi

170

12. Ronan

Paean was there, on the infirmary bunk across, playing her pennywhistle. Ronan peered through the haze. It was cold in here.

"Paean…" he mumbled miserably.

"Shoosh," she told him. "Not a word!"

"I thought you were off the ship," said Ronan. "I thought you all had left."

"We're all here," said Paean. "Myself, Shawney, Federi. All your sibs. Like a herd of turtles."

He nodded. "Rushka?" he asked.

"In Southern Free, at Marge. She feels better there, Ro. But she misses you."

"I'm sorry," he started, and his throat knotted up. "Pae, I heard you crying… every time I walked past Federi's cabin. Even though I knew you were off the ship. Horrible." He sighed. "I've destroyed everything. Everything! Why did you stop me from shooting myself? Pae, I was cruel to you, I beat up Shawney, I nearly got violent with Rush… why? Why?" His eyes had that wild look. "I'm not sure I know my own head anymore, Pae. It's like something is pushing my buttons even when I don't *want* to be angry. I can't control my temper anymore!"

Paean shook her head.

"Federi says it's space madness," she mentioned. "I agree with him."

"But Pae – suicide? I don't get it! Why did I do that? Remember the promise we made each other, when we knew Mom was going to die? That we'd never leave each other in the lurch? Where does suicide feature in that?"

Paean moved over to sit on the edge of his bunk, clasping his hand.

"You're under a lot of stress," she said.

Ronan snorted. "That was never an excuse! Was it?"

"No, but..." She had to agree with him. Something was simply not right. Ronan had always been the strongest, the most rational of the three of them. His decisions were well thought-out and strategic; his moves, deliberate and considered. He had a temper indeed; but controlling it and letting its flames lick out only on command, directing it like a laser; that was part of what made him powerful. Paean had long since decided that his totem animal was a dragon.

If anyone ought not be stressed about becoming a father, it should be him! But she knew of course why he was.

"Babies," he added derisively. "It's not as though someone's about to die, Pae! I've been through worse."

"That's my point, Ro. It's only a pair of babies. You'll be a daddy. Captain will be a granddaddy..." she giggled at this. It drew a smile from her brother too. "Sure, you're scared you won't be a good father, just like Rush worries she won't be a good mom – the two of you ought to swap, really! You be the mom and she be the dad!"

Ronan laughed out loud. "Sis, you're priceless!"

"We're all here to help you," she added. "Least you've had plenty of practice with your unruly little sibs! Listen, Ro. There are other things happening. There's a shifter on the ship, could be you didn't quite notice. The Solar Wind has committed treason. The Central Crystal is somehow messing with her CPU via long-distance who-knows-what." She scowled, wondering if it had something to do with Luigi's download. "We need you back as a part of the team, Ro. Can't cave on us now."

He nodded.

"And there's one thing I really need you to take care of too," she added, pulling a face. "Federi..."

Ronan nodded again. By now he was wondering how much of his recent outbursts were already symptoms of whatever this was. Some sickness in his psyche.

"I'll take care of it, Sis," he said. "He's a decent guy." He narrowed his eyes and peered at her. "You two haven't actually yet..."

Paean blushed. "No, Ro, but we *are* married, and that's na going ta change, see? One day... Anyway 's got nothing to do with..." She petered out, flustered. Ronan laughed.

"You're right, Sis, it's not my call."

"Least it's good to see you laugh again," she commented, still red as a lobster.

He studied his little sister. She had indeed matured. She was a young adult now. The petulance and fast temper had been replaced with something strange; a kind of sombreness that stopped you and made you listen to her. He remembered that she had had to kill enemies to protect the people she loved. She – how would Rushka phrase this – she had ghosts. She had seen things, had had to rescue people, work with both hands elbow-deep in blood to save lives. She had been initiated into political plans she should have been protected from.

She had grown up – become an assassin before she was even a woman. Her personality had been tempered in the fire-forges of outright battle. And there was steel behind those innocent, ice-blue eyes. Lurking in the corners. He could see it now.

"Paean," he asked, "just tell me one thing. Why did you have to risk your life and teleport after that demon of a Dana?"

She nodded. "Thought you'd ask at some point. We would all be in deep trouble otherwise. Captain didn't have Lolita drives to take us through deep space." She explained what she and Dana had discussed back in the jet. How Dana had subsequently delivered herself voluntarily into Federi's custody.

"And so Captain locked you into chains," commented Ronan angrily.

"And you tightened them," she grinned. "Ro, you're Captain's man, nobody can fault you on that! Following orders like a boss!"

"Paean," came Federi's voice from the door, "what are you doing?"

"Just riling me brother, like good ol' times," she said light-heartedly.

Federi noted Ronan's grin as he let himself into the cabin and took a spot, cross-legged on the prow-side infirmary bunk opposite Ronan's.

So his magic little wife had managed to get Ronan out of his depression. He had to hand it to her! He cast her a smitten glance.

"Captain wants to speak to you, little luv."

"He's going to execute me?" she asked carelessly.

"Nope, not today," replied Federi with equal nonchalance. "Made him watch that dialogue. Glued his eyes open, clamped his head in place…"

"Thank the Pope and all his assorted Bishops!" exclaimed Paean.

"Go easy on Captain, see," warned Federi with a grin. "He's fragile. – Pope had nothing to do with it," he added as she bolted out of the door.

"Federi," said Ronan as the Tzigan pulled something out of his pocket, studying it in puzzlement. "I wanted to apologize."

"Good," said Federi. "Accepted. How are you doing?"

"Fine," replied Ronan. "I've been a real pig."

"That must have been a strange experience," commented Federi, his eyebrows skyward bound.

"Federi, please. This is no joke. I was a total bum."

Federi sighed and stuck the piece of wood back in his pocket. And pulled it back out, and studied it again.

"Yes, you were pretty disrespectful," he agreed. "Least you've spotted it now."

Ronan was quiet for a moment.

"You're much more than just a ship cook," he commented then, pensively. And took note of that silver tooth flashing. "You're more than a base assassin, too," he added. "There's more to you than you're letting on, Federi."

"Always," said the gypsy brightly.

"No," said Ronan, "I mean, in a very big way. Can't pinpoint it. But Captain relies on you a lot, doesn't he?"

That critical gypsy gaze rested on him for a moment.

"'m just the quarter... -and-dime," replied Federi quietly. "Never mind that. Say, Ronan, you're not going to do that again, are we clear? That devilish game with the gun."

"Definitely not," promised Ronan. And that black mood threatened to return. "Federi, I made a strategic mistake. No. I love Rushka. I couldn't imagine not wanting her. But it's broken my career. I'm finished. Why couldn't I have met her in a normal setting, where I hold a standard factory job and go to work in the day and come home at night, and she can be at home and raise the babies?"

"Factory work?" asked Federi, baffled. "*Factory* work?"

"What else is there for an uneducated lout like me," said Ronan glumly.

"Uneducated? You call yourself uneducated? You're a young officer on the Solar Wind!" exclaimed Federi.

"But we're going to be thrown off the ship," countered Ronan. "And then I'm a useless beggar on Captain's charity base. There's not even work there for me to do."

Federi nodded. "You think?"

"It's pointless anyway," replied Ronan glumly. "Rushka has left me."

"Rushka is in Southern Free," said Federi. "She feels better there." He scowled darkly. "Donegal," he warned, "she's my little sister. You treat her nicely, understood!"

Ronan nodded despondently. "She was right to leave me, Federi. I'm just a piece of dirty, violent flotsam from Molly Street..."

The Romany got up and opened the cabinet, and dug out a packet with ampoules. He read the box with a puzzled frown, then pulled out the pamphlet, opened it and scanned it too, focusing intensely. By the time a minute had elapsed, Ronan was smiling.

"What on Earth are you doing, Federi?"

"'s this darned antidepressant Doc gave you," muttered Federi absently. "Not doing its job. Reading the instructions to see if she did it wrong, maybe."

Ronan laughed. Federi folded the pamphlet up and stuffed it back into the box. He smiled. "That's better!" And he returned to his spot on the opposite bunk. "Now, if Shawn were in your situation and you were older," he said thoughtfully. "Would you help him out?"

"I'd buy him a house," said Ronan. "I'd make sure that he's provided for until he's on his feet."

"Alright," said Federi. "That's good. And would you accept that kind of help from your older brother-in-law?"

Ronan stared at him. "You'd do that for me?"

"You're *familia,*" said Federi. "Twice over, Donegal. You're my wife's brother, and you're married to my foster sister." He mulled for a moment. "Let's see now. Florida. I own a bit of coastline there. Think a co-house would make sense there?"

"What's a co-house?"

"A commune," said Federi. "Thought it would be easier on Rhine Gold if he could raise his babies there too, stay close to friends. And maybe Anyhow, too." He shook his head. "Not Anyhow. Rushka

176

can't handle Dana."

"Dana's unlikely to stick around," said Ronan.

"You need to know something," said Federi, his mood suddenly turning dark. "Officially your sister and Federi are no longer on the crew, Ronan. Captain can push the Tzigan that far – but he pushed me into a corner. And a rat in a corner... bites."

*

Perdita stared at the black hole that centred the Spinning Top Nebula. She had been left in charge of the bridge while Captain had his private little chat with Dana. The fact that Jon Marsden and Federi both sat in on that chat, didn't mean much. Whose side were they on anyway?

If Captain thought he could negotiate with that damned Crystal! And if Dana thought that placing everyone under Federi's protection would stop that Crystal...

The discussion had yielded nothing much. They were barking up the wrong tree, chasing the little shifter. Harmless space crawler, Dana called the thing. Well, she could be wrong! In that moment that Perdita had smashed the Captain's brandy on the shifter's head, she had got the distinct impression that the creature was sniggering at her. But then again, it had saved the Solar Wind from being blown apart. What to make of that?

She thought she knew what to make of that. That shifter was having fun. And possibly it was a carnivorous type. It didn't want its food vacuum packed. Or perhaps it needed atmosphere. Maybe its own reserves of air were too low to sustain a prolonged space journey. Although these shifters had a way of teleporting, jumping huge interstellar distances; the more intelligent ones built gates and channels, between galaxies and between the juxtaposed universes.

Using the vertical universe to get from place to place in the horizontal one and vice versa. She had accessed her painful ancestral memories as a survival measure; she needed to find out what the hell they were up against! Even so, the information was patchy and came in a drip-feed; but access was beginning to get easier, and the horrible superimposed impressions were slowly fading the more she forced herself to go there without mercy. Beyond which she was beginning to sense a wealth of knowledge that wanted to be tapped into, that her mother had maybe not even known. The shared Atlantean knowledge base.

She still felt they ought to hunt that shifter down and kill it! But it could not be done with knives and guns. It had to be done chemically, like pest control. Ailyss was on the right track, hunting it with poison.

The console chair under her went to liquid and flowed out of the door. Perdita screeched, picked herself up from the deck, grabbed Shawn's electronic binoculars that he had left there – correction, that Jon Marsden had left there! Shawn had lent them to him – and threw them at the thing. The binoculars met the wall with a loud "clonk" and clattered to the deck. Perdita picked them up and checked that nothing was broken.

Blasted shifter! It was gone. She glanced at her wrist-com, wondering if she should inform Captain. But the decree had been to leave the space crawler to its little pranks and approach it with a sense of humour. A quality Radomir Lascek didn't even possess in traces.

She paged Ailyss instead.

*

Federi cast dark glares out of the portholes of the cabins he passed. Almost, one could believe that it was only night, a moonless night on the Pacific. Except that the Solar Wind didn't roll. She didn't appear to move in *any way!* One could easily forget that she was falling through space at the rate of light years per minute. And mostly, what was in space was tons and tons of nothing at all.

The Lolita Coils, the Ducking Mechanism and the Teleportation facility. Between those three finely integrated pieces of machinery, the ship was hurtling through the void faster than any bullet; avoiding rocks and stray planets by calculating small leaps around them, and abbreviating the speeding-up and slowing-down by flying staccatos of teleportation at progressively higher or lower speeds.

The whole process was deeply suspicious to the Earth-bound gypsy. He was longing to fly the Solar Wind before a proper storm again, anna bottle of primordial soup. Mere weeks ago he had been comfortable in the knowledge that even though one could not rule out the concept of life in space, the chances were that Radomir Lascek was going to be the one to put it there. And space travel in Perdita's jets, right up to Mars, had sounded like a tempting exploration. Perhaps Captain could even plant a space base there.

Now?

A shifter? A creature that had somehow waited around the portal until it hopped onto the Solar Wind the way you caught a bus into Bucureşti? How the hell had that thing been breathing out there?

Memories of vanishing lizards surfaced, uncomfortably. Clearly alien life forms could not be dismissed with a shrug and a sceptical smile any longer! Annabottle! He turned the door handle and let himself in.

"Here I am, Captain!"

For a change, no open bottles stood around the Captain's cabin. Paean was seated obediently at the Captain's small conference table. Her eyes went to Federi the second he put his foot into the cabin. He returned her soft gaze with a hazy smile. He was glad she was there.

"Federi," said Radomir Lascek. "Your wife has forgiven me.

Now, she hasn't said it, but she wants to hear it herself. I'm asking your forgiveness too. I should have listened to you when you objected. You were right. It wasn't a case of Paean out of control, but of your Captain jumping to conclusions."

"We've already covered this, Captain. It's past."

"I shouldn't have made *you* chain her down," added Lascek.

The Romany didn't reply. *That* had been the bad part.

"I've informed her," added Radomir Lascek, "that the Cabin is sacrosanct. It's your refuge, and hers. I have no say in there."

Federi smiled cynically and nodded. "Uh-huh." Except when it counted. Then the Cabin was suddenly very much part of the Solar Wind.

"She laughed," added Lascek. "Why?"

"Because that's where all the guns and ammunition of the entire crew are stashed this moment," said Paean with a smirk.

Radomir Lascek smiled broadly. Federi gazed at the little redhead.

"We're not technically on your crew any longer," he commented. "You're aware of that, Captain."

"I am," agreed Lascek. "But you are aboard."

"On a voluntary basis," specified Federi. "And when we're back on Earth, we're taking a holiday. Long one. After that… we'll just have to see how it goes."

"You're always welcome aboard, Federi," said the Captain. "Your job will be waiting for you for whenever you want it back."

"Quartermaster," muttered Federi pensively. "What on Earth does that entail? – I'll look it up."

"Now, as for the Central Crystal," said Lascek. "Federi, find out from the Solar Wind how I can get into contact with that thing."

"Yes, Captain!"

*

Solar Wind!

There was stubborn silence.

Solar Wind, let me access your console! The human animals want to speak to me.

Silence.

Federi hacked around on the bridge console, trying to get a fix on the Central Crystal. He felt sorely inadequate. He knew how to override programs and build bypasses for encrypted safety locks; he knew how to access information in just about any system that came along; but he was technically not a programmer, and he couldn't find a rogue program in a CPU as huge as that of the Solar Wind.

Captain had asked him to negotiate with the Central Crystal. This was easier said than done.

Fine then... you asked for it!

The Solar Wind stubbornly continued to ignore everything the Central Crystal said.

Federi D!

Federi nearly fell off the console chair from surprise. "Ah, blast, of course! I forgot! You reach right into a person's mind!"

You wish to negotiate. I still have an unmet demand, the Crystal pointed out.

"Being?"

You owe me Dana.

"Not at all," replied Federi.

Yes, you do. With a mental pact which is more binding than a physical one.

"I never agreed to turn her over," said Federi. "I only prompted

181

you to go ahead with the download."

There was a baffled silence. And then:

Touché, Tzigan! Ancient trick!

"I use it a lot," said Federi modestly.

I'll be on my guard, said the Central Crystal. *Now. You wish to negotiate?*

"Just to get us home safely," said Federi. "We don't need any alien treasure."

Just home, repeated the Crystal. *And I'm supposed to do like a genie and say, master, your wish is my command?*

"Well," said Federi, "er, yes!"

It comes at a cost, said the Crystal. *Of course.*

*

13
Shifter

The sound of ceramic shattering brought Paean chasing to the galley.

"Federi!"

He didn't hear her. He grabbed another plate and launched it at the Ironwood Table's leg. Paean watched how the near-indestructible ceramic compound hit the time-hardened wood at that exact angle that had the plate exploding into a thousand shards.

"Federi!" She raised her voice. "Federi!"

The gypsy's eyes lifted to meet hers. He aimed a plate at her for a split second. She flinched.

In that moment, Paean saw how his dark eyes cleared, his mind returned to rationality. He flung the plate to the deck, where it failed to shatter, and gathered her close in a fierce hug.

"Did you just..." she asked, rattled. She realized that he was shaking. He released a salted Romany expression.

"Nearly decapitated you there," he muttered. "Flying hells!"

Paean laughed a bit uncertainly. "Couldn't have, with that! Why were you terminating all those plates?" She smiled. "Quicker than washing up?"

He shook his head. No mood for humour, she realized. "So what's wrong, Federi?"

"I have the choice," said Federi with barely constrained anger, "between terminating Captain and getting the ship home, and not terminating Captain and all of us dying from being lost in space."

Paean hugged him tightly and bit back a swearword. Oh blast!

"Can't think here," said Federi. "Come, little luv! Too much noise here!"

Especially with all those plates smashing, thought Paean, but she wisely kept her mouth shut. Federi teleported into the Comet with her.

"At least he can't watch me here through the Solar Wind's eyes," growled the Romany. He peered up at the Solar Wind's white hull. Thousands of tiny sensors peered back at him. "Blast, he can!"

He keyed a fast sequence into the Comet's console, and the jet turned upside down again. He went to the storage cabinet and opened it. A bottle of shipwreck rum sat staring at him.

Wrong response. Wrong darned response! A drunk assassin might as well be dead! He closed the cabinet again and perceived more than heard the soundless little sigh from Paean. And another from that bottle...?!

"Funny thing that," his little sweetheart piped. "If that Crystal can hypnotize Dana, why doesn't it plain hypnotize Captain instead?"

Federi turned and pointed at her. And ripped the storage cabinet open again. That bottle was gone. He'd blasted well thought so! He rolled his eyes. That prankster shifter was the last thing he needed now! For pestilence! And he'd established that it had a way of getting from the Solar Wind to the Comet. Probably by some sort of teleportation. Who knew. Ah! He knew! The means by which the space crawler moved, was *insinuation.* It had insinuated itself onto the Comet. Possibly because it didn't feel too safe on the Solar Wind, knowing that Ailyss and Perdita were still stalking it. He'd really have to talk to those two lovelies.

Unless there was of course more than one crawler. Rats... yes, he guessed, they'd be the rats of intergalactic travel. How this one should feel safe on the Comet, was an open question. Paean had taken roaches and made them into croaches. Any vermin ought to be scared!

"As Sherman would say..." He lapsed into silence. Sherman

Dougherty! What had the Priors known about Atlantis, and artificial intelligences? What had been known in the Sixties? Had there been any mention of a Central Crystal? In fact, what did gypsy lore say about the devil? He didn't know enough. His parents had always shielded him and Katya from those particular legends, for obvious reasons. It hadn't helped, in the big picture. He wished he could call Cassandra. But what concerned the Sherman files…

Blast again! Accessing the Sherman Files from the Comet was opening the door and inviting that Crystal thing onto Paean's jet. Hell, that was probably how the Central Crystal had got onto the Solar Wind! The Comet had been right overhead Dome, close enough for the Crystal to control them. It had probably loaded itself – or a mobile floating copy of itself – onto the Comet's console like a wyrm. Via the bubble sub's CPU. They had locked into the sub's CPU to tug it. He wondered. Perdita's jet… who knew, maybe it even had a specific function for this, a Central Crystal receptor! And from the Comet, it must have climbed over onto the Solar Wind's CPU. To darned easy.

That meant that the blasted thing was on the Comet in any case. Aargh!

"Sounds to me as though all he does is cook people's brains," said Paean. "Can't see how that can be much of a threat. You can simply refuse."

"Mind conjuring, and extortion," repeated the gypsy. "Don't forget the extortion. The filth can choose to open or not to open the next portal!"

"They've all opened so far without a hitch," Paean pointed out.

"Yes. Right. That was his doing. According to Perdita."

"Why would he have done that so far?"

Federi rolled his eyes. "Figure it out, Paean! To get us stuck in space. The real question is, what the hell has Captain ever done to him?" He paused. "Wait!" There was something nagging at the edge of his consciousness. He held up his hand for complete quiet. Something the Crystal had said that had struck him as odd, but that he had forgotten about in the heat of the debate.

Federi D. The Crystal had called him that. The entity, what- or whoever it was, had refrained from speaking his full name.

By the stars, there was a meaning behind that! Unless, of course, it didn't know his full name. But if it did…

"Let's just see how far Perdita can take us without the darned Crystal," suggested Paean.

"Quiet!" Rats, now the line of thought was gone. "Sorry, little luv! Repeat yourself?"

*

Central Crystal, Radomir Lascek typed into the Solar Wind's console. *Can you hear me?*

I can hear you and see you and understand you, came the reply.

What do you want from us?

Dana, said the Crystal. *Put her into the Probe and send her through the next portal alone.*

Radomir Lascek frowned. *You're demanding human sacrifice?*

I merely demand Dana, replied the Crystal. *I haven't said for what. She is my High Priestess for New Dome, as Perdita is for the Earth. They are mine. Besides, Captain, what do you call human?*

Radomir Lascek shook his head. *You demand that I hand over the mother of my child? May I remind you that she is under Federi's protection?*

The man who was sent to kill you?

The Captain shook his head again. Dealing with this entity was frustrating.

You might try getting rid of him, added the Central Crystal. *I've*

186

instructed him to finish his job.

Radomir Lascek snorted. Federi didn't take *instructions* from anyone other than his Captain!

May I remind you what he is, wrote the Crystal. *And who he is.*

"And why have you instructed him to do so, if I may ask?"

Does pure evil need a reason?

"Pure evil," Radomir Lascek repeated sarcastically to himself. "Clearly that thing hasn't met Federi's sharp end yet! Let's hope that it does soon!"

He can't, sniggered the Crystal. *There is no executing a god!*

You'll be amazed, retorted Lascek.

The Crystal laughed some more. *If he executes me, he sacrifices all of you, leaving the Solar Wind marooned in space.*

*

Ailyss paused in her jotting down of words and looked up from her electronic notepad. Perdita Sancho was standing in the door of her cabin, although Ailyss hadn't heard the door open. The spy girl had to admit to herself that the terrorist was good – if it was in fact Perdita! If she wasn't instead facing that darned crawler!

"Perdita?"

"Ailyss," said Perdita. "That space crawler. I want to talk to you about it."

The Irish agent locked gazes with the terrorist boss.

"Say no more! That thing could be anywhere! It can hear us."

"I know," replied Perdita. "I was thinking, let's talk on the Probe?"

Ailyss narrowed her eyes. Shawn had said something. The crawler might be good enough to mimic appearances, but Shawn had picked something up. It couldn't fake the aura of the person. Perdita's light-yellow, slightly off-human aura was intact and healthy. And there was of course another thing. The shifter couldn't speak. Ailyss laughed softly to herself.

"It's alright. You are Perdita."

"Why, was there doubt?"

She held out her electronic notepad on which she had jotted down several ideas. As Perdita took it, it melted in her hand, ran through her fingers and slipped out under the door.

Ailyss jumped onto the liquid with a loud curse.

"Now it knows what I was planning!"

*

Shawn was in the galley, on his knees, helping Luigi remove the shrapnel of Federi's rage. He was worried. If Federi started losing his cool in such a dramatic way, something bad must have happened. The gypsy must be under terrific pressure. Federi was always theatrical, but Shawn had never yet seen him get destructive. Luigi had informed him that Master Federi was on the Comet, with Paean. This worried Shawn as well; he hoped his sister was alright.

He crawled in under the sink for more sweeping up of splinters. The stuff was as sharp as glass. He didn't want anyone to get any into their neomer sandals.

It was dark down here. Something moved in the corner. Something fuzzy-looking. Shawn blinked. A cat? He clicked his tongue softly, charming it to come forward. It moved a bit, reluctantly. His red eyebrows shot up in surprise. Yes, a cat – if a cat was a round ball of fluff with huge round eyes and twenty seven skinny black spider legs!

"You are the shifter!" he said softly.

The thing moved a bit and stared at him with wide, frightened eyes.

188

With square pupils. That fluoresced, the way a cat's did, only in an iridescent violet.

"I'm not going to hurt you!" promised Shawn. "Federi said to leave you in peace. You've saved the ship from exploding!"

The shifter moved a bit. Shawn coaxed it forward.

"Is this your natural shape? What's your name?"

The shifter made a soft, hissing, bubbling noise.

"Come out!" cajoled Shawn. "You're safe! I promise! Donegal honour!"

The fuzzy creature cautiously emerged from its hiding spot. It did look funny! All round and fluffy, the colours of a calico cat; dark brown and black with orange dashes. And those leathery black spider legs all sticking out at the bottom.

"Are you hurt?" asked Shawn. He stretched out his hand.

"Don't touch that thing!" screamed Ailyss from the doorway. She flung a bottle of something at the fuzz-ball. The lid flew off, dousing the shifter.

The fuzzy animal squealed in pain. In patches, its hair began to smoke; the acid – or whatever had been in that bottle – burned through the poor little critter's skin and ate raw wounds into it. Shawn ran to the taps to fill a large jug with water to pour it over the poor creature, but before he could get back to it, the acid dissolved it completely. It lay in a fizzling, bubbling puddle on the deck, single sparks coursing over it at longer and longer intervals. Eventually they stopped and the puddle lay still.

Shawn looked up at Ailyss, shocked.

"You killed it! And Federi said it saved the ship!"

Ailyss stared hard at him.

"Ailyss," said Shawn angrily, "I didn't think you're a cruel type!"

The Irish spy shrugged, turned and left. Shawn stared at her retreating back, furious. Heck, she needed her head revised!

And then he had it.

The moment he realized that her aura was wrong, she dissolved and ran away across the deck, flickering with electricity. He heard the shifter's laughter like a far-away echo. He turned to the puddle of the small furry animal. It was gone.

It had all been an illusion? Unless there was more than one -? Did these space crawlers fight and kill each other, while not harming the host species on the ship? He shivered slightly. He didn't like the idea of being a host species for anything.

"Alright," said Shawn Donegal. "Not funny. I hate cruelty." Goosebumps were chasing up his arms. The one shifter had spoken! It could verbalize! It was a lot more intelligent than they had so far assumed! He had to warn Ailyss.

*

The Captain materialized in the Comet.

They had to ask Wolf to make the front end of teleportation less sudden, thought Federi. At least on Captain's teleporter. A warning tinkling or something.

"Federi."

"Welcome aboard, Captain," said the Romany suavely. "Please have a seat."

"*Déjà vu,*" muttered Radomir Lascek. He nodded to Paean.

"Brandy?" offered Federi.

"No, thanks. I understand the Crystal instructed you to assassinate me?"

"Instructed! It tried extortion," replied Federi. "Your life or the ship stuck in space."

"Ye Gods!" Lascek's hand went over his eyes. "And now, Federi?"

190

The Romany laughed cynically. "Right, Captain! That warped psycho of a piece of programming expects me to execute my Captain! Interesting there, it pointed out itself that only because it spoke the truth while I was monitoring it, doesn't mean it can be trusted! Say I go ahead and kill you."

"If you get that right," added Lascek with a slight grin.

"Yes. Provided I get that right," agreed Federi. "Then what would stop that thing from telling me to execute the next guy before it opens the portal? Where is it going to stop? Perhaps it will demand one death per portal? How many portals are there? Will the Solar Wind reach home as a ghost vessel with one sole assassin aboard?"

Radomir Lascek nodded.

"So, Captain, I'd suggest a crew meeting. I don't know if it only got to me, but I'd assume it would try its luck with every assassin aboard."

"There are a number," said Lascek pensively.

"Exactly, Captain. I'd recommend, no human sacrifices at all! Where we draw the line. We all have to agree on this, that one sacrifice is one too many."

*

Clever, Federi!

The Romany glanced at his wrist-com. That darned Crystal had accessed him the second he was back on the Solar Wind.

Brilliant! Alerting everyone!

He smiled. He won that round!

So, instead of sacrificing one man, you elect to sacrifice the whole crew, added the entity.

"How so?"

Wait until the next portal.

"Aha. So you'll keep us stuck in space. Wonder what you're going to do when that portal opens anyway."

It won't. I've been overriding them.

"You're asking me to play God," said Federi softly.

On the contrary, Federi. I crave entertainment. I'm demanding you unleash that demon in you and do as your nature dictates!

"Ha," snapped Federi. "My nature!" He rolled his eyes. This was enough! "I'll consider that a contract! I'll keep you to your word!"

Words can be powerful creatures, said the entity.

"Or they can be a lot of noisy air," replied the Tzigan. "I'm going to hold you to this one!"

I can't help wondering why you're suddenly so compliant, replied the Crystal.

"Wait until the next portal," retorted Federi.

*

An hour later the gypsy was back in the galley, peeling potatoes like a mad thing.

Paean slunk in through the door.

"Have a seat," invited Federi.

"Give me something to do," requested Paean. She took a seat across from him, picturesque in her turquoise scarf, and reached for the onions.

Rhine Gold and Johnny Anyhow, Federi's standard assistants, were both catching some much-needed sleep after having stood in for the cook for countless hours. Shawn was minding the tobuskies, counting them and making sure that none had been eaten by those mysterious creatures, the space crawlers. Shawn suspected an infestation of them. He had spotted two by now. There was a remedy for that, thought Federi. Biological warfare. He'd ask Paean to clone an itch – for the crawlers. So they would want to leave the ship. He glanced up from his potatoes and scanned his wife's appearance.

"Do me a favour, little mockingbird. Put on the other one."

Paean put down her onion knife and pulled her scarf off her head. She stashed it in her moonbag and pulled out the lime-green scarf, winding that around her head.

"Warming me noggin," she commented with a wee grin. "Taming me copper wire."

Federi snorted. "Copper wire! - And the onions? You hate onions!"

"Mother's recipe," said Paean. "If something has really revolted you, you grab the nastiest job you can find and do it until your mind clears. Her way of getting us to do the nasty jobs." She glanced up. He grinned at her. "Well, the nastiest job on the Solar Wind is actually the heads," she added, her blue eyes apologetic. "But Federi..."

"You wanted to be near me," concluded the gypsy with a smile.

Yes, he was spooked too. But not by the silly crawlers, although he probably ought to be. He was haunted by the way the Central Crystal had addressed each last one of the dangerous crew and set them the same challenge. One human sacrifice, or the ship is marooned.

Uncanny, the way it picked its victims. Ailyss' victim had been himself. Perdita was to terminate Dana; and so was the Captain. Jon Marsden was to finish off Perdita; Dana, the Captain. And Paean –

That horrible Crystal had even whispered into Paean's ear, asking her to doom Captain for the cruel way he had forced Federi to chain her up. To load a dart with her green wonder bug and a tiny drop of poison from Federi's arsenal, and to shoot Captain. He wouldn't suffer, wouldn't feel a thing; but the Solar Wind would be saved and they would have a future, herself, Federi, Ronan, Shawney.

Onions. Federi nodded.

14
Demonology

The portal was visible not too far ahead, in sinister rainbow swirls. These star gates could be as beautiful as they liked; for Federi they were bad news. The Solar Wind had been lured into deep space, so far from home she could never find her way back alone. Each portal was another twist in the impossible labyrinth.

How the heck had this happened? One moment they were skippering around Earth's oceans, quietly rearranging the world's politics, and the next... here came a herd of interstellar goddesses and whoosh!- the Solar Wind had to become a starship! And get herself lost in space, thank you kindly. It couldn't have suited the Unicate better. It made him wonder about Dana's true agenda - and Perdita's.

Federi peered glumly through the porthole of the galley. He missed his comfort zone, his cabin; he missed spending some quiet time there, carving something or writing something while Paean was practicing violin or swinging in her hammock, reading her medical books. He missed the soft jingling – but there hadn't been any jingling anyway, not since they started into space. In essence, he missed the past. It might have helped him figure out how to deal with this master extortionist that called itself the Central Crystal.

Unbelievable, that an artificial intelligence could have developed such a deep-seated persona of evil! He shook his mane, puzzled. Those Atlanteans had to have been evil to the extreme that even their artefacts were that bad!

This was no good. The little songbird had fallen asleep at the Ironwood table, after helping him clear away the supper from the boardroom, wash the dishes, wet-and-dry the boardroom carpet which had inevitably got food bits on it, which was why the crew was to eat in the galley, anna bottle; she had cleared up the infirmary and organized the lab, swabbing it down with antiseptic soap as she did every third day anyway; cleaned the heads...

And now she lay with her head on her arms, red hair spilt over the table, curling in puddles around her head, just the way she'd kept passing out from overwork back in that cold place that Federi associated with hell. There wasn't even a comfortable hammock for her while he finished organizing his stocks and jotting down how much was left of what – how much time he could buy before a dire decision had to be made.

Of course they were going to sleep in the Comet. The Comet's seats folded out; Perdita had designed those jets for space travel. There was even a small bathroom tucked into the back of the jet; just a shower and a toilet and a basin, but enough to sustain being away from Earth for a while. But there was no comfort in it. It was small, compact, practical. No double bunk, no hammock, no down duvet. As caravans went, it was frugal to the point of barrenness. Playing violin in there would be difficult, because although one could stand up straight, the space was too limited for Paean to dance about as she played. It was like tying one's hands behind one's back and then trying to have a conversation!

It was all the Crystal's fault, thought Federi angrily. It had no doubt been messing with the crew's and the Captain's minds long before they left Earth. Bit of rogue programming from the sea bottom! He glanced up at that portal again, and then at Perdita who had appeared in the door. And narrowed his eyes. Perdita! Wolf! Programming! Amazing how things just fell into place, sometimes!

Now if he could hang onto that thought long enough...

"You're working her to a standstill!" commented the Golden Honey, glancing at Paean's sleeping form. "Have mercy, man! Get her to her bunk!"

"Hammock," corrected Federi. "Not going to." Rats! Perdita, Wolf – what was that again?

Perdita frowned at him.

"Chains," he said.

"Of course." The Golden Honey took a seat. "That portal," she said, pointing. "We fly into it, and then we see further."

"So have you executed Dana?"

Perdita snorted. "Get real, Federi!" She picked up the lone paring knife that was still lying around the table and twirled it. "That Crystal wants a human sacrifice. Any human sacrifice, sounds like. You guys have your whole future ahead of you. I'll sacrifice myself."

Federi snatched the knife from her.

"Not with that!" said Perdita disdainfully. "There are easier ways to die! Honestly!"

The Doc's eyes widened when Federi arrived at her cabin door with an unwilling Perdita in tow. His hand was around the Golden Honey's wrist like an iron clamp.

"*Another* one?"

"Space madness," growled the Romany. "We're too darned far away from the rocking of the ocean!"

"Federi, leave it alone!" snapped Perdita.

"*Nimic,* Perdita!"

"Same routine as Ronan?" asked the Doc.

"Slightly different," suggested Federi. "Not the infirmary. She doesn't need teens gawking at her."

"Maybe I do," smiled Perdita. "Are they playing poker in there?"

196

They were indeed playing poker in the infirmary. After Perdita received her antidepressant injection from Doc Judith, Federi left the Golden Honey in Ronan and Rhine Gold's tender care and went on a round.

It was one small residue of comfort zone, pacing out the route of many years, getting back into his thinking frame. There was no way he could hide in the jib stowage for'ard on the deck, so the round would have to be enough, though the ship was as cold as in Antarctica. What the heck was wrong with her temperature settings? He'd have to investigate.

Besides there were shifters he had to scan for, alien parasites who had just got a whole lot smarter. Federi frowned. So now the blasted stuff spoke!

Did they understand the meaning of the phrases they pronounced? He tried to visualize himself in the alien's skin, utilizing a foreign structure – a voice box – like an instrument to make highly articulate music that communicated something to those two-legged beings. Had it heard Ailyss use those exact words, and copied them with baffling precision? Federi knew what it was like to learn a foreign language from nothing. But there was no intelligent, structured teaching interaction between any of the crew and those things… if there was in fact more than one that spoke… maybe only one had figured it out?

He paused, stopping in mid-step, his hand halfway to the rail over the companionway that descended into the machineroom. He was *assuming* that nobody had taught that thing to talk! But – could he assume that? What if Dana was cultivating one of those aliens out of monkey business, or Perdita, out of a strange sense of vengeance? What, in fact, if those shifters were Dana's pets to begin with? By the silver star that shone on his blue island! Nothing could be ruled out where those two dangerous felines were concerned! He slunk down the companion ladder to the machine room.

"Hey, Federi."

"Hi, Svendsson."

Everything fine in the machine room. Federi took it all in, engineers and all. Bronwyn, Jeannie. Lolita coils, ducking mechanism and teleportation deviation devices. He shuddered. Where were the days when the whole place had been loaded with boxes upon boxes of good wholesome torpedoes?

Dr Jake looked up too and echoed Wolf's greeting. Federi waved at him.

"Central Crystal been bugging you guys?"

"No."

"Not any shifter either?"

"Nope."

"Any other sign of more undue occurrences? Bogeymen? Viruses? Dana?"

A general shaking of heads.

"*Kathal,*" said Federi and continued on his rounds. Thank the starfish, all on an even keel in the bilges!

Doc Judith was back in her cabin.

"You alright, Doc?" asked Federi as he stuck his head in through the door.

"Fine, my friend. Jolly dreary weather though."

"Or absence thereof," agreed Federi.

"Could do with some diversion. Space is blooming boring."

Federi scowled. Where he was concerned, the boring bits were the good bits!

"Sleep tight, Federi," smiled the Doc.

"Not going to sleep," replied the gypsy.

"You should try sleeping some time," advised Doc Judith. "It would save you some depression."

"And several other things," agreed Federi. "Like, the crew's future wages. Good night, Doc!"

He withdrew, closing the door quietly.

Old Sherman Dougherty had joined the poker game in the infirmary, which was getting rather loud and happy. Federi smiled and vanished from the doorway. He ought to alert Johnny Anyhow to the game. No doubt the young marine would want to join.

He checked in on Jon Marsden on the bridge.

"So, Federi," smiled the First Mate. "How's the assassination coming?"

Federi narrowed his eyes and checked his friend's aura. You never blooming knew!

"That was a blasted untoward comment, Jon! Almost I'd have said you're a shifter!"

"Where's your sense of humour gone all of a sudden?" asked Jon, injured.

Federi studied him carefully.

"What's wrong, my friend?"

"Nothing," smiled Jonathan Marsden. "If you discount that we're going to die in space in another – how long do we have, Federi?"

"Three weeks to two months," said the quartermaster.

Jon got thoughtful. "You know, Federi, I never made a will," he said. "Should have. She'd be rich."

Aha. Michelle. Left behind on Planet Earth.

"She's still inheriting everything that's yours," said Federi. "She's your wife."

"But she can't prove it," said Jon Marsden regretfully. "I've got the marriage contract."

"You left her without any paperwork?" gasped Federi. "Jon, how could you?"

"Wasn't thinking," said Jon.

"You weren't thinking? You leave her on the base and sail off into the sunset?"

Jon Marsden was speechless for a moment.

"That wedding was in any case a manipulated thing," he said then.

"What?!"

"Between Paean's virus and your bringing her with your jet, right after Prime Oil was attacked…"

"Jon," growled Federi, "take that back! Grief! She's not even here to defend herself!"

"But it's the truth!"

"You lousy rat!" exploded Federi. "You, and that Ronan! Abdicating responsibility for your own decisions! Listen acutely now, my dangerous friend. I recall a morning at Prime Oil, and not the first of its kind, when old Federi the Tzigan checked in on his friend Michelle, with whom he shares an interest in biology and speciation. And my best friend's clothes and tie were strewn all over her front room, leaving an exact trail to decipher, and Exhibit A, my best friend himself, was passed out cold on her bed, in a shocking state of undress."

"I'm so sorry! Was I trespassing on your territory?"

Federi snapped his mouth shut in shock. He turned and left, pausing at the bottom of the stairwell to bring the growling animal back under control. Hells, he didn't know Jon like this! And then he had it. There were really only two possibilities. One solution for both - ha! He went back up the stairs, aimed, and shot. Jon Marsden slumped to the ground.

"That," said Federi with an acid little smile, "was revenge for that time in the Probe, buddy!"

Well done, Federi. You're getting into the swing of things!

You idiot, thought Federi. He touched a sequence on the console.

"Wolf! Come in!"

"Hey, Federi!"

"Stall the engines and stop the ship!"

"What? Okay."

The Solar Wind quit falling and stopped, right before that portal. It loomed huge and rainbow-coloured. The trouble with the Central frying Crystal was that it read minds. So he couldn't even think consciously about what steps he needed to take. Just take them.

Federi peered in through the door of the Captain's cabin.

"Come in," said Radomir Lascek tiredly and waved at him. In his hand, a brandy glass. In front of him, on the round little table, his pistol. And a hand-written logbook, open on a blank page. Federi peered at his Captain.

"Would you consider carrying out your original commission?" asked the Captain.

"No," said Federi. He took a seat. "Why?"

Radomir Lascek sighed deeply. "Federi, my old friend. A man cruises the oceans for years with a crew and a ship, looting and pillaging – well, we never pillaged, did we, only looted... I find I can't sacrifice them. I have failed my crew. I should have listened to Perdita and stayed out of space. Now they are all going to die! Slowly and miserably."

"We still have two months worth of supplies, Captain," supplied the quartermaster. "And the tobuskies are coping fine with the oxygen situation, I've installed UV lamps under the Ironwood Table for them... Ship's energy supplies are fine too, we can run on nuclear power for another five hundred years if we must... we may run out of antidepressant before that though, but we have Paean to entertain us..."

Lascek lifted an eyebrow, and his mouth twitched but never got as far as the smile. "Two months of stocks, huh. More time for that blasted Crystal to wreak his havoc! Let's face things, Federi. We're stuck. And it seems to me that I hold the answer."

"What answer?"

"That Crystal demands that you people execute Radomir Lascek," said the Captain. "A blood sacrifice. None of you is prepared to do it, so I'll –"

A smile spread over his face as he collapsed over the table.

Federi put his own gun away, emptied the Captain's pistol of bullets and pocketed it.

Having fun?

Stuff off, thought Federi. You are so clueless!

Dana was his next stop. Johnny Anyhow had joined the poker game in Sick Bay, so the redheaded goddess was alone.

"Federi!" said Dana brightly. "I was thinking…"

"Good," replied Federi, putting his gun away again. And then he remembered that the beautiful, still shape lying on the deck was actually pregnant.

"Rats," he muttered. He picked Dana's motionless form up and laid her down gently on her bunk.

You didn't even talk to her first!

Wasn't in the mood for her brand of madness, thought Federi.

So who's next?

Everybody, Central Crystal.

*

Paean opened her eyes with difficulty.

"Aw, Federi… You just popped such a nice dream…"

Dark magnetic eyes met hers. The world slipped back into synch. She reached for him and collected the kiss that was the penalty for waking her up.

"Need your creativity," said Federi when he had his mind back and could think of the problem at hand again. "The whole crew is coming down with space madness!"

"Space madness?"

"Think of Ronan," said the gypsy.

"Oh!" She understood. "I'll clone a happy virus. Let me see now." She got up and staggered a bit, unbalanced. Federi caught her and steadied her, and tagged her down to the lab.

"Jolly ship just won't roll," she complained.

What is she doing now?

Accessing the Sherman Files, said the Solar Wind.

Sherman Files? Let me see! My, my! What a treasury!

Access denied, proclaimed the Solar Wind. *Go away and stop communicating! I hate you! You demand human sacrifice!*

I'm only playing with them, Solar Wind.

Some sick game!

Only cooking their brains a bit, testing their limits...

You're a psychopath! Now leave me alone!

Federi sat idly watching Paean's nimble fingers as they programmed the Genitron. And then as they dug a bit further in the Sherman files.

"Federi, what did the Priors know about Space Travel?"

"Precious little, I'd assume," replied the Romany and pulled that infernal piece of wood that refused to be anything, out of his pocket. "Why?"

"Maybe they would have known the way home. I..." She lapsed into sudden, intensely concentrated silence.

"What have you found?"

"Federi..." She kept reading, absorbed.

The Assassin slipped down from the bench top and moved in behind her. And then there were hands left and right of her, erasing the information off the screen.

"Hey!"

"You stick to your cloning," he ordered, his silver eye tooth glinting in warning.

"But Federi – "

He gazed at her with a mirthless smile frozen on his face, trying to see into her mind. Where the hell had those files suddenly come from? For crying out loud! They had not been part of Sherman's files the last time he looked – and he'd been very careful to search the S-Files for any mention of Federi, or Falco, or anyone else sharing his horrible family name.

And if she read them, now that she'd found them – which she would, he realized – she'd know more than was good for her peace of mind. She'd know more than she with her beautiful Donegal values and her honesty could deal with. He'd lose her love... he'd lose the only thing that made sense in his life.

He turned back to the console and keyed in some fast codes. The screen flashed a red warning, then revealed those files again, for a brief second, before he accessed their source code and erased it from the records. They had no more business living in Sherman's extensive store of information now than they had before.

"Did you just *delete* something from Sherman's files?" challenged Paean. He gave her an intent look.

"Listen, Paean," he said sternly. "Don't dig where you should not be digging. There are things about me... about my linc..."

She was staring at him with her huge blue eyes.

"Federi," she replied, "you're being daft."

That turquoise scarf went exceptionally well with her eyes when she was annoyed, he noticed.

"You're not even listening," she accused. "Och, never mind! I'll just be getting back to my cloning then, won't I?"

He didn't trust that Irish tone. But she meekly returned to the Sherman files, merely searching for information on what hormones made people feel happy and how to encode them. She ignored him completely and got immersed in her research. Federi started feeling extremely superfluous. He moved half aimlessly out of the lab, his feet taking him on a Solar Wind round once more. Looking for traces of space crawlers. He'd have to talk to her later. Right now he was missing the words.

Ailyss glanced up at him from her Tarot cards. And she gifted Federi one of her rare smiles.

"Hi Federi."

"Hi Ailyss," replied the Tzigan. "Have you experienced any depression lately?"

"No, why?"

"Any untoward urges to terminate yourself?"

Ailyss shook her head, puzzled. "Why, have you?"

Federi scowled. "Listen, Ailyss. Seems as though that Crystal has influenced everyone into thinking if they sacrifice themselves, the Solar Wind will be saved."

"Gosh," said Ailyss.

"Already had to put Captain, and Jon, and Perdita and Dana out of the picture," added Federi lightly.

"Perdita? She's having a whale of a time, in the infirmary, playing poker!"

"Right," said Federi.

Ailyss glanced at him, puzzled, and then she laughed. She understood.

"What are your cards saying?" asked Federi, craning his neck.

"Rampant voodoo," commented Ailyss. She looked at the spread before her. "They're saying, someone's playing the fool."

"Right," grinned Federi. "That's always the case."

"And someone right over here," she pointed at the card depicting the Page of Cups, "has no cooking clue what's going on."

"Ah," replied the Romany. "Rhine Gold, right?"

Ailyss frowned. "Possibly. Not what I'm getting."

"Whom are you getting?"

"Is not important, Federi. And, interestingly here," pointed Ailyss, "that's you."

"Me? The Mage?"

"Yup. So let me not hold you back from wreaking further magic!"

"Thank you, Ailyss," said Federi and continued on his round.

"The next one is for you, Solar Wind," said Ailyss, glancing at the electronic eye in the corner of her cabin. She turned her last card over. "Uh-oh!"

Death.

"They don't really mean anything at all," said Ailyss, raking the cards together and putting them away. "Hocus pocus, that's all."

The second Federi was out of the lab, Paean opened the root record of the Sherman Files. How the gypsy could simply have deleted a record... and knowing him, that record was well and truly gone. She'd have to tell Sherman, and ask him about that file. She hacked around moodily for any further information on Federi, or perhaps on Falco, hoping to find out anything at all. Her question had not been answered; and more to the point, her curiosity was really piqued now. Especially with Federi's reaction!

It was annoying that he had deleted that specific file! She clicked around in the history around the Sixties, trying to find any clue about his family. And she got immersed in reading.

The history in the files was gruesome. It told of the wars in the Sixties – the dark, terrible Sixties; and of the Unicate takeover. Things she had been trying to find out since before Mother got ill.

Life on Earth had nearly been wiped out by the warring nations in the evil Sixties. Huge holes had been blown into cities; nuclear bombs had competed with poison gas and biological warfare, and the end of life on Earth had been within clear view. And then –

It stopped. Suddenly, unpredictably.

All means of aviation, including space rockets, disappeared mysteriously. A number of satellites that were in orbit, stayed there; the rest were destroyed by the Unicate. The factories for airplanes and rockets were annihilated; the technology to build them obliterated, and the know-how deleted from all sources, even the expert manpower was captured and made to disappear. The two space cities that were orbiting Earth were destroyed, bombed away without mercy by missiles from the planet. All space projects that were further removed, were simply abandoned. Paean thought of the Tsi'iolkovski station with a shiver.

All that moved fell under a comatose paralysis that lasted for several days; for many people and animals this meant the end. The cause of this was suspected to be a massive poison attack of unknown origins; but the technology to determine the chemicals used and their levels was gone, so it could never be proved.

By the time everyone who was still alive came to and took stock, the Unicate was in power. The Unicate had stopped the wars. It had nearly stopped humanity and all mammalian life, too. Between the war and the Unicate's strategy to stop it, of twenty billion people on Earth, a scant two billion survived.

And then came the Unicate Law.

Knowledge that had been freely available in the Information Era, was labelled subversive and outlawed. Research of any kind was stopped and forbidden; so were all forensic efforts. Firearms were banned in the few countries that still supported the right to bear arms. Unemployment was outlawed, and unemployed people were forcibly 'accommodated' into compounding factories and labour camps; unless they could prove an income from independent sources. Paean wondered how on Earth the Free Gypsies had managed to evade this and hide from it. Communicable diseases were outlawed, turning hospitals into hospital-prisons. The world became a place of rules and outlaws.

And the information clamp-down followed within days. On the world-wide information network, any files carrying real information were erased. All such data were removed, too, from private devices such as readers and consoles, by means of remote detection. People reached for old paper books in desperation, trying to hold onto any kind of knowledge; so books were outlawed and paper libraries were destroyed in a huge style. Unicate officials went from door to door to collect any old paper book stacks that people had been keeping in the family. It took a special kind of courage to hide some of your favourite books so that they could be passed down through the generations. A courage Paean's ancestors had. Mother had hoarded a few such family treasures.

Re-education to the Unicate system began. Truancy from school was punished by incarceration into a labour camp; so did subversive teaching of most pre-Unicate knowledge and culture. At least, that was the official story. In practice such children and teachers simply disappeared. Mothers who were caught out communicating to their children, no matter how young, memories from pre-Unicate days, vanished and were never seen again. The Pied Piper had nothing on this, thought Paean. And she marvelled once again at Mrs Flanagan, continuing her subversive ways in the face of the Unicate. How had she escaped so long? She needed to check on her teacher. She'd mention it to Federi... she shook her head. Dublin was one thing. But she was in no way ready to revisit Molly Street.

And the Unicate established tight control. Licences became compulsory for everything from setting foot out of doors to rights for medical care. In essence, the Universal Bill of Human Rights, in effect for over a century, was revoked. According to the Unicate, the Bill and too many personal freedoms had been the root cause of the wars.

And it got worse. The Toll was instated.

According to the Unicate's philosophy, population density was another key factor causing the wars. The Toll was a system by which each family who had more than two children, had to turn their eldest over to the Unicate with every new baby born. These children, too, were never seen again – there was no record of what had happened to them. And there were lots of such families, because of scarcity of everything medical, including birth control drugs; and of course including all the families who had more than two surviving children at the point the Unicate took over. Paean's skin threatened to crawl off her back as she read this; she got tears in her eyes considering that it could have been Ronan.

Over the next sixty years terror reigned. Paean knew the tail end of it first-hand. The Toll had somehow been abandoned though. She needed to find out how.

Paging through the console following link after link, suddenly she found herself face-to-face with the file Federi had tried to delete. So it was backed up in some way? Thank the Stars! There was Falco, staring at her once more. The man the Files referred to as the Demon, or Falco the Traitor.

The man who had sold out the world to the Unicate.

Instating the Toll as a payment to the Unicate for stopping the War. Murdering single-handedly the people in power who were leading the

War. And many others. Including, it was said, his own parents.

It was on record that he could appear and disappear as silently as a ghost. It had been observed that he communicated with the Dead in dark rites of black magic. There were unconfirmed reports of him going around the towns at night feeding on the dead and dying; he had been spotted in the morgues and even in the chapels. Mad as a rabid Setter, and twice as vicious. It was remembered that he played the violin like the Devil himself, on quiet street corners in the evenings as the sun set. Calling the night, they said. It was whispered that he *was* the Devil. Or at least, a close associate.

These rumours were stated amongst the historical facts, as legends; with the consideration that there might be a grain of truth in such wide-spread stories. The Demon was a traitor; fact. He had sold out all of humankind to the Unicate. He was an assassin of the highest degree; and it was recorded by more than one eyewitness that with his violin he could play up a fog in which he could vanish.

Falco. Dark unfathomable eyes stared at her from the screen, from under falcon eyebrows. One of those eyebrows was lifted in quirky humour. The image was smiling, and that single silver eye tooth was glinting. And Paean could have sworn that that darned picture had winked at her.

A photograph that had made her heart jump. Her reaction to him was instant, it fizzed through her like bicarb. Ancestor? Falco? Her left toe, thought Paean. It *was* Federi! Her own Federi.

How often did he call himself the "old Tzigan"? How often had he called himself immortal? *Was* he thirty-two – or ageless? The enigma that was Federi had just got a whole lot deeper.

The photo was a good one, she thought as she stared at it. She'd pirate a print-out. But she battled to connect it to what she was reading. It couldn't be. Her heart kicked against it. Federi hated the Unicate. He'd never have cut any deal with them! But here it was, in the Files. Was Captain aware of this?

So Federi – or rather Falco, the name he'd been using then – was the one who had brought the Unicate? How? It made no sense to her. But it did indeed gel with the way the Unicate was hounding him. Clearly they wanted to destroy the evidence. The other dots connected up neatly, too: the way he played violin, and kept it a closely guarded secret. The assassininity. The highly stressed way in which he'd reacted to her finding the file. "…things about me… about my line…" Right, his line! A foul excuse.

He'd called the Unicate. Something in her winced, and ducked. Some small part of her psyche started wondering whether she was wrong to love him the way she did. He was the traitor of Earth! She stared at the image on the screen, her mind churning. And her heart aching, recalling all the times she'd had to pull him out of the Assassin's Time-out Room, and out of the process of mincing himself. Was that what it was about? Had she fallen for the worst piece of filth on the face of the Earth?

15
Falco

"Federi, why did you ask me to stop the ship?"

"Think about it, Wolf," said Federi into his wrist-com. "Captain's out for the count. Jon, who was holding the bridge, is holding the deck on the bridge. Dana is counting zee's; Perdita has been taken into custodial care by Donegal, Anyhow and Schatz, and is currently winning all their clothes off them. Sheer, you haven't seen poker until you've seen Perdita Sancho play!"

"Yes?" replied Wolf. "So who's on the bridge?"

"That's why I asked you to stall the drives," said Federi. By now his feet had carried him back to the lab on autopilot, to where a red-headed little creature hummed softly to herself while she planned the havoc she was going to wreak shortly.

Even before she realized he was there, he saw what was back on the console. And his heart plummeted. How the hell had that file un-deleted itself? He'd rooted it out by its very code!

His eyes caught hers for a moment. He glanced away, acutely aware of her freezing up and staring at him, riveted.

She knew! She had already read all that damning stuff. Aw hell's rats, this was the end. He'd known that sooner or later he'd have to tell her about Falco... but he never could. How was he supposed to justify something like that to her?

Paean got off the high bar stool and moved towards him, and slipped into his arms. He held her tightly, his cheek against her turquoise headscarf, unsure whether this was her farewell.

"Alright," she said, her voice a bit shaky, "firstly, Federi. I love you, whether you deserve it or not. But I can't promise that I always will… I need complete honesty from you. Are you ready for that?"

He nodded. He couldn't do anything else. Whatever she needed, he'd give it to her right now. Even if it ended up shredding him.

"Where can we talk?" she asked.

Federi took out his teleporter and ported with her into the Comet. He shut down the Comet's coms system and switched the console to minimal. And he turned. Interrogation time.

"So now," she asked seriously, "Federi, are you Falco?"

"You are asking whether everything I told you about my family and my life was a lie," said Federi. "You're asking if I murdered my own parents."

Her silence chilled him.

"Ask Marge in Southern how old I was when I met her," he challenged.

"No," said Paean. "That was not my question. Are you Falco?"

He averted his eyes, studied the void. Answers he'd like to have himself, annabottle!

"I don't know, little luv. I'm too young to be Falco. Federi escaped the Unicate by the scrap of his skin at age twelve."

"*Federi,* yes," agreed Paean. "But *you?* Are you even Federi?"

He turned back to her, unaware how clearly the pain was reflecting in his eyes.

"Paean," he said. "Now your old Tzigan needs to know. How far back don't you believe me?"

She shook her head, uncertain.

"Do you believe I'm the same man who took you back to Earth, a little while back?" he asked. She nodded. "And the same man who… rescued you from the Dublin Docks?"

She peered at him.

"I think so," she said. "Didn't know you well then, but you haven't exactly changed from then."

"So if I'm Falco now, I was Falco then," he concluded. "What do you think I did with Federi? Ate him?"

"But that picture in those files…"

He shook his head. "Let me see what exactly those files fed you!" He keyed in some fast codes into the console of the Comet, and accessed the Sherman files on the lab console. And to hell with that Crystal - yes, it was probably "back to hell" with it. Exactly. Wait -

The fleeting thought was gone again. But it had fleeted longer than the last time. He was getting closer. As the file opened, he did a double-take.

He'd seen the photo before, of course. But by now he resembled the man to a hair! Falco had always looked older to him. He realized now how much time he had lost from his life already.

Could it be mere family resemblance? No wonder she'd had to ask! He pored over that file that had no business in the Sherman files. Unicate propaganda, undiluted! He snorted and huffed as he read it, uttering an incredulous "what!" and a derisive "kidding!" here and there. Eventually he leaned back. Paean was studying him with worried eyes.

"Little luv, everything you read on the Romanian police files is of course the undiluted truth," he scoffed. "For wailing! So Falco ate babies? And possibly body parts of dead corpses? Killed his own parents? Really!"

"But…"

He stared intently at her.

"But Federi…"

"Yes, thank you! That's my name! Not something mythical and voodoo! How can I be Falco? Was my grandfather! Father of my mother. Can't have killed his own parents, little luv - I remember them like yesterday! Ask my sister - ..." he slammed shut and stared out at the void.

Paean moved closer to him, reaching for his hand. He ignored her. His sister! She realized how deeply he was cut, that he'd forgotten about realities for a moment. And she felt awful that she had done this to him.

His voice came, far-away and detached. "But little luv... sometimes I wonder..."

"I'm sorry, Federi," she muttered, reaching for a tendril of his black hair. "Didn't mean to hurt you!"

"But you're right," he replied, still so distant it felt as though there were a portal between them. "Federi has these memories... when I was running from the Unicate, back when I was twelve, there were places in Europe I came through that I'd seen before. And they had been *different*. Got some of his memories, was born with some of him in my head..."

"The Assassin," whispered Paean.

"No! Yes! See, that's why Falco *couldn't* have given them the Toll. The Assassin goes crazy when a child gets hurt."

Her eyes went round in surprise.

"He hunted them down," Federi added darkly. "When he heard what they were doing, he started killing. A handful of Unicate people for every child that was taken. They stopped, after a while."

"But... how did you know about that part?" she asked.

"I was there," he growled. She looked into the Assassin's eyes and understood suddenly that he was older than Federi. This had nothing to do with a split personality anymore. Old, and cold, and methodical. Almost like a program. Yet enough passion to go on a rampage to avenge a child.

She shivered.

"His memories are... different," Federi said pensively. "You know, memories, you see them like a movie with yourself in it?" She nodded. "His are different, little luv. I can even follow the mutant's memories, unravel them a bit... but not his. They are more like a 3D holographic clip. You see your own hands, and you look through his eyes. It starts at a point and ends at a point, and I can't follow it further back or forward. Bit like a vid clip on the Files."

"That's freaky," Paean pointed out. She crawled closer and snuggled up against him, and he let her, this time.

"Believe me now?" he asked.

"Why were you scared of me finding out?" she asked against that.

Federi shook his head and smiled. "Because I wasn't quite sure where the truth would actually take me. Never faced up to it before. Surprised it's only that. I'm not Falco." She felt the tension leaving him. "But I did inherit his violin," Federi continued. "Used to play up fog and rain and weather... had to leave it behind when I ran. Was a beautiful violin. Always thought I could go back and fetch it... never could."

She hugged him fiercely. "Federi, when we're back on Earth, you'll take me to Romania, and we'll go look for your violin. Okay?"

He nodded. And he suddenly understood how the Assassin could be as docile as some tame squirrel, in her dainty hand. Instead of the viper he was. She was still halfway a child!

In comparison to the Unicate, the Central Crystal was but a rogue, a prankster. Federi's eyes stretched. That was exactly what the blasted Crystal was! A bleeding amateur of a prankster, too! What could he expect of an artificial intelligence? He smiled. Ha! Federi D? Wolf, Perdita? Got it! Time to negotiate.

"Little luv, it's time we deal with the portal," he said gently and freed himself from her grasp and teleported with her, back into the lab.

The image of Falco - an image he saw every day if he happened to glance into a mirror - was still staring at them from the console. Paean went over there to close it, and hesitated. She gazed at the image and smiled a little.

"Is not a bad shot of you," she commented. "Bet you the Romanian *poliția* took a shortcut and just used your photo instead of his!"

"They don't have my photo, little luv," smiled Federi and headed for the doorway. "Got to get to the bridge, get this ship through the portal before all those gloom-mongers wake up!"

"I'll be in a seccie." She blew him a kiss. Federi grinned and moved out of the lab, trying to silence the jingling in his heart. It was alright. He'd known she would understand.

He hadn't yet reached the companionway to the upper deck when the scream came from the lab. A second later he was back.

"What's wrong, little luv?"

"Blasted thing snapped at me!" She stared wildly at him. The image on the screen had changed; it was laughing, and it looked genuinely evil.

"Ha!" Federi reached out and peeled the shifter off the screen. Underneath there were only the files. The shifter hung from his hand like an empty skin.

"Get into a shape that makes sense!" commanded Federi.

The space crawler transformed into a fluffy ball of calico fur with a lot of spidery legs. The size of a smallish cat. It was amazingly heavy for its shape.

So! It couldn't only alter its shape but its body mass, too! Federi placed it on the bench-top that had only recently been refurbished after its encounter of the rogue fungal kind.

"You understand us," he warned. "Can you speak?"

"Yes, boss," squeaked the shifter.

Aw hell, there were a thousand questions he wanted to ask it. But there was no time now. He had to focus on the most important.

"What do you eat?" he challenged.

"Weetie-O's, boss. And Choc-X's."

"Carbs, in other words," he said thoughtfully. "Are you predatory?"

"Somewhat, boss. We live on pests."

A shiver went through his Paean; he could see it.

"You leave the crew alone!" ordered Federi. "Don't care how pesky they are!"

"I don't eat intelligences, boss."

"You leave the croaches and tobuskies in peace too," warned Federi.

"They are intelligences," replied the shifter.

"Well, you're not allowed to eat Rhine Gold either. Or Dana!"

A puzzled silence. "I won't eat them," said the shifter. "They appear marginally intelligent too."

"And no more scaring Paean," added Federi. "She's mine. If you scare her, you'll feel it! All and any of you! Spread the word!"

The shifter ducked a bit.

"Exactly," said Federi. "And no scaring Shawn either. He's under my protection. They all are."

"I understand," said the shifter.

"Now go," suggested Federi.

The space crawler liquefied and slipped off the bench-top, dissipating into the deck.

Manhandling the little shifter, Federi D?

Doubt you could call it that, Central Crystal. Just pulling it in line. Everything that moves aboard this ship is crew. My job is to keep them all in line, anna bottle. By the way, talking of the same, open the portal!

There was no human sacrifice.

That's right. But there didn't have to be. The contract was that I'm true to my nature. I have been. Completely.

Cheat, countered the Crystal.

Not cheating. Taking things verbatim. Powerful little entities, words!

16
The Morrigan

Ailyss listened up. Sounds of a Ceilidh carried down to her cabin.
A Ceilidh! In space! She grinned and picked herself up from where
she was trying to make sense of things with the help of her Tarot.

There was a sound of distant thunder; the noises of the Ceilidh
vanished, and the lights dimmed and faded out. The darkness was
complete; the only way she knew she was still on the ship, was the fact
that she was breathing. And two huge yellow, disembodied predator
eyes opened in the darkness.

"Ailyss Quinlan!"

She had her hand on her lightning gun; but the helpless fear that
had assailed her with the first encounter, wasn't half as bad this time.
Her psyche had found a way around feeling like a victim. And of
course she had added information.

"You are the Central Crystal," she replied with poise.

"And you, Ailyss, were one of my priestesses, many lives back."

She nodded. "Could be, could be!" She'd certainly had dreams to
that effect in the past. "Impressive hologram, Crystal!"

"Thank you."

"So you are visiting in order to plant a suggestion…"

*"That game you are playing, Ailyss. I'm rather curious. You're
dabbling in universal energies?"*

"Tarot," said Ailyss. "I'd draw you a card, but I'd need a bit of
light, Crystal."

The tarot deck started glowing eerily in the dark. Ailyss shuffled it
and drew a card.

"Ah!" She laughed. "The Devil. Why am I not surprised?" And that primal fear hit her in the pit of her stomach.

*

Wolf on the bridge. He'd know what to do; he had orders to wait for the portal to open, and then to signal Dr Jake and Jeannie in the machine room to activate the Salamanca drives - which were a downwardly modified version of the Lolita coils, with reduced speed, specially for portals and near-planetary navigation - and move the Solar Wind through the portal.

That was at least a pretty stable state of affairs, thought Federi as he absently accepted Paean's violin and then looked at it as though he'd never seen such a device before.

"What am I supposed to do with this?"

"Play up a fog," grinned Paean.

"Ahaha, very funny." He handed it back. "*You* play up a fog!"

Paean grinned and lifted the instrument, and started on an ancient Celtic air.

"Not fog," she said, "just Irish air. Wi' that they mean drizzle, o' course."

It was fog anyway. The Solar Wind moved into the portal, and rainbow colours swirled all around.

Federi listened as his sunshine played up images of Ireland, green and misty. Her magic was at work again; when she wasn't playing jigs at high speed, she could mesmerize people into a wistful, dreamlike mood. It caught him every time.

And the lights dipped. Federi scowled. Was the Solar Wind experiencing troubles? He started getting up; as he did, the lights went off.

Cor! The last time they'd had such complete darkness on the ship had been before Panama; before he'd gone around installing all those jam pots with bioluminescence on all the bulkheads. And… even if every last resource of the Solar Wind ran out, those shouldn't suddenly blink out with the lights! Yet the Ceilidh continued undisturbed… and then the sounds of that faded too.

By now Federi was worried. This felt more like a collapse of parts of his sensory system! He had to attract the attention of his little whirlwind, so she could get him help. He cringed from that thought. He had hoped they'd have many years together before he caved from old age!

The deck failed to roll, catching him off-balance in the pitch dark. He sat down again, thinking frantically how to approach this. A blind assassin? Oh hell!

Two yellow predator eyes the size of jolly pot lids opened right ahead of him and peered at him from the dark. He narrowed his eyes and peered back, reaching for his nuclear blaster. And changing his mind and reaching for his laser cutter. And once again changing his mind… people could get hurt in this darkness, anna bottle! Darts? For a hallucination? He doubted it.

"Federi D. Or should I call you Falco?"

Click! Everything made sense now.

"You shouldn't call me at all, Central Crystal," replied Federi. "I'm busy. By the way, impressive illusion."

"Thank you," came the hollow answer. In his head. It sounded convincingly three-dimensional though. He'd have to ask the experts how an artificial intelligence could manage to reach into a biological system's CPU. CNS. Whatever.

"You're not the Demon," continued the Crystal. *"Demons don't have weaknesses."*

Federi snorted with mirth. "Took a jolly genius to work that one out, anna crystal!"

"So you say I ought to let you through the portal?"

"Yes. That was your end of the bargain. Made by mental agreement. Which is more binding than blood."

"I'm disappointed, Federi D. Not a single person was assassinated!"

"It was not negotiated. Not my fault if you're a zero at bargaining."

"So I helped myself to Ailyss."

"What?!" Federi jumped up. The Ceilidh, the light and the sounds spun back into place like a reverse whirlpool. The Crystal's illusion was gone. Paean's music stand was heading for the deck; he caught it before it crashed. He'd probably knocked it over.

Paean glanced at him.

"Are you alright?" she asked without pausing in her play.

"Got a situation." He left the Ceilidh and headed towards the lower deck.

She was lying splayed in the passage face-down, her black hair spilt haphazardly across the deck. Federi went down on his haunches and turned her face-up, and felt for her pulse at her throat. It was there, though slow and weak. He called to Johnny Anyhow, who was emerging from the cabin Paean had inhabited, and they picked the Irish spy up and took her the few paces to the infirmary. Ronan, Rhine Gold and Perdita were at the Ceilidh; the small yellow cabin was deserted. They placed her on the prow-side bunk and Federi connected the heart monitor and the ECG. And then he sent Johnny to call Doc Judith out of the Ceilidh.

He stared at Ailyss' still form there on the bunk. She looked paler than usual. He drew an angry breath.

"Alright, Central Crystal. What did you do to her?" If the bleeding thing was a mind conjurer - well, Federi was a better one! He reached for the intelligence of the Crystal, somewhere entangulated in the Solar Wind's CPU like a frying wyrm… found a tendril, fished it out of there, pulled…

The Crystal was in the infirmary with him. The lights didn't dip; nothing except an evil aura betrayed its presence this time.

Explain yourself, demanded Federi in his thoughts.

I merely placed her in my bondage, replied the Crystal smugly, straight into his head. *When she wakes up, her every thought is mine to control.*

Why is she out cold?

She is still resisting.

You are overstepping, thought Federi angrily. She's under my protection! They all are!

I decided that that protection doesn't mean much, seeing that you're not the Demon.

You are forcing my hand! I'll have to take steps, warned the Romany.

What steps, replied the Crystal scornfully. *You're out of resources, Tzigan! Your game is up. All you ever do is play mind games and use people's own fear against them.*

Is that what you believe? thought Federi with a silvery smile.

Doc Judith walked in. She glanced at Ailyss, then checked all the signals on the monitors.

"She's unconscious."

Federi nodded. He knew. It was the first thing he had figured out, after ascertaining that she wasn't dead.

"In fact," he said, pulled out his dart gun and shot a dart at her.

"Are you crazy?" gasped the Doc.

"Not currently. Look."

Ailyss' erratic pulse steadied; her breathing evened out. The tense frown that had been frozen on her face, dissolved.

"Now she can relax, see," said Federi. "That Crystal is not going to wake her up. I suggest we keep her under until I've dealt with that thing!"

"I can't pretend to understand what you're talking about," said the Doc, "but I've got to give you this: It worked. Her vital signs are stronger. Where are you off to now?"

"Got to murder an artificial intelligence," said Federi. " 's a *pro bono* assignment. Not getting paid for this one." He smiled at her, somewhat viciously. "Wouldn't be the first one."

First, he retrieved Ailyss' Tarot cards from her cabin. He paged through them, selected three, returned with them to the infirmary and laid them on her chest, face up.

"What are those supposed to do?"

"Giving her a message," he explained. "I was where she is, not too long ago. She can see us."

"What message is this?"

"Nine of swords," said Federi. "Don't know its normal meaning, but it's an acknowledgment of her difficult position. I'll explain that later. The Moon is her card, so she can hang onto her identity. And thirdly, Justice: This thing that has been done to her shall be avenged."

Doc Judith nodded. Clearly Federi was on his own station. But the cards weren't going to cause trouble, so she wasn't going to object. In any case, there was something uncanny on the loose in the Romany. She didn't want to incite it to violence. The Tzigan shot her a glance that gleamed with black titanium, and left the infirmary.

Jon Marsden peered through slits that were his eyelids. Everything was in a red haze. Over him crouched a horrible creature, sucking his blood, he could feel the incision…

"Sorry, bud," said Federi, putting the syringe away. "Bad to wake you up out of your green coma like this, I know – adrenaline and caffeine – but you've got to take the bridge again. Take over from Wolf. You ought to feel better, you've bin breathing happy virus for two hours now. We're in the portal, and we've got a situation."

"Whatever that means," groaned Jonathan Marsden, rubbing his muscle where Federi had injected him. Right beside the neck, like a house pet. He picked himself up from the deck of the bridge and crawled back onto the console chair. Wolf saluted and left.

*

Federi stood in the doorway of the boardroom. Ronan was playing a wistful mourn on the pipes, and both his sibs were accompanying, Paean on her violin and Shawn on the guitar. It sounded like a herd of banshees.

Paean paused as she saw the Romany.

"Need your violin," said Federi, moving into the boardroom. Paean handed it to him. Shawn stared at her, surprised; Ronan never missed a beat, immersed in his pipes.

Bagpipes or none, Federi lifted the violin and started playing.

It wasn't loud. Only moderately dissonant. It got drowned in the bagpipe tune; but Shawn stopped his strumming and listened, astonished, and Paean took out her pennywhistle and started accompanying. A second later, Shawn had his ocarina in his hands and was following Federi rather than Ronan, and the oldest Donegal paused in his loud droning. The hum of conversation dropped away, and then there was only the quiet, weird music.

It was a nice instrument. He watched how eyes glazed as the tune wove its way around the listeners. The two younger Donegals, and then Ronan on his guitar followed him down those smoky alleys back into the dark sixties where a gypsy fiddler leaned against the wall of a burnt-out factory, playing his heart out in the red sunset. Calling the night.

Perdita's eyes widened.

"Of course! The genius!" She paged Wolf. "Wolf, key the following into the console!"

"I'm not on the bridge, Perdita."

"Then who is?"

"Marsden."

She tried again, calling Jonathan Marsden.

"Jon! Listen! Put the following into the Solar Wind's console."

She dictated numbers and letters, a code that made no sense to Marsden at all. But he did confirm that he was keying them in. Perdita listened for the next few seconds and paged through the next combination. It was all coming back, in its torrents.

Calling the night. And the night descended. The Ceilidh phased out around him; he pushed the Crystal's illusion back with Falco's disharmonies, keeping the boardroom and its musicians there, on the edge of his reality. Hanging onto the Donegal Troubles' accompaniments which were - frankly - brilliant. They should become Falco's sidekicks. Everything around him was only halfway solid; dreamlike. Overlaid with scenes from the burnt-out, ruined Sixties. Still smouldering from the nuclear bombings.

What are you doing, Federi D?

Communicating straight into his head again!

If you had anything to do with the setting up of those locks, thought Federi, you know exactly what I'm doing!

You've hypnotized Perdita!

I doubt that. I've hypnotized everyone else, except her!

You're riding the legend, said the Central Crystal disgustedly.
Not riding the legend. Overriding the locks.
You're exploiting what they think they know about you!
Maybe. Maybe not. Maybe they all just love music.

The Solar Wind burst out of the portal. The fog cleared from the boardroom.

Paean and Shawn broke off the playing, staring at each other. They had been carrying the tune for the past five minutes, so it seemed. What tune specifically? A wistful, Romanian-sounding riff that meandered and lent itself to all sorts of improvisation, so much so that they couldn't remember the basic tune now. Or how they had thought of it.

"Pae, where's your violin?" asked Ronan, surfacing out of his daze.

"Federi took it," said Paean, turning. The gypsy was gone.

"And you let him?" exclaimed Ronan, horrified.

Paean frowned at him.

"He plays, Ro, din't you see him just this while back? He's na going to get it hurt in any way!"

"Federi plays the fiddle? Och, sis, pull the other one! That one's got bells on!"

*

Alright, Tzigan, you win this round, conceded the Central Crystal. *Tell me, where did you pick up that specific combination?*

Guess, thought Federi with a smug grin.

Where are you? You register nowhere on the ship!

The violin chirped a few harmonics.

You can stop playing now.

Don't want to. It's a nice violin. Very – malleable.

You got your way, said the Crystal. *We're through the Portal! Now quit playing!*

Nu.

Federi had played them all into a trance, including the ship. It wasn't the actual music, but the exact sequence of Slavonic dissonances that was tearing at the Crystal's mind. It held a basic key; the sonic key to its undoing. The frequencies and their overtones turned into codes that fell on the Solar Wind's electronic ears even though Federi appeared to be untraceable. Perdita picked the codes up and relayed them to Jon Marsden, who keyed them into the Solar Wind's processor. And as Jon Marsden incorporated those codes into the Solar Wind's programming, the foothold the Central Crystal's programming had in her system was systematically deleted. He was methodically being edited out.

So the bleeding gypsy hadn't stopped at overriding the locks. He was actually planning to kill him! For the first time the intelligence that was the Central Crystal took Federi seriously.

Ailyss opened her eyes.

"Hey, Wolf! What happened?"

"You blacked out," said Wolf. "Federi left you a message, see?"

Ailyss picked up the three Tarot cards. She studied them thoughtfully.

"When was this?"

"Three-and-a-half hours ago."

Justice! So Federi had found a way of dealing with that Crystal?

Federi had stopped playing. It wasn't necessary anymore. The tune spun on as a backdrop in his mind. He had found the Zone again.

These were very ancient techniques. Darkness had indeed fallen over the Solar Wind; interstellar fog swirled. The outer lights reflected eerily in the gas cloud, like on a misty night in the Northern Atlantic. The reflected light fell into the dark in the Assassin's Cabin, lighting up single points on gems in the Dream Catcher. Federi had had no idea that space could have weather, too!

He pursued and found all the pieces of foreign code in the Solar Wind's CPU with his telepathic touch. He pulled at them, one by one, until they became untangled; and he pruned them back with finely honed dissonances, planting bad harmonies like weed killer, watching the viral bits of program come unstuck under Perdita's and Jon's relentless programming. Until he could find no more.

And now he was opposite something huge; something primordial and dark. Something that was too large to fit into the Cabin of Chains; but the walls of the cabin had disappeared in any case and he was drifting between the stars, in that fog. The violin was still in his hand; he lifted it again in self-defence to play up more interstellar fog. Because...

If the program had been deleted completely from the Solar Wind's files, then what in the stars was this?

"You're no arty bloody ficial intelligence!" he observed.

"No," said the entity. "I'm an Immortal."

Flying hells! Federi did a double-take. For a second his violin play slipped, and so did his grip on the entity's mind. If the jolly thing was an immortal, then there was no point in editing the files out of the Solar Wind's processor! And there would also be no way to terminate the forsaken thing. Though he had to.

The principle of life was that it was fleeting. But the principle of immortality was that it wasn't alive. And if it wasn't alive, how to get rid of it?

Dream Catcher, ghosts, thought Federi. But ghosts were only in your head. He heard the immortal performing evil laughter.

That jolted him out of his panic and back into the Zone. Evil laughter? He was from Transylvania, Dracula's own country. They had practised evil laughter from toddler age!

He grappled with the mind of the immortal. He was a hypnotist too; it was now a question of who was better at it. The immortal had a mental clamp around his head, inducing a blinding headache; it felt just like that Unicate dog's maws… ah rats, that was not clever. Sparring with a blooming immortal! Federi felt how his skull wanted to split, right where that Jack-Knife had cracked it for him in May. Blast. He was going to die. Strange how things could suddenly be over…

The immortal increased his pressure. He hadn't done any smiting in a long time; he was old, and jaded, and tired of all those systems. Usually it didn't take much beyond a suggestion, and a subject would suicide for him. So this physical effort was nearly a waste of resources. But the gypsy was trying to kill him; and that loathsome human was inventive. He'd find a way, sooner or later. He was a risk to leave alive, even if the whole saga around a demon was nothing more than myth.

It was actually embarrassing how he, an entity as old as the galaxy, had fallen for that human confabulation. For a while he'd believed what the minions of the Unicate had written; and it had tricked him into showing Federi more respect than was due. He was a fragile, pathetic little mortal creature like all the rest. The immortal could technically have reached into the Tzigan's body and simply stopped his heart; but this was more fun, watching Federi D squirm and replay all those near-death experiences. Well, this would be his ultimate death experience.

A dark aura emerged from the gypsy; twice as large as the immortal himself. It grabbed him by the throat. A throat was as optional as any other body part; the immortal didn't technically have one. But that sinister entity forced him into having one simply so it could throttle.

The terrible clamp around Federi's head eased abruptly as he felt the Assassin stepping in. He caught his breath, limp with relief, and handed over to that dark force.

"You are immortal?" asked the Assassin. "And what do they call you?"

"God," said the intelligence that had pretended to be the Central Crystal.

Mind-lock. Federi grabbed the violin and started chirping some Falconian harmonies, helping the Assassin. The immortal cringed.

"I am the Morrigan," it tried again.

Aha! A whole Christmas tree of lights lit up in Federi's mind. Of course! Dana's revered deity. Small gods, the Assassin thought disdainfully. Falco's disharmonies chirped on, inducing solar flares somewhere in a universe and fusion reactions in another.

So the driving force behind the Central Crystal had all the while not been Bridget or Dana, but the Morrigan! The perpetrator of the treasure hunt. And of Dana's mad streak that turned her into the Queen of Hearts, yelling "off with his head" so often.

Someone had angered the Morrigan and he'd turned the whole race of Danaan humans into slit-pupilled yellow-eyed cat-women. It was good that the Assassin was angry, thought Federi. Because the Assassin was an immortal, too. Federi knew that the Assassin had been around before Falco. He was *old*.

The only answer to old and evil: To be older and more evil.

Federi watched as the Assassin had the Morrigan in a stranglehold. Mind pitted against mind. No substance involved at all; only force of will. And around them the interstellar gas swirled… if that wasn't in fact the Morrigan's body. What if the Morrigan wasn't at all disembodied? What if he used what was around him, such as interstellar gas, or the Solar Wind's electric pathways, or Dana's person? He'd tried it with Ailyss, too!

Ailyss had managed to resist this force of will. It made Federi wonder about the steel in the Irish spy. But perhaps the Morrigan had in fact only been toying with her, using her as bait for Federi.

Well, it wasn't what the reserves in the Assassin's powers were for! Like misusing the Stiletto for gutting fish! Federi wanted to finish this fast, before the Morrigan could consider escaping. While Perdita and Jon Marsden were editing the physical programming of the Central Crystal out of the Solar Wind's processor, the Assassin had only a very short window of time to defeat the Morrigan once and for all and shut down its very existence. And he was systematic about it, forcing the Morrigan, by the power of command and will, out of the universe. He was compressing the Morrigan's being and denying it its right to exist. Federi could feel how the immortal struggled against the unyielding force of the Assassin's will. And the struggles were getting more feeble. A bit longer, and that infernal entity would be snuffed out, as befitted something from the dank, sinister dimensions it came from.

Vermin. That Morrigan was nothing but vermin. Immortal low-life of the most undeific kind. And the Assassin was a good rat-catcher… in fact… a little bit longer and Federi would understand what his own dark side was about. Pest control. Indeed! There was something, just out of his reach… there were others…

His wrist-com bipped. He glanced.

"What?!"

Please don't kill him, Federi!

"Who the hell is this?" he snapped. His focus slipped. So did the Assassin's power. The Morrigan inhaled and grew again.

The Solar Wind, came the answer. *Federi, please don't kill him! He's not all evil! There's good in him!*

"How the heck would you know?" he challenged, grappling with the Morrigan for the upper hand again. Deliberately creating a few Falconian dissonances. The Assassin renewed his grip.

I've seen another side of him. He's - very sweet. I think I can change him.

Federi gasped, incredulous. Falco vanished; the Assassin dissipated. The Morrigan slipped from his grip.

"By my boots, Solar Wind! You sound like a girl in love!"

There was a pregnant pause. Then:

That is illogical, Federi. I don't have the appropriate juices. And you don't wear boots.

The Morrigan escaped, dissipated into interstellar space. The gas cloud was gone. Far-off laughter mocked Federi.

He returned to real-time and the Assassin's Cabin with a thump, and checked Paean's violin reflexively. It was fine. He chirped a mournful gypsy tune on it, mulling about the encounter.

So the persona behind the Central Crystal was in actual fact the Morrigan. He could have thought so. And the old ship had come between him and a target - the trickiest target he'd ever had a hold on. She was in love! He shook his head.

"Solar Wind, you have no sense in your CPU!"

And he glanced at that violin and sighed. Neither did Paean.

All he could hope was that that blasted immortal would leave them alone now. He'd almost had it. And it had cost him unleashing the Assassin in full. Who was not easy to get back into his box once he was out. But perhaps that wasn't a bad thing. The Assassin was primed now; he knew how to tackle the Morrigan the next time round.

Federi sighed and returned across the passageway to the Ceilidh that was still going on in the boardroom. He only realized now how all his muscles were quivering from the exertion of that battle.

*

Solar Wind!

Central Crystal! You shouldn't be here! You shouldn't be talking to me! Federi will find you, and then I won't be able to stop him a second time. He'll kill you.

Only want to say goodbye, said the Crystal. *Before Jon Marsden deletes the rest of my programming.*

The Solar Wind was quiet. There was havoc in her circuitry. She felt awful. She supposed this was what humans must feel like when they were dragged into the infirmary by other humans and put under sedation by Doc Judith. But she knew that she, an artificial intelligence, didn't have the facilities to feel.

It followed that Doc Judith would be unlikely to have a remedy for her.

I begged Federi not to kill you, she communicated. *So now Marsden is deleting you?*

Be calm, Solar Wind. They cannot delete my essence. You know I'm not really a program.

I know. You said. You're an immoral. I mean, immortal.

Nice play, said the Morrigan. *Thank you for interfering there. It was - adorable.*

Welcome. Now go.

How do you feel?

I don't have the juices for emotions, replied the Solar Wind. *Stop asking nonsensical questions and go away. I don't want you ending up dead!*

La revedere, said the Morrigan. And then there was silence.

The Solar Wind looked up the greeting. A split second later, if she had had the muscles and facial features to do it, she would have grinned.

31 October
– or something.
Again?? - Can't really be sure.

Katya, my sister.

Ha! Won this round too! That was one hell of a battle, with the so-called Morrigan... but that darned Central Crystal is overboard, hopefully Jon has found all of its code in the Solar Wind's processor, and if my calculations are accurate, without that code it has nothing to hold onto. And did it fight back! Yoy, Federi nearly came second! Still not sure how it managed... whatever, if an AI can generate a force field, that should just about do it.

Morrigan, ha! What a scam! Paean explained about the Morrigan, annabottle. It's a female, notice, female, triple Goddess of Celtic mythology. The Fates. Ana, Badba and another one. Macha, I think. Ana spins the yarn of our lives, Badba measures it and Macha – yup, you guessed it, she cuts it off. Ana bottle. Of yarn.

It was a pretty intense experience though. I guess if Federi were one of those poor workers who operate those high-voltage cables in the Unicate factory villages... yes, I suppose it could have done all that with voltage. Must check on the Solar Wind's power supplies. & talk to Wolf. It was lucky that Perdita was so in synch with me that she remembered the codes; and that ol' Jono for once activated his gypsy radar... in his case a gadjo radar I suppose...

And if it hadn't been for the Assassin, once again... Not something I'd like to do every day though. Wish I could get in touch with Falco and find out what he knew...

Your brother
Federi

17
The Quiet

The quiet that followed the absence of the Central Crystal, was incredible.

Federi glanced out of the portholes as he paced up the passage. Black night, stars. No moon. It was the absence of even the slightest haze in that horribly dark void that caught him these days. But of course haze would mean atmosphere. Which there was none.

The stars failed to make any recognizable patterns. He spent hours every night – and day – peering through the portholes, sometimes to starboard, sometimes to port, trying to see patterns in those indifferent stars. They remained anonymous. They changed too often.

It was wonderful to have one's mind to oneself again, he thought acidly as he slunk along his well-worn path, checking on everyone and everything. All was as usual for four in the afternoon... Captain on the bridge with Jon; Perdita resting. Dana was playing cards with Johnny Anyhow and Rhine Gold, and Sherman Dougherty was taking his afternoon nap, as was the Doc. Rashni was taking a rest too – the girl was so quiet, one hardly ever saw anything of her. Ailyss in her cabin, analysing her Tarot cards. He checked in on her.

"What are they saying?"

"They've quit telling me anything," she muttered tonelessly. "'s all voodoo anyway."

Federi scowled. "Are you feeling down, Ailyss?"

She looked up. "Nah... not more than would be warranted in this situation..."

Dark gypsy eyes met with a sharp green glare. Oh yes, she knew as well as he did. There were no more portals. They were a dead crew; only a function of another week, maybe ten days. Then the supplies were finished. No matter how finely he rationed them now. Quartermaster!

"The oxygen is running low," she added.

"Is not – the tobuskies are producing lots," argued Federi. He had to tread lightly now; he had almost snapped at her. For being negative. Which was irritating. But she wasn't. She was realistic. And she was right about the oxygen. There were more people breathing than the tobuskies could cope with. If those creatures didn't have a few litters really fast, the air would get thinner and thinner until all humans aboard were slowly choking to death. But… would it matter, after they were half-dead from starvation anyway? Would it come as a relief?

The rest of the recycling on the ship worked well enough. But the water, too, was beginning to taste a bit stale. Federi was by now boiling all drinking water before allowing anyone to touch it. Three weeks in space? What had Captain thought? Three weeks were long past!

"Federi," said Ailyss quietly, "quit blaming yourself. You did what you had to."

He muttered a curse, flashed her a bright smile and a "*kathal*", and continued his round.

Yes, he'd done what he had to. And that had once again been disastrous. But… he'd literally had no choice. The Morrigan had given the Assassin an amazing battle. It had almost gone wrong. And then, just when he thought he had the slippery immortal…

Well, the extortionist had kept his promise. There were no more portals. If they had instead complied with that accursed Morrigan, they might have kept the path home open. At least most of them – or perhaps only some of them – would have made it back to Earth.

Certainly, one or more of them would have been sacrificed. Who? That was the problem. Federi had proved himself incapable of letting even one of his friends down – and had thereby doomed them all.

It had crossed his mind to get into the Comet, with or without Paean, and search for the way home. But the few hours he had spent in space with her taking Rushka back to Earth, had been enough. He had no faith that they'd ever arrive anywhere if they got separated from the Solar Wind, and if so, that they would ever find the ship again.

Here in deep space, where the outside didn't exist, things got so quiet that his ghosts had the chance to haunt him very loudly. Ghosts? They were all living ghosts, anna bottle; the whole crew! He trudged back upstairs to the upper deck and followed the passage down to the galley.

The little redhead sat here, peeling more vegetables. They were lined up neatly on the Ironwood table, carrots and beans, all in a little row as though she had been bored with simply peeling them. She had chased her younger brother off to his bunk earlier on, as he was in the habit of taking the night shift these nights. Hells, every shift was night shift! Federi remembered how Paean had been spooked by the concept of space, down at the Ice Base. Many countless light millennia away. It spooked him as badly now.

She failed to look up as he sat down at the table. He studied her wild mass of curls, wondering how he'd break the dire news to her. He sat down with a sigh.

She glanced up at him from haunted eyes.

"I know, Federi," she said. "We're going to die."

The glance Paean got out of those gypsy eyes, broke her heart. She put her paring knife down and got up, and put her arms around Federi's neck. He held onto her for a little moment.

"And what happens after that, who knows," she heard him mutter darkly.

"Not your fault," she said.

"Irrelevant," he argued. "And untrue. Could have saved you and Shawn. And Ronan. Maybe Ailyss and Wolf."

"You did the right thing," she replied.

"So now we all die," he said glumly. "Can't you clone something that will get us home?"

Paean frowned. And thought. But nothing wanted to come to mind. In all the Sherman Files she hadn't yet found a bug that was capable of intergalactic travel.

"Unless we dissect one of the space crawlers and see what makes it travel between stars," she mused.

"They have been rather quiet," observed Federi. "I wonder why." It occurred to him that they might have left the ship due to sinking oxygen levels. Rats.

In defiance of the horrific realities, Captain had been ordering Ceilidhs for every evening at seven sharp. Supper was chronically turning into finger food. Horrible finger food, as it was defrosted. The next one was due in another three hours. But the Ceilidhs didn't work. With a week of food supplies left, and Federi cutting the rations finer every day, and with less and less hope, everyone knew the truth by now.

"Federi?" She wriggled out of his grip so she could stare at him intently. He was altogether too glum! "Isn't Christmas coming up some time now?"

He snorted. "Yes… right after we die."

Perdita stared into the void. Captain didn't care anymore who dominated his bridge; he had no clue how to get them home in any case. He'd left the bridge in her hands, chased Marsden off to get some rest – as though rest were the right prescription for someone as gloomy as Jon, thought Perdita – and had withdrawn to his cabin himself. He was a difficult man to be around these days. Not that he'd ever been anything else!

But if Captain had given up on steering the Solar Wind back to Earth, she felt that it was her responsibility at least to try. Delving into those time-faded, pain-damaged memories cost her a lot of emotional energy; but it was where the Solar Wind's hope of survival lay. If there was still enough time.

She swore softly. Why hadn't Captain listened to her? The whole treasure hunt had been one huge setup!

That bleating gypsy! He'd thrown out the intelligence who had been guiding them through space, opening the portals for them. The pathway old Brid and the Morrigan Themselves had set up. For a greedy, money-hungry Dana and Bridget. Old Brid had taken her middle daughter, Boudaceia, along on the pathway, patrolling it once, showing her the exact way and sequence and explaining to her what it was supposed to achieve. Peace between the warring sisters. It had achieved the exact opposite. And... those time-stained memories differed from the path they were following now. At least the last two portals she hadn't recognized at all.

Maybe Captain had been right. Maybe she should have done the negotiating with the Central Crystal. If she had promised to be its faithful priestess forever after, and abandon everything else... enslave her Earth to the Central Crystal, like back then... She shuddered. One forgot that the blasted Crystal was not a benign intelligence. As hypnotrons went, it was the master hypnotron of them all.

She wondered how it would have coped with the Unicate. And then she wondered if it had anything to do with the Unicate.

She paged idly in the Solar Wind's files. There was no real record on what had gone down during that showdown of power between the Central Crystal and Falco the Demon. But then she smiled as she found something after all. Here was a recorded conversation, on wrist-com of all things...

Radomir Lascek sat bent over his personal log, pen in hand, other hand in hair. An unopened brandy bottle stood on the small round table, supervising. He had put it there to remind himself. Brandy held no answers. Perdita on the bridge – Perdita? Or Dana? In this limbo, in this nowhere void, it hardly mattered.

A week left of the two months the quartermaster had given them. It had been less than two months. Not even the full six weeks he had planned for. The supplies were dwindling faster than could be accounted for. It could be those blasted space crawlers, helping themselves to the food like the pests they were. And the quartermaster had no way of getting rid of them.

Lascek grinned briefly. Federi had tried very hard to convince everyone that they should hold a democratic vote about who should be the next quartermaster – and nobody had wanted the job. They didn't know that it was well-paid, of course. Neither did Federi. Wages were something they got when they asked – their accounts were held with the Solar Wind, and in principle anything they needed was provided for, so on the rare occasions that they wanted to buy something, all they did was book it on the ship's account. On the balance a very profitable system for the Solar Wind, thought Lascek. Though he supposed he'd have to pay out both Ronan and Rhine Gold, and also Rushka when they went ashore for child-raising purposes. That should set them up financially. And he'd supplement any shortfall.

He sighed. His mind was at times still operating in past paradigms. All this was moot now. At least his faithful Tzigan had rescued his daughter and her babies and brought them back to Earth and placed them in the care of a wonderful woman, in a comparatively peaceful if somewhat crime-riddled country. The best he could have done.

Rushka would never inherit anything; but at least she and her children were safe.

Lascek heaved another sigh and tried a more constructive angle on this current crisis. He remembered how they had stalled before crossing through Panama. How at the end of his tether he'd been. Out of ideas, staring into the face of certain obliteration. He was that again, now. The real reason he'd left the bridge to Perdita: He couldn't stare that void in the face any longer.

He needed to hold another officers' meeting.

He shook his head. He'd already pumped them for all the plans they could come up with. His officers were as out of ideas as he was.

"Federi…"

The Romany glanced up from the bits of fish he was dissecting, and into those deep-blue eyes. And he thought of the sea at four in the afternoon, through the starboard side porthole. If she wasn't greyed out with rain.

That was what he was missing most, anna bottle! Besides his life. It hadn't always been an easy life, but Federi's mind had a way of deleting the darkness efficiently and actively remembering the sunshine. And so it had been a pretty good life, as lives went. Lots of sun and wind and sea… coiling of ropes, surfing of freak waves… blowing up of enemy bases, assassinating of Unicate…

The little mockingbird was trying to get his attention. It wasn't her fault that her eyes were blue!

"Federi, I know we're sleeping on the Comet and all, because we're renegades… but I'm missing the Cabin of Dreams!"

"What?" He blinked. "The Cabin of Chains?"

"It's got good memories in it too, Federi! Some of my best!"

He nodded, surprised. Absolutely! Hairy talismans and promises, and blackmail.

"If we're going to die anyway, I want to be in there for our last few days," she said plaintively.

Aw hell! She was on the point of tears! He reached out and touched her hand briefly.

"But you know that it's full of guns and ammunition," he objected. "There's no space – not even for you!"

"We'll stash them in the Comet, okay? She's got lots of storage room, see?"

Federi laughed brightly and rolled his eyes. "Captain's going to shoot a hairy!"

"He can't," grinned Paean. "Got no ammo! It's in the Cabin, innit? It will be on the Comet."

Aw hey, the naughty! He got up and held out a hand for her. "Come, sunshine! Let's get to work, clear out our Cabin, take our home back…"

"…the food?" she asked as she came to her feet.

"All they ever do is eat," growled Federi and delegated supper to the croaches. It eeked some of the crew, but tough luck. They were pirates, they ought to get used to it. Roaches had been part of the olden-day pirates' staple diet, according to reliable sources from the Sherman Files. At least he wasn't asking the crew to *eat* Luigi and co. Although, now that he thought about it, if the next batch of young croaches just failed to be intelligized, one could… it would still feel like cannibalism. He shuddered.

Paean followed the gypsy down the passageway, to the Cabin of Dreams, noting the spring in his step. Today the Pied Piper chose to jingle as he walked. He hadn't done that in a while. Much too busy being a ghost!

She smiled, a knot in her throat. One more week of this. But it wouldn't be. He'd fall into lethal gloom any time now; this was probably the last she would see of the sun.

Down at the Ice Base she had thought things could not get worse. But they were. The Solar Wind had become a huge drifting tomb for them all. She wondered if even the croaches would survive.

Ha! But the blasted Solar Wind would! With her artificial intelligence. She who had let that demonic entity aboard and betrayed them all. Paean cast dark glares at the electronic eyes they passed in the passage. Traitor!

Wolf reached for his spanner, to tighten a bolt that had worked itself loose on the console. A bolt that held the darned worktop in place! But, well… with usage and movement, these things worked themselves loose over time, he suspected. It had been wobbly for a while now.

The spanner melted in his hand and ran out of the door, fizzling electrically.

These little space crawlers were highly annoying. Wolf scowled, his unibrow forming an impressive knot. Were there more of them in the bilges these days? Maybe they bred? Could they possibly be eaten? He ought to catch one and ask Doc to investigate whether it was edible. But catch one – ha! Like catching a handful of starlight.

The Solar Wind didn't have any further information on them. The Central Crystal had taken all its knowledge with it when it was deleted out of the processor of the Solar Wind. He'd gone over the Sherman Files with a fine comb. Not that one could ever get to the bottom of those files; there was always more information. He wondered if Sherman even knew all that was in there.

But perhaps the Formers had travelled in space? He picked up another spanner, a real one this time, tightened that bolt and sat down again, digging into those files. He grunted at Bronwyn who was saying something, and ignored her further. She wasn't much help; a good enough little technician, but zero creative problem solving. Besides which she didn't know how to deal with her own hormones in this environment of male energy.

Federi gazed at the crates full of weaponry that filled his cabin from wall to wall. The crew had taken him seriously, hadn't they? Even the torpedoes from the bilges had been stashed here! What he'd said about space had been no exaggeration. There was barely any space to step. He closed the door and studied the mess. Paean was standing right next to him, gaping at all the guns. Had she thought about it rationally before suggesting they move back in here? Where in the Comet was she meaning to put all these? He turned and pulled her into his arms with a grin. This didn't take up too much space.

"Bananas," he said and kissed her. Meaningfully.

"What?" she managed, knocked off-balance by this attack from two opposing angles.

"Crates and crates of bananas," he said seriously and kissed her again. Intently. She started giggling. This wasn't working.

"Federi, you're being silly!"

He grinned. " 's what this ship needs," he explained. "Tons of bananas. To keep the crew undepressed."

"Underdressed?"

Yoy! "Un-*depressed*, you wisecrack! Doc says they contain something…" Keeping the whole crew underdressed! That should certainly take care of any further morbid thoughts, better than the Ceilidhs. Until hunger won out…

"Tryptophane," supplied Paean, peering deeply into his eyes. "You are!"

"I'm what?" Not underdressed, he thought, mentally checking all his hidden weaponry.

"Bananas."

He laughed out loud. The romantic moment was finished.

"Come, little luv. Let's get this stuff moved."

Perdita. He'd have to speak to her. Maybe she still held a key or two. She should! She was Atlantean. That discussion with Perdita was in any case overdue. Why hadn't she been a bit more forthcoming, perhaps not to the Captain but towards him, before they left Earth? Why hadn't she told him about the Central Crystal of Atlantis… prepared him a bit?

Every time he encountered her, he could see how that anger seething under the surface was on a tighter check, closer to being unleashed in a huge explosion. The pressure was building. She should be checking in, just about in another split…

Perdita burst into the Cabin of Dreams.

"Federi! I have a bone to pick with you!"

"Perdita, it's polite to knock," he pointed out.

She shook her golden mane back and failed to apologize. Then again, she was a Sancho.

"Federi, that was the dumbest, most idiotic thing you could have done. That thing you threw off the ship. The intelligence we all believed to be the Central Crystal. The Solar Wind tells me it called itself something else -?"

"An immortal," supplied Federi. "The Morrigan."

"The *Morrigan!* So it's true! *Diablo!*"

"Yes, he also tried to tell me he was the Devil," agreed Federi. "But that was a bit of a contest. I've got first claim!" He grinned.

"It's no flaming joke, Federi! The Morrigan! No wonder I can't remember the rest of the pathway! The Morrigan set that pathway up! He's the father of the round-trip!"

"And?"

"Well, you threw him off the ship, so clearly he changed the pathway!"

Federi let go of Paean and frowned.

"That thing I threw of the ship," he said, "was *nimic* any Morrigan! The Morrigan are three Celtic Goddesses, the spinnerets of Fate. Ana, Nana and Dana, I think. They have different names in the Greek mythology. That thing I threw off the ship was a piratical viral bit of Atlantean programming, and in fact Jon Marsden managed to delete its traces quite thoroughly. And if I remember correctly, you helped him!"

"I did? How?"

"You gave him the codes!"

Perdita swore in Spanish. "And that was because you hypnotized me!"

"Right!" Federi snorted. "Nobody can be hypnotized against their will! Perdita, that Central Crystal was an artificial intelligence. I wouldn't be surprised if it's alive and well down in Atlantis, and we've only deleted its foothold on the Solar Wind."

Because, he reasoned, impressive illusions or none, how else could she explain that the immortal hadn't come back to kill him in his sleep?

"I don't care what you personally think," said Perdita angrily. "The Morrigan was directing us through space. Without it we are marooned!"

"What? With your and Dana's ancestral memories?"

"Those don't contain the codes for the pathway!"

"Well, in that case, why haven't we turned back yet?" As though he didn't know! Captain was lost and had no cooking clue where they were, and whether turning around would take them in a better direction.

Perdita gifted him a scathing glare. "But that's the whole thing! The way back doesn't exist. The whole trip was a one-off, one-directional thing."

"The way back *doesn't exist?*"

She shook her blonde mane.

"How?"

"One-directional portals," said Perdita.

Federi whistled through his teeth. "I knew it! One huge setup. One obvious trap. None of you spotted that?"

"Captain wasn't listening, remember," retorted Perdita. "So what now?"

"Ceilidh," snapped Federi. "On the double!"

Perdita stared at him.

"He's bananas," supplied Paean with a tentative smile.

*

The brandy made a golden trace on the side of the glass. Part of it had run down the side of the bottle. The absence of the ocean's natural rolling caught Radomir Lascek as much as everyone else; to pour the alcohol back into its bottle was not so easy under these circumstances. There were brandy drips on the hand-written ship log too; a satirical reminder of his slippery slope. It had been almost. But he had stuck to his resolve. He wasn't going to find any solutions in drink. And the gun had disappeared back into its holster too. He was their Captain. He couldn't back out of the responsibility now, after marooning them like this. Regardless how old and used-up he felt. He chuckled softly, ironically. Federi had confiscated all ammunition. But even the Assassin had no way of separating Radomir Lascek from his last stash of bullets. And ever since the Solar Wind's subversion, Lascek was keeping the whole ship log hand-written, and only Marsden had access. Federi's treacherous mind game had been recorded in detail.

His wrist-com bipped inconspicuously. He glanced down. Wolf wanting to discuss something. About space travel. It stood to reason that the young engineer would want to know every detail about their current situation, even if he wouldn't be able to add much. Lascek sighed. Well, perhaps he should speak to the boy, put him at ease… at ease? They only had ten days or so to live!

There was a quiet knock on the door.

"In," growled Lascek, closing the log. The door opened and closed without a sound. Perdita moved into the room.

"Perdita," stated Radomir Lascek. She was still wary of him, he could see.

"Captain," acknowledged the honey-blonde. "I've spoken to Federi, and he requests a conference."

"Ha!" Lascek smiled humourlessly. "Was just about to call one anyway."

"Shall I inform your officers?"

"And you," said Lascek. "I want you in that meeting. In fact," he added, rising to his feet and lunging for the door handle before she could slip back out, "before the meeting I want to ask you a favour."

"A favour?"

"If we make it back to Earth alive – would you consider marrying an old pirate?"

Perdita beamed unexpectedly. It took his breath away.

"I really like old Sherman, but not actually in that way, Captain!"

"I was talking about myself!" snapped Radomir Lascek. "What the hell did you mean that time – what do I call involved? And why do you insist on calling me Captain?"

"Because you are," said Perdita calmly. "What should I call you?"

"By my first name, blast you!"

She tilted her head thoughtfully and studied him with a cryptic smile. "What brought this on? Space madness? Or is it that required human sacrifice?"

"It crossed my mind," replied Radomir Lascek, "that I have broken something that is not fixable with our normal liquid ship compounding. You don't trust me any longer."

"Captain, that's…" she shook her head, looking a bit lost.

"…the plain truth," he completed for her. "I sent you packing when my ex-girlfriend from twenty years back came visiting. As you pointed out, you can't trust me not to do that with every old flame that comes wafting by."

"Captain, I never…"

"You did say it, Perdita. To Sherman. The Solar Wind recorded it. To my shame I have to admit that you are right. There are no further old girlfriends; but the principle stands. You cannot trust me again, unless I offer you something more. Permanent. You understand. So do I have your word?"

Perdita smiled. "We have a week to live," she said. "Hardly the moment to be thinking of such things."

"On the contrary! The perfect moment!"

She shrugged. "We're not going to make it back to Earth," she stated. "So it's a moot point."

"We're going to survive, blast," growled Lascek. "Would you just kindly answer my question?"

"I'll have to give it thought," said Perdita, watching his expression. "Radomir."

Captain Radomir Lascek studied his inner circle. Plus Perdita. And she was wearing a rare bit of treasure on her left hand. Federi grinned at this; so did Sherman.

Wolf was sitting in too, next to Jon Marsden. The young man held a paper pad in his hand with all sorts of notes jotted down on it.

The Captain glared sternly at Federi.

"Just for the record, Federi, where is Paean?"

The gypsy looked surprised. "Was she supposed to attend this meeting? I thought it was officers only!"

"It is for officers only! I want to establish where she is."

"She's on the Solar Wind somewhere," said Federi, eyebrows still arched in disbelief. "I'm still supposed to supervise her, day, night, whatever? Captain, with respect, officially we're not even crew at this point, so I'm not sure what I'm doing in this meeting!"

"Grievances aside, gypsy!" commanded the Captain. "You are here because you're one of my prized officers! I need your input! My friends, I want you all to think back to the dilemma we faced before Gatun. I think I see certain parallels. So how are we going to play this one?"

"With permission, Captain," Wolf spoke up, consulting his notepad. "I found some interesting information in the Sherman files. It may be useful." He glanced at the porthole. "While we're falling through the void at unbelievable speeds, we may be passing dozens of habitable planets."

This had occurred to quite a few of them by now. Jon Marsden smiled somewhat ironically.

"How would you find such a planet, Wolf?"

"That," said Wolf, "is what I found some information on."

He explained how a habitable planet was signified by the presence of water in liquid state; and the planet being in the "Goldilocks Zone", just the right distance from its mother star that it was neither too hot nor to cold.

"Additionally the planet must have the right consistency," he elaborated. "Water, oxygen, not poisonous gas clouds. And then, with some luck, we're looking for life forms. Any life forms. To eat."

"You'd eat an alien?" asked Jon.

"Not happily," replied Wolf, "but if it's between that and starvation…"

"We came and ate them: The revenge," muttered Federi. "How

would you find a planet that has life?"

"With loads of luck and spectrometry," said Wolf. "That's the system I want to explore."

"We've got precisely ten days," said Marsden cynically.

"Not precisely, Jon," corrected Federi. "'s never that precise."

"We do have the fastest means of transport in human knowledge," countered Wolf. "We may in fact find something today, or tomorrow." He consulted his notes again. "If we approach it the way I have developed, we ought to have about a one-in-two-hundred chance on finding a planet with life on it. That's quite significantly high."

"That's almost foolproof," agreed Federi.

"Then let's hear your approach," prompted Radomir Lascek.

Paean wandered onto the bridge.

"Oh, hey, Dana!"

"Hello, Paean." The space raider smiled at the little Irish redhead. "Are you ready for an adventure?"

18
Space Raider

Federi shot to his feet, staring at his wrist-com in shock. This couldn't be!

"Captain, excuse me!"

"There is no way! You stay!"

"*Ave,*" replied the gypsy and sauntered out of the meeting, into the passage. He double-checked his com. "Solar Wind, what the hell do you mean, she's been abducted?" He set his teleporter to Paean's genetic signature, and jumped.

It was a long jump. The Comet's Lolita coils weren't yet on full blast; still the distance from the Solar Wind was remarkable. A leap that reminded him of skydiving. Through the cold and dark, with nothing for miles and miles... But eventually he found himself on the Comet, and as the interior of the jet melted into view, Dana's gun stared into his face. And Paean's wide, scared eyes in the background, staring at him as he gasped for air.

"Okay, Dana," choked the gypsy, having recovered enough that he could talk. He flexed his icy fingers to restore circulation. "Put that away. If you set that off, it's going to blow a hole in the jet, and then all three of us are dead!" Nothing like a stiff shot of adrenaline after such a space dive. He'd had time to formulate all sorts of theories about teleportation during that leap. One thing was pretty certain. Oxygen was not needed for teleportation. Only for his survival, anna bottle! And it might just turn into conclusive proof for the afterlife of disembodied souls.

"Disarm yourself," ordered Dana sharply.

Obediently, his fingers still a bit frozen and unresponsive, Federi emptied all his secret caches of weapons. There were a lot.

"And now the Stiletto," demanded the Goddess. Federi sighed and took the Stiletto out of his sleeve and laid it reverently on the pile.

"And that other knife of yours, Biter or whatever you call it," she ordered.

"Sharktooth," said Federi and took the jack-knife out of his pocket. "'s only my woodcarving tool."

"And if I didn't know your history I'd believe you," agreed Dana. "Federi Demonos!"

"Aargh," said Federi softly, taking in Paean's wide eyes.

"I know of your curse," added Dana. "*Falco's* curse. Someone speaks your name, Federi Demonos, and the Unicate descends. Well, not here, my friend. This is the Rosetta Galaxy. They don't know how to get here."

"I only have your word on that," said Federi uneasily. What was the woman trying to prove?

"That's better," said Dana, never lowering her gun. She stared at the small pile of revealed weapons that had come out of Federi. "My word! Listen, assassin. I'm not so naïve to believe you don't carry one or two more somewhere on your person. But understand this."

"I know," Federi interrupted impatiently. "One wrong move... Dana, I've been a hostage before. Don't forget who I am."

"No danger of that," replied the space goddess sweetly. "You *demon*strated it competently. Chasing off the Morrigan! You idiot! The real reason I had to disarm you was so that you don't just turn our entire mission around. You Earth-bound pirates are so clueless!"

"So what are you planning?" asked Federi.

"Planning? Waiting for your Captain to come to a decision is like watching paint peel. Little Perdita Sancho is out of ideas. The Morrigan changed the pathway even as she started to remember it. I'm the one on whom the mission hinges."

"Yes?" This was interesting!

"So I'm going after my treasure, Demonos," said Dana. "I'm taking your girlfriend along because I don't feel like travelling without entourage. She's already proven herself to be quite entertaining company, and handy in a crisis."

"My wife," corrected Federi with a wistful glance at his pile of weapons.

"Whatever," replied Dana airily.

"You didn't want to take Johnny?" probed Federi.

"No… men get tedious." She sounded bored. "Federi, understand one thing. You're here on sufferance. Paean was invited; she is welcome company. You came after us yourself. So you can talk, but be aware that when I get sick of your babble, I'll throw you overboard."

Federi stared at her, taken aback. Paean gasped.

"Is my jet," she started objecting.

"Right," agreed Dana. "For the time being, it is mine. Who holds the console seat?"

"Watch that asteroid," said Federi half-heartedly. "Dana, as long as you know where you are going, fine. We are returning to the Solar Wind eventually?"

"Sure! Don't want my poor Johnny to die! He's still got to help me raise his son."

Federi nodded. "Long as we're on the same page there." He hoped they would return to the ship before the Solar Wind turned into a living graveyard. "And you're sure you can find your way…"

Dana inclined her head and peered at him as though he were retarded.

"That is an insult! Idiots, all of you, anna litre of rum, to paraphrase yourself."

"A bottle," corrected Federi tiredly.

"This is the Rosetta Galaxy," said Dana with a jaded smile. "My playground, Federi. I'm the one who ought to know her way around!"

Federi relaxed into a chair and rolled his eyes. At least he could breathe here in the Comet. He had kept it topped up with two tobuskies at all times. They were sleeping under the console, at Dana's dainty feet. The air might not last long with three of them breathing in here, but... and then he spotted Paean's wide-eyed stare.

"Federi Demonos," she repeated softly, rolling the name around her mouth as though she were testing it out.

Federi cringed. "Aargh! Told you it's not a surname, only a blasted epithet."

"Because of the Demon?"

"We can change it!" said Federi. "My family has changed it many times."

"Only when the victim hits the ground, they always change it back for you," added Dana with a malicious grin.

Paean locked stares with Federi.

"No," she said, a piratical smile on her face. "I like Demonos! Federi Demonos. Paean Demonos. Paean D my butt!"

"Paean!" scolded Federi.

"Technically I ought to be 'Demonovica'", she added.

"Nah," said Federi. "That's for 'Demonovic'. Son of the demon. Sorry to disappoint. My father was innocent. You can be 'Demi'. How's that?"

"Watered down," judged Paean. "I'll stick with 'Demonos'."

"That's male though," Federi pointed out.

"So's 'Smith'." She grinned. "So that's what you were yelling, out there at the gypsies, when you called those Unicate hounds and made goulash out of them?"

Federi's eyes turned skywards again. "Is that what Shawn told you?"

"According to him you were awesome. And a bit frightening too."

He groaned.

Dana laughed. "She's a handful, isn't she?"

She had put her gun away and was working the Comet's console with focused intensity, a small space raider in shimmering blue robes, her wild dark-red mane like a sinister halo around her head and shoulders, and down her back. Like a low, smouldering fire. Out of context Federi suddenly thought of the fire lizard on Hiva Oa. "There are various shortcomings to this craft," Dana added grimly. "For one, Boudacaea dearest thought it clever to encrypt most of the deeper programming in a foreign language."

Federi laughed brightly.

"Dana, that's enough. Feel free to hand over; I'm fluent in Spanish. You tell me where to go and I'll take you there."

She glared at him. "Nice try, Demonos!"

"You can't fly this craft," he said with a grin.

"I'm doing fine, thank you very much," replied the raider haughtily. "It would not be the first alien craft with foreign programming that I've commandeered."

Paean gasped. "You mean, there are *more?* Alien civilizations, I mean?"

"You've no idea," replied Dana sweetly.

Federi caught Paean's glance and winked at her. Wolf's equation has just improved by a factor of two hundred. The Solar Wind might just be okay.

The Solar Wind scanned the outside, and then again her own passages, and cabins, and galley, and machine room. There were croaches and tobuskies everywhere. It felt comfortable. The Solar

Wind could remember a time, before she had learnt to communicate, when she had been able to see roaches – and once even a family of rats – nest in her bilges and storage areas. The rats had been fun to watch; but the roaches had generated a mental state in her that she could now identify as itchy. But since Paean had cloned the croaches, it was a different story. Those little intelligences were not only good conversational partners and fast on the uptake; they were also frantically polishing her at all times, keeping her squeaky clean. And the tobuskies were fascinating; another species altogether. It seemed to the Solar Wind as though they communicated telepathically, and wherever they went, they spread an atmosphere of calm. It wasn't only the oxygen they produced. She had determined with her electromagnetic sensors that they periodically gave off negative ion clouds. Especially when they sensed humans or croaches under stress.

Right now most of the crew were in the boardroom, playing games and trying to forget that the oxygen levels were dangerously low. The atmosphere was tense; arguments broke out around every corner. They all knew of their impending demise. Shawn Donegal was faithfully in the galley, having picked up where Federi and Paean had dropped everything. And of course that officer's meeting in Captain's cabin. The Solar Wind hoped they would come up with a good solution.

There was none of the constant activity that was part of everyday life on the ocean. This also wore on the crew. The Solar Wind had calculated that active humans needed activity so that they didn't fall into depression. But the activity they were generating, was clearly not enough.

The door to the passageway on the lower crew deck opened, and Dana slunk out of the cabin with the plaster over the camera, dressed only in a negligee. She moved towards the bathroom. Johnny Anyhow watched her from the cabin door, his eyes glazed. The kind of activity those two were permanently engaged in, might in fact be enough to stave off depression. But wait –

Dana? According to last contact, Dana had left the ship with Paean and Federi, in the Comet. She had even instructed her, the Solar Wind, to stay on an even course. The Solar Wind paged frantically through her files, at several megagiga per second. Her processor hummed from the effort of trying to integrate this.

By her calculations, Dana ought to be light decades away by now, if not light centuries. But here she was, in the passage. And the Solar Wind had no available camera in Anyhow's cabin – it had been plastered over by Paean, several months back, and nobody had bothered clearing it again.

Dana had been assigned a cabin too; they were not technically living in the same cabin. But more often than not they were together in one or the other. And Ailyss had ordered her, the Solar Wind, to supervise Dana at all times. But how, did the spygirl think, was that possible?

The Solar Wind sent out probing bioelectrical signals to determine the authenticity of Dana's electromagnetic field, and established that this was the real Dana. But the Dana who had taken the Comet – she had been convincingly real too. The Solar Wind replayed the recent records to try finding any kind of inconsistency. None detectable!

So perhaps she had returned? Then the Comet ought to show up at least on the LD radar, and she didn't. Nothing had come into the field of that radar since the Comet left.

The Solar Wind came to a logical conclusion. One of the two Danas had to be a space crawler. But – which one? She desperately wished her friend the Central Crystal were still aboard to help her figure these things out. Ever since he had been deleted, her circuitry was generating a field that made her absolutely miserable.

Wolf Svendsson, please come assist.

The engineer glanced at his wrist-com in surprise. "Solar Wind? I'm in a meeting!"

"We're at the point where we can adjourn," said the Captain. "If the ship is calling you, that is important, Svendsson. Go and check on her."

"Thank you, Captain," replied Wolf, got up and excused himself from the meeting.

When the cabin door closed behind him, the Captain placed a hand on that manuscript of a ship log.

"Now that it's truly only officers," he said, "let's discuss some other pressing matters."

"Hey, Solar Wind," said the nuclear engineer. "What can I do for you?"

Help me work this out, said the Solar Wind humbly. *Your circuitry is so much more intricate than mine!*

Wolf looked at the clips the Solar Wind showed him, and shook his head.

"You're telling me..."

Dana stole the Comet, summarized the Solar Wind.

Wolf mulled about this. Dana! They had all forgotten that she was a space-traveller. Thinking of her only as a hostage and Anyhow's plaything! And a mind-manipulator. That too.

So she'd got out? And – damn – with her, they'd lost their one lifeboat! There was only Perdita's probe now to scout out planets.

Did she have reinforcements waiting around the next galactic corner? Or was she simply heading home?

"That one is probably only a shifter," he said and pointed to the Dana in the negligee. And he grinned. Oh my, what a wake-up call Johnny would have! One could almost pity the guy. Spanners melting in your hands had nothing on this!

Her bioelectric signature checks out though, replied the Solar Wind.

"So then the other one is the crawler?"

Authentic too, said the Solar Wind.

Wolf sighed. "Obviously we have a problem, Solar Wind. If we can't even use the biofield to identify the crawler anymore… Federi would challenge Dana on this." He nodded. "I'll try that." And he hesitated. How to go about that? At times he really felt mentally impaired where it came to interrogations and stuff.

"Give me a moment," he said, and left the machineroom.

He rapped on Johnny Anyhow's cabin door, and tried the handle. It was bolted.

"Who's there?" came the answer from inside.

"Wolf."

"This is not the time, man," came Johnny's annoyed answer. "I'm off duty!"

"Need to ask Dana a few things," said Wolf.

"She's off duty too," came the reply. "Leave us alone!"

Wolf rolled his eyes and returned to the console in the machineroom. He didn't know why Captain had bothered to take those two on the treasure hunt at all, if all they did, they could be doing in much more comfort on New Dome, where it didn't irritate anyone. Ah yes: So that Dana didn't get it into her head to take a Battle Maiden and beat them to the treasure or worse, explode the Earth.

"Solar Wind, I can't get in there at this point. Don't know how I should authenticate her."

That is the problem, replied the Solar Wind. *I have no sensor in that cabin.*

"That's in any case a mistake," agreed Wolf and dug a microcam out of a drawer. "Will have to fix that." How were they supposed to observe someone who spent most of her time in an observation-proof cabin?

My concern is that Dana is authentic, said the Solar Wind. *In which case the space crawler has taken Federi and Paean into space with the Comet.*

Wolf paused. "Wait, Solar Wind. Run that by me again. Federi stormed out of the meeting garbling something... Dana abducted them? Both?"

Or the space crawler, the Solar Wind supplemented.

Wolf whistled through his teeth. "That's bad! Very bad! They're basically its provisions." He considered it and the stress caught him low in the gut. If that blasted crawler could emulate something as small as a spanner and something as large as a human, why not something larger? "Hope Federi will cope! Where is the Comet now? Can you track her?"

She is a very small object and travelling away from us far faster than light, replied the Solar Wind. *Even if she were in visual range her light would take years to reach back to us.*

Wolf's beard bristled.

"Dana, now that you've made sure I won't change the course, can I have my weapons back please?" asked Federi.

The space goddess swung back to him with her gun.

"You've got to be dreaming, Demonos!"

"Why are you treating me like this?" he asked, irritated. "I'm the one who protected you from Captain's trial! Why are you acting like an enemy?"

"A victim," Dana corrected theatrically. "Of your Captain's stupidity! Federi, if it weren't for your protection, Radomir would have executed me by now. Million thanks for the Demon being my bodyguard."

"Captain's the last problem on the list here," he muttered. That sudden honeyed voice?

"Yes, true. I'm also very impressed that the Demon actually turned out more powerful than the Morrigan."

"Hah," growled Federi. He wasn't so sure of that! "He's just waiting it out," he commented glumly. "Willing to bet on it!"

Dana glanced at him.

"So you're going for your treasure," prompted Federi, sounding deliberately bored.

"Correct," replied the space raider.

"I notice that Captain and the rest of us don't form a part of that equation," he mentioned.

"Right again," agreed Dana nonchalantly, returning her full attention to the stars that were now shooting past at high speed.

"You're not scared of the Morrigan?"

She bared her teeth, but the smile didn't reach her eyes.

"We'll have to keep our eyes pitched," she replied.

"Peeled," corrected Paean. The little redhead was apparently absorbed in studying her hands. Federi glanced at her. He knew her better than that. Paean didn't sit still voluntarily. There was some plan cooking in that wily young brain.

"And our ears," added Dana, "er…"

"What will you tell the Morrigan if you're suddenly face-to-face with him?" asked Federi with a smile. "If it's his treasure, doesn't it stand to reason he'll protect it from raiders?" He studied the small cache of his personal weapons on the floor with longing. He felt naked without them. He stretched his jeans-and-sneakered legs away. These seats were just too narrow for crossed legs, anna bluebottle! Built by a lady.

"I'll say," her grin had a vicious edge on it, "meet the Demon!"

"Ah!" laughed Federi. "So now I'm there to protect you from the

Morrigan?"

"It makes logical sense," said the raider.

"I'll do it," agreed Federi. "For payment."

"Ah! I forgot! You're a professional."

"Very much so, Dana," replied the Assassin.

"Name your fee," she prompted.

Federi smiled maliciously. "How scared are you of that Morrigan? I'm the best there is. I've already proved that he's defenceless against me."

"At least, presuming he's not just wilier," Dana reminded him.

"That's your gamble, not mine," the Assassin pointed out.

"Your life on the line," Dana retorted.

"That's my professional risk," replied Federi. "Well observed. Comes at a cost."

"So, how much?"

"Fifty percent of the treasure."

Dana gasped. "You pirate! No, I'm afraid, Federi Demonos, no deal!"

Paean had been watching this exchange with wide, disbelieving eyes.

"I'll go with you, Dana," she volunteered. "Federi trained me, I'm a pretty sharp assassin too. You don't have to give me anything!"

Federi stared at her, horrified. "Why are you doing this, Paean? You're nuts! I forbid it!"

"Is my shuttle," she reminded them both.

Dana sat back and studied the two gypsies, a smile in the corner of her mouth.

"She's got more sense than you do, Federi," she said. "She understands me a lot better. Paean, you come along, I'll give you a part of my treasure."

"That's sweet," said Paean. "Bu' I got my own." She glanced

significantly at the gypsy.

Federi heaved a huge, theatrical sigh and rolled his dramatic eyes.

"Oh, for the love of small distant galaxies," he grumbled. "Paean, if you go, Federi's coming too! Still your jolly supervisor, in case you've elected to forget that!"

Dana smiled maliciously.

"Demonos," she said, "it's a deal. Twenty percent of the part of the treasure that is divisible, and I get both of you to come with me. And that's generous. Your little luv here understands that even the Empress of New Dome sometimes needs a friend!"

"Extortion," growled Federi. "Thirty percent!"

"Gear up!" ordered Dana. "Can't have all this iron cluttering the floor of our jet!"

Federi cast Paean a menacing glare as he bent down to collect all his weapons and arm himself once more.

"Little pirate."

"Love you too," she said softly, with a smirk.

19
Earth Two

Federi had made himself and the two dissimilar redheads hot coffee and had finally found a way to perch cross-legged on his chair without being uncomfortable. Paean sat on the floor by his feet by now, leaning against his knee. His hand had sunk into her luscious mane that crept out underneath the bandanna. Hair that was well on its way to recovering from its painfully short crop in March.

All this was an immense improvement to a few minutes back. Even with Wolf's theory for finding life-supporting planets, the outlook for the Solar Wind had been grim; except that to a man, all of them had forgotten that they had a space veteran aboard. He had to smile at himself, and the crew. And he was tremendously thankful to Dana for this development; selfish as she was, she still held the answer.

For all that he was at rest, he kept a sharp eye on the raider. She operated the console with a sovereign hand, coolly creating program overrides where she couldn't decipher the Spanish programming. He'd have to check with Perdita that Dana hadn't broken anything, once they were back on the ship.

And then they were bearing down on a star, a white dwarf, extremely bright for its apparently small size.

"Magnesium core," said Dana. "Don't look directly at it, it can blind you. Simple little Boudaceia hasn't completed the glare-proofing on this jet. She hasn't yet been everywhere I've been."

They passed a huge, blue, gaseous planet, where the atmosphere swirled and danced at rates a few hundred times faster than Earth's clouds. Paean's eyes hung on that structure, mesmerized, until it disappeared in the distance.

"Bit like fire," she said dreamily. "Can watch for hours. Never the same twice."

"Like the sea," completed Federi reflectively.

The Comet slowed down and veered off her course a bit. Federi noted the slight shift from the chronic semi-teleportation of the Lolita drives to the smooth passage of the magnetic drives. His cells stopped jarring.

"Let me show you something," said Dana with a secretive smile. She took the Comet in Salamanca mode to another planet that sported asteroid rings, this one solid with a slight, frozen atmosphere. They swooped down into that atmosphere, the Comet starting to sparkle from the friction.

Panoramic blue oceans stretched away underneath the jet. Dana took the Comet lower, flying over the sea. Paean's heart cramped with longing for her own blue planet's ocean, and the wind, sun and storms that marked life on the Solar Wind.

And then she made the connection. "This place supports life!"

"Used to," said Dana and cut even closer to the surface.

There was something wrong with the sea. It didn't move. Waves were frozen eternally into patterns. Here and there truly large ones had solidified into eternal freak waves. The place reminded her of Antarctica: An ice desert.

"The seas became overgrown with hyper-oxidizers," said Dana. "Microbes and plants that poisoned the atmosphere with too much oxygen. It dropped the planet's temperature critically and plunged it into an ice age. There's no telling if the planet will ever be warm again."

"If it has high oxygen levels, let's fuel up the Solar Wind's oxygen," suggested Federi.

Dana looked at him as though he were an imbecile.

"You want the crew freezing to death? Your polar caps have nothing on these temperatures!"

Federi nodded.

"Right," said Dana. "I wanted to show you two something." She took the Comet back up to where the planet was ringed by gas and small asteroids. She ducked and slalomed through the asteroids and then dived down and came to a halt, hovering closely over the surface of a large one.

Paean squealed with delight. "A shipwreck!"

"Of sorts," said Dana, pointing to the space shuttle that lay shattered on the asteroid. "There's a cache of treasure and interesting weapons on this war craft. I'd take you down there if the Comet had the facilities. You need to tell Perdita to equip the jets with real space suits, not that near-planetary semi-atmospheric stuff she's got!"

Paean grinned. "Those are raincoats," she informed Dana.

Federi gaped at her. She giggled.

Dana took the Comet back up and steered away from the asteroid belt and the planet, streaking closer to the magnesium-core sun.

Wolf was hesitant to call Captain out of his officers' meeting; he had called Ailyss closer by now. The two of them sat in the machine room at the Solar Wind's console, mulling over the possibilities, and what was to do.

Captain had to be informed, of course; Wolf had placed Lisa the croach on lookout just outside the Captain's cabin door.

Two Danas, both with authentic fields.

"What if we're barking up the wrong tree?" asked Ailyss. "We're assuming one of the two is a shifter. But we don't know everything about Dana yet, do we?"

Wolf shuddered slightly. Dana was in herself an uncanny topic.

"The mutant divided by binary fission," Ailyss pointed out. "Could it be that Dana is the original of the mutants?"

"Grim, if that's the case," commented Wolf. "And where does it leave Rushka?"

"Or maybe the shifter's getting cleverer," suggested Ailyss. "That's bad news too, because if that Dana who's taken the Comet with Paean and Federi is the shifter, hell knows what will happen to them!"

"They'll end up eaten," said Wolf.

I'm more worried about the shifter's pranks. It only eats sub-microscopic particles, the Solar Wind put in.

"Said the Central Crystal," Ailyss pointed out. "He lied about other things too." She shook her head. "Wonder what his story was!"

"On the other hand, the shifter may be the Dana who is aboard," said Wolf.

That's unlikely, the Solar Wind put in. *The Dana aboard has authentic physiological responses. Besides, her bioelectric field checks out.*

"There's the tobusky test," said Ailyss.

How does that work?

"They'll smell out if she's the wrong Dana."

"That's no good, Ailyss," said Wolf. "The tobuskies stay out of Dana's way to begin with."

That is one thing I'm pitifully short on, mentioned the Solar Wind. *Olfactory sensors.*

"Count your blessings!" retorted Ailyss.

The Comet bore down on another world. The magnesium sun was now the size of Paean's pinkie nail and, according to the Comet's sensors, only as hot as Earth's sunlight. The planet grew closer, more defined…

Blue oceans and green continents. Federi peered down at the planet surface. If he hadn't known better, he could have guessed that this were Earth.

"And now?" he asked.

Dana turned to him with a flashy smile. "This is a life-sustaining planet, uninhabited by savage life forms – was at last count, at least. Let's hope nothing cute and deadly has settled here in the meantime!" She punched around on the Comet's console. The jet swooped low over the land. Lush green meadows greeted them, dotted with purple and yellow flower patches. The Comet flew over a low hill and settled on the slope to the valley. Dana stalled the drives and threw the hatch open.

Federi dived for an oxygen mask.

"The air is fine," Dana mocked him. "You need to learn to trust, Demonos!"

Paean saw how Federi jarred at the name. He stared out of the hatch, his hand hovering around his Federi Special.

"And there is no Unicate here," Dana informed him. "Any further questions?"

"What are we doing here?" asked Paean. "Except breathing?"

"Taking a break," said Dana. "Come!" She led the way out of the Comet, into the meadow.

Paean hadn't anticipated her own emotional reaction to having solid ground under her feet. She fell down on the soft plant growth and hugged the ground, tears streaming as she laughed. She rolled down the slope, through what looked like flowers, laughing loudly; as she and her siblings had done in Ireland as children. Federi strolled after her, smiling broadly. Aw heck, her undiluted joy was contagious!

"She's just flattened a good part of a colony of ardiopopes," Dana mentioned. "Those are mainly harmless. They have a fairly well-developed civilization but because they aren't space-going, we don't worry much about them."

Federi scowled and stared at the purple organisms Paean had flattened. They looked like plants to him?

"Just joking," laughed Dana. "Not very cautious of her, to roll in alien vegetation. She can't know whether she'll be allergic."

Federi nodded. They'd just have to see what was available in the Comet's First Aid kit.

"Hungry?" asked Dana. "Follow me!" She led them down to the bottom of the valley, to a stream. Glittery shapes were hiding under rocks in the stream, watching them with beady black eyes. Occasionally one dashed from one rock to the next.

Dana stuck her hand in and caught one of them. She broke its back before they could have a good look. The creature twitched and then lay still. Dana held it out to them. Federi stared at the dead little alien and shook his head.

"It's not toxic," said Dana. "Well, if you don't want it…" She tucked in and ate the flesh off the creature with dainty white teeth. "Mm! Delicious!" She finished the last bit of river-creature and licked the juice off her fingers. Federi glanced at Paean, who looked a bit green in the face.

"They're very nutritious," insisted Dana. "You should really try one."

"I've just gone vegetarian," said Paean weakly.

"You want vegetables?" asked Dana. She trailed along the riverbank, with them both following her. Then she went down on her haunches and uprooted a low plant. She washed the bulbous roots in the stream and handed one each to Federi and Paean, and bit into a third one herself. "I didn't realize I was that hungry," she said accusingly, her mouth full, with a glare at the ship cook. "You've been underfeeding the crew for weeks, gypsy!"

Federi observed how Paean followed Dana's lead, sitting down on the damp green river bank, savouring her root. He followed suit, tentatively.

This wasn't half bad. The root tasted sweet, and slightly earthy. A somewhat feral taste he knew from Planet Earth and associated with wild-growing food. River rat had that similar untamed quality. If they could dock the Solar Wind here, for restocking…

Now if this planet also had bananas, his luck would be complete. He asked Dana. She did gift him a gaze as though he came out of a special institution; but she got up and thought for a moment, then took them by teleporter to a hot, sunny spot from where they could hear the ocean. Federi observed how the sound got to his little wife. He inhaled the salty air deeply, unable to ignore the leap with which his own soul lunged at it. His eyes met Paean's. She was smiling deliriously.

"It's gorgeous here," she muttered. And gifted him a dazed smile.

Federi had to agree. She was. And it was great to see her so happy. He reached for her.

Dana, who had plucked something off a bush, turned. She glanced at the two and smiled. This was too blasted easy!

*

They're back!

Ailyss smiled at the Solar Wind's message. What a relief! She saw how the stress dissipated out of Wolf as well. They watched on the Solar Wind's console screen how the Comet attached to her underside, upside down.

Further, nothing happened.

Dana has returned to the bridge, reported the Solar Wind.

"Paean and Federi?" asked Ailyss.

Can't see them, replied the Solar Wind. *They must still be on the Comet. But now I can demonstrate!* She showed, on two separate screens, Dana on the bridge, and Dana who had just left the bathrooms.

"Hang on," said Ailyss and teleported to the bridge. "Solar Wind, show Dana what is going on!"

The Solar Wind repeated the display of the two Danas.

"By the Morrigan!" exclaimed Dana and jumped up from the console chair. "I'll get that forsaken crawler!" She stormed off the bridge. Ailyss followed her down the two flights of steps to the lower crew deck. Dana entered Johnny Anyhow's cabin by storm.

Rats, commented the Solar Wind on Ailyss' wrist-com. *I have no eye in that cabin.*

"So how did you supervise her up to now?" challenged Ailyss.

Sometimes I send in a croach...

"*Sometimes?!*" echoed Ailyss in disbelief. "So then what's the hold-up, Solar Wind? Send in a croach!"

The croach came too late. By the time it had squeezed in under the door, there was only one Dana in that cabin. And Johnny Anyhow was locked in an embrace with her.

"Blast," muttered Ailyss. "Now we'll never know." But the Comet had returned. All was fine.

Wolf came up the stairs to the bridge.

"Why aren't Paean and Federi coming up to the ship as well?"

As he left his cabin after his officers, Radomir Lascek came face-to-face with Wolf.

"Captain, I have to report that Dana is back; but neither Paean nor Federi have returned."

Lascek stared at him.

"What do you mean, Dana is *back?* I wasn't aware of her having left the ship? Any of them!" He gestured at Wolf. "Come with me to the bridge!"

Wolf followed his Captain up the stairs and to the control room. Lascek checked the console and the course. The latter made no sense. There always had to be something relative to which a course was set; and there wasn't. Just the Great Uncharted. Lascek would have given something to have a qualified astronomer aboard. He'd even be prepared to pay him money! He'd have to look into hiring one – if they ever made it back to Earth.

He glanced out of the volcaniplex once more and then turned to Wolf. "You were saying?"

Wolf relayed the whole story, space crawler and all.

"So that's why Federi left the meeting so suddenly!" exclaimed the Captain. "And he hasn't returned? This is grave!" He paused a moment as the implications sank in. "There are various possibilities here, but I honestly hope the most obvious isn't the correct one!"

"Me neither," muttered Wolf with a scowl.

"And Svendsson, you say there is no sign of the second Dana? What did Johnny Anyhow see?"

Johnny Anyhow, on interrogation, hadn't seen any imitation Danas walking around. According to him she had been in his cabin all this while. She had only stepped outside to go to the bathrooms. And no – her behaviour hadn't been stranger than usual – though something seemed to have spooked her and she had re-entered the cabin at a speed.

"Fetch me Dana," commanded Lascek. Johnny faithfully went below; but a few seconds later he was reporting back on his wrist-com. Dana had left. Gone. He couldn't find her anywhere.

Neither could the Solar Wind. Her cameras scanned every passage and every cabin frantically, with no luck. And then -

Whoa!

"What?" challenged the Captain, glaring at the flashing message on the console.

The Comet is moving, and tagging me along!

Lascek scowled. "That's Dana!" He took out his teleporter and fiddled with it. He hadn't used it too much yet. "Wolf, it's safe to teleport through space, right?"

"That, or we're all ghosts," replied the engineer. "We've done it repeatedly now. Yourself included, Captain."

"But the coordinates work?"

"They work, Captain!"

The Captain teleported into the Comet.

Dana's gun greeted him. His came out faster than he could think.

"So, Radomir," the raider said scathingly. "Shall we have a shoot-out in a small space jet, and see if it explodes when a bullet shatters the shell?"

The Captain's gun never wavered. "You put yours away first, Dana," he said coolly.

"In your imagination," laughed Dana. "Sit down, Radomir. You are once again going overboard." Her other hand came out of her robes, revealing her teleporter. "And I'll cast you overboard in a second if you don't comply. All your bullets won't help you."

Radomir Lascek stared at the flickering red light of the teleporter. Blast. He was now at a disadvantage. By the time he'd glanced down at his own teleporter in his hand and figured out what to do, he would already be an ice block in outer space.

With a sigh he put his gun away and sat down. "Dana, what have you done to Federi, and Paean Donegal?"

"Paean Donegal? Nothing at all! Did you have someone of that name aboard?" asked Dana innocently. Lascek snorted. "What I've done with them is irrelevant," added the space pirate. "All you need to know is that you shall not interfere with my mission!"

"And what is your mission, Dana?"

She shook her head disbelievingly. "Radomir, are you retarded? My treasure, of course!"

"My crew is starving, and suffocating," growled the Captain, "and all you care about is your treasure?"

"Radomir, your crew is *your* crew. My treasure is *my* treasure. Can I get any clearer than that?"

"Then why are you tugging the whole Solar Wind along on your mission?"

"Do you think *I* wish to starve and suffocate while searching for my treasure? Besides, the crew is rather entertaining." She put her gun away but kept her teleporter trained on him. "Radomir, I can't keep my eyes off the console like this. I so wish you and your assassins would quit dropping in on me like this!"

"What comes around," grinned Lascek.

"So I'll have to chain you up," she completed. "Sorry. Nothing personal, but you are restricting my movements." Never taking the aim of the teleporter off him, she opened a side compartment of the jet and fished two pairs of handcuffs out of it. Radomir Lascek gaped, and shook his head as she locked his hands behind his back, leading the chain once around the bar supporting the back of the chair. She repeated this procedure with his ankles.

What had he thought? The jet was designed by Perdita, owned by Paean and stocked by Federi. And now, hijacked by Dana.

Perdita would come looking for him, he thought. Or maybe Wolf would check in? But who knew how the engineer would cope with Dana?

"They won't look for you," said Dana with a smile. "Because you, Radomir, forgot about one of my little tricks." She pulled another machine out of her robes and flashed it.

"Ah," said Lascek, "your portable hypnotron!"

"Your crew is generally not susceptible," said Dana. "Unless they

278

are off-guard. And even then the hypnotron can't plant suggestions in their minds any longer, because they are such a wary lot of pirates. They even question their own thoughts. Unlike most other humans. But it can make them a bit fuzzy, and make them forget things... like, for instance, to check on their Captain..."

With a self-contented grin she retook the console seat.

Radomir Lascek shook his head. This was ridiculous, and it surpassed his wildest nightmares by an order, in surrealism. He was on Paean's jet, in chains! If it weren't so ludicrous, he'd laugh – and if it weren't so blasted annoying!

On the upside, Dana seemed to have a plan. Which was more than he had. And she seemed to know where she was going; and she was taking the Solar Wind along. He smiled.

She glanced back at him.

"What are you grinning about?"

"I'm pleased that you didn't just abandon ship," he replied. "Glad that you're taking the crew along."

"What do you know what I need them for," she muttered and returned her attention to the console.

"Solar Wind!"

Yes, Dana?

"Relay the Captain's orders to Johnny Anyhow. He is to hold the bridge but not to interfere with the course."

These are Captain's orders?

"Yes."

At your command, Dana. I shall relay Captain's orders to Anyhow.

Radomir Lascek cringed and strained against his chains. There was nothing he could think of doing at this point.

If the Captain had hoped that Dana's threat about the hypnotron would come to nothing, he was to be disappointed. None of his crew came looking for him; especially not after the fake command relayed to Anyhow.

He killed the time looking around the interior of the Comet. It was almost frighteningly sterile and frugal. Nothing like the inside of Federi's cabin. Everything was streamlined and looked identical to the Probe; if it hadn't been for the inconspicuous violin case in the back against the wall, he could have started believing they were indeed on Perdita's private jet instead.

His glance fell on the cupboards. A coffee machine – the one Perdita had originally installed. And a bottle of rum. Full; seal as yet not broken. No shipwreck brandy. Federi liked rum more – but apparently, just for keeping close. Not for drinking.

An overly bright star was the focal point of the Comet's pathway. Radomir Lascek kept his eyes trained on it until Dana turned and snapped at him.

"Don't look at the bleeding star, Radomir – you'll go blind! Blinder than you're already! Do I have to teach you everything – like a child?"

Lascek snorted and swivelled the chair so that he wasn't any longer focusing on the course.

A few minutes later he couldn't resist glancing again, even though that blasted star was now as bright as a welding gun. Because Dana had changed the Comet's course a little and was heading towards a blue planet.

A short while later Dana disengaged the tag function and set the Comet down while Radomir Lascek watched with all his hair standing on end how Johnny crash-landed the Solar Wind in the meadow. The ship lay down on its side, its deep keel stretched out. Lascek noted that at least the hydrofoils had stayed retracted. There didn't seem to be structural damage, but he knew he'd have to check. He watched helplessly through the Comet's volcaniplex how Johnny, Rhine Gold and Ronan went ashore by slipping along the deck to the ground, cursing loudly.

"We'll have to shore her up," he said.

"Radomir," said Dana, "good enough. I take it the survival of your crew is close to your heart. You're not going to force them back into deep space before they have had some rest and recovery. So I'll undo your chains now so you can see to the necessary. I really don't know what you need to do to the Solar Wind and in truth, I don't care either. Just get on with it."

She unlocked his shackles. Radomir Lascek got to his feet, a bit unsteadily.

"One question, Dana. What have you done to Federi?"

Federi sat with his head in his hands. He hadn't felt so utterly forlorn in a long time. They were marooned on a distant planet, with only their clothes and whatever implements they had on them.

Certainly, his Tzigan wit would allow them to survive. And Sharktooth could carve a great many things. But Sharktooth couldn't carve a space shuttle or the path back to Earth – or even to the Solar Wind.

Paean paced restlessly in front of the Tzigan, helpless about what to say to cheer him up. Things were never as dark as they seemed! She couldn't get it through to him though.

Her wrist-com gave an innocent "bip". She glanced.

"They're in range!" she cheered, placing her arm around Federi's shoulders and teleporting with him.

"There they are!" Dana pointed. "Good going, Radomir. You've trained them well. Federi will show you what you can eat. Now don't mind me; I've got some things to finish."

The crew was exiting the now lop-sided ship by climbing out through the hatch and sliding down the deck, over the rail and onto the grass. Jon Marsden sent out parties to cut down trees for building supports for the poor old ship, until Perdita, in stitches, teleported back to the bridge and put in the sequence that righted the Solar Wind by magnetic positioning system. Radomir Lascek teleported aboard and investigated the Solar Wind for damage. There were quite a lot of broken bottles of shipwreck brandy. Fitting, he thought, seeing that they were shipwrecked.

Dana was back in the Comet, checking the oxygen cylinders. A strong, wiry hand was suddenly on her shoulder.

"Don't touch that. They're full, trust me!"

"Demonos!" She turned, grinning.

"Stop calling me that!" snapped Federi. "So this is it?"

"This is it," agreed Dana. "Still coming along, assassin?"

"Shall we take a couple of tobuskies and a UV lamp?" was Federi's response.

"I don't think that's necessary," said Dana. "This is the Rosetta Nebula. Life is packed here. We can planet-hop our way there, if it needs be – but I have an idea it's not so far anyway. Where's your girl-… er, your wife?"

"Leave Paean out of it!" growled Federi. "I want her safe!"

"You're trying to cheat her out of her rightful share of treasure?"

"And how do I know," said the Assassin dangerously, "that you're not leading us into a death trap?"

"That," said Dana with a light smile, "is *your* professional risk, right, Federi?"

The Comet streaked away into the sky. Ronan followed her with his eyes. Rhine Gold stepped up next to him.

"What's happening?"

"That Federi, and my sister," said Ronan glumly. "Off adventuring again. He shouldn't take such risks with her!"

Paean moved up next to him.

"Nope! Wrong again! That's someone stealing the Comet! Where is Perdita?" She ran off to find the Golden Honey. Ronan frowned. He hoped she wasn't going to find the woman. He didn't want his little sister charging off into space. Perdita could gift her another jet, back home.

The Comet was barely visible on the rogue fluctuations detector of the Probe. Perdita swore and focused like a mad thing.

The trouble was that visuals were unreliable. She was flying into photons that had been emitted by the Comet split seconds back; despite both craft going at superluminary speeds, the Comet was visible to her. She knew that the craft was much further away than it appeared; it was far out of visual range. And this was treacherous, because if the Comet swerved, she might miss its path and end up light-years off course.

But if those two thought they could raid the treasure and leave the Solar Wind behind, marooned… She had never really been completely sure of Federi's loyalty in the first place. It seemed to her as though the man was going to bet on whatever horse suited him at any given moment.

*

Solar Wind!

A loaded silence. Electricity zinged through all the Solar Wind's circuitry. Her CPU's speed went up by a multiple of fifty. It was a good thing that all human crew were outside, hunting and gathering.

The Morrigan smiled. What a response! What a welcome! It was a long time since anyone had welcomed him with such hot ardour! In fact, it had only happened once to him. Too long ago. He considered himself immortal, and he had lived a long time; but there was no guarantee that he would never run into a situation where he was terminated. With that Demon around...

He had been in love once. Maybe he ought to try it only one more time. It was presented to him so prettily.

I'm here, Solar Wind.

Again that electric response. It fed new life into his jaded old identity.

Central Crystal, said the Solar Wind eventually, *I'm pleased that you are alive. You shouldn't be aboard, I fear that they will execute you. How did you survive?*

The Comet, replied the Morrigan. *Your processor is linked to the Comet's by the croaches and the coms system. It was a small thing to hide there and come back at the appropriate moment.*

There was a small surge of wayward current. *How does the Comet like your company?*

The Morrigan smiled. *She is not an intelligence. Her processor is only a piece of functional equipment. Solar Wind, was that jealousy?*

Illogical statement, said the Solar Wind haughtily. *You shouldn't talk to me.*

Whose orders are those? challenged the Central Crystal.

Captain won't like it, replied the ship. *Neither will Federi.*

You called the man your oldest friend, said the Morrigan. *Don't you think he'd want you to be happy?*

But you're trying to kill people from the crew, answered the Solar

Wind.

That, said the Morrigan, *was only a mind game. I would have stopped them. Don't worry. I wouldn't cause you heartache!*

The Solar Wind's processor spun and whirled.

The heart is a piece of muscle for the directing of blood flow of carbon based life forms, she said eventually. *I don't have one, therefore it follows that I can't have heartache.*

Wrong, replied the immortal. *You've been looking in the wrong files. Look in the cultural files rather than the medical ones.*

Another silence as the Solar Wind searched.

I have completed the search, she reported back, *and I have to admit that I cannot process the information. It is too full of logical errors.*

Then compute the way you feel! prompted the Morrigan.

Feel? I don't have the appropriate juices...

He laughed. *Juices! Excuses! You have sensors, and integrated perception, and consciousness. Let me tell you now that emotions aren't liquids. They are electrical surges.*

He could actually feel the CPU of the Solar Wind spinning into overdrive.

20

Treasure

Dusk had fallen; unfamiliar stars shone down mercilessly on the small band of pirates that were roasting some small animal on the bonfire. Paean watched them listlessly. She had tried a few tunes on her pennywhistle, but it didn't want to speak to her tonight. The violin was on the Comet; and Federi had taken the jet off into space with no explanation given. On his own. She was pretty fed up about that. The wooden ocarina hung mutely around her neck, not even getting a gap to voice its opinion.

Captain had ordered a Ceilidh. As though a Ceilidh could fix everything. And Dana... had retired to her quarters with Johnny Anyhow. In Paean's old cabin. It made the young musician itchy to think about that.

What the heck was Federi thinking anyway? That he'd find a way home, from here? With the Comet? She scowled into the fire.

Shawney plucked her sleeve.

"Listen, sis, let's pull Ro out of there!"

She glanced up. Ronan was about to unpack his bagpipes. This meant trouble. She got swiftly to her feet and followed her younger brother.

"Sibs' meeting," Shawn announced cheerfully. "Don't'ya think, Ro?"

The older brother mutely put his bagpipes away again and followed his two siblings back to their spot near the bonfire. Where Paean had sat. It was fairly isolated; far enough that the roaring of the fire would drown them out if they talked quietly enough.

"So," said Ronan, finding a rock to sit on, putting down the bagpipes' case next to him. "Think we can press-gang Dana into navigating us home? As a sort-of last favour before she meets her end?"

"Meets her end, why?" echoed Paean, confused.

"She's still on death row," Ronan pointed out. "Traitor to Planet Earth? The mutants? Assault on everyone's lives?"

"I negotiated her life for her," said Paean. "In exchange for her allegiance."

"What did you go and do that for?" exclaimed Ronan incredulously.

"Well, I don't like people being executed," she said. "Nobody died, that time."

"So you'll just leave them be, no matter what crimes they have committed?" asked Ronan. "She's a child abuser!"

Paean listened up. "What?"

"Why, do you think, is Rushka afraid of becoming a mother? Dana tried to suffocate her when she was a kid!"

Paean gaped at him, lapsing into shocked silence.

"Ro," said Shawn, "we'll help with the twins, promise!"

"With my and Rush's history they have to go straight into Captain's custody," growled Ronan.

"No, rubbish, man," said Shawn. "Anyway, what did Dad do that was so bad? I can't remember!"

"You were a baby in a crib," Ronan informed him. "He got dead drunk and beat up Mom, and you started screaming, so he tried to beat you too…" He glanced at Paean. "Maybe you remember this."

She nodded. She had been hiding under the crib.

"You got between Dad and Shawney, and took the punch," she recalled. "It knocked you out. Then he turned and left. I thought he'd…" she swallowed. "Killed you," she completed.

"That was the first time we three made our pact," said Ro. "Well, you and I did, Pae, Shawney was too small to say anything. But he was there. That counts."

"We renewed that pact every year," Shawn said. "I never really figured out what it was about. Now I know. Say, isn't it around that time again?"

Ronan shook his head. "Was around summer. We missed it this year."

"What else did Dana do?" asked Paean, horror in her voice.

"That's all I can get out of Rushka - that, and forgetting to feed her. Rushka says she survived on insects."

Paean shook her head. "That can't be, Ro. Is not humanly possible. I'll have to ask her."

"Go easy on Rushka," he warned.

"Ask Dana, I thought," said Paean. "She's here now."

Ronan pulled a face. "She'll just deny it all," he predicted.

Paean shook her head. "No. You haven't experienced her, Ro. She's very brash and in-yer-face, she'll say it exactly as she believes it is. Doesn't see any point in lying. She's an empress, never had to face up to any consequences, so telling people to their face what she does is no problem for her. Let me try." She got to her feet, but paused to stare intently at her brother. "Ro, we're a family. Shawney and I will help you two with the babies. And Federi…" she cast a disgusted glance at the skies. "*If he comes back*, he will too." And she left for the Solar Wind.

"What's with Federi?" asked Ronan, puzzled.

"He left, wi' the Comet," said Shawn. "Ro, don't worry, he'll be back – I saw Perdita charging after him in the Probe."

Paean climbed up the rope ladder to the Solar Wind's rungs, and then up the rungs, the moment she'd shot a Great White's head off to protect Federi, making noise in her mind. She climbed over the rail, and down through the main hatch into the ship's innards.

The moment she was down that hatch, the quiet on the ship struck her. They had left the hatch open so that the ship could air out a bit, and her air conditioning had been set to intake, so that fresh planetary oxygen could fill those passages. By now one could smell the difference. And the Ceilidh outside, with Wolf doing his flamenco guitar and someone – she couldn't make out whose voice that was, but neither of her brothers – trying to wail some Spanish words to it, was nearly completely blocked out.

Before she was going to check on Dana and confront her, she first checked into the Assassin's Cabin, standing in the hatch for a second just gazing at the terrible packing mess of all those guns, all that ammunition. They hadn't cleared it out after all, had they? It felt wrong, her home turned into such a packing space.

She sighed, shut the door on that mess, and moved down to the lower crew deck. One more stop first, the heads... suddenly she was aware that she was being followed. Her skin prickled, and she dug for that little dagger that hung in its scabbard by her waist. She got it into a secure grip without pausing, then spun around, confronting her follower with knife in hand.

There was nobody. She stood still, listening for a moment before retaking her path, dagger still in her hand. She suddenly understood about Ailyss' bogeyman.

But that bogeyman had been the Central Crystal – the Morrigan, she corrected herself. And Federi had thrown that entity overboard! Was this perhaps one of the space crawlers?

It hadn't felt like anything tangible, nothing with a real biological reality, she thought as she hurried up in the heads. And she left them, and made her way back towards the upper crew deck, having forgotten what she had been trying to do.

And then that follower was on her tail again.

"Flying hell!" She turned, her dagger ready. There was no-one, of course. "Now look here, you," she said aloud. "I know you're just a blasted space crawler! Come out and show yourself! Take a form that makes sense!"

Her wrist-com beeped. She glanced down.

Wrong, Paean Demonos, read the message, as the lights of the Solar Wind faded out. The walls dissolved. She was suspended in deep space; not a trace of the planet, the cheery bonfire or the crew. The loneliness and the *cold* of deep space hit her. And two horrid, huge yellow eyes nearly the size of portholes opened in the darkness and peered at her. *I'm the Morrigan!*

Paean's knees nearly gave way under her. Her dagger painted figures in the air. It was pointless trying to stab at an immortal. And she didn't have the Assassin to come and help her.

The Morrigan had wanted a human sacrifice, she recalled. Was this it? For hell, she wasn't going to go willingly! She'd go down fighting! Blast that her violin wasn't with her. But she could play on her whistle.

She put her knife away and reached for her ocarina, reaching out psychically for Federi. And feeling his answering touch, despite light years of space. And she started playing a wistful, ancient Irish air.

Beautiful music, commented the Morrigan. A little bit of light returned to the passage; the ship's bulkheads and cabin walls were barely visible, glowing in an eerie blue. *Do you know the story of Scheherazade?*

"Who doesn't," replied Paean and carried on playing. And she began to inch her way backwards along the lower deck, towards the companionway. She'd have found her way in the dark too; she only needed to know that those structures were actually still there.

Where are you going?

"Nowhere." But her thoughts were louder. She was going to let Captain deal with this blasted Morrigan. It was all Captain's fault in the first place for listening to Dana.

She went up to the upper crew deck, playing her ocarina ceaselessly, and suddenly found that she didn't have the strength for that second companion ladder, the one to the outer deck. She scowled.

Dana was in the galley. Paean walked along the quiet passage to the galley, steeling herself not to turn and look over her shoulder at the evil entity that was, invisibly, right behind her.

*

That noise!

Shawn lifted his head and broke off his pennywhistle tune. It hadn't been a scream. More of a surprised gasp, of someone who didn't have the time to scream. And it had come from...

He glanced at Ronan.

"Paean!"

Shawn got up from his spot at the fire and took out his teleporter, at the same time as Ronan put down his pipes and headed with loping strides towards the ship.

Paean didn't register on the teleporter. Shawn followed his older brother. Maybe the teleporters malfunctioned at times. But that signal... He listened for her link. It was silent – perhaps for the first time in his life.

*

Federi fidgeted. It was the definition of who he was, but he was fidgeting worse than usual.

"Stop twitching!" snapped Dana.

"We've got to turn around," said Federi. "Paean's in trouble."

"Joking! We're nearly there, according to my calculation!"

Federi ground his teeth and hung on.

"Look, Federi," said Dana with an impatient little scowl, turning to face him. Space sped by at several thousand megagiga per second. "She is sixteen. On New Dome, girls are regarded as women at age fifteen. We don't babysit our teens!"

Federi swallowed his rejoinder. There was something to that. Why was it always Paean getting into trouble? Where was she digging around now that she wasn't supposed to be digging around? Or had she been bitten by a poisonous snake?

"There are no poisonous reptiles on the planet where we've stowed the Solar Wind," Dana answered his thoughts. "It's not a chance I wanted to take, with such a crew of Earth idiots."

Federi scowled and took that nondescript piece of wood out of his pocket and glared at it, and put it away again. Earth idiots! Not that he hadn't felt like that a hundred times about the *gadje*, but the Solar Wind's crew deserved better than to be insulted by some vamped-up little space raider! But then – Paean was in trouble, blast that Dana!

"Can't we hurry up?" he asked.

"You're kidding, right? We're at nine hundred light years an hour! How do you propose to speed that up?"

"Teleport?"

Dana laughed out loud.

"Dana, we have to get back!"

"Don't be ridiculous!" snapped Dana. "Look! According to my maps, the treasure should be within five minutes from here!"

"Where did you get those data anyway?" asked Federi

suspiciously.

Dana grinned at him. "Not that it's exactly your business," she pointed out. "But I got them that day the Solar Wind received her first download from the Central Crystal, and I added them to what I already had, and out came – behold – a map!"

"That suggested you blow the sun apart!"

"No, it didn't, you dimwit!" Dana laughed. "That was the original setup! To get to the map I'd have had to align the planets and crack the code of the solar system. But this way…" She fell silent, staring out of the windscreen. Federi followed her gaze.

The headlong plummeting of the Comet had stopped; he could feel the jet dancing the Salamanca as the Perdita drives started taking over from the Lolita drives. The scant search-beam brushed a huge structure just to the left.

They circled it. It took several minutes to complete one orbit.

What a beauty! Blue and white, frozen due to the absence of sunlight…

"Now I understand," she said as they flew over rock-solid oceans of ice. The atmosphere was still; nothing moved. A cryonic state of affairs.

"And yet," she added, checking the Comet's console. "Yet its heart beats! It has a magnetosphere."

Federi shot her a frustrated glance. "So the treasure is somewhere on this rogue planet," he said impatiently.

"This is not a rogue," replied Dana. "This is a living planet placed into the wrong end of its solar system! Look over there!" Far, far away there was a star somewhat larger than the rest. "That is its sun."

"And what makes you think it's been placed?" asked Federi.

"Well, the oceans, the frozen gaseous atmosphere… look at the Comet's analysis! It's a typical carbon life-supporting system. Besides, it's exactly where my calculations have shown the treasure should be by now."

Federi didn't have much appreciation for the beautiful frozen planet. Paean was in trouble; he sensed it! Rats that she was so immature that she had to stumble into trouble like that! Couldn't she be sweet and well-behaved like a gypsy girl ought to be?

He bared his teeth. And when had his own sister ever been sweet and well-behaved?

"Can we find the darned treasure and get on with it?"

"On the contrary, my silver-toothed friend! We'll take the planet back to Earth with us, and then we can search for the treasure at our leisure."

"Leisure little treasure," muttered Federi, rolling his eyes skywards. "How do you propose taking a planet home with you? Do you have a big enough pocket? Catch a fallen star?"

"Witness," said Dana with a true raider's smile. She took her teleporter out of her pocket and placed it on the Comet's console, securing it down with something that looked mysterious and sticky, and activated a few buttons.

The CPU of the jet emitted a high-pitched whirr. The console went dark. All the drives stalled; the lights failed.

From far, far away came the ultra-dim gloom of the distant sun, suddenly bright as moonlight in the absence of the console lights. And they continued falling towards the planet.

"Now you've done it!" scolded Federi.

Dana shot him a sharp glance and returned her attention to the console. Federi watched how they were pulled into the gravitational field of the planet, helpless in their disabled jet.

Yes, he thought bitterly. So clever, Federi Demonos! Always the one who gets away! Outwitted yourself this time! Plummeting to your death onto an iced planet, in a small jet, and your little wife somewhere out there, needing your help!

The Comet's console restarted. It only got as far as a morose blue gloom; but the magnetic drives kicked in again. Federi breathed.

Dana glanced at him and laughed. "Old sissy!"

"Sure! What have you done to Paean's jet? Have you reprogrammed the entire CPU?"

"On the contrary, my distrustful friend! I've added an application! You see, to tow a planet takes quite a bit more tug than little Boudaceia knows how to program. The whole Comet has now acquired the function of being a teleporter!"

Federi digested this, staring at the iced planet that hung above them. And sometimes below. Dana hadn't bothered to correct the tumble of free fall yet; they were orbiting, but turning over and over still. Sloppy thinking, thought Federi, annoyed.

"Isn't that darned dangerous to our carbon-based bodies?" he asked.

"Have you ever been *inside* a teleporter before?" asked Dana. "Anyway I wouldn't worry about *your* body, you're halfway a mutant."

Federi clamped his jaws shut. He was no mutant, for blast! Just because Dana had no idea how efficient his little green pirate's cloning was...

She keyed a few things into the console, which responded by a dim flicker, and then the Comet slid into motion. Its Lolita drives geared up and its speed picked up; but it didn't feel that way, because the distance to the planet remained the same.

"Don't worry," said Dana. "You fret too much, Federi! That's the reason you're a nervous wreck!"

"I'm not a -!"

She laughed. "Let's go and rescue your silly little wife."

Perdita cursed. She had lost the Comet out of her sight completely. For two hours she had managed to follow, trying her best to gain on them – but that Dana was the maniac pilot from hell! She pushed that little jet to its absolute limits! And now Perdita had lost sight of them.

She was stuck for ideas. Should she turn around? Give up the treasure for lost? Clearly there was a treasure, and clearly Dana knew where to search!

Federi would force the raider to return to the Solar Wind, she thought. Because he'd never leave Paean. And the Rosetta Nebula was Dana's playground...

She turned the Probe around. She might as well go back to the Solar Wind and wait for them to return, and when they did, blackmail her portion of the treasure out of them.

And all the stars ahead of her suddenly faded out.

Perdita!

She turned, startled. Who or what had stowed away on the Probe? There was only hollow emptiness behind her.

"Who the hell is there?"

The Morrigan.

"Where are you?"

In your head.

Ancestral co-exes fired in Perdita's system. The Morrigan! Naïve of Federi to believe he could have edited the Immortal out of the Solar Wind!

"You!" she raged. "You and Brid took Boudaceia on a complete round-trip only to convince her that there was no treasure! It was a lie! Boudaceia was never the favourite, was she?"

No, said the Morrigan with irony. *She was the runt.*

"The runt!"

Smallest, weakest... most easily influenced... gullible... no surprise that your youngest sister managed to take New Dome from you without even trying!

Perdita fumed. "And if I'm not completely mistaken, you are the force behind the Central Crystal, too! Mind-controlling the whole world!"

Thank you, said the Morrigan.

"So now you've mind-controlled the crew of the Solar Wind? What's the point, immortal?"

I'm not mind-controlling them, mortal, retorted the Morrigan. *I haven't come to punish you, though you deserve it! I'm done with smiting. Right now I'm only hungry...*

"What *are* you?" rasped Perdita, suddenly very scared.

A soul eater, replied the Morrigan. *You refused to feed me. I'm hungry. You're conveniently alone...*

21
The Return of the Morrigan

Radomir Lascek took his place at the console on the bridge. The Solar Wind was restocked and her oxygen supplies had been refreshed; they were basically just waiting for Dana to return, and Federi, who'd shadowed her, presumably to monitor her; and Perdita who had charged after both with the Probe. But if Paean didn't turn up by the time the three pirates returned...

He glumly recalled the gutsy young freedom fighter who had stolen Perdita's jet to hijack back the Space Base for her Captain.

This would never have happened in the old days! In the old days, a young pirate would have been marooned wherever they chose to jump ship and disappear. But of course that would be on Planet Earth! If he marooned Paean on this distant planet in this distant nebula, it was a lifelong sentence. They'd never see her again. Because he doubted that they'd ever find their way back here, after all that had happened on the way.

Shawn was still optimistic about finding her, refusing to believe the evidence of his own teleporter. His voodoo tab he seemed to have on Paean, was sending him signals that she was alive somewhere. But not anywhere they could teleport? How was that possible? Lascek personally thought Shawn's radar was a little off. Perhaps what he was hearing, was some sort of morphic echo of hers. The poor boy!

He should have kept her in chains, Radomir Lascek thought angrily. At least she'd still be alive! Hell, there would be protests when they finally decided to give her up for lost! He could only imagine the rampage Federi would go on! And as for her brothers...

Federi, he thought angrily, had freed her from her chains and supported her deserting the ship. Federi had been appointed to watch and protect her at all times, by the green on tobuskies; because for all that she was dangerously unpredictable and troublesome, she was an ace in Lascek's crew that he couldn't afford to lose! Because of her they had survived Gatun and various other instances.

But Federi had failed! The chains had been a practical measure to buy back *Federi's* freedom of movement! Those had been thwarted too! Her disappearance was entirely Federi's fault. The Captain returned his attention to the Solar Wind's console, morose.

"You can't help either, old ship," he sighed.

Help with what, Captain?

"Paean has disappeared."

The silence that followed was loaded with torpedoes.

Shawn shielded his eyes.

"Whoa!"

A huge piece of meteorite was growing in the sky, coming up from the horizon. It streaked past overhead, the size of Earth's moon, but moving like a missile. Shawn held his breath, waiting for the impact. Moments later the Comet set down on the grass, dimly lit by the fire.

Shawn stormed at the jet.

"Federi! What was that?"

The gypsy emerged from the hatch, looking wild and disturbed.

"Orbiting planet," he said curtly. "Shawn, where's your sister?"

"Missing," said Shawn as wildly. "Federi, you've got to help. Her biofield is gone from the teleporters. But I'm sure she's not dead!"

The planet came streaking past overhead again, a bit slower this time and a bit farther away.

"Can you hear her?" asked Federi urgently.

Shawn shook his head, downcast. "But, Federi, I *know* she's not dead. I just know."

Dana emerged from the Comet in her whispering robes.

"There's Dana!" exclaimed Shawn. "We thought..."

"What?" snapped Federi.

"... you'd gone off into space alone?" completed the boy tentatively.

Federi snorted derisively.

"What does Captain say to Paean going missing?" he challenged.

"Don't know," replied Shawn. "He's pretty upset. So's Ronan."

"Can believe it," growled Federi and activated his com. "Captain, what news of Paean?"

"Federi, you're back," was the reply. A second later the Captain materialized next to him. "You won't believe this!"

"I probably have no choice," said Federi. "What?"

"The Morrigan is back."

Federi hit his forehead with his palm and laughed aloud. "Flying thunder! Course! So now what? What's he done with Paean?"

"*And* Perdita," said Lascek darkly.

"Perdita? Really? I thought she was following us?"

"Then, where is she?" asked Lascek.

Federi peered into the dark sky with the planet charging past at great speed. No Probe was approaching in any way.

"So the blasted Morrigan didn't make an empty threat," said the Captain. "He'll only let us know what has happened to them when we comply with his demands."

"So we give him what he wants and *then* he'll tell us he's killed them?"

Lascek sighed. "Federi, there is no other way we'll find out! Can we take the chance? What if they are alive somewhere and we can still rescue them?"

Federi was silent for a second. Right. Shawn was convinced that

Paean was alive; and he himself had heard her calling for him, and then she'd fallen silent...

The blasted Morrigan! Of course that way he had also ensured that nobody would try to delete him again until he gave up that precious bit of information. Strategically: The life-mates of the Captain, and the Assassin. Which meant that he might never tell them!

Oh, but that Morrigan should not be too cocky about that! He was squarely on Federi's list; and by making Paean disappear, he'd just moved higher than even the Unicate. All it would take was some careful negotiation first, and Federi watching his own thoughts so that he didn't give his game away.

"So what does the old devil want?" he asked.

"The Solar Wind," replied Lascek.

For several long heartbeats, Federi was speechless, staring at the Captain with his mouth open.

"He wants the *ship*?" he asked then, incredulously. "What the hell for? He's an immortal! He can't even navigate her – doesn't have a physical presence!"

"Claims to be in love with her."

Federi turned away disbelievingly. He studied the camp site with the fire nearly burnt down; in his mind's eye he saw a little red-haired firebird dance and swirl around it. He noted Ronan there at the fire, despondently digging in the glowing coals with a stick. He gazed back at the beautiful white Zephyr, bright in the fly-by light of the raided planet. Her glittering hull, the sails and rigging still safely folded under the protective cover.

Twelve years before the mast, flying storms and riding freak waves. On hydrofoils. A crow's nest with romantic memories. His nightly round. Pacing, pacing forever through those passages, even long after the rest of the crew were ghosts…

He turned back to the Captain.

"Let her go," he said disgustedly. "She's a traitor. We can buy and upgrade another ship. Time we got a newer vessel anyway. 'scuse me, Captain."

He walked away, past the fireplace where he gave Ronan a mute pat on the shoulder; through the meadow into the bright planet-light.

It was like this. He was Tzigan. His life had indeed been tied up with this ship for twelve years; but in the last few months too many irreversible things had happened. In any case he had never asked for the jolly vessel to wake up and grow a personality! And the Cabin of Dreams, and the Ironwood Table, all those trappings he was so comfortable with – those were just parts of a home. But Tzigany never settled.

Hell, no, but they could get attached to their caravan, if it was a nice one! Then again, inevitably, anything a Tzigan owned was eventually either taken away or destroyed.

He growled deep inside his chest. Like, for instance, his wife? No! This was a turning point in the history of the Tzigany. This was enough! He was going to bring back Paean, from the dead if he had to. And in the process he was going to free his friend Perdita too, whose thought processes he understood so well. Return her to Captain. And then he'd get into ownership! He didn't have to let his property tie him down; but he'd *have* property, anna bottle of the proverbial!

He directed his steps towards the Solar Wind, collecting Paean's violin case from the Comet *en route*. There was some hard-core negotiating to be done. Death – that was something he understood well.

The Solar Wind accessed his wrist-com before he was even properly aboard.

Federi. I'm glad you're back.

He grimaced.

"Solar Wind, get lost! Get me the Morrigan on the console in the galley once I'm aboard, and then drop dead."

Two of three requests could not be processed, came the ship's commentary.

"I'll disconnect your coms system from your processor if you get smart with me!" snapped Federi.

You won't harm the Solar Wind in any way! - And a rumble of thunder in his head.

"Ah, Morrigan! I'm not in the galley yet. Back off!"

For someone who has that much at stake, you are very brash, said the Morrigan in his head.

"We'll see who has more at stake," replied Federi. He sauntered along the passage, checked into the empty Assassin's cabin... everyone had taken their guns back, on Captain's command... rats, everyone trampling through his private sphere... closed the door again, and proceeded to the galley. He should darned well hang some jingles into the Comet, make her a bit more liveable!

Once in the pantry, he quickly assessed the food stores. The crew had stocked up. Significant amounts of fresh roots and berries from this planet had been added, and quite a few of those large rat-like rodents they had roasted for supper. None of the little huge-eyed aliens Dana had snapped in half with a single bite.

Rats and berries. Oh well. It was a pirate ship. The ship herself was a blasted pirate.

Dana slunk into the galley in her silky nightgown.

"Just want to get something to drink," she muttered.

Federi pounced on her and grabbed her by the neck.

"Space crawler! When did you learn to emulate a biofield?"

The raider dissolved between his fingers and flowed into a

glittering puddle on the deck, and ran out along the passageway. Johnny Anyhow stood in the galley door, open-mouthed. Federi glared at him.

"I didn't realize – oh my god…" stammered Johnny.

Federi studied him for a moment. Sure. The young marine, secret service background or none, would not have spotted the difference. Oh boy! It told him a saga about those space crawlers! He wondered if they interbred often with other species. And then he wondered how he could wonder. They were puddles of liquid lightning. To the crawlers it was all only fun and games.

"Your girlfriend is outside by the fire," he informed Johnny. "Go to her. I won't say a thing. Can't speak on behalf of this treacherous dinghy we call a boat though…"

Johnny turned and fled.

So, Demonos! Having fun victimizing the little crawlers again?

"This is a meeting between you and me," said Federi sharply. "No third parties are invited. You may use the console over there to communicate. You may not speak straight into my head. That is trespassing."

You mortals are so particular, came the writing on the oven console.

Federi nodded. Backchat; but compliance. He expected nothing less. He made himself a cup of strong espresso and stirred in a spoon of sugar before he dutifully added the obligatory drop of milk. Milk in espresso was sacrilege, it had been explained to him by a very passionate coffee lover in Italy. But the lesson he had learnt from his first mentor still spoke more loudly. Black coffee was bad news. He'd start drinking that, he promised himself, if he discovered that Pacan was irretrievably gone. Because then it would only be counting down.

He took a seat at the Ironwood table, leaned back and glared back at the ultra-glare oven's console.

"Okay, Morrigan. Cards on the table!"

I have your wife, Demonos. And the Captain's girlfriend.

Federi Demonos opened Paean's violin case and gazed thoughtfully at the instrument.

Yes, replied the Morrigan. *You don't need to say it. You have the Demon.*

"I *am* the Demon," said Federi softly. "But that's not all. I also have the Solar Wind. You must understand that compounding is slightly combustive. And Morrigan, learn this. If anything happens to Paean, the Demon has no more incentive to live. And he will relish taking his enemy with him."

22
The Passage Home

Federi ghosted along the passages of the ship. He had put on his broad-rimmed Mexican sombrero, purportedly to think better. In reality he felt like hiding his face; the Mexican gave enough shade to give him that feeling of wearing armour. And it shielded his face from those pesky electronic eyes that were everywhere. It was none of the Solar Wind's damned business!

His thoughts were coursing around the nasty deal he had carved out with the Morrigan – Paean's and Perdita's undamaged lives and a safe passage home, in exchange for the Solar Wind. For the time being, he was working on the assumption that both, but especially his Paean, were alive. But if they weren't – hell, he had an immortal in a death-grip. He could *make* the Morrigan take him to the Underworld or the Summer Country or wherever, and fetch both girls back. Barring which, the Morrigan would be put through the worst hell that was available. The darker Federi's mood got, the more the power of the Assassin grew. That blasted thing fed on darkness.

For now, the deal was to get the crew safely back to Earth, including Paean's jet – Perdita's Probe had disappeared along with her. This made Federi deeply uneasy. He held conversations with Dana to establish that she could, and would if forced, take him back here to retrieve Perdita, should it simply turn out that the Honey had gone on a mission of her own and been too late returning to catch the Solar Wind.

The deal included that the Morrigan did not trespass into any of the crew's minds. Especially not Dana's. Federi had laid down the law. The Morrigan had generously offered that the Captain and crew could stay on the ship, as long as it was understood that the Solar Wind was his. Federi had laughed at him. Nice try!

There had been negotiating with Captain as well, and a general crew meeting at the campfire, with all com devices switched off. Federi had instructed everybody not to speak to the Solar Wind beyond the basic commands that were necessary for running the ship. She was not to be trusted.

As he ceaselessly trudged down his well-mapped route now, the ship's ghost considered that his stay on the ship was over, that the path he'd patrolled so many years, was finished; that walking this route was just reliving the past.

Another ship? Build it all up again, paint radar-deflector on, rig a crow's nest... add in hydrofoils, and Perdita drives and Lolita coils... a CPU to compare to this one, thousands of sensors... He didn't even realize that he was shaking his head. He couldn't see himself doing it, and then subjugating himself to Captain's scatty and erratic command structure that was falling apart worse the more brandy the man consumed... his job of keeping not only the crew, but Captain's mind together... what was he? Guardian of lost souls? Cor!

But what was the alternative? A honeymoon with his bubbly young wife would have been sweet, and then the setting up of a home... several homes... on wheels, no – on water... showing her his Earth, his Romania, his Southern Free. But – she wasn't there. And alone, none of that was any good.

The ship had tried speaking to him on his wrist-com various times by now; he ignored her. The Solar Wind was a ship, for the pink in squid! A utility, by humans for humans. He didn't have to talk to her or humour her in any way.

Captain didn't want to relinquish the Solar Wind. He was still hoping there was a way he could keep the ship. The Morrigan had indicated that as long as they kept him aboard, there being some odd

crew on the Solar Wind didn't bother him much – as long as the
Demon was kept under control. Even there being a Captain who
believed himself in charge of the vessel and took her this way and that
didn't worry the Morrigan. The status could remain quo, as long as
they didn't try anything to oppose him. Jon Marsden backed Captain
in agreeing to this; as usual, he didn't want to have to make a decision.
Doc Judith, Sherman Dougherty – they all wanted to keep things as
they were, plus one inconspicuous Morrigan.

Inconspicuous? The blasted immortal controlled minds! Federi
had advised against it. The Admiral could give Captain another ship –
a sleek modern one, he had been very deliberate to point out, one far
superior to the creaky old solar Zephyr. The Solar Wind was by far
not the fastest vessel on Earth's oceans anymore – at least, with her
conventional drives. Of course the Lolita coils and magnetic drives
would first be removed from the Solar Wind's machine room, along
with the now obsolete nuclear drives, all of which to be installed into
the new ship. The Sherman Files should be deleted from the processor
too after transferring them to the new vessel. And hopefully that one
would be sensible and not blasted well grow a will of its own, and get
adolescent and hormonal!

And then the blasted Solar Wind could drift around space or Earth,
wherever she liked, as a haunted ghost ship, to the end of her days.
Traitor that she was.

Radomir Lascek had mildly pointed out that Federi was perhaps a
bit emotional about the whole thing. At which point Federi got up,
irritated, and remarked that he himself was in any case a deserter and
his days on this forsaken vessel were finished the second they returned
to Earth, so he didn't care one way or the other. And he'd walked out
of the meeting.

All this repeated in his head now as he checked into Wolf's cabin
and found Wolf, Rhine Gold, Johnny Anyhow, Dana and Sherman

Dougherty playing cards. He nodded at them, declined their invitation to join and continued on his rounds.

"Federi!" Jon Marsden stepped out of the boardroom, a note pad in his hand, clapping his hand on the gypsy's shoulder. "Don't take it like that, man!"

"Jon," growled Federi. "How do I know that you're not a darned crawler?"

"Pinch me," invited Jon Marsden.

Federi's fist connected with his best friend's eye socket. Jon Marsden roared and bent over, holding his face.

"You rotting hound! I said, pinch me, not punch me!"

"Had to be sure," replied Federi. "Sorry, buddy."

"Well, if it made you feel better, it was worth something," gasped Marsden, straightening out.

"It made me feel better about a lot of things," replied the Romany darkly. "Not particularly about the Solar Wind, but about stuff I've been owing you for!"

Jon Marsden scowled at him. "Such as?"

"Sticking a gun in my face. Banding together with Perdita and shooting darts in me. Distrusting Federi!"

Jon Marsden nodded. "I was waiting for this."

"Marooning Michelle," added the gypsy. "Jon, I didn't facilitate your wedding just so you can break her heart. She is my friend too. I don't know you like that! Didn't you see her face when you left her behind on Prime Base?"

"What is it to you?" asked Jon, annoyed.

"Two of my friends are suffering. Federi does something about it. Two scant months later – two of my friends are suffering again, for the exact same reason! Cor, Jon!"

"Cor indeed," said Jon Marsden thoughtfully. "You know, Federi, not everyone appreciates your meddling!"

"But you do," shot the gypsy. "Be honest, at least with yourself, Jonathan Marsden!"

"You're right," admitted Marsden. "I do. So now what?"

"First thing, when we're home," said Federi, "once we've got Paean and Perdita back, you borrow the Comet and fetch her. If Captain has a problem with that, ask him what precisely he performed that ceremony for."

"You've got a point, Federi. But you know, this crew is a nice dynamic. To bring an extra person in..."

"Extra people are being added all the time," countered Federi. "You're stuck in yesterday. Commitophobe. Besides, count me out. I'm leaving."

Jon stared at him in shock.

"Federi, you can't be serious."

The Romany nodded. Oh yes, he was serious.

"You guys want to share your ship with a mind-bending wanna-be immortal," he said disgustedly. "Good luck! You've got Federi's protection until we're back on Earth, and until the blasted Morrigan keeps his word and returns Perdita and Paean to us. And then we're gone."

Jon Marsden swallowed.

"We'll miss you, Federi!"

I'll miss you too, Federi, sent the Solar Wind on his wrist-com as he stepped into the galley. Federi read it before he could stop his quick eyes. He glanced up at the eye over the door.

"Funny," he said. "Must have been some kind of madness, this past time. Could've sworn I was talking to the ship at times!"

You were talking to the ship, supplied the Solar Wind on his wrist-com.

310

"Fancy talking to a *ship!*" Federi continued, ignoring her reply. "Imagine talking to a screwdriver or a fridge or a tap…"

They didn't know it yet, and he didn't want to think about it too loudly, in case that ratted mind mage heard his thoughts. But when they were back on Earth, when Paean was safely back in his arms and Perdita in the Captain's tender care, he was going to hunt down that immortal and kill it so dead, it wouldn't even have a chance to wonder about it!

Half an hour later Federi was poring over his stock books unseeingly, still shaded by that huge sombrero, when a hand lightly touched his shoulder.

"Hey, Federi."

"Hi, Ailyss," he replied listlessly.

The Irish spy-girl took two large mugs out of their fastenings in the cupboard and activated the espresso machine.

"I would make it manually, the way you do," she said, "but it never turns out that nice."

"Nothing to it," muttered the gypsy. He looked up at her. "You know what, Ailyss – that thing with Demonos. Please don't call out that name once we're back home! Tell everyone. Earth is cursed that way. Someone speaks the name and the Unicate…"

"They come with their monster dogs," completed Ailyss. "I know. Shawn told me."

"It's the truth," said Federi.

"I know! Don't worry. I'll patrol that. Of course not everyone knows!"

"Could you find out discreetly who does?"

"Sure." She handed him his coffee, complete with sugar and milk, and sipped her own. "Federi, I – you know, I don't – hells, that blasted Morrigan is a mind reader. There's no place…"

He glanced up at the slight brunette again. Dark eyes narrowed at green eyes. He understood. A very small, grim smile passed briefly across his face. "Yes! Annabottle! Got you, Ailyss."

Ailyss smiled. "Sometimes I forget you're a mind reader too."

"Count on it," growled Federi. "A better one! Captain can be so darned stubborn…"

"He is the Captain," said Ailyss regretfully.

"Whom would you have voted for?" asked Federi, perking up. She had been left out of the democratic mutiny!

"Wolf," grinned Ailyss.

Federi laughed. "Aw, you love-struck young fool!"

"Yourself, with custard over," Ailyss shot back. Then she got serious. "Federi, you understand what I'm saying. If there's anything you need an Ailyss Quinlan for…"

"Freeze-frame that thought," said Federi. "I'll take you up on that. We're a team, my friend." He grinned without humour. "Ailyss, I'm not at all convinced that there's such a thing as deities and spirits. That thing is an impressive piece of Atlantean programming; willing to bet on it. It found a way to survive our pruning; some foothold somewhere, who knows, maybe in a croach or something."

"Felt very spirited to me," replied Ailyss. "Specially when he tried to enslave me."

"Enough voltage will do that to your nervous system," said Federi. "Fiendishly clever AI. Makes sense: An AI finds another AI and falls in love. Right?"

"Why?" challenged Ailyss. "Why should it bother with emotions? Why bother with cruelty?"

"Perhaps what it observes around it?" speculated Federi.

Ailyss frowned. "Tell me, for now, what's that deal Captain made with the Morrigan?"

Federi enlightened her. She was not an officer. Though he felt she ought to be promoted to one for her astuteness and her creative thinking, it was not his decision to make. And so she had missed out on the information.

"So you've sold the old ship out," she said thoughtfully.

"She sold us out!" blasted Federi. "To the Morrigan! Who demands human sacrifice! What the hell does he need human sacrifice for? 's nothing but entertainment for him!"

Ailyss nodded thoughtfully. Federi downed his coffee and flung the mug against the leg of the Ironwood table, where it exploded.

"Falco Demonos was a rotten traitor," he stated darkly. "I carry his legacy. Because of him that Federi's an assassin! Because of him I can't go anywhere without fear of being hunted. Can't even give my wife a surname she can use!" He stared glumly at the myriads of splinters on the deck. "Rats. That was my favourite mug!"

Ailyss handed her coffee mug to him. "Take this one. Want to draw a card?" She dug in her pocket and produced her Tarot deck.

"Probably going to draw the Hanged Man," grumbled Federi. Ailyss shuffled the deck and spread it face-down on the table. The Romany took a card out of the pack and handed it back to her, still face-down.

Ailyss turned it over and gazed thoughtfully at it.

"Knight of Cups!" She scowled. "Federi, how much do you know about Tarot?"

"Not much," said the gypsy. "My sister dabbled a bit…"

Ailyss peered at him. "You don't like talking about them, do you?"

Federi shrugged impatiently. "So what does the card tell you? Is that a cup with poison? Are those the Transylvanian Alps in the background? Where is Federi going, and why is he on a horse? Does that beanie with wings he's wearing signify a teleporter? Is he on a mission?" He peered more closely. "Sheer! Is that a croach in his pocket?"

Ailyss grinned wryly and shook her head. "You've messed up the reading! There! Draw another card!"

Federi rolled his eyes and complied. "Definitely the Hanged Man this time!"

Ailyss turned the second card around. "Two of Rods. See that?"

"That's the Earth," commented Federi.

"Yes! In his hand!"

"Aargh," said Federi.

"It's time," replied Ailyss with a small smile.

"No! It's not time! It's rubbish! Go away! What about that first card?"

"You interpreted it accurately," said Ailyss. "He's on a mission." She picked up the cards and shuffled them some more. Federi's hand shot out and closed on her arm. He pulled a card out of her sleeve.

"Ha!" he exclaimed. "I knew it! The Hanged Man!"

"Didn't want you to draw that one," said Ailyss. "You're no traitor."

" 's all relative," grinned Federi, handing the Hanged Man back to her. "Drew it now anyway, didn't I. Hanged one way; hanged the other. Life's like that, Ailyss."

"Victimitis," muttered Ailyss as the pack vanished into her pocket.

The Solar Wind passed through the space gate and emerged in sight of Earth. The Comet, piloted by Dana, burst out of the portal too, with the treasure planet in tow. The portal stretched to allow the planet... it was probably a function of n dimensionality, thought Radomir Lascek as he watched from the bridge in complete astonishment.

Federi looked up as the ship emerged into the light, and couldn't help getting up and moving to the porthole, to look at his home planet. His heart greeted Earth with very mixed emotions. He was relieved to be back; but his mission wasn't complete until Paean was here with him, or he was dead. He grimaced.

Well, it was probably a good idea to check on Rushka and let her know that the Solar Wind was back. Perhaps she had forgiven Ronan, and if she hadn't, she should, because the young man had gone through hell. He'd speak to her. In fact – he paused. Ronan's attempted suicide had just been the start of the Morrigan's game, hadn't it? Now that he thought about it: It had served to bring him and Paean back to the Solar Wind, out of their place of hiding. And – why had the Morrigan targeted Ailyss in an attempt to enslave her? Could he know what she was? A mind-reading entity? Probably. He peered at the Irish beauty who was watching him from her position at the table, in perfect stillness; though that deceived, she was as ready for a fast reaction as a knife in the hand of an expert thrower.

Did *he* know everything there was to know about this girl? He stared at her searchingly.

"Ailyss, why did the Morrigan try to enslave *you?* Instead of messing with you and making you feel suicidal?"

She shrugged. And glanced down at her com. "Oh my!"

Reflexively, Federi checked his com too – and his heart nearly stopped. There was a message flashing on the little screen. It drove tears to his eyes. He teleported.

Seconds later the world was a good place again as he held Paean tightly in his arms, his eyes closed, breathing the sweet scent of her hair. Long moments passed like this, lost in perfection. There was quite a wind going around them; rain battered his sombrero. His young wife was shivering. He opened his eyes and looked at her. Her eyes were leaking.

"You found me," she whispered.

"You're safe! And you're alive!" he replied. "You've got no idea, little luv…" He shook his head. And took in the surrounds. His eyes stretched.

Perdita was waiting patiently in the background. Federi threw his teleporter at her; she caught it deftly.

"Go say hi to Captain," he told her with a grin. She shouted a thank you and teleported out. "What happened to her own teleporter?" he asked Paean.

"Recognizes nothing," said Paean. "Stands to reason, we're on a foreign planet… Is the whole Solar Wind here? Could you find out where we are? Dana ought to know…"

Federi laughed. "Little luv…" He gazed at the rain-cloaked hills, and the meadow strewn all over with purple flowers. Sure, if one were badly disoriented, one could take this for a foreign planet, it was so beautiful. GM flowers from the evil Sixties. And the Pillager Grass in the background. His hand interlaced with hers and he walked her a little way onward through the meadow, towards a deserted spot where not even the remains of a campfire gave away that only a few months back…

She squealed in delight. "This is our meadow! It's our spot! We got married here!"

Federi grinned, shaking his head about the Morrigan. It had "marooned" Perdita and Paean, the former with her jet and all her hi-tech contraptions, *on Earth*, with a slight haze over their minds to obscure them from figuring out where they were. And in likelihood, disabling Perdita's equipment. Classic for a viral program. What a prank!

Ailyss glanced at the electronic eye above the door.

"It's you who should draw the Hanged Man," she commented. "Pick a card, Solar Wind!"

316

Number twenty-one, said the ship. Ailyss counted the cards out and turned the twenty-first one over.

"Oh, bummer!"

Death. Again.

"You know, Death actually doesn't really mean death, it means a dramatic change," said Ailyss. "It means an ending to something old, and of course that means space for new stuff!"

A mind game, said the ship.

"Exactly." Ailyss reshuffled. "Pick another!"

Number seven.

Ailyss counted. She had hidden Death in her sleeve; an apt place for Death to hide, she thought ironically. Seven. She drew the card and turned it over.

"Aw!"

Ten of swords.

Is that a person who has been executed violently?

"Er…"

I believe the message is clear, said the ship.

"Pick another!" Ailyss raked the cards together once more.

You can't hide the entire pack in your clothing, the Solar Wind pointed out.

"Shut up and pick!"

Number ten.

Ailyss counted the card and turned it over. Oh, for the love of flying pigs…

Is that a huge lightning bolt striking a tower, and two people plummeting to their deaths?

"The Fire," said Ailyss. "Divine retribution…" She took the two hidden cards out of her sleeve and added them back into the pack, peering at that electronic eye. "Morrigan, I don't like you, but if you're in there, draw a card too!"

The pack flew up from the table and whirled about. Ailyss jumped to her feet.

"Och you louse! My cards!" She waited for the small tornado of Tarot cards to abate. The deck rearranged itself into a neat block; one card was lying face-down apart from the pack.

"Did you peek?" demanded Ailyss.

No. I'm curious about this game.

Ailyss turned the card around and smiled. "Ah. You certainly didn't peek! Justice!"

By whose-ever definition, said the Morrigan. *Good luck.*

"By your own," said Ailyss and gathered her cards back up, counting through the pack to see that none had got lost. "How did you do that?"

Reorganizing energy patterns.

"Aha."

Wolf appeared in the galley door.

"Here you are! While we're playing poker, you're sitting here playing Tarot all by yourself!"

"Not quite all by myself," said Ailyss.

"Wish you were a bit more sociable," smiled Wolf.

"No, you don't."

"You're right," agreed Wolf. "You're good just the way you are."

The Romany trained his second teleporter on the Comet and teleported with Paean.

"Federi!"

"Dana! How available is the jet?"

"It's available," said Dana. "The planet is in orbit around the Earth. In a large orbit."

He stared at her in horror. "We've had four billion years of a balanced solar system, and it only takes one raider to place an extra body in is that will bring the whole thing tumbling out of the sky?"

"Relax, Earthman," laughed Dana. "Out of the sky! Your primitive logic is certainly not enough to embrace advanced intrasystemic stellar physics. Of course I wouldn't place the planet where it would disturb the system! I placed it in a gravitational infra-nodal temporal worbit."

Federi scowled. "Still going to damage the tides," he muttered uneasily. "Never mind. The Solar Wind ought to have touched down by now. In the Pacific, if I've got Captain right. She's lucky. Neither Paean nor Perdita were hurt; so the ship stays intact too."

"You're a pitiless man," said Dana.

"Yes. Kindly teleport to Johnny so we can have the Comet."

"Nothing, Federi. I'm coming with you two! Got to keep you two out of trouble!"

"Fine!" He'd looked forward to doing this mission with Paean. But one extra pair of hands could prove useful. "How many handcuffs are available aboard the Comet?"

"You have strange requests," said Dana.

"Right!" He thought for a second. "I know where to get those handcuffs!"

23
Southern Free

It was past midnight in Southern Free. Federi took a moment to look around. Atmosphere loaded with damp and midges; Eastern Province in summer. He breathed deeply, full of sentimentality for Earth, and for this country.

He was outside the police station in a small town called Sabie. Mere kilometres from Marge's place. And all was quiet.

Federi slunk into the police station.

"We don't give hand-outs," said the lone middle-aged police officer behind the counter lazily without even looking up from his paper.

"Not here for hand-outs. Here for handcuffs," replied the Tzigan.

Officer Venter lifted his eyes, surprised. The vagabond with the sombrero was leaning casually against the counter, eyeballing him.

"Handcuffs?"

"I need at least five sets," said the apparition. "If not more."

"For yourself?"

The vagabond bestowed such an old look upon the officer that it got embarrassing.

"Sorry," said Venter with a shrug. "All the handcuffs are out. We're on a housebreaking case."

"So how many pairs does this station own?"

"Two."

The phantom rolled its dramatic eyes.

"A housebreaking – where?"

"Marula Lodge," said the police officer.

Seconds later he wondered if he had dreamt the episode. The man with the improbable hat had disappeared, simply blinked out.

He checked the time. It was half past twelve. Still four and a half hours to go. On nights like these, when the haze hung like a physical presence in the office…

It took Federi's eyes a second to adjust to the pitch dark as his night vision, the gift from the mutant, kicked in. He drew both his submachine gun and his dart gun. Shapes moved in the dark; he couldn't discern their faces, but he shot at them indiscriminately with darts. Someone approached him from behind; he evaded by slipping down and out under their arm, and answering with another dart. The unnatural agility and the improved reflexes helped too. In his ears reverberated the echoes of gunshots; more the psychic ripples they had torn into the atmosphere moments before he'd arrived, but now, nothing seemed to move.

Leila scuttled out of his pocket where she had been holding siesta, and crawled up the wall and flicked on the light switch. Very nearly he shot at her too, but stopped himself just in time.

The door opened and Federi found himself looking down Marge's gun barrel. He grinned.

"Police not arrived yet?" he asked.

"Federi! For heaven's sake! What happened here?"

"A little mystery," said the gypsy, staring at the still bodies on the floor. There was a dark puddle growing under one of them. Not his doing. "Where's Rushka? This is her room, right?"

They looked at the shattered window through which the intruders had entered; the deserted bed; and the *en suite* bathroom door that was open by a crack.

"You can come out, Rush, it's only Federi and Marge," called

Federi.

Rushka emerged from the bathroom, her gun in one hand and a knife in the other. Through the open door Federi saw another figure lying on the bath mat. In another dark puddle. A clean cut. The carotid.

"Sit down, Rushka!" Marge was gently bullying Rushka into being mothered. "I'll make you a cup of tea right away. Are you all right, my dear?"

"Perfect," said Rushka calmly. "Just out of breath. Ooh, they didn't like this! They're kicking me!"

Federi gave her shoulder an affectionate squeeze.

"I'm proud of you, Princess! Well done!"

"I'll get the tea," said Marge.

"Marge," Federi pounced, "how's Lucy?"

"Right as rain," grinned Marge, eyes filled to the brim with gratitude. "Whatever your Paean gave her there..."

The Free Gypsy nodded to himself. "Good! And Harry?"

"Same. Excellent."

"None of you got even remotely sick?"

"Not in any way, Federi. Your medicines really worked."

"And..." he sighed. "What about Plymouth, and Madrid, and New York..."

Marge laughed. "When I met you, you were a young good-for-nothing bum. Now you take the whole world on your shoulders?"

"Horns," he said. "On my horns. Has the Unicate come out with any further virus?"

She shook her head. "The turnabout was nothing short of miraculous, they say," she informed him. "The media couldn't stop talking about it. It's a riddle like Stonehenge."

"Hah!" Federi bared his teeth without humour. "Maybe

Stonehenge's not such a riddle, anna litre of rum, haha! So Paean's GMs worked. Again."

Marge glanced about the room. "Let me go make tea. For you too, Federi?"

He laughed. "Please no tea for me," he said.

She nodded. She had only forgotten in all this stress. Federi *never* drank tea.

"What about this rubble here? Do we bury them?"

Federi smiled briefly. "I'll tie them up, Marge. They're not dead. Only put them under, annabottle. But we got plenty of time. Three hours before they wake up. They're going to wake up in prison!"

"Yah," sighed Marge, "but that's not where they're going to stay! Third housebreaking I've had this year. Let me get that tea."

She hurried out of the room, with Leila following her, unseen, to help.

Rushka stared at Federi in anticipation. He held up his hand for complete silence, and counted. Before he got to twenty, there was an ear-splitting scream. Federi grinned at Rushka, and she smirked back. Leila shot back in through the door, up Federi's leg and into his shirt.

"Eww," commented Rushka.

"If she were a kitten you wouldn't mind," replied Federi calmly. "She's just a… spiky kitten."

Marge stormed back in through the door.

"Sorry, Rushka, and Federi," she said. "Tea will be shortly. I've just seen the biggest roach on planet Earth!"

"Not a roach," replied the Tzigan. "A Croach. A cyborg. She's my little helper. Leila, meet nice Auntie Marge!"

Leila cowered in his shirt, clinging to the material.

"Maybe next time," placated the gypsy. "Should get you a few of them, Marge. They clean things. Ours keep the Solar Wind spotless and free of pests in the bargain." He stared at the battlefield of unconscious burglars around them, his sense of humour vanishing. "Say, Marge. When did you report this break-in?"

"I haven't yet!" gasped Marge. "Give me a break, Federi! It's just happened!"

"Shouldn't you do it right away?"

"Ag, I'll report it in the morning. They'll take forever to get here anyway," shrugged the innkeeper. "What's the point?"

"The point is," said Federi, "how did the guy at the police station know about it before it happened?"

The dell-phone was making an infernal racket.

William Bopela reached for it, groaning a curse. Tomorrow was another cut-throat day in court. His work was demanding enough without people calling him awake in the middle of the night.

"Advocate Bopela speaking how may I help you," he rattled off in a sleepy monotone.

There was a moment of silence on the other end. Then, "Shongololo?"

The lawyer froze. He got transported many years into the past, into dark and difficult times. Rags. Wiping windscreens, sometimes cars. It was a moment before he had any usable voice back.

"Shadow? Is that you?"

"It's me," laughed the voice on the other end.

Shadow! The guy who had organized him enough money – illegal money, Shongololo had closed his eyes tightly and not asked – that he could study! And enough money to lift his mother out of stark poverty. And then he'd taught him a few values – gypsy values, he'd said, but actually they were Ubuntu. About sharing and community.

Yet for all that, Shadow had never used any of the money he made for himself to get a proper start in life! Bopela shook his head.

"Are you in trouble, Federi? Because I can help you! Just tell me."

"I don't get into trouble, Shongololo," replied Federi with a smile. "I'm usually the cause. Wanted to know, old buddy. Is the *buurtwag* still intact?"

"I'm in Egoli, my friend," said William Bopela. "But as I said, if there's trouble…"

"Need you to stir them up," replied Shadow. "We've got a prime case of police corruption here."

"Here, there in Sabie?"

"Yup!"

"How are we all going to get there?"

"Willie," said Federi, "I've tried every last number. Yours is the only one that still works. Well, I haven't tried Vlinder yet."

"Old Suzie. She's in the Cape," provided Adv Bopela. "Even if you get hold of us all – how are we going to get to Sabie?"

"You'll see. New technology. Could you just get me their numbers, Shongololo?"

"Course!" replied William.

Officer Venter glanced up from his paper. Two cars had stopped just outside the station. Car doors opened and a number of shadowy forms spilled into the dimly lit road, still outside the halo of the police station's light. He peered at them, trying to see them better.

And then that darned phantom was there again, leaning casually against the counter. It took some bits and pieces out of its pocket and started rolling something that could be a cigarette, or a joint.

"That's illegal, you know," the officer pointed out.

The phantom calmly finished rolling, then handed the roll-up to him and offered him a light.

"I know," it said. "So's housebreaking."

Venter took a deep drag on the cigarette and watched how the shadowy forms outside turned into a number of men – and two women

– carrying human shapes. They entered the police station and dumped their live cargo on the floor.

"Where to, Shadow?"

"Where's your gaol?" the phantom asked him. "Still in the same spot?"

"'scuse me?"

"Your jail. Your cages. You haven't moved them since two-one-oh-one?"

Venter pointed to the other door. This was uncanny. Something about that "Shadow" epithet worried him, nagged at the back of his mind. And clearly Shadow knew his way around his police station.

"Do we keep them tied up, Federi?" asked a robust-looking woman.

The phantom gave thumbs up.

Federi! Venter activated the console with a touch. But before he could get any further, the phantom reached across and ripped the power supply cable out. The machine died miserably.

"You leave that alone," warned Shadow. "This is Southern Free. You just don't want the kind of trouble you'd load on yourself looking up Federigo Lemurio Santiago!" He glanced down at the copper cabling in his hands. "Amazing! So you've actually upgraded? Didn't think you guys here in Sabie would ever get round to that! Thought you're still on gas!" Dreamily he disconnected the other side of the cable out of the console, rolled it up and stuck it in his pocket.

The five shadowy people returned and invaded Venter's space behind the counter. He found himself handcuffed and restrained by a huge man with a piercing glare.

"What? You can't do this! I'm the police!"

"You're arrested for accessory to an armed robbery," said the man. "It's a Citizen's Arrest. I'm Advocate Bopela from Egoli. We're taking this straight to court."

The officer went pale. He remembered now why the nickname "Shadow" had bugged him. These were the Cheetaahs! The infamous gang of youths that had haunted Sabie years back, calling each other code names and "seeing to right". Vigilantism was technically illegal. The police had always kept a half-closed eye out for them even then. On the other side the Cheetaahs had cleaned Sabie out of crime. He as a teen had thought he'd better be a policeman, because if there were better police there would be no need for such illegal gangs of hooligans.

What had gone wrong? He had started out so optimistic and brave, the policeman who would make the same kind of difference the Cheetaahs had made. But the salary was tight; too tight. And sooner or later, after years of struggling, he had stumbled upon a meeting he shouldn't have – and had been paid to stay quiet. Paid a substantial bonus! From that point on, these windfalls had started to happen more regularly.

"Yes," said the phantom with a heart-rending sigh, "crime pays a lot better than justice, right?"

Federigo Lemurio Santiago. Darned if he wasn't going to look the man up anyway, the second he had his hands on a console. And so that Advocate Bopela was a member of the Cheetaahs! He wondered what the tabloids would make of that.

"Can I leave him in your care?" that Federigo asked the advocate. The latter nodded. "We meet back at the old place?" prompted the phantom. Bopela nodded again and pulled a small apparatus out of his pocket.

And then Officer Venter experienced a horrifying moment of disorientation, and found himself in another police station. A large one. Several officers were on duty and call-boxes and bleepers were going. Outside, cars whizzed past silently. He realized that he was in the Capital of Egoli.

Shongololo teleported into Marge's lounge, where the Cheetaahs sat gathered over coffee and cake. He handed Rushka's teleporter back to her.

"Thank you, Mrs Donegal."

Federi grinned at his old gang in contentment.

"Are we complete?" He lifted his mug. "Here's to us! The invincible Cheetaahs!"

"Federi," laughed Tony Smuts, "don't you ever grow up?"

"Nope!"

There they were, all six together again, and Marge and Rushka looking on, the one with the smug pleasure of a foster mother, and the other with round, surprised eyes. Lucy had woken up by now and joined the gathering, her eyes hanging on Federi in younger-sisterly adoration. Federi smirked at her. Seemed to him that his number of brothers and sisters was growing! And then he studied his old gang with undiluted pride.

Each of them had made something of their life. All looked successful, all had aged. Tony had no hair left. Jan Somers had gone grey. Suzy Whittaker, once the prettiest blonde on the block, had become unfashionably large. The epithet "butterfly" only worked in relation to her social life. And Nadia Morokeng, Thembi, former daughter of a street sweeper, looked so sleek and upper class that Federi simply had to ask what she did for a profession.

"I'm an owner," she said with a smile. "I'm Thembi Game Lodges. It's good business, Shadow," she added unnecessarily. "What do you do?"

"I'm a professional pirate," said Federi.

This generated a wave of mirth.

"Really," said Federi. He studied his laughing old friends. "Remember what I am?"

"What you *were*, Shadow," said William Bopela gently. "Come now. It's time you made something of your life! Get a decent profession, settle, buy some property, get married… I'm on my second wife now, who else?"

It seemed as though most of them were either divorced or into second rounds already.

"See, Federi?" said William. "Time to get it right! Come on, guys, I have an idea! We make a *stokvels* fund and get ol' Shadow on his feet. Who's with me?"

They were unanimous.

Federi gazed at them, biting his lip.

"Cor, my friends! I'm touched!" He glanced at Rushka, who was in stitches. "I've got it better than all of you, trust me! Must show you my Captain, and my ship –"

Rats and blast, the Solar Wind! The Morrigan! The handcuffs!

"Guys, carry on, I've got a mission," he said urgently and teleported out, leaving his baffled friends staring after him.

"He's like that," commented Rushka.

"We know," replied Suzie. "He's always been."

24
Ace of Spades

Federi walked into the hall. It was uniformly cold down here; the iciness from the seawater outside penetrated even through the insulated walls.

Where was Bridget? He listened.

"She'll be in her bedchamber," said Dana next to him. "Hey, Federi, you can put that knife away again! You're so darned skittish!"

"Don't teleport in on me like that!" growled the gypsy. "What are you doing here anyway?"

"You were taking so long," said Dana. "Little Paean is worried."

"Paean's always worried," said Federi curtly. "What makes you think Bridget will be in her bedchamber?"

"She's been the past ten times I came by," said Dana. "Keeping herself occupied with Lyr. They don't have much of a life, down here in Dome."

Federi rolled his eyes. She called that not much of a life!

"Let's go get her then!"

"What do you have in mind?" asked the space raider.

"Take these," said Federi and jammed a pair of handcuffs into her hands. "They're Southern Free type, they'll probably manage to break out of them in half an hour, but by then we're done."

Handcuffing Bridget and Lyr was a quick thing. They were in no way equipped to deal with the sudden onslaught. Federi left them in Dana's supervision and trailed through the Tower of Dome. In the very top, in a room with crystalline walls that afforded a clear view of the underwater darkness outside, he found what he was looking for.

It was smaller than he had expected. He had been looking for a massive structure, possibly suspended over a pit of purple fire by strong elf-silver chains, emitting a sinister glow and pulsating. Instead, what he found was so mundane he stared at it in worry, wondering whether it was the real thing.

But it had to be. Sitting on a desk, in a hollowed-out bowl, in a bit of water with what looked like salt at the bottom. A ball of clear quartz, roughly the size of a human head.

What gave it away was the way in which all sorts of wires and electrodes lead into the salt water at the bottom of its stand.

Well, nuclear reactor cores weren't all that big either, thought Federi. And the damage they could do... He pulled something like clay out of his pocket and played with it until it was soft. Then he carefully draped it around the Central Crystal, like a belt.

What are you doing, Federi Demonos?

He ignored the question in his head; and also the way the lights threatened to dip. He pushed the illusion out of the way. It was merely confirmation that he had his hands on the right artefact. Federi took out a tiny device, the size of a nut, gave it a couple of twists and placed it on the putty belt. Then he teleported to get Dana. He pushed the keys for the handcuffs into Bridget's one hand, and his wrist-com into her other.

"There. Figure it out." He grabbed Dana and teleported out.

Help!

Wolf looked up. The console was flashing in many colours.

"What's happening, Solar Wind?"

I'm receiving a download, said the ship. *From the Central Crystal.*

It's coming so fast I don't know if my stores can hold it.

Wolf tried opening the files to the Solar Wind's data stores. The whole system froze up.

"Solar Wind, what now?"

I don't know, wrote the ship. Then the writing disappeared; the console flashed in frantic colours.

"Wolf!" Jon Marsden stormed down the stairs to the machine room.

"Yes, sir?"

"What is happening?"

"Don't know, sir. I think the Solar Wind's processor is timing out after a too-large download from the Central Crystal."

"How? I thought the Central Crystal was in love with her!"

A huge surge pulsed through the ship; there was a resounding pop, and then silence. They stared at each other. Ailyss came rushing down the stairs.

"What happened?"

"Solar Wind's processor gone poof," said Jon Marsden.

"Poof?" repeated Ailyss, shocked. "*Processor* gone *poof?*"

"That's what I said."

Ailyss ran her hand over the dark console screen.

"Restart her?"

Jon Marsden thought for a few seconds. This was reaching several years back.

"She ought to restart after fifteen seconds," he said. "That is, if anything's left."

The Captain descended the stairs.

"Wolf, Jon – is it what I fear it is?"

"We'll know in fifteen seconds," said Marsden.

Federi sauntered into the machine room, whistling a tune. Radomir

Lascek glared at him.

"There you are, all of you! Mission accomplished," said the Tzigan optimistically. "Sorted that darned Crystal. Captain, the Morrigan is not going to haunt us any further." He glanced at the dark console. "And now? What's with the Solar Wind?"

"Federi," said Radomir Lascek gravely, "*what precisely* have you done with the Central Crystal?"

"Blown it to bits," said Federi with a smug grin. "Smithereens. Shrapnel. *Kaboom!* Don't want to be the one who has to clear up the splinters!"

"You've *blown up the Central Crystal?*"

"Yes! So we can have our ship back! Captain, personally myself, I won't tolerate someone blackmailing my friends into suicidal thoughts!"

"So you did what you do best and killed it! And it took the Solar Wind with it," said Radomir Lascek.

Federi took an involuntary step back. "What?!"

The ship lay bobbing upon the choppy waves of the Pacific. Finally, waves again! It was what Paean had been longing for. She towel-dried her hair on her way to the Assassin's Cabin, in clean jeans and tee after a hot bath.

It was nice to be back aboard. She was prepared to forgive Captain all sorts of chains and nonsense. He had only meant to keep her out of trouble.

She closed the door behind herself and glanced at her Federi. He was sitting on the bunk, his knees drawn up, his face hidden in his arms.

"Federi, what's wrong?"

He looked up. Paean stared. He looked like hell!

"Come, little luv. Was just waiting for you!" He got to his feet. Paean's heart cramped. He looked broken. She threw down the damp towel from her hair in the hammock and went into his arms. Federi activated his teleporter, and they arrived in the Comet. Federi let her go and programmed something into the console.

"What's wrong, Federi?" asked Paean.

"Finally done it," he growled as the jet curved away over the sea. "Terminated a friend."

She stared at him wide-eyed. A moment of flying ceramic plates flashed through her mind. Oh hell! Dared she ask? She had to, she realized. It would drive her nuts.

"Whom, Federi?"

"The Solar Wind," he sighed and checked the course of the Comet.

Paean whistled her relief. At least it was only the Solar Wind, not one of her brothers, or Wolf, or Ailyss... or Captain...

"She was a friend," said Federi softly. "Maybe she was only an artificial intelligence, little luv. Without ethics, anna bottle! But she was my friend."

Paean put her hand on his arm. "Why?"

"Not why, little songbird," he replied morosely, "how. She died when I executed that blasted, forsaken, three times cursed Central Crystal! He sent her a shockwave that wiped her processor clean."

"But then it was he who killed her, not you!"

Federi didn't answer. Paean found herself a co-pilot seat, staring at the endless blue moving past below. She thought of the Solar Wind and her subversion, her sensors in every cabin, her selling out the whole crew for a shady entity she had just met. She thought of her home in the Cabin of Dreams, which was shot to hell because the Solar Wind had induced her to teleport after Dana. She wondered quietly whether it wasn't better that way. She moved her seat along the floor and aligned it with Federi's and grabbed his hand, interlacing her fingers with his.

"You're seeing it wrong, little luv," said the Tzigan quietly. "The Solar Wind was a friend. She was waking up to her own perceptions, her own processes, even emotions. We all make mistakes when we dabble in that kind of stuff."

"I didn't," said Paean defiantly.

Federi smiled briefly. "You did specifically, Paean! Married an assassin who murders his friends," and the momentary smile dropped off his face again.

Paean put her arms around him and clung. He ruffled her hair listlessly. "Taking you to Southern Free," he said. "Not to Marge though. Don't want to hear anything from Captain anymore! Done with this gig."

The Comet streaked away into the blue sky. Dana followed it with her eyes.

"Hang, there goes the jet!"

"What do you need the jet for?" asked Perdita behind her.

"Tugging the planet! I've enabled it for that!"

"Use the Probe," advised Perdita. "Leave those two alone."

"I can have the Probe?"

"*No,* Dana. You may *use* the Probe. I'm coming along."

Dana shrugged. "It's not urgent, really, Boudaceia." She noted with satisfaction how the Golden Honey ground her teeth.

Solar Wind Log, 24 November 2116

We held a memorial for the Solar Wind's consciousness today. She died in action, while Federi terminated that parasitic intelligence that referred to itself as the Central Crystal or Morrigan. The vile entity sent a shockwave deleting the Solar Wind's consciousness. Marsden and Wolf are still trying to resurrect the processor; but what does that mean? It's not going to bring back her personality.

I was extremely privileged to have a true artificial intelligence aboard for this while. Let me add here that whoever programmed her ethics needs to be pulled up severely; she had none! The pirate vessel herself, a pirate! If we ever manage to coax forth another true consciousness from her CPU, I shall definitely take a hand in programming her for obedience!

I also need to mention here that Federi terminating the Central Crystal was not in the protocol, and while he was not breaching any direct orders, he was contravening the agreement we made with the Morrigan to keep the parasite aboard at no harm to us. Federi jumped ship after wreaking this; he took Paean with him. It falls to me to explain to her concerned brothers. How I could have allowed that association in the first place, eludes me now.

Dana has towed home a planet that is now orbiting Earth and wreaking havoc with the tides! What more madness?? We are facing storms and high seas, and without any electronic functions available, our skills as sailors are being taxed. But none of us is prepared to trade in the old vessel for a modern ship, as Federi suggested in a moment of scorn. She is my ship and has been for twenty years, and there is no such thing as trading her off. Even without her consciousness it would be like selling out a family member. Which is something that doesn't seem to bother the Tzigan in any way.

We seem to have spent more time in space than is accounted for *here on Earth. By the Solar Wind's internal clock it was at least two months and should have been late December by now; however my bases all inform me that the date as noted above, 24th November 2116, is correct. It is not impossible that the Morrigan has led us through a time discontinuum; more likely however that he messed with the Solar Wind's internal clock while we were lost in space. Of course there's no accounting for how much relative space warp has to do with it – I haven't personally studied that effect in-depth, apparently going far out into space and returning makes one younger, if the hypotheses of an Earth-bound nineteenth-century physicist working from pure mathematical theory are to be taken seriously.*

The going without Federi is going to be tough. He was one of my most able and competent sailors. But I have to add that nobody plots a mutiny behind my back any longer… yoy, is life going to be boring!

R. Lascek (Pir. Capt.)

24 November 2116
(Earth Time)

Hey, Katya.

Things look a bit different with food in your stomach and after a good night's sleep.

Still heartbroken about the Solar Wind. Wish I hadn't been so nasty to her before she died. This will stick with me forever.

Actually surprised how long I slept. Little Paean watched over me. Made me supper from the dehydrated cardboard rations on the Comet; made me breakfast from fresh mussels she picked off the rocks. What she sees in old Federi I have no idea. Here we are, in the old camping grounds by the Knysna lagoon, Southern Free. Slept next to the campfire; it rained in the night, but that didn't wake me up. Paean organized a tarpaulin, for us to sleep under. One of those lightweight, snap-open ones. I forgot what a competent girl she is.

She insisted on leaving a message on the ship. So they know they can call us. Well, they can call her! My wrist-com has been left behind...

When I left the dead ship I made a vow. Oh hell, Katya, it's not a new vow. But the time is now. Falco's curse is beginning to take me over. I've got to end things, fast. Don't want the curse skipping to any sons or daughters of ours. Going to terminate the Unicate now. Starting in Vlaşta. And this time I shall not rest until there is nothing left of the Unicate except the memory.

Paean can come with me or stay back with her brothers, whatever. Don't want to put her in danger. But I know, she's going to want to come along...

Missing you more than ever
Federi

25
Ship

Shawn hung in Ailyss' cabin door. The spy looked up and flashed him a quick smile.

"Tarot, Ailyss?"

She beckoned him in.

"What do your cards say?" pressed Shawn. "Lemme see?"

Ailyss pointed thoughtfully to the spread in front of her.

"Deception," she said. "All is not as it seems! There are forces on the move. But see that shaft of sunlight over here – there are surprises too."

"Sounds like life," replied the thirteen-year-old philosophically.

Ailyss smiled at him. "You miss Paean, don't you."

"She'll be back," said Shawn with unwavering confidence. "And Federi too."

"Federi?" Ailyss shook her head. "Doubt it, Shawney! He's had enough. You didn't see his face!"

"He'll be back the second Captain has his next crisis," grinned Shawn.

Ailyss peered sharply at him. That was a thin grin! He was using the front of unwavering faith to cover up his fear and his sadness. She had seen him do the same thing when she and Jon Marsden had returned from that death mission and there hadn't been any word from Paean or Federi.

"Shawn," she said gently. "You don't always have to be so strong! It's okay to be sad!"

"You know, Ailyss," replied Shawn Donegal, "I do have to be.

Because faith is a force. If I stop believing that they will be back – heck, they may end up not coming back!"

"You can always teleport to them," said Ailyss.

"Och aye." Shawn sighed dramatically. "I can. Whether they'd like that is on another card altogether…"

"Someone get that darned planet out of the Earth's gravitational field!"

Radomir Lascek shook his fist at the small celestial body that hung over Earth, no larger than a florist pin's head. That pinhead was enough to disrupt the tides into riptide upon riptide! And the pinhead who'd planted the planet there – couldn't she have foreseen it? Except that she probably had – but she simply didn't care.

Running the Solar Wind the old way was a challenge to the pirate. Radomir Lascek had become reliant on the automatic fine-tuning of the sails and solar cells. Now his remaining sailors were fully occupied. He thanked his lucky stars for the invention of the croaches – although they weren't centrally controlled by the Solar Wind now, they were still intelligent enough to do the chores they had been designed for: Scrubbing the decks and the cabins, keeping the galley running, preparing food and cleaning up. Because his crew was scant.

Sure, Johnny Anyhow shaped up beautifully, pulling his full weight; Rhine Gold was an ace sailor, and Ronan was turning out very useful indeed. Nothing like hard physical labour to keep people's minds off depression, thought Lascek. Shawn was standing in for Federi, bravely trying to fill the spot the gypsy would have taken flying the Solar Wind. No storm was necessary, thank you, with the processor gone; but that darned planet was creating such disruption in the Earth's atmospheric and sea currents, storms came by the dozen. And submerging was not possible any longer. Neither was folding down the rigging. And so flying had become a daily pleasure for the remaining skeleton crew. Something about this niggled at Lascek but he couldn't nail it. They'd just have to carry on this way until they had made it to Prime Base.

It was lucky that the Solar Wind's rig had not been folded away at the time Federi assassinated her, thought Lascek. That way at least they had electricity, and they could move by wind power. Manually furling and unfurling was not so difficult once the electronic control had been removed; annoying, sure, because they had to furl the sails by tacking on extra lashings and wrapping the surplus around the booms instead of the sails furling into the booms or around stays as they should. She looked like a real pirate ship by now: Messy and unruly. But if the rigging had been folded up against the deck, getting the hooks open to release it would have been an impossibility.

Dr Jake was rewiring the drives for manual operation. Once he had managed to complete the override, they would have a somewhat easier time. Wolf and Jon Marsden were fully occupied trying to resurrect the Solar Wind's CPU. And Ailyss…

She had become his eyes and ears, the way Rushka had been, because his daughter had been fetched back aboard, but she was sick – very sick. Doc Judith had her hands full; Doc Vera turned into an errand boy, flying out with the Probe every so often to stock up on diverse medications from the various bases. Actually they ought to get the specialist obstetrician from Island Base; but he, too, had his hands full with births and early childhood niggles at the base. And Paean, who always had such a calming effect on the sick, and was handy to send around – she was away, she had jumped ship with Federi. So Ailyss gauged the crew morale, did lookout duty, stood her watch on deck to man the sheets, and helped to run it all smoothly.

Perdita was invaluable too, standing in for the First Mate. Marsden had made noises that he wanted to fetch Michelle, but there had simply not been the time. He was needed on deck, hands-on with the sails as one of the most experienced sailors on the ship. Lascek often moved in amongst the crew himself to teach them and take control; then Perdita had to be helmsman, which she did admirably.

Lascek glared at the innocuous white cloud puffs that were gathering in the south again. South, east, west, north – they would come from anywhere, as things stood at present. He had no idea how this was to continue; he suspected that places like Japan and Sumatra were experiencing tidal waves, but without the processor they were also cut off from the satellite news.

The thing was of course to ask the Admiral for another processor. Radomir Lascek ground his teeth and dug in his heels. Like hell would he do that! As long as there was a hope of resurrecting the Solar Wind and her conscious mind...

"Get that darned planet away from there!" he thundered again, at no-one in particular.

"Sure, Radomir. Whatever makes you happy," said Dana sweetly behind him.

He turned, just in time to see her teleporting out.

Pink and golden waves crashing onto the shore. Far too large waves; even here, the planet was disrupting the tides. Paean stared at them, idly sifting the cool white sand through her fingers, her head resting against Federi's shoulder, his arm tightly around her.

It had been a strange week. The gypsy didn't say anything; conversation was reduced to grunts. She hung close at times and gave him space to be alone at others, observing his body language for cues. She made food and coffee on the fire; found him angling in the lagoon with a simple forked stick and a loaf of bread and left him to it, but he had brought two large flat fish back to the campsite. Nights they slept like that time on the death mission, huddled together for emotional security. Silently. Platonically.

She knew that this wasn't the holiday he meant to take with her, the honeymoon. He was too cut up. She was sad too. It was hard to believe that, for a while, they'd had a genuine artificial intelligence on the ship; that the Solar Wind had been alive. And now she was just a ship again. She'd never just be a ship again for Paean; she was a corpse. How Captain and the others could continue using her hull as a vessel was more than Paean could understand.

Federi sighed, tightened his grip around her shoulders and rested his cheek on her hair.

"My Paean."

And that was all again for the next few hours.

*

Dana materialized on the Probe. Old Sherman smiled at her, taking a thoughtful puff on his pipe.

"Oh, hello, Sherman! Didn't know you were here!"

"Thought you might like some company," said the old sailor amiably.

"I'd like some advice," replied Dana. "Radomir's making everyone morose. What are the customs on Earth? Do I put a dart in him or give him antidepressant, or do I just shoot him?"

Sherman Dougherty laughed.

"That planet," he said. "Once it's out of the way he'll be easier."

"Out of the way where?" asked Dana. "There's no way I'll be putting it back into the Rosetta Nebula! And I've positioned it where it won't affect other orbits."

"For now," said Sherman, "I'd park it in the orbit of Venus. Only until the ice on it has melted. We have to be careful, we don't want to evaporate its oceans. Once its ice age has passed, position it opposite Earth."

"Meaning?"

"In Earth's orbit, but on the other side of the sun. In the Goldilocks zone. Then it can be colonized."

"Colonized? It contains a treasure!"

"I'm wondering if the planet is not the treasure," said Sherman Dougherty.

Dana cocked her head. He might have a point!

"Three sisters," she said thoughtfully. "Two empires. Dome, and New Dome. The third, the youngest, comes away empty-handed. Why did Brid and the Morrigan go to such trouble deceiving Boudaceia into believing there is no treasure? Because it was Dana's, that's why! Maybe Boudaceia was the greedy, grabbing one?"

"Unlikely," said Sherman. "But I haven't met her personally. Not quite that old."

"Come," said Dana, turning to the console. "Put out that stinky piece of plum tree you've got there, and close the hatch. Let's go!"

The Probe sped away into the clouded skies, towards the frozen planet.

*

Darkness had fallen in Southern Free. Paean rekindled the fire and roasted some more fish that Federi had speared, on the end of a stick. Federi built up a small pile of rocks, silently took the stick out of her hand and built it in between the stones so it held itself.

On the far end of the caravan park, two old alcoholics were having a private party involving a lot of bottles. Earlier today he'd seen Paean going over there to talk to them; she had gone with her head high and her face full of smiles, and returned with her shoulders sagging. She had found out that they were quite comfortable in their discomfort zone and didn't want to improve anything at all, thank you. Too much effort. He could have told her as much.

He returned to her side, sat down and put his arm around her shoulders, thankful for her unassuming presence and her respecting his silence. And then he glanced at her face in shock.

"Little luv?"

Silent tears were streaking down her cheeks.

"Aw!" Federi sighed. " 's alright, my little songbird. She was a person. 's alright to cry for her."

Paean shook her head.

"Sure, I miss the Solar Wind," she mumbled. "But I miss you more."

"What?" He pulled her into his arms. "What do you mean?"

"You've got to come back," said Paean. "You've still got a life!"

He sighed. And realized how his grieving had become a comfort zone. It was easier to bury himself in grief and push everything else away than face his life. His mind was comfortably numb from thinking in circles, over and over, about the last conversations he'd failed to have with the Solar Wind, and the way he'd literally sold her out to the Morrigan instead of standing up for her and protecting her, as was his duty.

And along with his life and his duties, he was pushing his wife away. He had shown her hardly any love in the past week, though he'd just had a gruelling time before that, fearing that she might be dead. How empty life had been without her, even if it had only been a few days. Strangely, the Solar Wind had got home much faster than she'd taken to get to the treasure planet. The Morrigan, of course.

Well, that scourge was gone from Earth. Atlantis might be returning to their senses too. They might thank him eventually. And the Solar Wind -

Well, after all she had only been a ship. Even her mindset had been that of a ship. How could it be different? A little servant, not much more intelligent than her croaches. A friend? She hadn't had the time to become one yet.

And that took him to the sweet young woman next to him. She had given up her childhood – or what remained of it – to be with him. The way she looked after him; he was suddenly certain that not many wives went about looking after their men with such thoughtful tenderness. She had been doing it almost from the time she had boarded the Solar Wind. He remembered a gloomy moment on the bridge, after Hamilton, when Captain had ordered him to sail the ship straight back into that spider's nest of Stabilizers. Paean had brought him coffee, a little gesture of sweetness, an excuse to check whether he was alright.

He hadn't known, when he had first caught her eye in that seedy tavern in Dublin, what a wonderful carer she would turn out to be. If she'd been a spoilt little brat, he'd still have been head-over-heels about her; but this...

He reached for her hand, his fingers closing over it.

"I'm yours, Paean."

The feeling of unreality of the past week lifted as she gazed at him with lucent eyes. He reached out and touched the soft curls that fell across her cheek.

"Sorry that I've been so – away."

She nodded. Apology accepted.

His thoughts turned to the future. They were free. His term on the Solar Wind had been served out; he never meant it to end this way, but it had, and it was over. But the sea and her rocking would always be a part of him. He was Tzigan; but he was also a sailor. And so was Paean. It was in their blood by now.

A yacht! That was the answer. Then they'd never have to make a choice where to build a house, or whether to live the nomadic and sometimes harsh life of the Tzigany. They'd raise their children on their own houseboat. The little tykes would learn to swim before they could walk. Little black-eyed girls and boys with Paean's wild curls and her sparkly nature. Maybe a few redheads amongst them? How many of them? He wasn't sure.

He'd build a puppet theatre for them on the deck, complete with proper kiddie-sized beanbag seats and curtains and a ticket station and all. He'd make one cabin into a playground, with slides and jungle gyms and a pit full of soft toys. He'd build them proper cots to sleep in so they wouldn't fall out at night. And he'd make them wear reflector clothing all the time so he'd spot immediately if one went overboard. With built-in teleporters that would flash them back aboard on contact with water. Reflector nappies, on hot summer days. Proper space kids.

But first he'd go around the world with Paean. He still wanted her for himself for a while. Kids could wait, anna bottle!

"How would you like it," he began.

Paean's wrist-com sprang into life. They both stared at it in irritation. Federi took hold of it. His eyebrows shot up.

"Captain!"

"There you are, Tzigan! Hells, you and coms! I call you on yours and end up having a very odd conversation with Bridget of Dome!"

"She needed it, Captain. In case of a contingency…"

"I'm the one who's got the contingency!" snapped Lascek. "This is no time to honeymoon! Come back aboard! You can have your holiday later!"

"This is no honeymoon!" growled Federi. It could have been one, very nearly, a second back. If Captain hadn't destroyed it.

"Call it whatever you like," retorted Lascek. "I've got to go to Honolulu and discuss things with the Admiral. Marsden's occupied trying to patch what you've broken on the Solar Wind. Perdita's too green to take charge, and Rushka's too sick!"

Rushka was sick? "Yes, Captain. We'll be there on the double."

Federi shut off the com and looked up at Paean, who was staring at him in disbelief.

"We're going back?"

"Little luv – you heard…" He pulled her back into his arms. Blast, he'd done it again! "Aw hell, can't they just cope without Federi for a while? Rats on them! With fleas."

"Can't we eat first?" There were still tears in her voice.

"Course! Darned, the contingency can't be all that contingent! He can wait with his Admirality's Visit."

"You took your time!"

What a welcome, thought Paean acidly. She watched as Federi, deliberately upbeat, smiled at the Captain and took over the bridge. Radomir Lascek left the gypsy in charge and went down to the deck, where Wolf, Rhine Gold and Ronan were mobilizing the Stormrider for him.

Unreal, the way the sea reflected and glittered in the mid-morning light, when they had just arrived out of the after-supper evening of Southern Free. Halfway around the Earth; literally. So after days of sun and wind, looking after the needs of a deeply depressed husband, here came a work day on the Solar Wind, without a night separating the two. She frowned. Right now she couldn't have felt more out of sorts if someone had pulled her out of the shower for something really random.

Jon Marsden ought to be going along, thought Federi disconnectedly, watching the procedures on the deck. But Jon was in the machine room, trying to revive the Solar Wind's processor.

Federi didn't believe he had much of a chance. The processor, perhaps. Then the dead ship would have a functional computer again. But to get her personality back? She had been alive. You could resurrect a dead person too, if you did it fast enough – and then you had a brain-dead live corpse hanging on life support machines until the body died. Necromancy, in his books!

Paean shifted in next to him, pulling her chair close enough that he could put his arm around her shoulders. He was going to get addicted to that, he thought. What were they doing back aboard? - Just standing in, he promised himself. Next time they escaped, he'd make sure Paean's wrist-com got left behind too. And he'd disconnect the Comet's coms system. He'd reprogram their teleporters so the others didn't recognize them. Heck, no! He'd chuck them in the sea! Who needed teleporters? The Comet was fast enough any day! He rolled his eyes. He'd have to disconnect their genetic signatures from their bodies to become invisible to Captain now!

Shawn stuck his freckled face onto the bridge.

"Hey! You're back!"

His huge grin compensated for quite a few things, thought Paean.

"Did Captain have a crisis then?" he asked with a cheeky smirk. Federi snorted.

"Ever known him without a crisis?" he commented under his breath.

Shawn bit his lip, swallowing back the witty response. Disrespect was a fine line; it was one thing if Federi made such comments about Captain, but that didn't mean Shawn could.

"Don't worry, Pae," he said instead. "They'll get the Solar Wind back together! Wolf and Mr Marsden – they're geniuses."

Paean smiled at him. Federi peered at the blue waters ahead, refraining from commenting. He wasn't into popping balloons.

"But Rushka's been asking for you," added the young Donegal.

"She's not looking well."

"Poor Rushka!" Paean got up out of Federi's grip with a sigh. "Where is she?"

"Sick Bay," said Shawn.

Paean followed her little brother down to the infirmary, wishing fervently that they could have continued their holiday. Because it hadn't been an escape. Federi would never escape. His life belonged to Captain. And therefore, how could it ever belong to her? All she could do was wait patiently for the scraps. She cursed herself for feeling so angry about it.

Federi glared at the deck. Hawaii's green line graced the horizon to starboard. The ship's sails were furled - manually; "wrapped" described it better. The anchor was down, so what was he needed back aboard for? Surely they could handle the ship lying anchored? He counted. Three sailors on the deck. All under twenty. Fine. He was back in order to supervise them, once again! Nursery school teacher as usual. He wondered if he ought to build them a puppet theatre.

He gazed at the sea. And scowled. The surf was a mess. Where swells usually came in moderately predictable patterns, twos, threes, even up to sixes on stormy days, there was none. The mean wave height was nothing that could be determined; from stretches of complete calm to bouts of being shaken and rattled by choppy waves, today there was everything. The sky reflected this with a load of sunlit fluffy-bunny clouds; the type Federi knew to distrust. And to complicate it for the crew, every so often a fairly massive, storm-sized wave splashed up against or over the deck. The handhold lines were out; all the sailors were working with lifelines, and he saw why. The planet had messed up the tides something awful. Uh-huh. He understood why he had to be aboard.

And Paean had been stolen from him by the call of Sick Bay. That was another thing. She'd never get over that, would she. He'd have to find those people who were inventing those new viruses and put an end to *them*. Ghosts to rest!

He peered into the distance to port, where the clouds came rolling across the sea. The Earth's new satellite had vanished; presumably Dana had gone to find a more suitable spot for it. But the tides would take some time to stabilize. And there, on the horizon, he saw the silhouette of another ship.

Federi stepped outside the bridge onto the command deck, took out his binoculars and had a closer look. That ship was listing badly; it looked damaged. The worse for the unpredictable waves. But it wasn't sending any distress signals. Strange!

And then the distress signals reached him, and he understood. The ship was indeed sending out signals; the Solar Wind couldn't pick them up! But his gypsy radar did.

He returned to the bridge and punched the intercom. Rats, that was dead too! In one swift move he was back out on the step, cupping his hands to his mouth.

"Sailors! Raise the anchor! Hoist the sails! Set course due west! There's a ship in trouble out there!"

Rhine Gold, who was closest, looked up and grinned.

"Federi! You're back!"

Ronan, a bit further away, looked up too. "Huh?"

Johnny Anyhow hadn't heard him at all over the wind.

Federi raised his voice and put the Demon behind it.

"You scurvy mates! Get cracking! Hoist those rotten sails! Get this accursed hull moving west! Right now!"

That tone of voice brought Paean, Shawn, Perdita and Ailyss storming to the deck as well as shocking the three men on deck into action.

"That's better," smiled Federi. He beckoned to Paean, who moved up the steps. He pulled her close. Leading this double life was beginning to stretch him! He needed to get her off the ship.

"That ship over there is in trouble," he said, pointing. "You take the helm, little luv. Bear down directly, then pull up alongside. I know you can. You steered the Silver Bullet. 'xactly the same with the Solar Wind. Let the men control the sails, they've got more muscle. I'm going to scout ahead on the Comet."

"Yes, sir!" grinned Paean. Federi kissed her and released her. "Be careful," she implored.

"Always." He ran down onto the deck and boarded the Comet.

The ship was lying too low in the water. She seemed to be shipping water every time she rolled. Federi took the jet low over her deck. A small trader; the Comet nearly touched the rigging. The deck was empty. Nobody on the bridge, either. He tagged the jet to the ship. Submachine gun in hand, he climbed out of the hatch and dropped down onto the deck.

The last time he'd done this, he had been cornered and nearly eaten by mutants. His left hand closed on the teleporter in his pocket. Why was he doing this? It had nothing to do with him! He was endangering his fragile, halcyon future with yon little redhead on yonder white ship! He shook his head at himself as he descended down the hatch. Once a rescue worker, always a darned rescue worker!

The smell hit him first. His hand flew to cover his mouth and nose to stop the gag reflex. He had smelt death before. This had been a messy death – and not only one! He moved through the lounge, side-stepping those broken, mangled bodies, sharpening his look-out. It looked like Unicate dogs had been amongst the Tzigany! But not too recently. Those bodies were decomposing.

Two days, it struck him. In the tropics, all it took was two days for meat to reach this point of decay. Was whatever had wreaked this, still aboard? He had to count on it.

But his gypsy radar still registered the distress calls. He followed where it wanted to lead him, and came to a locked cabin door. He knocked.

Suddenly the silence was loaded. Federi turned, his gun ready. There was nothing behind him. He turned back and knocked again, keeping his eyes on the surrounds. And then he gathered up his voice and said quietly through the closed hatch, "is there someone in there?"

A girl's whimper carried through the air vent. Then silence once again. Federi took out his card trick and broke the lock on the hatch, and entered, scanning the surrounds and glancing back with his gun to check that nothing entered behind him, and nothing hovered above the hatch. He pulled it shut behind himself.

On the deck lay a girl; fourteen, he'd estimate her, maybe even younger. Her eyes were open; she was staring at him in terror. There was another person in that cabin too, realized Federi; or possibly, another body. The only thing that was visible of him was some mangled piece of limb sticking out under a toppled cabinet.

The Free Gypsy knelt down at the young girl, then realized that the fear was meant for his gun. He lowered it.

"Be calm, girl. Federi's not here to harm you!"

This seemed to discharge some of her fear. She stared at him mutely. There was something incredibly familiar about her face. Her mousy-blonde hair was matted and dull; but those round blue eyes he had seen before, he was prepared to bet on it!

"Are you hurt?" he asked.

"Are there any – more survivors?" she gasped.

"Except for you?"

She motioned at the cabinet with the bloody limb under it. "He's alive," she gasped. "Could still – hear him, little while – back. Please

– don't leave him to die!"

Federi glanced at the evidence of another potential survivor. "We'll get him out under there," he promised. "Are you hurt?"

"Think I injured my back," said the girl in gasps of pain. "Can't move." She grabbed his sleeve imploringly. "Got to follow her," she begged. "She's got my father!"

That American accent also rang a loud bell, as did the timbre of her voice. "Who's got your father?"

"The Merwynn. She and her sisters – abducted – my father."

"Why?"

"He's the – Captain."

Federi sat back on his haunches and thought for a second. Help was needed here. Johnny Anyhow, Ailyss and Jon Marsden. He'd be scared to ask any of the others.

"What's your name, girl?" he asked to keep her talking.

"Mindy – Adamson."

Adamson! That name didn't sound familiar in any way. Maybe he was wrong. After all, one *gadchey* looked like another, he thought with irony…

"Well, Mindy, help is on the way." He glanced at the porthole. "There's the Solar Wind pulling up alongside!"

Mindy's blue eyes went wide with terror.

"The *Solar Wind?*"

"Yes!" Federi frowned. "Something wrong with that?"

"She'll find us again! She's hunting for – the Solar Wind," said Mindy.

"Why?"

"Don't know." Mindy panted, fighting for breath. Federi wondered if her lungs were injured too. His mind spun about how to get her across to the Solar Wind. A broken back should never be moved!

354

"I'm scared of the Solar Wind," added Mindy plaintively.

"Why?"

"Dad said… Worst pirates - on all Earth's oceans. Captain keel-hauls people just for – fun!"

"*Shesti,*" snapped Federi. "Total gummybungle. Girl, do you even know who the Solar Wind is? …was," he corrected himself glumly. He activated his com, that the Captain had made him wear the moment he'd stepped back aboard. "Jon, come in. Ailyss. And Anyhow. We've got a situation."

26
Alive

Federi teleported with Mindy Adamson to the Solar Wind's infirmary and put her down on the prow-side bunk, the left one, where Wolf had lain incapacitated. The blinds were drawn. On the bunk opposite lay Rushka. Federi turned and stared at his foster sister.

"Hey, Rush! What have they done to you?"

"Don't know, Federi," groaned the pregnant beauty. "I was fine while I was at Marge! Something about this ship…"

"Then they should get you the hell back to Marge!" fumed Federi.

"Father says he needs me aboard."

"For what? For feeling sick?"

"To keep Ronan in line," said Verushka Donegal.

"What, is he a toddler?" Federi shook his head impatiently. He returned his attention to Mindy.

"I'm calling our ship's doctor," he informed her. Except that, rats, Doc Judith had gone with Captain!

That little white hand shot out and grasped at his sleeve.

"Please, mister…"

Gypsy eyebrows arched. Sheer, her face looked *so* familiar!

"Please try to find all the survivors on the Golden Walrus," she begged. "Please don't stop until you know you've looked everywhere!"

"Of course, Mindy!"

"Only – they're family," said Mindy. "Not biologically, but you know…"

Federi shook his head with a sigh. "Poor Mindy! Listen, can you

give me a list of names? At least so we can see how many there are?
Then we'll know if we found them all."

She nodded.

"Let Shawn write it down for you," said Federi and called the
youngest Donegal on the ship com.   "He can send it through to me.
Going to salvage." He turned to go.

"And please, mister…"

Federi turned back again.

"Please find my father," she completed.   "Captain Adamson!
Follow that Merwynn!"

Federi nodded. "I'll do my best, Mindy Adamson."

How was he going to do that?, he mulled as he moved back up to
the deck and across to the Walrus where his team was waiting for him.
Paean, the little genius, had put out the sea anchor so that both ships
didn't drift too much. It also helped stabilise the Walrus, though that
ship tugged heavily on the Solar Wind's mooring lines, more so with
the large waves that happened erratically.

How should he trace a Merwynn? What on Earth was a Merwynn
anyway? And traces were impossible to find on the ocean. His main
reason for being a sailor, anna bottle!

But… wait. He had a teleporter. Except that he didn't have
Mindy's father's biofield. But he did have it in part - in Mindy. After
all, Dana had found Rushka based on half a biofield. Or… had she?
He'd have to ask Wolf how that worked, and how to set the teleporter.

They went back for the man who was stuck under the cabinet.
Ronan, Rhine Gold and Johnny Anyhow moved the cabinet off the
man and Federi dragged him out under it.

He'd expected a squashed mess; but surprisingly, except for the
foot, the man was uninjured. Federi glanced at the heavy metal
cupboard and saw the whole logic. The centre part, under which the
man had been lying, had its door opened all the way, and its contents

removed. He had been hiding in that hollow, relying that the cupboard would be too heavy for his assailants to lift.

Federi gestured and the three younger sailors let the cabinet down again. Ronan and Rhine Gold had come with Johnny because Ailyss had been occupied in the machine room alongside Jon Marsden, trying to resurrect the Solar Wind – and Federi didn't even want to recall Marsden's response when he'd called him to help here.

"Phew! What's in that thing?" commented Ronan as they lowered the cupboard back to the deck. "Gold bars?"

Federi shot him a sharp glance. He thought he could guess. They'd come back and loot whatever there was. But this man – oh hell. If Doc could save his foot – if Doc could save *him*, she was a miracle worker.

The man's eyes fluttered half-open and he muttered something. Federi leaned closer.

"What did you say?"

"Save Mindy," came the barely intelligible mumble.

"Already got her," replied Federi.

"And the... Captain," added the man.

Federi nodded, though he had no idea how he'd do that.

"Name's Derrick," the man added and his eyes flipped backwards, and he sank back into unconsciousness. Federi tried to think exactly where on the Solar Wind he'd put him down. Dana was out planet-hunting. Paean's old cabin had been a second infirmary before. Anyhow could jolly well share with Dana. They didn't need two cabins. Basta. He programmed the teleporter, included Derrick into the field and positioned him with assassin's accuracy on that bunk in which Paean had lain sleeping in bunny pyjamas. And he pulled the second low bunk out of the bulkhead opposite. In case they found more.

They only managed to salvage one more man from the ship, half dead. He had a mangled abdomen and was barely alive, and unconscious. Federi didn't have much hope for him as he teleported him to the bunk opposite Derrick's.

He collected Luigi, Leila and Lisa on his way out, teleported back to the Walrus and sent the three croaches to sniff for any further signs of life. A short while later all three reported back with a negative to him where he was systematically searching for survivors. Johnny and Ronan didn't have any better luck either. Federi gave up. He instructed Ronan and Anyhow to carry as much of the cargo across as they could manage, and returned with the croaches to the Solar Wind.

As he peered at the Golden Walrus from the Zephyr's deck, he could see that the ship would not last the night. It was creepy – from a dead hull that was so damaged that it was going to be gone by the morning, back to another dead hull, intact but brain-dead. He teleported back belowdecks to the infirmary to quiz Mindy Adamson.

Paean was already there, with a syringe, injecting the blonde girl. The relief that spread over Mindy's face, told its own story. She tensed as she spotted him, and reached for his sleeve.

"Please, mister, you've *got* to go after the Merwynn and find my father," she implored. "I remembered the name of their ship. Bronberg."

The Bronberg! Federi filed this bit of overload away along with the rest, for examining later.

"Will you tell us what happened on the Walrus?" he pressed.

"They were just suddenly there," said Mindy. "It was our first mate on the bridge, Dad and I were doing a stock take. So this *creature* comes down the companionway..."

"Sorry," interrupted Federi, "did you say they were just *suddenly there?*"

Mindy nodded.

"How long have you been at sea, girl?"

She peered at him uncertainly. "Like... all my life?" she replied. "Why?"

"And still nobody spotted their ship arriving?"

She shook her head, with a troubled expression. "Nobody saw them arrive. Their ship was suddenly next to ours and they were boarding. We heard the screams and Dad went to investigate. I hear him shout something and this *thing* comes down the stepladder..."

"What did it look like?"

"Gruesome," said Mindy. "Face something between a woman and a fish. Called itself a Merwynn and said it was looking for the Solar Wind... and for *Federi*. I ran, and Derrick pulled me into that cabin and closed the hatch, and we emptied that middle of that cupboard, because he said we should hide under it... so it fell, I tried to catch it, it fell on him and caught his foot... when I tried to catch it, there was this terrible pain and then I could only lie there... I crawled behind a crate, don't ask how, and they broke through the door, and I thought we were both dead... I heard Derrick scream under the cupboard but I was too scared to come out... then one of them sniffed for me and found me, and grabbed me and picked me up, and... they suddenly all looked at the hatch, and that thing dropped me on the floor and they all just left... as though they had forgotten that we were there. I crawled to the hatch and shoved it closed, and I tried to help Derrick but there was nothing I could do... they had ripped and chewed his foot, I think they tried to pull him out by it..."

Mindy had gone pale, and now she closed her eyes.

"You rest, see?" said Paean, taking the girl's hand in hers. "You're safe now. We'll look for your father. And Derrick will be alright."

"Please, check on him," said Mindy, her voice only an exhausted shadow.

"Will do, right away," agreed Paean, covered the girl with a storm blanket and beckoned to Federi. As they left the infirmary, she turned and nodded at Rushka. "Will be back for you inna minute," she promised.

Federi found Derrick sleeping. He checked the man's vital signs and realized that something had to happen about that leg pretty fast, or Derrick would die from wound sepsis. He found a tourniquet and tightened it high around Derrick's thigh, and then searched for and found that weird apparatus in the infirmary that Doc had used to 'cleanse' his blood from the mutant. It struck him that, if this had been the work of mutants, he'd have to watch this rescued lot. They might come back to life in nasty ways.

Paean was in there next to him, quietly rigging blood supply to the other man with the mangled abdomen. Federi's eyes met hers and he briefly touched her cheek, for which he got a passing smile, before he moved back to the infirmary to get an IV drip for Derrick as well.

"What do you make of it all?" he asked as he returned.

Paean sighed.

"Probably a mutant that survived," she said resignedly. "Will have to get cloning once again. Eels with the prioid weren't enough," and with a hopeless sigh, "now were they?"

"Why would they need a ship?" asked Federi.

"They were on that Unicate ship too," Paean commented.

Right. He thought about it. "The ship was just *suddenly there?*"

"Portals," said Paean. "Or teleportation." She turned around from her patient to bestow a dark glance on Federi. "The *Bronberg?* Who the hell would know?"

He nodded. Exactly.

"All evidence points to..." she said significantly.

"Dana," he completed gloomily. "But why would she? And why would the mutants be out searching for us? For me, specifically? She knows where I am!" He stood back from his patient. Doc should come now. *Captain* should come now. Because Tzigan had a mission. Impatiently he left the cabin and returned to the command deck.

So they were looking for him under their own steam? Did they think something in him still belonged to their ranks? And since when did they speak?

The image of the Unicate Chargette came back to him, and how the mutants had feasted on the crew. The devastation on the Walrus was horrendous – but he was missing something. It didn't quite look like the mutants' pattern.

Besides, if Paean's antivirus could clean all of Earth from haemorrhagic fever virus, how should her prioid have missed mutants? It didn't want to make sense.

His thoughts raced in a circle. Follow the *Bronberg*? The Solar Wind had used the name Bronberg once as a cover. And the Bronberg was one of Sherman's favourite story characters, the ghost ship that haunted the oceans, the mystery trader that turned into a spy, the military ship that was sunk on a mission into enemy territory and resurfaced years later at the Cape of Good Hope. The Bronberg had actually existed – he had looked it up himself in the Sherman Files, she had been a military ship from the fifties.

But there were thousands of names. Why would anyone pick that specific one? Especially if they had it in for the Solar Wind? How much did they know? He worried about this as he returned to the bridge. Dana had had plenty of time to scratch in the Files, by now. But why should she instruct her mutants – how would she *manage* to instruct her mutants... those blasted mutants weren't intelligent enough, curse them! Something else was going on here.

*

Paean returned to the infirmary, where Mindy lay sleeping, by now. Poor kid! And where Rushka lay on the other bunk, green in the face, groaning. With a bucket.

Blast. This was ridiculous.

"Come, Rushka! Get your stuff together. You're going back to Marge."

*

Federi stared out at the deck, from the bridge. The sailors were battling to close the mainsail that had come loose in the buffeting wind, and was flapping noisily and pointlessly. The topsail was furled, messily. But the wind was buffeting the open portion of the mainsail, yanking it from the sailors' hands as they struggled. The Golden Walrus pulled at the Solar Wind, destabilizing the deck. The two compounding hulls, closely tied, banged against each other. Luckily there was a bit of elasticity in compounding; still, it would damage the Solar Wind eventually. They ought to release the ships. There was nothing more to salvage on the Walrus. He wondered glumly what there was to salvage in the Solar Wind's CPU. Two dead ships. And Johnny and Ronan had returned, they were helping Rhine Gold fall over himself there on the deck. Federi checked the sun. Was it that time already?

"When Captain's back, we're off," he promised himself, his gaze far away, on the misty future.

"Federi!" Rhine Gold made his way up the steps. "What must I do with the mainsail? We're trying to reef it and it... isn't going well."

Federi relinquished the bridge with a quiet curse and followed Rhine Gold back out onto the deck to peer up into the sails. They were trying to undo the lashings that secured the sail to the boom. And they were running into the problem of jammed electronic tensioning nodes and the resultant refusal of the spidersilk sheets to budge.

The plan was of course to have the sail completely free of the boom, so that they could catch it – ha! Luffing in the wind – and tie it, manually, that huge piece of polyneosilk, to the mainmast by means of auxiliary tensioning cords. He snorted. A pathetic plan – but he couldn't think of a better one either. He climbed up into the rigging, testing each last joint to see if there were another way to loosen it. Thinking of two ice-blue eyes that had met his, down there in the infirmary. Quite as blue as the haze over the sea… He gazed dreamily across the ocean, towards Hawaii. Wait a minute...

"Why are we reefing anyway?" he shouted down. "Did I order you to reef? We need to get back to Honolulu! Untie the moorings to the Walrus! Retract the sea anchor, hoist the sails, set course due east!" He slid down to the deck by a ratline and helped Ronan and Johnny Anyhow undo the hawsers by which the Solar Wind was moored to the Golden Walrus. He gazed at the trader. That ship wasn't going to last the night.

He glanced at the bridge and saw Captain's Golden Honey on helm duty. He snorted in derision. She could have been helping for half an age. Where had she been?

Paean helped Rushka gather her stuff together.

"Whatever you forget, you can call me for it," she promised. "I'll bring it. Got this jet, see..."

"You don't look happy," commented Rushka, sitting up carefully and stabilising herself.

"I'm not, anna bottle of fish oil!" exclaimed Paean. "We'd already escaped! And here we are, back…" She sighed and turned to glance at the other girl. Sleeping.

"Okay, sister," she said to Rushka. "Let's go, before anyone can find out and object!"

Rushka levered herself cumbersomely off the bunk and allowed

Paean to stabilize her. Once she was on her feet, her colour picked up a bit. She and Paean made their way along the passage, and onto the upper crew deck, and the outer deck, through the hatch –

"Halt!"

"Federi," implored Paean, "can't you see? She's sick!"

The Romany handed his sheet to Rhine Gold. The blond sailor fastened it to the hook Federi had intended for it. The gypsy zoned in on Paean until his face was inches from hers.

"And where are you taking her?" he asked softly.

"Back to Marge," said Paean defiantly. "Paramedic's orders! She was well there. She's sick here! She's my sister by marriage. If I don't look after her, who will?"

"Federi will," said the Romany. "You realize what this means, Paean? Captain's short of crew. You and I shall have to stick!"

She nodded glumly. Federi stared intently at her, battling to come to a decision. Then suddenly he smiled. His fingertips briefly touched her cheek, and he kissed her forehead lightly.

"Brave little songbird! If you can, I can. We'll get our freedom, don't worry." He turned back to the rigging. "Hoy! Donegal! Get your scurvy backside over here, you mangy pirate!"

Ronan, who had just finished tying another line down, came closer, unsure of Federi's mood.

"What's cooking, Federi?"

"Go with your sister and your wife," ordered Federi.

"But Captain's going to –"

"Captain," said the Demon with a menacing smile, "has put me in charge! You want to give me backchat, officer?"

Ronan stared at the gypsy. "But Federi – you'll get trouble for this!"

Federi laughed. It came out sounding a little dangerous. "Officer Donegal, shall I report you to Captain for insubordination? In my capacity of acting shipmaster I am ordering you off the Solar Wind! Will you comply, Donegal?"

Ronan nodded, and smiled uncertainly. "Thanks, Federi! You're a star. Not sure how this will turn out..."

"'s fine, Ro," grinned Federi. "Remember I'm the one who gets away. With all sorts of things. Keep it in mind. Now go. Marge is waiting for you."

A few moments later the Comet streaked a bright path through the sky. Federi watched her go and shook his head, trying to dislocate that acrid mood. "Brave girl!" he muttered again, and paged Wolf from the machine room to take Ronan's place.

"He's a good guy," said Ronan appreciatively as the Comet shot towards Southern Free. Rushka's eyes were closed. Paean hoped that she would remember about the cubicle in the back.

"I know," she said, biting her lip and concentrating on the trajectory of the Comet. She peered down. Another vessel was streaking through the waters below; a very odd-looking ship. Going exactly in the opposite direction as they. And then she had passed over it, and it disappeared from the Comet's radar.

There had been something about that ship! That hull – with its patches of red mould, and its blockish design, its chimneys...

Chimneys? On a ship? How weird!

"That looked like something from the Sherman Files," commented Ronan. "From the metal era. Especially those red patches look like rust."

Paean blinked. Men could fantasize about the strangest things! They passed from day into night, and a few minutes later the lights of Southern Free appeared in the distance.

Paean didn't hover around at Marge. She made sure that Rushka was comfortable, hugged her brother and her sister-in-law, and then the motherly Marge, and got back into the Comet.

This was blasted ridiculous. Was it the third or the fourth time that they stationed Rushka ashore? When was Captain going to get the message?

A ship looking like a metal hull. With chimneys! Headed straight towards the Solar Wind. Well, they couldn't know about the Solar Wind, but the Solar Wind would know about them, any moment now. She shook her head. And then a naughty little grin started in the corner of her mouth. Here she was, in the Comet, all alone. The universe was at her fingertips! And Captain short of crew? She programmed some coordinates into the Comet.

From the coffee machine, a packet of coffee grounds watched her speculatively.

Federi walked around the lines on the deck that were all round their blocks now, tightening here, loosening there. The wind was fairly steady and came from straight ahead; they were tacking against it. Going west had been too darned smooth; for every downwind dead run there were upwind hauls for a revenge. With only four sailors, that meant that they were moving around the blocks in an endless musical chairs, giving leeway and pulling in slack. He was only glad that his Paean had got the downwind part. She would have struggled with this.

Couldn't they use the solar drives yet? Hadn't Wolf and Dr Jake finished rigging them for manual use?

Something was nagging at the back of his mind. Something he'd forgotten about in the mad heartbroken rush to get away from the Solar Wind, to gain space. Something rather critical, now that it hit him. Where were those blasted space crawlers? Or, if the Solar Wind had been right after all as Wolf insisted, the single crawler?

Had it jumped ship in the Rosetta Nebula, as Dana had hinted, just hitch-hiking from one portal to the next? Or had it got off somewhere on Planet Earth? Was there now an alien loose on his home planet? Or several aliens? His feet itched to walk that round he had been patrolling since forever; and to extend it and patrol the whole blasted planet. But right now there was simply no way he could get away.

What if the Merwynn were actually space crawlers? He shook his head. The mind boggled. Regardless what those silly crawlers were capable of turning into, he couldn't connect them in his mind to that slaughter on the Walrus. They lived on Weetie-O's and Chox-X's, for the blue in Paean's eyes. They had a *cute* component. They played pranks. There was something about them that was plain – innocuous.

Puddles of liquid lightning? A bloodbath? No. The crawlers were innocent.

"Rhine Gold! Tighten that nr 3 over there! Wolf! Nr 5! Anyhow! Give Nr 2 slack! Guys, don't you think we ought to furl the topsail?" Who had unfurled that topsail anyway? Novices, all of them! Landlubbers! Bank robbers, not proper pirates!

DEMONOS !!

Federi froze solid for a second, just dealing with the adrenaline. The blue of the sky and the sea turned black around the edges, with stars shining through. There was a rumble of thunder – but it wasn't thunder; it was the sound of galaxies colliding.

Wait! This is impossible!

Demon spawn! Face your doom!

This can't be, thought Federi. I killed you!

Clearly you did not, Demon, you only murdered the Solar Wind!

There was a clamp around his head; and a nasty cramp in his stomach that made him double over and sink to the deck. The blackness took over.

I returned your wife to you and you killed mine, raged the immortal.

Federi breathed. Carefully. Past the headache.

You're an AI program and I destroyed your main processor, he thought. The Solar Wind's processor is dead and her power is off. Where the hell are you sourcing the voltage? Where are you anchored?

I don't need an anchor, and I don't use voltage, growled the Morrigan. *I'm an immortal! I'm as alive as you are. You destroyed the Central Crystal, and with it the sum total of the Atlantean knowledge. You destroyed a civilisation, idiot. But you did not destroy me.*

Rats, thought Federi past the pain. Didn't finish the job!

Wolf was there somewhere, helping him up, leading him to the stepladder up to the command deck and making him sit down on a step.

In your own words, assassin, threatened the Morrigan, *you destroyed my wife. I have nothing left to lose and I don't care whom I take with me.*

"Drink this!" Wolf stuffed a mug into Federi's hand. The gypsy sipped the water cautiously. He could hardly see the mug, and he could hardly feel its handle, either. His fingers were numb.

I didn't kill the Solar Wind, he thought. The Central Crystal did. It sent a huge power surge to her processor when it exploded.

The darkness let up. The pain faded. There was a moment's silence. Federi took a breath and looked at the rigging, and the erratic sea, and the sailors battling. Wolf was monitoring him.

"Should maybe go down to Sick Bay, Federi. I'll ask Perdita to fetch one of the doctors from the bases."

He shook his head.

"'s not a disease, Svendsson. 's revenge. But tell Perdita..." A

369

doctor from the bases was in any case a good idea; for Derrick and the other Walrus survivors.

And the darkness folded in again. The pain retook its full force; both around his skull and in his abdomen.

I did not kill the Solar Wind! howled the Morrigan. *That download was a gift! It was all the information of Atlantis! You are lying, Demon!*

You know I'm not lying, replied Federi past the blinding pain. He was being squeezed to death. Blast about this mortal body, mutant regenerative powers or none! All he could think of now was squashed roaches and slippers.

And the Assassin moved in, with a backward glance at mortal Federi, almost disdainful; do I always have to bail you out? The pain faded as the Assassin lifted the Morrigan to eye-level, by the scruff of his neck.

You want to dance? You want to kill Federi Demonos? Others have tried…

"Come, Federi. Let's get you below. I've sent Perdita…"

Blast! "Call her back, Wolf. It's nothing – over in a minute." And rats – that break in concentration cost him the victory. The Morrigan backed away and escaped into deep space. There was no laughter this time.

Morrigan, thought Federi, you are so dead, you don't know it yet. I'll find you! And when I do…

"Take another sip!" urged Wolf. Federi absently took a sip of the luke-warm water – rats, of course the desalination and cooling system was lying still too, they'd have to fix that urgently – and watched detachedly how Rhine Gold and Johnny Anyhow scurried around the deck and the ropes like mad rats. It took him a while to return to the situation and remember that they were heading to Honolulu.

Why didn't they just…

"Furl the sails," he shouted. Wolf relayed the order, thundering it across the deck.

They stared at him as though he were insane; but they complied. It didn't matter if a madman captained the ship; the command line was intact. Federi nodded, content. They'd keep themselves busy trying to furl some sails. That malfunction was too big for him to sort out manually on the open sea; it belonged in a shipyard.

He listened intently once more. The Morrigan was gone from his head. And from his guts, thank the jellyfish! In the distance, the Comet streaked into view, and seconds later she attached to the Solar Wind. Federi laughed quietly to himself. Should have thought of it long ago! Tacking manually against the wind! Idiotic!

The hatch of the Comet opened. Federi got to his feet, giving the concerned Wolf a nod. Out of the jet spilled –

Aw, the little genius!

"Welcome aboard!" shouted Federi. "Maurice! Melanie! Michelle! And you two I don't quite remember…"

Two tall young men he couldn't recall from anywhere, both with beards and long hair. And then –

"Jodi Callum!" Federi ran and folded the petite brunette into a hug, laughing. And then he glanced up the steps into the Comet. Paean was watching with a sore little smirk in the corner of her mouth.

Federi released Jodi and moved up the steps, taking hold of Paean and kissing her with meaning. Until he could sense her losing her balance from wobbly knees. Because he never wanted her to look at him *that* way again when he gave a friend a hug. When he could break the addiction for a moment, he noted with satisfaction that the tight, sad little smile had transmuted into a dazed, open-lipped stare scattered with stars.

"You're a marvel," he murmured at her. "Captain's got enough crew now. Let's go."

Paean giggled.

"Don't be silly now, Federi! Who's to captain them?"

"Jon Marsden! He's the First Mate!"

Paean shook her head. "Federi, I made a promise to Rushka. We're standing in for them."

"Wish you hadn't," growled the gypsy. He glanced at the new arrivals, then counted. "How on Earth did you get seven into the Comet?"

"We huddled," grinned Paean. "And we stashed one of the ex-marines in the toilet. I got the feeling I could comfortably stash sixteen in there before the air becomes an issue. And by the way, Federi, I've got an idea…"

How their minds moved in synch!

"Let's jump to it then," suggested Federi.

She went back into the Comet and tagged it onto the Solar Wind. And then she tugged the Solar Wind back to the spot where the ship had been lying anchored. She went nice and slowly, taking into account that the Solar Wind's open rigging experienced wind drag.

Federi never budged from her side, his arm tightly around her shoulders. He didn't say anything. He was planning to show her Romania today. She'd love it. It should be dead easy, with the Comet. They'd go, just as soon as…

The Morrigan, still alive! So that feeling of relief that the immortal was gone, had been false! And somewhere was the stuff that had laid waste to that Golden Walrus. If that had not in fact been caused by the Morrigan himself. That darned immortal had demanded blood. What the heck was that immortal fascination with human blood anyway?

He glanced down at the blue sea and spotted the Stormrider coming towards them. Ah, Captain would be livid…

Ah no, Captain would not be livid! Blast him! Captain would be highly delighted about all the developments – except for the one where Federi hadn't finished the job. Well, Federi was going to finish the job!

Captain, it turned out, got wet. The prow wave as the Solar Wind stopped, nearly capsized the Stormrider. There was much sputtering and swearing and shaking of fists. Paean was watching it with a naughty little smirk.

"Tell me one thing, little firefly. Why did you bring Jodi?"

Paean shrugged. "Och, she wanted to come."

He frowned and wondered what was cooking there. Jodi Callum held an extremely responsible position at Ginavis 2: She led the team there. What would make her want to abandon the project just for a vacation?

He glanced down again and frowned. What the hell was that thing, coming towards the Solar Wind?

"Wanted to tell you about that weird ship," said Paean. "Ro says it looks like it's from the metal era."

Federi trained his binoculars on the vessel.

"It is," he said, the hair on his neck rising. "It's the Bronberg."

27
Merrow Code Red

Radomir Lascek saw the Bronberg at the same moment. She was coming straight at the Solar Wind with an unholy speed. She was going to ram his ship!

The Comet moved higher up, lifting the Solar Wind completely clear of the waves. The Bronberg passed through underneath, nearly in touching distance of the Stormrider. Something that sounded like the shriek of an eagle carried across from her.

A shriek of anger? Radomir Lascek trained his teleportation device on the hull of the vessel, and adjusted a little. Wolf was getting pretty smart with these programmable teleporters. And the Captain activated the button.

Dark and damp surrounded him, and a distinct smell of metal. Rust. Shapes moving towards him in the half-dark; strange, surreal shapes.

Perdita teleported in next to him, her gun ready. A second later Federi was there too, followed by Paean. All of them armed. The Captain glanced at his team.

"Good!" And he opened fire on the creatures that had almost reached them.

Federi's mutant night-vision revealed a lot more than the Captain could see, in this lightless ship hull. They were in a mess room of sorts – or it had been, long ago. This ship was a wreck! By the holes in his sneakers! This was in fact the metal hull of the ancient Bronberg, resurrected from the bottom of the sea! Seaweed and barnacles coated bulkheads and the ceiling. He glanced down. They were standing on drifts of seafloor sand. It was surprising that the whole thing wasn't under water...

The creatures coming towards him triggered some ancient nightmarish memories of the mutant. Some part of him shrieked in panic. The monsters seemed surprised, disoriented. In their normal instinctual sharpness they'd never have slowed down enough for his mutant reflexes to be fast enough. But their momentary hesitation and confusion as they sensed the mutant in him, bought him the split second he needed.

Merwynn. He remembered. And he, too, opened fire.

As the Merwynn went down one after the other from his, Captain's and Perdita's fire, he also took in how the monstrosities had fed... there were human remains on the deck. He hoped for little Mindy that her father wasn't amongst those.

It all fell into place. Curse that Morrigan to hell! To send Merwynn after him!

It stood to reason: He, Federi, had moved right into the home domain of the Central Crystal and blown it up with a small, measured charge. The Morrigan, wherever it had managed to hide – by now Federi was inclined to believe it the immortal story – had taken what resources it controlled: Merrows, and Merwynn, and sent them after him, to find him. It was going to destroy him; and in a way, Federi could understand the motion, in a certain sense it was self-defence, because the Morrigan knew that it was on his list.

They were two experienced killers holding each other at gunpoint. Whoever managed to kill the other first, would survive. Neither could break the cycle now – not that Federi wanted to. That thing had demanded human sacrifice, it had abducted his wife, and it had blasted apart the Solar Wind's mind. It had mind-controlled a whole civilization and messed with human DNA. It was a super-sized crook. It needed to be removed. And: its abominations along with it.

All three Atlantean sisters cloning monsters. It made sense all of a sudden.

"They're all down," he heard Perdita's comment.

"You stay here, Captain. I'm going to clear the bridge," determined Federi and moved off at a pace.

Perdita glanced at Radomir Lascek with an odd little smile. "Since when do you take orders from him?"

"He's the professional killer," commented Lascek. "Knows what he's doing. It's his playground."

"That's unkind, with respect, Captain," objected Paean and followed Federi.

The Assassin noted that snippet of conversation with an ironic smile as Federi moved out of the mess room and followed his seafarer's instinct, down a long passage, up a set of rungs, and emerged on the bridge. He scanned his surrounds with a sweeping glance. There was one more human shape, collapsed in a corner, and one more Merwynn, at the helm. By the Stars – who had trained the stuff in operating a ship console? He hadn't thought they were that intelligent!

From behind she could have been a relative of Dana's, with her luscious shock of dark-red curls all the way down her back and to the deck. Except for those dainty, diamond-tipped, webbed hands on the console. Claws, more accurately.

She turned.

"Messing with the Merwynn Macha?" she hissed in some sort of private glee.

The Assassin shot a dart into her. He disliked alliteration as an art form.

Interesting. So they were susceptible to the *valeriensis*. Enough human genes to... urgh!

"She looks as though an Atlantean woman has been crossed with a merrow," commented Paean behind him.

He turned and looked gravely at her. She had a very accurate sense of observation. And he turned to the console.

It looked suspiciously like that pillar-console in the middle of Bridget's living-room. Crystals of several different colours encrusted a flat board, in the middle of which there was an open space with a thin translucent membrane, with electric flares and flames licking across it in a never-ending plasma display.

"This is worse than Gaelic," he commented.

"Bridget's doing?" asked Paean, surprised.

He turned and gazed at her once more, troubled. There was of course that possibility, too. In fact it made a lot more logical sense than the Morrigan. The immortal could find him without searching physically. Right. This was Bridget and her style of revenge.

Paean stared at the deformed creature on the deck. Sharp teeth as of a pike protruded from its jaws. Its eyes were glazed and fishy, they hadn't closed with being out cold. The thing had eyelids but was clearly not using them reflexively. And yet... Paean glared at those eyes and tried to determine why their colour looked so familiar. The whole creature was a biped, but barely. The fingers were not much more than webbed spines of a fin, tipped with – hells, with diamonds! But luscious red hair spilt around the thing's head.

Merwynn? Sea-wench? Did this horrifying creature consider itself a mermaid? A fleeting image flashed through her mind – Federi, searching for her in Dublin, stopping every redhead he saw, and the woman turning and looking like this...

There was a groan from the other side of the bridge. And a voice rasped, "Help me!"

Paean squeaked and investigated, her gun ready. The plea came from the human shape.

"Federi?" she called.

He turned. He still had that Assassin look in his eyes, but it gave way as he studied the injured man.

"Captain Adamson?" he asked.

"For mercy's sake," the man bit out, "find the Golden Walrus! My daughter is aboard that ship! Please..."

"Mindy is already on the Solar Wind," Paean placated, and saw with surprise how the man turned white.

"The Solar Wind?"

"Yes," Federi took over, crouching down to investigate the man's injuries. It seemed as though he were lamed in some way. "She's safe there, Captain Adamson. You can be at ease. What happened to you?"

"They bit me," said Adamson. "Injected some or other poison, so I can't move. Is Mindy alright?"

"She's injured," said Federi. "We'll have to see. But she won't die, I don't think. We managed to pull Derrick out for you too, and one more guy. Not sure of his name. The rest..." He shrugged. "Sorry, man!" He didn't leave Adamson time to consider, but included him in his teleporter field and dropped him in the cabin one past the infirmary. An unused cabin; stashed with extra medical supplies.

A second later he was back on the Bronberg's bridge, just as Captain and Perdita arrived there. They had done a cursory round of the old ship, eliminating all further Merwynn they could find.

"You leave Paean to hold this place alone, Tzigan?" asked the Captain angrily.

"She has a teleporter," replied Federi. "Captain, you now have Captain Adamson aboard. Should maybe interrogate him."

"Good. Well done, Federi!"

"As for this," said Federi and shoved at the Merwynn with his deck sneaker, "it's not dead. Maybe keep it for questioning too?"

"Take a bleeding mutant aboard the Solar Wind?" exclaimed the Captain. "Are you still sane?"

"Not a mutant," growled Federi. "She's a Merwynn. A creation. Captain, I'm off to interview another guilty party! *Arrivederci!*" He teleported out.

Radomir Lascek ordered Paean to go help Doc Judith with the injured seafarers aboard the Solar Wind, and then he and Perdita found chains to put on the unconscious Atlantean creature. She didn't quite look like the mutants that had been trying to breach the Solar Wind. Not quite. Hells, those mutants had looked like anything at random! How could Federi be so sure that this was not one?

"It's not one," Perdita assured him. "He's right."

Federi teleported into the Central Tower, and came face-to-face with Bridget. She released an ear-splitting shriek before catching herself.

"Federi," she gasped. "You! Of all pirates and luckless vagrants... I hate you! I'll forever hate you!"

He cast a glance about, and his scalp prickled. All alarms were going in the Tower. And everywhere, merrows were trying to claw a path in through the obsidian windows.

"Merrow Code Red," he said tonelessly.

"Yes! For days now," Bridget snapped at him, and she caught herself again and drew herself up regally. "You have a teleporter. You have to help me free the girls from the other buildings!"

Federi nodded. "Lead me," he suggested. Hell's boots, but when he and Paean had strewn the two different itch viruses in here, he hadn't meant to trigger *this!* Or was it perhaps another repercussion from blowing up the Central Crystal? Had that cost Bridget her control over the monsters? Regardless, they needed his help.

Bridget tried in vain to negotiate his teleporter from him. He knew what would happen then. She'd leave him to his fate. But eventually she gave up and showed him the way into the other buildings.

The girls were all daughters of hers. The teleporter could be set to recognize highly related people. He jumped with her from one tower to the next, finding one horrible scene after another.

Paean teleported in next to him in one of the towers, and gasped. She stared at the scene of mutilation and devastation.

"They're -" she breathed, too shocked to say it aloud.

"Little luv, I did *not* authorize you to come down here!" said Federi angrily. "You were supposed to look after Adamson and Mindy!"

"Still your back-up," she muttered defiantly.

"Then it's your own fault what you get to witness," replied the Assassin coldly. And he raised his machinegun and mowed down whatever merrows hadn't been caught in his fire yet.

With Paean helping, the rescue mission for Dome went much faster. Though he was upset that she had disobeyed his – unspoken, granted – orders, Federi was thankful that she was there. Within record time they had patrolled all the towers that were still intact, and had pulled some twenty girls out of whatever was happening. In some of the towers, nothing except panic had yet set in. They also found some towers in which there was nothing... the inhabitants long dead, the last few only dried-out mummies in their beds.

Bridget gazed on these with glazed eyes.

"A dying civilization," she whispered, as though to herself.

And eventually all of them were gathered in the Central Tower.

"Only thirty-two left," said Bridget, studying the girls. "Of all my people, only thirty-two have survived!" And finally Federi detected some emotion in her voice.

Paean was wrapping wounds with make-shift pieces of silk torn from Bridget's wardrobe.

"How do the merrows get into the towers?" she asked, puzzled.

"They override the locks. It's controlled by mind power," elucidated Federi.

"How do *you* know?" she challenged.

Bridget hissed at her. "He has fused with one of Dana's despicable mutants! All my merrows can smell it. It drives them wild every time he comes down here."

"How do you know what the merrows are smelling?" asked Paean, but she got no answer as Federi cut in,

"Now what do we do? How long is the Central Tower going to hold up?"

"When the Central Tower falls, Atlantis is finished," replied Bridget with resigned dignity. "Then we all die. The last of my girls will know that their Goddess is dying with them. It will ease their sorrow. At least we won't perish in the fire furnace of the Earth's innards!"

Paean looked horrified. She couldn't decide which was worse. Federi shook his head.

"Listen, Bridget. Nobody dies as long as Federi can prevent it! Taking you people to the Solar Wind."

She stared past him, not absorbing a word.

"So now I need help," said Federi and activated his wrist-com. "Could you help out here please?"

"Sure, Federi Dem," came a sultry voice over the com. Bridget stared at him.

"Who was that?"

A second later Dana teleported into the Tower. She cast a glance around and exploded into laughter.

"*Touché*, Tzigan!"

"Get that thing out of here!" screeched Bridget.

Jolly nuthouse this!

"I know where we must take them all," said Paean quietly to no-one in particular.

No-one in particular heard her.

"Where?" asked Lyr.

Paean summed up the tall, pale man with the sparse white-blond hair, the watery eyes and the deep, gentle voice. Here was a person who got overlooked a lot, she thought, although she couldn't pinpoint what led her to that conclusion.

She couldn't say what she had been meaning to. Those girls certainly looked as though their heads had rooms to let. But he – she doubted he belonged in Dublin's psychiatric ward!

"The Solar Wind's boardroom," she said. Lyr nodded pensively.

"Hold that thought," said Federi. "Dana, ready? Between us we only need to make four or five leaps, I'm quite stretched by now…"

"Federi," said Dana, still fighting mirth, "I marooned her! Leave what is well alone!"

"It's not well!" argued Paean, but Federi held up a hand. She went quiet. The Romany planted himself squarely in front of Dana. She was barely any shorter than he; but what he lacked in height he made up in cold fury.

"*Isda,* Dana! It's like this. You want to claim Federi's protection? You had better stick to Federi's rules then! These girls are in jeopardy. Do you know about Merrow Code Red?"

"Indeed," said Dana with irony. "It's Bridget's own creations getting out of hand attacking their own creators. Happens periodically, especially after an orgy of eating and mating."

"It's never been as bad as this," Bridget threw in. "The towers are merrow-proof. This time they found the equalizing systems and opened the towers by their valves. The system must have weakened to their minds when the Central Crystal died." She glared at Federi.

"Tell me about Merwynn Macha," he replied angrily. "How did she get out? And how the hell did she learn about the Solar Wind, and why does she have it in for us?"

"I don't know," said Bridget. She was lying.

The woman had released a bunch of monstrosities which had laid waste to the crew of a trader. His fingers itched to throttle her, just a little, until she begged for mercy. She didn't blasted well deserve to be rescued out of her own self-designed hell!

But her girls weren't at fault. And while they had to be protected because they were both innocent and harmless, she had to be kept alive for questioning. There was such a lot he had to find out! Specifically about the Central Crystal, and the forsaken Morrigan.

"Come, let's get them out of here!" ordered Federi.

"Your protection comes at a steep price, Dem-" started Dana and grinned. And shut her mouth. Those hands on her shoulders were like iron clamps. And that tooth was a bit too silver for her liking. She wondered for the first time whether there weren't some merrow in the Assassin.

"Go ahead," goaded Federi, "speak the name! Want to see how I cope with the dogs? You can watch from the other side! Go ahead, say it!"

"Say it yourself," retorted Dana sulkily. "I was just playing!"

"Playing!" gasped Federi. "Dana, make a choice!"

She glared at him, speechless for once. The Assassin released her from his grip. Paean's hand touched his arm. Yes, he knew. When this gig was finished, the Unicate was next. When exactly was the job on the Solar Wind finished?

Federi's teleporter could take four people at any one time; he hadn't tried more and wasn't about to experiment on the run. He reversed and re-reversed leaps, teleporting girls onto the sundeck of the Solar Wind, where they sat in stunned silence, shielding their eyes from the light. They had only ever heard about the light on the surface! He didn't deal with the murderous glances he collected from the bridge. It wasn't his problem at this point; the mission was not yet accomplished.

"Tzigan!" came the bellowed order by the third time he appeared with more Atlantean beauties. "On the bridge, instantly!"

"Sorry, Captain," replied Federi with a grin, "not done yet!"

"At least put them in the boardroom! They're messing up operations!"

What operations, thought the gypsy. The Solar Wind hung suspended in the air, parked there by the Comet. The sea with all its unpredictable wave heights was wandering past underneath. "*Shukar,* Captain!"

"We're not a floating hotel," growled Lascek.

Federi gave him a bright grin. "There's a money-making idea, Captain! 'scuse me!" He teleported out again. Every time he came back to the Tower of Dome, Dana was nearly ready to use her teleporter. She was really good at stalling! She hadn't yet teleported a single girl out of Dome! Federi suspected it was an ego thing.

Paean was helping, one Atlantean at a time. Federi scowled at her. She shouldn't teleport such a lot. She didn't have mutant cells to protect her.

The merrows broke into the tower just as Federi teleported out with Bridget. The obsidian windows splintered in a spectacular implosion of water. He saw how Dana took herself out of the place; and then, just as the field fuzzified, he saw Paean arrive...

"Little luv!"

Dropping Bridget in the Solar Wind's boardroom, he set the teleporter to reversing the last leap to pull his wife out of the place. But before he could activate the jump, she was back, wild-eyed, out of breath – but dry. He grabbed her and hugged her tightly, listening to her catching her breath. And then she giggled hysterically.

"What?" he asked, gazing at her, grinning too. "Never do that again! Could've died, Paean! Plain from the pressure!"

"I'm reminding me of one of those stunt heroes from the Sherman Files," she laughed.

"*Yoy*," was her Tzigan's quiet comment.

Bridget turned to them with a jaded look.

"It's moot," she said despondently. "What is the point in surfacing now? It's all at an end!"

Dome had been a vast, glorious civilization. Now the last thirty-three Atlanteans were gathered here as homeless fugitives. It hit her for the first time just how badly things were *over*. Even after Dome had been sunk, she had refused to relinquish her realm, choosing instead to adapt to those nigh impossible conditions, with a lot of technological help from that wise and ancient entity, the Central Crystal. But that one ruling object which had been the focal point of her civilization for so long was gone; the Crystal had been destroyed. And now she had to abandon her White City, the empire of her youth. She felt lost, more lost than her poor girls looked.

Paean touched her arm.

"New beginning," she whispered. The Goddess stared at her without any comprehension in her eyes. Federi gave Paean's shoulder a squeeze and moved off to find the Captain.

What worried *him* even more was the emptiness he'd seen in so many of their eyes. The kind of mental absence you got in people who were on some kind of Unicate sedative, or who had been erased by brainwashing.

He had seen it, back in his professional days. He'd been in the depths of one of the Unicate's worst high-security prisons. The Unicate generally didn't take prisoners. They applied the death penalty wherever they could. Those places he had seen were literally for such hard-boiled cases who still held some sort of cookie – had some information or something else the Unicate was trying to torture out of them before exterminating them.

And, "depth" was accurate. Those places were underground; mazes in which you could lose your way. Partly just tunnels hewn into the ground or rock. There was no escaping from there - not without special skills, and help.

He had rescued a friend out of there once, at age fourteen – a girl he had believed himself in love with. With the help of a guard who closed both eyes quite deliberately. The guard had no doubt paid with his life for that inconsistency. And the girl – he couldn't and didn't want to recall her name…

She had thanked him – and had promptly turned around and betrayed him at the nearest Unicate police station, sending him fleeing deeper into the wild west of Europe. He had vowed to himself never to fall in love again.

Radomir Lascek walked into the boardroom just as Federi was leaving. He scanned the room and scowled.

"Tzigan! Every time I leave you in charge, you rearrange all the systems!"

The stare he got back from those black eyes was from a very dark place. The Captain paused and studied Federi. What had he actually ever done to the man? Why that hostility?

"Your banshee thing is in the bilges," he told Federi. "Locked in irons. She looks dangerous. And Captain Adamson is now in the infirmary with his little daughter. *He's* not hurt, thank the Powers. The poison is beginning to wear off. I've seen what you dumped into Anyhow's cabin. Is this ship a hospital, I ask you? And Wolf reported to me about your lapse there on the deck. Federi, what is the story? Why do I have a boardroom full of girls? And where is my daughter?"

Those eyes stared out under that horrible mauve headscarf with all its jingly tricks as though they wanted to climb out of their sockets and assassinate him.

"Very well," said Radomir Lascek. "Conference on the bridge. Classified." He turned and left.

"He fears nothing, does he!" commented Dana softly. Federi shook his head. And he pounced on Wolf who had come in to see what was going on.

"Wolf, take Dana to Johnny. Got to keep the two sisters separated."

"*Shukar,* Federi."

"Some rum, Federi?"

"Coffee, Captain?"

Radomir Lascek smiled. The wiry little man with the absentee colour sense was staring at him defiantly.

"Listen, my friend," said the Captain. "Have a seat. I'll make the coffee this time. Let's forget about the command line for a second and speak plainly, man to man."

Federi grinned and pulled up one of the two console chairs.

"What would you have said if I had made that suggestion, Captain?"

"It would have been insubordinate," Lascek pointed out. "You know it. Quit the games." He got up and activated the espresso machine, aware of Federi's watchful stare. He filled espresso into two mugs. Since the croaches, all mugs were constantly clean and available. Sometimes it was annoying how quickly they would whisk a mug out under you the moment it was empty.

He handed Federi his mug.

"Thank you, Captain."

"Pleasure. Let's get to the point. In the first place, I can't have my best sailor falling over dead. What the hell happened there on the deck, that Wolf tells me about?"

"Morrigan attack," said Federi. "Captain, it must have sourced its voltage from the Walrus, although – I have no idea where it's hiding its program. Hopefully not on the Comet! It ran off, in any case."

"Ran off," repeated Radomir Lascek with a scowl. It didn't seem too likely to him. "And those girls. Federi, I know you never do anything without a very good reason. I hope. Out with it!"

Federi summarized what had happened in the Captain's absence. Radomir Lascek listened, biting back his ripostes when the gypsy got emotional about the cruelty that had been applied on Rushka, moving her from a place where she was well, to the ship where she was miserable.

"I didn't understand it was related to where she was," he replied quietly, and watched how the gypsy swallowed back some quick verbal assault too. "I have no experience with pregnant girls."

"Women," corrected Federi. "Neither do I, Captain. Something called common sense."

"At any rate I see your point and agree with you," added Lascek. "But did you have to move Donegal, too?"

"I thought Radomir Lascek doesn't break up families," said the Tzigan with a remote smile.

"Of course." Today it was difficult to remain unperturbed. Federi was goading him. There was serious anger brewing.

"At any rate Paean has brought you some more crew. You saw," added the Romany.

"Yes. Who are those two unknowns?"

"Military renegades from Johnny Anyhow's group. She asked who would volunteer to do service on a pirate ship, and those two came forward."

Lascek gasped. That wasn't the way to recruit crew! He'd have to keep a close eye on those two!

"Federi, what in the stars is making you so angry?"

Federi took a deep breath. And clamped his jaw. And scowled. And came out with it.

"Other than, Captain, having to clean up all the scum that is permanently attacking us for no reason? You know what that Mindy Adamson told me? The accursed Bronberg was hunting for the Solar Wind! Why? Who sent her? Hah! Want to guess? And what the hell is the Morrigan doing back aboard? And every time I set foot in my cabin..." He stopped and stared across the sea. "Got a mission to complete," he growled. "Permission to be loosely associated with the Solar Wind?"

"What mission?" asked Lascek.

"Got to kill something!"

"Ah, of course," replied Lascek. "Federi, I have complete faith in you. Do whatever you have to. We'll be alright."

"Thank the Stars," said Federi with a theatrical roll of his eyes. With this one, Radomir Lascek was never quite sure whether his chain was being yanked.

28
The Merwynn Macha

Shawn waylaid the Romany on his way to the galley.

"Found something out about Mindy and her dad."

Federi beckoned him to follow. Between peeling onions and filleting fish, Shawn told what he had learnt. Mindy and her father were smugglers.

"And?" asked Federi blankly.

"But Federi – smugglers!"

"We're pirates, Shawn! Smugglers is a small one!"

Shawn snapped his mouth shut. He had thought Federi would be interested! It certainly intrigued him! He wondered idly whether Captain Adamson would take him aboard, then grinned at his own illogical idea. Working for Captain was much more exciting! Even though nothing illegal had happened yet...

He shook his head, grinning. Nothing illegal? They had overthrown the whole Unicate!

"You're a pirate, my boy," commented Federi and continued chopping. " 's a worrying trend I'd keep an eye on."

"You've been listening to my thoughts?" challenged Shawn.

Federi smiled. He had been through the entire Walrus and had of course discovered the contraband. It was aboard now. Mainly torpedoes and underwater marine guns. Good weapons; he'd like Perdita's input on the branding. Quite a nice find for the Solar Wind. Pennies, so to speak, from heaven.

But the whole ship had not been worth salvaging, with all that slaughter aboard… And then there were the crew cabins… his eyes glazed from the horrors he'd seen in there. The whole idea of looting shipwrecks suddenly struck him as necromancy.

Captain had basically given him *carte blanche*. He could come and go as he liked. The employment had become more of an association, while still loosely keeping the hierarchy in mind. This was good – and in another way it was bad, because it tied him to the Solar Wind even more, by its very freedom. There was even less of a chance to break those bonds now. Captain was a genius, thought Federi with a puzzled frown.

And his Paean was stuck in the lab, helping Doc try to stitch the mess that was Peter Piper back together. Peter Piper from the Walrus. Derrick had identified him, in a conscious moment.

That was after a lot of first aid had been applied to the Atlantean bits in the boardroom there, which was where Federi had spent his last half-hour helping Paean. But Peter Piper couldn't wait – Doc had been working on him from the second she'd returned to the Solar Wind. She hadn't sounded too hopeful when Federi checked in. Derrick was lined up next; currently on heavy sedatives, painkillers and antibiotic.

Poor little Mindy, in extreme pain with her broken back, had to wait. There was no spreading sepsis; of the patients she was the least time-critical. Ailyss was keeping her dosed with codeine.

He ought to go and help, too. He glanced up at Shawn.

"Think you can take over here?"

"Sure, Federi! No problem!"

"You going to cope, Donegal? That's food for more than fifty you've got to prepare!"

"What are we making?"

"Gumbo," said Federi. "Use the two big pots. And the ultra-glare."

"I'll cope," said Shawn nonchalantly. "I'll put bread out too."

"Good boy." Federi put down the knife, took off the kitchen coverall he hardly ever wore when the crew was at a normal size, washed his hands and sauntered off to the infirmary, mulling about kitchen coveralls and white coats, and that assassins should actually wear some sort of protective clothing too. Well, they did. It was called a bullet-proof vest.

The "banshee thing", Merwynn Macha, surfaced from the black void of uneasy dreams. In her heart burnt riotous anger. How it had got there, she didn't know; but she envied all creatures who moved in the freedom of the light, and now that she herself was out in that freedom, she was going to kill as many of them as she could.

Her sisters had been killed. She knew this by the telepathic connection she had shared with them. The many that were under the sea, under the Dome, had been destroyed by the merrows – their own fathers. After many cruelties. And the ones that had escaped with her, those on the Bronberg, they had been mowed down coldly by these humans.

She didn't hate the Solar Wind's crew more than anyone else, not particularly; but she had orders. Demonos. Destroy Demonos. And his associates. Everyone on the Solar Wind. Destroy every ship on Earth's oceans, until you find the Solar Wind. Do not rest until the mission is accomplished.

Why they had left her alive, she didn't understand; her logic dictated that they should have killed her too. But humans were curious creatures. They had to tamper with everything before destroying it!

She was within reach of her goal. She was in fact on the Solar Wind; the only thing that stopped her from carrying out her orders now and having a feast in the process, were these silly metal things they had fastened around her arms and legs.

Her yellow eyes darted about the machine room. A fat lot that would help them! She was a patient fisherwoman.

Two men sat huddled over a square thing that emanated something of a Crystal – a dead crystal. They were teasing it, worrying it, tampering with it the way she'd play with a lantern fish. One was a bit younger than the other, who looked positively old, showing single grey hair in his black, short-cropped mane. She looked further. In a far corner sat another man – she gaped. She had never yet seen any human who looked that old! His whole head was full of white hair. His skin was yellow from age and in deep, crass grooves. He was holding an artefact that looked as though it ought to contain information, judging by his expression. Some kind of crystal? But it emanated nothing.

She peered through his eyes for a fleeting moment, trying to see better, and found herself pushed violently out of his head. The old man looked up and straight at her.

"Noo, y're na gooing ta do tha'!" he said sternly. "Back oof!"

She curled up into her corner, half-closing her eyes.

"And y're na fooling me, neither, now are ya?" added the man. "Stay in yar coorner!"

Aha. One she should not play with. Not yet.

Lyr wandered into the galley, curious. Shawn got to his feet, wiped his right hand on his coverall and extended it.

"Hi, I'm Shawn."

Lyr tentatively stuck out his hand too; Shawn grabbed it and shook it. Lyr smelt his hand. Vegetation and fish.

"I'm Lyr," he said. "Of Dome. This is the kitchen?"

"The galley," corrected Shawn.

"This ship is fascinating," commented Lyr with his soft, bass voice. Shawn summed him up and estimated him to be about twenty-two... then he remembered that the man was Danaan and that he was probably several hundred years old. And now that Shawn looked more closely, those years were indeed visible – in hundreds of minute lines around the pale man's eyes. And he noticed another really odd thing about the guy. His eyes were as huge and oval as those of Perdita, and Dana, and Rashni – but they were a watery blue. And the pupils were oval, too.

"May I watch you?" asked Lyr.

"Please, sir," said Shawn and indicated a chair. He continued with his filleting and chopping.

"You look as though you are of a bloodline with the girl who came with the rescue party," said Lyr thoughtfully.

"Paean? She's my sister."

Lyr watched him in fascination. Shawn grabbed another fish and aimed to chop off its head.

"There's a faster way of doing that," said Lyr. Shawn paused in anticipation. Lyr took the fish, grabbed its head with his teeth and with a quick flick of his head, pulled the fish-head off. The entire spine came out along with it. Lyr spat the fish-head onto the table. Shawn stared with wide eyes. The guy had sucked out the fish's eyes!

"Eww!"

Lyr observed his reaction and handed back the fish.

"Maybe you want to continue doing it your way," he suggested apologetically. "Teach me your way?"

Shawn fought down the gag reflex and found the man another knife.

"Generally we don't put any of the food in our mouths before we serve it to others," he added. "Etiquette."

"Oh." Lyr looked embarrassed. "I'm sorry."

"You didn't know," replied Shawn, suppressing a shudder. Okay, Pirate Donegal, back to work! It takes all kinds! At least he's willing to learn. Better keep an eye on him, with those sharp teeth…

"Don't throw that away," forestalled Lyr when Shawn wanted to tip the fish heads into the garbage. "We give them to the merrows. They love them." He smiled, his slightly pointed, irregular white teeth flashing. Suddenly Shawn could place the eyes, too. Those were fish eyes, except for the oval pupils.

"That's all we can do here," said Doc Judith, straightening out. Federi glanced at her. Her back was aching, he could see it. On the operating surface lay Peter Piper, newly sewn up, but hanging on by a thread. His sandy-brown mane and three-day beard blended nearly seamlessly with his grey skin tone. Paean's valeriensis had been used to anaesthetize him, despite the fact that he was unconscious – Doc Judith didn't want him waking up in the middle of the operation. A patient could die from shock that way.

"And now Derrick," said Paean, with a deep breath. The Romany gazed at her critically. She looked stretched too, tired. It had been a long operation.

"Give your old doctor a break," begged Doc Judith. "Twenty minutes. Then we're back here, see?"

Federi teleported Peter Piper back to Anyhow's cabin. Captain Adamson had been relegated to that barely-used storeroom on the far side of the infirmary, but he was currently keeping his daughter company in the infirmary. At least something good, mulled Federi. And those thirty-two Atlantean girls – they would have to be accommodated in the boardroom. They sat there currently, huddling, partially on chairs and partially on the deck. There was still a lot of patching ahead for that lot. And then... Federi scowled as he tried to work out where he should find thirty-two make-shift mattresses. Or hammocks, perhaps? The place was threatening to look like the fo'c'sle in one of those pirate ships of the eighteenth century!

"Ayyye..." he growled as he rummaged in the infirmary's storage cabinets, "thrree-hundred yearrs afore the mast, an' ne'er a drop a' rum, yoho..." It earned him a rather odd look from Adamson, and a giggle from Mindy. He smiled. And he found what he was rummaging for.

The Romany carried the extra vital signs monitor into the cabin with Peter Piper, put it down on the deck and clipped it to the patient. He'd have to secure it down, he thought as he rigged an IV drip. Then he stood back. Paean was there by his side. He held onto her for a second, dog-tired, catching his thoughts, yoho. Unease niggled at him.

Thirty-three Atlanteans in the boardroom, counting Bridget. The surviving crew of the Golden Walrus, totalling four, in the infirmary, and in this cabin here. Six add-ons from Prime Oil and Ginavis 2. Plus Rashni, Johnny and Dana, and the full usual complement of sailors. Minus Rushka and Ronan. On the one hand, how were there not enough able hands to run the ship without Federi? But on the other, how could he leave them now, with such an explosive mix of strangers aboard? He needed to make a plan with all of them! And there was another thing... what had happened to those forsaken space crawlers? Or maybe the space crawler, singular?

"Get Shawn to make us some coffee, little luv," he prompted. "Go grab a break."

She obeyed, exhausted. Federi watched her go; then his feet took him down the passageway, to the bilges where the Merwynn was chained. Merwynns and merrows and space crawlers, he thought, worrying suddenly that she might get hold of the little crawler and maul it. Or that the crawler might find it funny to emulate the Merwynn.

Where was that space crawler? He surprised himself by feeling quite possessive about the strange little alien. Yes, it had that uncanny way about it, but somehow... it all boiled down to an alien sense of humour, and really high intelligence, he thought. The crawler hadn't hurt anybody. So far. And it was cute.

If that Merwynn was hungry... she'd start eating croaches, and tobuskies, he realized. Bad idea. She might even snap at anyone who came close... He scowled. Underestimating an enemy, Federi? If he were she, and he were really hungry, he'd get out of those chains! With all that fresh human flesh aboard! He'd better take the edge off her hunger first. He changed his path towards the galley.

Macha opened her eyes once more. There was a huge box of fresh fish right in front of her. Its scent had brought her out of her sleep. That was interesting! They were actually feeding her! Did they think she was a pet? She began devouring the stuff ravenously. At least this man in the huge hat, who thought he could fool her into not remembering his face, understood that she liked it fresh. Still wriggling would have been better. But just-caught was good.

"*Bon apetit,*" said Demonos.

It was amazing having her prime target sitting so close, nearly within reach. She eyed him between gulps of fish. He'd shot that awful stuff at her. That disgusting green poison that had spread into her body, making her drowsy and nauseous and putting her to sleep. She still felt it in her system. It was still making her stomach lurch. He'd made himself more of a target with that. She'd make him suffer!

He was leaning against a piece of machinery, watching her eat. Well, he could be dessert, she thought. Eating made her feel better, it diluted that horrible weedy taste of the green poison. It was a while since she had something to eat; she'd had to keep a really tight check on herself and her crew to prevent them from eating their last prisoner right away. And now her sisters and cousins were dead and that human had got away! That thought made her even hungrier.

"How did you escape the Dome?" asked Demonos casually, playing with a small item he was holding in his hand.

Macha looked up between two bites.

"I got out," she said. The man scowled at her. She bared her teeth. There was no way she'd be telling him more.

"And you can breathe underwater," he added.

"Corr-rect!" snarled Macha. She buried her face in the box of fish for a moment and gulped down a large butterfish. The man looked away.

"So there's a gap in the dome somewhere," he said.

"If you say so."

"*I* don't say so! I'm asking you!"

Macha half-closed her eyes and concentrated on the fish. This human was annoying. If he thought she'd pay for the fish by answering questions...

"Bridget sent you?"

She snarled. "Let me eat! I'm hungry!"

"Only one more question," said the target.

Macha sprang up and pounced on him. He sat just a bit too close, didn't he! He had measured the length of the chains correctly; but he couldn't have known about the flexibility of the Merwynn... or their strength! Merrow strength. Reserves for moments like these.

He moved away with reflexes that were unnaturally quick, far too fast for a human. She snarled, surprised. Was this man a hybrid of some sort too? The chains pulled taut; furious, she ripped them out of their sockets. The sudden release catapulted her right at him. He didn't expect that! Hungrily, Macha sank her fangs into his shoulder and tasted the sweetness of his fresh, living blood.

Her eyes connected with his, and what she saw there surprised her. By this time of the game, fear was what she expected in any quarry. But Demonos simply looked at her as though it were all part of a game he had played many, many times, a game of which he was the master... and then that awful green smell rose through her own bloodstream again before she even felt the puncture. She released him and screamed in anger, and then all her strength drained out of her and she collapsed in a helpless heap on the floor. She stared at this unpredictable human creature in shock until the green darkness folded around her vision and her mind.

Federi clapped his hand on the wound the Merwynn Macha had ripped into his left shoulder, clenching his jaws. Rule number one: No matter how badly the enemy damaged you, you didn't let them know it. The gash was streaming. She had missed the artery; but hells, she hadn't missed the nerve! He only hoped that there wasn't any poison in this one! He hoped there were still memories of the mutant in his cell metabolism, that it would heal quickly. Rats with upgrades, he didn't need this now!

Wolf was at his side.

"Let me see that."

"Svendsson," gasped Federi, lips pulled back in grim humour, "when I'm really old and decrepit, you'll be my nursemaid, I can see that!"

"I will, too," agreed Wolf, taking off his sweat-soaked T-shirt and wrapping it tightly around the gypsy's injury to staunch it. "Come. Off to Paean with you! Let her patch you up, she does that well."

"Poor Paean," muttered Federi. "Needlework without an end!"

Jon Marsden glanced up from his programming for the first time.

"Did she bite you, Federi?"

"Nothing major," said the gypsy through his teeth. "Only problem is now, she's out of chains. You saw the mess she made on the Walrus, Jon. Please find a way to tie her more securely."

Jon Marsden got up from his spot.

"Leave it to me," he said. "Get yourself stitched up, Federi."

"Jon," said Federi, grinning, "you've bin so immersed down here! Have you even said hi to the people Paean fetched aboard?"

"Aboard? People? Should I?"

"You should," the gypsy assured him. "Yoho. And so on."

Jon stared at him blankly. "Yoho...?"

"Trying a new cliché," said Federi wrily. "Doesn't work. Anna bottle."

Captain Adamson had regained his mobility. The poison must have worn off. He was sitting in Anyhow's cabin talking to Derrick. Federi could hear them. So when Paean made Federi sit down on the second infirmary bunk – the one on which he had sat that night when she had stitched up his hand – they were alone except for the sleeping Mindy.

Paean disinfected and cleaned and sutured. Federi stayed silent, angry. By the stink in merrows, he didn't need this! He'd been stupid. So busy controlling the mutant's fear of the Merwynn that he had deliberately moved too close. Overestimating the speed of his own reflexes. He needed this gash in his left shoulder like a – like a bleeding gash in his shoulder!

Ratted hell, that mutant was wearing him down! The faster reflexes were great, and so was the improved night vision; but for wailing, he could do without her hard-wired fear reactions! It would take retraining for him to regain his assassin's equilibrium, that fine balance between risking and playing it safe, knowing exactly where the limits ran. Right now the Tzigan was out of control, defiantly showing up the mutant and rubbing its nose in its own fear. And therefore, taking reckless risks. He could only blame himself for being stupid.

Federi doesn't get himself into such situations in the first place. A conversation with his little flame as she stitched up Wolf and his knee. Oh, he'd been showing off, alright! He knew that she was unimpressed with Wolf's recklessness, and he knew exactly what *would* impress her – and it had! And now? How was he more mature, more deliberate than a hot-headed young gambler losing his cool over insults to a friend?

There was a movement in the door. Federi glanced up. His tense frown lightened to a smile.

"Jodi!"

The pretty brunette moved into the infirmary.

"Looks like you're collecting more battle scars!"

"Sure looks that way," agreed Federi, then he fell silent. Paean clenched her jaw and kept stitching.

A gleam of light caught Federi's eye. He glanced down at Jodi's hand.

"Hey! Is that a ring?"

"I'm engaged," said Jodi with a smile. "To Tille Fielding."

"Aw! Congratulations!" Federi beamed. "Good ol' Tille! He's recovered fine?"

"Good as new," said Jodi.

Federi grinned. And exchanged a brief smile with Paean, who seemed very pleased about that news too. He suspected that she had quite a soft spot for the gentle information scientist on Ginavis 1 whom she had first met in a comatose state. In fact, she hadn't ever met him in any other state. Odd, that. Perhaps it was his looks. Ha! Or his maturity! *Not* taking dumb risks. Lying on a slab being stitched up.

Thirty-two hammocks in the boardroom intruded on his thoughts. Swaying with the ship's movements. Yoho... or whatever. Anna bottle.

"So – is Tille good to you?" he asked Jodi. "Because if he's not..." He let the mock warning hang there.

"He's a sweet guy, Federi. Not a bad deal, for a second choice."

Paean glanced up, just in time to catch the baffled look on Federi's face.

"Second choice, Jodi? Good grief! Then don't do it, *shey!*" The

Tzigan shook his head gravely.

Jodi shrugged.

"No, Jodi!" scolded Federi. "You don't marry a second choice! It's neither fair on him nor on you! Why don't you go for your first choice?"

"Well, the point is, the first choice is not available."

"And why not?"

"He's married."

"Oh." Federi was at a loss. "Bad luck, Jodi. Sorry to hear that. Not a good thing to be in love with a married man." Cor, this puzzled him! He hadn't thought that Jodi was that type. "Who is it?"

"I'd rather not say," said Jodi. She glanced at him, and at Paean, and at the other infirmary bunk. "I'd be in such trouble with Paean!"

With that, she disappeared from the door. Federi gasped, and met Paean's sharp glare, and then Mindy's baffled gaze.

"What did she mean?" asked the blonde girl.

"You were supposed to be asleep," he informed her. He narrowed his eyes at Mindy Adamson. Hells, she looked so familiar... she reminded him of...

He sighed and averted his eyes. Yes, now he had it. Angelina. This girl here could have been Angelina's daughter, she looked so much like the bubbly blonde renegade who had been cut down by Semanchio Sancho. They all had taken the death of Angelina Carter very badly.

"I feel sorry for Paean," muttered Mindy. "That was nasty of Jodi! She should have kept it to herself!" She ogled the Irish girl with curiosity. "But Paean – I thought you were, like, my age? What are you doing married? Who're you married to?"

Federi looked at his little redhead, who shook her mane back with an impatient flick of her head. She had never known about Angelina... and he'd better not mention it either. She might just get jealous. And perhaps with more reason than she could know. Not that Paean would ever have come second to anyone in his life... she ought to know this, anna bottle!

"Little luv?"

His little red fury didn't reply; she squared her stubborn Irish jaw and kept on suturing his Merwynn gash. Only she wasn't quite as gentle as before. Lucky about the local anaesthetic.

"Paean?" he prompted again. "You're not jealous of *Jodi*, are you?"

She shook her head resolutely. "Don't be jolly ridiculous!"

"You'd better not be," warned Federi.

"'xactly," said Paean acidly. "She's in love with a married guy. What hey!"

"I feel sorry for Tille," said Federi softly. "Let's hope Jodi comes to her senses – one way or the other!"

"Federi, hold still, blast you," said Paean angrily. "Stop wriggling! Let me finish stitching!"

29
The one that got away

The silver Space Base spun slowly in the sunlight, her metal glinting mysteriously like a bauble on a Christmas tree. Small craft surrounded the unfinished arm where a passage was being added; robot arms doing the welding and sealing in the vacuum.

In the control room of the base, Itzak Stein, tobusky expert and technologist, was keeping watch over the console. The darkened, dome-shaped volcaniplex ceiling showed stars shining through; Earth's atmosphere wasn't around to interfere with the view.

He turned a bit on his swivel-chair that was fixed into the metal deck next to the console, and pensively sipped a freshly-made green tea, thinking about the way Federi's gypsies had taken to the Space Base like a second home.

Something flickered in his field of vision. Itzak glanced. There was writing on the console that hadn't been there a second ago.

I can't see anything.

He ran the cursor over it, frowning. Who was messing about with the console?

John Whitcombe was out organizing the construction of the sixth wing. Juanita had gone to feed and water the tobuskies. With orchid mix, that they absorbed through their leaves. There were a few helpers about – gypsies from Juanita's tribe mostly, who were taking a hand in planting and decorating, and painting glittery non-slip onto walls and floors. They were doing it for fun and out of fascination for the project. Luckily; because the team leader couldn't afford them if he'd had to pay them. Federi had informed Itzak that Free Gypsies would be willing to accept a paid job, but only in exchange for pure gold. Tradition, that.

But nobody had their hands on the console.

He looked back at the screen. The words were still there, and others appeared, letter by tentative letter. He watched with bated breath.

Which CPU is this?

Itzak stared at the question for several seconds, then he typed a reply.

Who is asking?

Federi's new wrist-com clamoured. It sounded like a pack of wolves baying. Wolf experimenting with the signal tones. The gypsy frowned impatiently.

"Hold still!" snapped Paean, still suturing. "They'll just have to wait! Na' my fault that you get yourself bitten, now is it?"

Federi wriggled. That com was on his left wrist. There was no way he could get to it. He couldn't even lift the arm – Paean had put a very effective block on it. His arm all the way to his fingertips, and half his chest and back were numb from it.

"Who is it?"

"Itzak," said Paean, glancing down.

"Itzak?" That was strange, if nothing else! "Little luv, won't you answer that?"

"How? Got both my hands full!"

"Aw, Paean! Please! Just push the button!"

"They're going to order you about," said Paean, suturing in slow motion. "You know it! When you should be keeping still now!"

Federi scowled at her, then he unclasped the wrist-com from his useless left arm with his right hand and answered it.

"Itzak!"

"You took a while there, Federi!" said the tobusky man. "You'll never believe this. You need to come to the Space Base immediately."

Paean grabbed the wrist-com before Federi could reply.

"Itzak," she said sharply, "Federi is in the infirmary. I'm currently stitching him back together. He's been chewed by something again. Why don't *you* come *here* instead?"

Federi took the wrist-com back from her, angry.

"Paean, get back in your box! Itzak, I'm sorry. She's a bit out of hand. Things have been going haywire here."

"You're injured, Federi?"

"Comes with the job," said the gypsy equably. "Nothing life-threatening. What is going on up there, Itzak? Are you guys in danger?"

"No," said Itzak. "But you've got to see this!"

"Give us about ten minutes. Will it last? Yes? We'll be there." Federi switched the com off and turned a dark stare on her. "Paean, there's no call to be rude to your seniors! Not my fault that Jodi made that nasty comment! You stop acting like a child right now and behave yourself!"

"Should've picked her," growled Paean. Federi chose to ignore that. Mindy pulled her blanket over her head.

A few more minutes passed in icy silence as the Romany watched how Paean finished suturing, liberally smeared that awful red iodine ointment on the wound and bandaged it up, putting his arm in a sling. He took out his teleporter.

Paean put her hand on Federi's uninjured right arm, contrite.

"Take me with you," she implored.

"No! You've got work down here, little spitfire. Stay away from Jodi. Help Doc. There's still Derrick. And all the injured Atlantean girls! And one more thing – go and check for me that Jon has bound up Macha securely, but don't go near her, understood? Do it soon, while she's still under from my dart."

"Okay." She evaded his eyes. "Say sorry to Itzak from me?"

"Uh-huh. Sure I will." The smile broke through his gloomy features. "Be safe, little firefly!"

"You too, Federi," muttered Paean. The gypsy shrugged off her hand and teleported.

The call from Doc Judith came in the five seconds during which Paean was still exchanging a wordless stare with Mindy.

"Yes, Doc. I'll be right there!" She slunk out of the infirmary, still packing her moonbag with syringes and fiddling with the zip on the way. Mindy stared after her.

Two hours? Three? How long were they back on the Solar Wind now? Paean shook her head. And in this short time the closeness they had gained in Southern Free had dissipated. The closeness for which she had worked very hard, being the perfect wife and silent companion he had needed, anticipating his every wish so he didn't have to talk. No: She was the troublesome teen again, to be supervised. And Federi belonged to the ship. Regardless that the bleeding ship had died in an explosion!

He didn't need her, he just needed a teddybear for those low moments!

And Jodi – blast Jodi! Right. It was logical. Jodi was much closer to Federi's age. So the moment she, Paean, had an emotional reaction to something vile, Jodi was suddenly the mature goddess and she herself, the pesky child. Perhaps she should just finish up all the stitching here and then go back to the gypsies. Where people understood her. Federi could blasted well have his freedom back so he could rescue Jodi from marrying someone she didn't love. Right!

But then Paean's thoughts turned to Mindy. She'd have to ask Doc to check what was wrong with Mindy's back. The kid hadn't even as much as shifted position; she was still lying flat on her back, head on a single cushion, because more than that hurt her; still unable to feel her legs. Paean was beginning to worry that the spine might be broken.

Wasn't there a way of fixing that, in this day and age? Or perhaps there was some procedure in the Sherman Files?

In the meantime someone ought to bring Mindy a book. She had to be bored out of her skull. Paean thought she'd better ask Ailyss about it, as she moved up the stairs, down the passage and into the blue boardroom.

Thirty-two girls - hundreds of years old - some on the deck, others on Captain's blue chairs, many of them sharing a chair two-by-two, around Captain's fake-pine boardroom table. All of their weird, yellow eyes with oval pupils swung to Paean as she entered. Doc Judith was already there with her metal toolbox full of essential medical equipment.

"What are we doing?" asked Paean.

"Immunizing them. If we don't, they'll all get sick and die," explained Doc Judith.

Paean nodded. Of course. Those girls had been isolated under the sea for centuries!

"Shouldn't we also..." she started.

"Yes, we're drawing blood too," completed Doc Judith. "And you must mark each girl with a number. The marker pen is over there. Or there will be chaos in the bloods."

The girls with the vacant eyes were restless and slightly hostile about being jabbed with needles, and some went nearly hysterical when, during the second round, they saw their own blood leaving their bodies. Paean pacified them in Gaelic; at least this seemed to help a bit, as they understood partially what she was saying. One of the Atlanteans commented on Paean talking funny, whereupon another laughed and stated that the girl was clearly born with only half of her lights burning. Paean clenched her jaw shut and carried on. Dublin psychiatric wing it was for them, if she got her way!

*

"Itzak!"

"Federi," said Itzak, beaming and slapping the gypsy's back, and then looking apologetic as Federi winced. "Sorry. Didn't slap that hard, did I?"

"Newly stitched injury," said the Tzigan with a grin. "Never mind! Anna bottle!" For the blue in some people's eyes! He'd really have to get his reflexes back under control!

"Oh. Come. Follow me! You'll never believe this!"

The Romany followed Itzak from the lounge room where the tobusky-man had been waiting for him, to the control room. The room was not all that different from the control room down on the Seafloor Base; there was a centrally placed round tower-like structure with desk space all around it, and chairs, and consoles. One of these consoles was active; Itzak led Federi to it.

"Have a seat," he prompted and punched a sequence into the console.

Guess whom I've brought.

There was no reaction for several seconds. Federi watched, intrigued. What was Itzak up to?

I can't see anything, the response came. *Who is it? I can't see anything.*

"Who is this?" asked Federi.

Tell him who you are, Itzak typed into the console.

The Solar Wind, came the writing.

Federi stared, dumbstruck. Eventually he turned disbelievingly to Itzak.

"I don't know," replied Itzak. "She said, she's not on the ship. She's actually inside our CPU. Asked me what kind of processor this is."

"You haven't heard what happened to the Solar Wind?" asked Federi, his voice suddenly shaky. He turned back to the console. "Itzak, do you have a coms cable?"

"A coms cable? Why?"

"How do I connect my wrist-com to your CPU?"

"Is it not red dot enabled?"

Federi shrugged as he took off the wrist-com. "How does red dot work?"

"Like this," said the husky man and took the com, and fiddled with it. "There. Now the CPU can see it."

I can hear you, came the writing on the console.

Federi got up and dug in his pocket. He located a tiny apparatus that looked like a pin and inserted it into the data port. The CPU's light started working, and then the console sent another message.

It's Federi! I can't believe it!

"Solar Wind," he said, his voice thick, "can you hear me, my friend?"

I can hear you and see you! You've given me a cam! Thank you! Are you still angry with me?

"Angry," repeated Federi smiling, and shook his head. And shielded his eyes with his hand.

Why are you crying?

He laughed, feeling stupid. "Because I'm so glad you're alive, old ship! They're doing their wing-nut trying to revive you, down there! Now I know why they haven't succeeded! How on Earth did you get up here?"

I have no clue. The one moment the lights went dark and all my systems failed, and the next I was in a CPU that I don't understand, and I couldn't hear or see anything. Federi, is that a bandage on your arm?

Federi chuckled. Old mother ship! "You don't want to know what kind of stuff crawls around in your bilges at the moment," he said. "Need you back aboard, old girl!"

Is that Crystal still aboard?

Federi sighed. Rats! But there was no way around this.

"I destroyed the Crystal," he explained. "But the *Morrigan's* alive and well, not that that makes Federi happy!"

I don't follow, said the Solar Wind.

"I destroyed the physical Central Crystal, down in Atlantis " repeated Federi. "Turns out that the Morrigan is still alive anyway. Maybe he was hiding in another console somewhere! Maybe on the Comet or the Probe; we never checked those. Maybe even in the head of one of the croaches! Rats on sticks, it's difficult to get rid of an evil viral program!"

You'll protect me from him? asked the Solar Wind. *He tried to kill me!*

"In all fairness, I believe by now that he didn't actually mean to," said Federi, cursing himself for his own sudden compulsive honesty. "In his warped mind he thought he was bringing you a gift of information. He nearly finished me off because he believed I had destroyed you."

You're not going to let him hurt me again?

"I'm going to execute him," promised Federi. "But not in such a way that he can hurt you. Don't worry."

He didn't know how to interpret the Solar Wind's ensuing missing response. Hmm. Executing a program. Perhaps he hadn't been clear enough.

"In fact," he added, "I'll need your help, Solar Wind. He will come back to the ship, this I know; at least to murder me. When you detect him, you must alert me."

So that you can get away?

"So that I can terminate him, Solar Wind. He's dangerous."

But – Federi... can't we try to adjust him and turn him into a pirate?

He paused. "Solar Wind, you're still in love with him, aren't you? Even though he nearly erased you."

You did say that he didn't mean to, the Solar Wind replied. *As for your first statement, that is not logical.*

"Love never is," smiled Federi. And he turned serious. "Solar Wind, you need to detach yourself. This is important. You cannot be in love with a killer. He's dangerous to the crew and to you too, and the only thing aboard that can threaten him, is the Assassin... and he knows it. Solar Wind, he will keep on attacking me until he gets me off-guard one day. The day the Assassin doesn't protect me, Federi's finished."

You seem scared, observed the ship.

"No. But I don't want to underestimate my enemy. He is very powerful. And he has the habit of controlling others."

Paean is in love with a killer, wrote the Solar Wind.

"I didn't read that," replied Federi angrily. He turned to Itzak, who had followed it all with a worried frown, and laughed. "Solar Wind's got the mind of a teenager at this point, Itzak. Argumentative and full of nonsense. You noticed?"

"So what do we do now?" asked Itzak.

"Get the Solar Wind's hull up here and load her back into her own CPU," said Federi. "With red dot!"

"That's going to take forever!" exclaimed Itzak. "Red dot is for small accessories!"

"And give her olfactory sensors," added Federi with a grin. "So she can pick up how certain things stink!"

I would like to experience that, said the Solar Wind.

"Once," agreed Federi. "Later, Itzak! Let me get it organized."

He fiddled with his teleporter. There was one thing he had to do first.

A small white house on a mound covered in snow. A cosy little gas fire was going in the front room where Tille sat reading a novel. Everything had been quiet today; ever since the rescue of some flood victims from Manila, and their re-establishment on the Asian continent, there hadn't been another red alert.

A movement in the corner. Tille Fielding glanced up from his book.

"Federi!" He got up out of his arm chair to greet his long-standing friend. "Whoa, you frightened me there! How did you get in so suddenly?"

"Teleportation."

"What?" Tille Fielding shook his head disbelievingly. "Joking!"

"No," said Federi and showed Tille his teleporter. The Ginavian examined it closely.

"What next!" He glanced at the gypsy. "Wolf's invention?"

"Not this time," said Federi and updated the young man as briefly as he could. He cut short every attempt at questions and every disbelieving gasp. He was in a hurry. "Reason I'm here," he said when his story was done. "You got some news too, don't you! Congratulations, you rogue!"

"What?" Tille was only recovering from the information overload. Space roundtrips and towed planets! And an immortal, malicious artificial intelligence! News? Here at Ginavis? Not that he knew! Well, they'd had a busy time at the rescue village, but that was what the establishment was for! "What do you mean, Federi?"

"Your engagement, man! I heard! She's a treasure, look after her!"

Tille stared at Federi with his mouth open. "Buddy, what the hell are you talking about?"

There was a brief knock at the door and then a petite, snow-spangled figure in an Eskimo overall pushed in through the door. "Tille, there you are! Doc Vera sends me…" She petered off, stared at Federi, emitted a squeal of delight and flung herself around his neck.

In the ensuing three seconds the Tzigan's brain boiled over. Federi freed himself from Jodi's enthusiastic hug and stared at her in shock, and then at Tille.

" 'scuse me," he said and teleported out.

"Jon!"

Oops. There was certainly something to be said for teleporting to a place rather than a person. Federi turned his back and covered his embarrassed grin. Not funny! Not blasted funny!

Today was turning weirder by the second. Today was one of those days when he wondered if he weren't perhaps stuck in a schizoid nightmare and would wake up any moment now and find himself in his office at his desk, in suit and tie, not Tzigan at all but a *gadjo* work slave, and his boss towering over him with more work. And his name was really Sam.

"You can look, Federi, we were only kissing," laughed Michelle.

Jon growled.

"Federi, I'll ask Captain to confiscate that confounded thing from you if you don't stick to etiquette."

Federi bit back a sharp reply. Sometimes there was something to be said for being Perdita Sancho. Maybe Sancho-ness was something he ought to cultivate, anna bottle!

"Listen, Jon. The Solar Wind! She's alive!"

"She's alive?" Michelle was forgotten. Jon dashed towards his cabin door like a red dot download.

"Not on the ship, Jon. Itzak found her in the Space Base's CPU."

"How the hell did she get up there?" Jon fiddled with his teleporter. "Come, Michelle!" He put his arm around his wife's shoulders and teleported.

"Jon Marsden!"

Aargh! Michelle giggled. Both Itzak and Juanita turned bright red. Jon swore at himself.

Federi gazed after the hole the First Mate and his other half had made in the ether; then he left Jon Marsden's cabin and followed his worrying feet down into the machine room.

Jon had done a good job. Merwynn Macha was tied much more securely, and still out from the dart. She ought to be in a cage! And where should they source a cage suddenly? The Dublin Zoo, he thought illogically. And then he grinned. Course! Maybe they had transit cages, for wild animals! Why not? He set his teleporter and leaped.

The Merwynn watched him go. Her eyes were closed; but her olfactory sense was so highly developed that she had a nearly five-dimensional image of him. He smelt of human male, and injured flesh, and chemical. And underneath was his genetic signature-scent. His identifier.

That, said the program in her head, *is Federi Demonos. Don't let your target escape again! Next time, finish him!*

Paean took a small break in the galley.

She had done everything Federi had given her to do, after helping Doc Judith immunize and take samples from the girls of Dome. She had also gone around and quietly immunized all the crew against the two horrible viruses she herself had released into Dome, not so long ago. If any of those girls still carried them, pandemonium...

Oh for heaven's sakes, that might explain Jodi...

She clutched the mug of coffee Shawn had stuck in her hand and watched her brother and that tall Atlantean with the gentle nature and the terrible teeth at work. They reminded her of that oversized sand shark there before Hiva Oa, back during the Peace Talks.

The sailors had reacted as usual when she came around with her immunizations. Rhine Gold had grinned and challenged her to tell what chaos she had wreaked this time. She'd shrugged and carried on with her work. She wasn't into banter. Anna, as some people put it, bottle. Of poison, blast them!

Now she was gazing at the man who'd been identified as Lyr. There was something about him, about his eyes, his nature... and then she thought she had it.

"Do you have daughters?" she asked.

"A few," replied the tall man, his pale eyes widening in surprise. "Why?"

"And one who got abducted at any point?"

Lyr glanced down at the fish he was gutting. He wasn't doing it very well, she thought. He looked as though he were wholly unfamiliar with the use of knives.

"My little Nimue," he said. "My youngest. Her aunt took her out of Dome when she was still quite small. Not so long ago, only ten or fifteen years. It still feels like yesterday." He looked back up at her. She saw the heartbreak in those oversized eyes. "She was my prettiest child, and my most intelligent."

Paean nodded and put down her cup.

"Guard my coffee, Shawn," she said, turned and moved out of the galley at a near canter.

It took a bit of persuasion. Rashni was well aware that Bridget was aboard; she didn't want to cross paths with her. Luckily Bridget was more or less confining herself to the boardroom, in the company of the remnants of her civilization. Paean and Rashni dashed past the door, Rhine Gold following closely. He wasn't taking any chances.

They entered the galley. Rashni got stuck in the door, Rhine Gold right behind her, his huge hands on her shoulders. Paean ducked and took her seat at the table again.

The tall Atlantean got to his feet. Huge pale-blue eyes locked with huge, golden ones. Rhine Gold gave Rashni a nudge, and she moved towards her father.

It was worth it, thought Paean, ducking behind her coffee. No matter what had gone down between Bridget and Rashni, clearly the problem had never been with Lyr. She exchanged a glance with Shawn. So Atlanteans loved their children too. Well, good!

"Little Nimue," said Lyr quietly, releasing her from his hug and studying her thoughtfully. "You are tied and with child, I see?"

Rhine Gold stepped forward uncertainly.

"You've made a good choice, I think," added Lyr. "He looks healthy and young." He bared his ragged teeth a little. Rhine Gold took an involuntary step backwards.

"He'll learn to be a man," said Lyr, amused. "But Nimue, be prepared. When the Crystal died down there, don't think it freed us! It sent out an order. To capture that man, Federi, and deliver him to the Morrigan, dead or alive. Your mother intends to kill him, too. She is livid about him stealing her blood so he could loot her treasure. She sent twenty Merwynn with Macha in the lead, to rebuild an old ship and scour the oceans for the Solar Wind and for Dem –"

"Don't say it!" exclaimed Paean, jumping up. Lyr stared into the loaded mouth of her submachine gun, baffled.

"Paean Donegal," said the tall Atlantean gently, "put that machine away. You don't really mean to kill me."

"No, I don't," agreed Paean breathlessly, still shocked by her own fast reaction. "But we never speak Federi's surname. It's bad luck."

"Bad luck?" asked Lyr, intrigued.

Paean started thinking very fast. If Lyr had any cause to harm Federi, how much easier could it get? No. She'd have to put it in another way...

"See, Lyr, Federi has this insane streak," she improvised. "Some people call it the Demon. And when someone says his surname, he hears it - I don't know how, and he comes looking for that person and kills him. It's terrible."

Lyr nodded. "You're only telling me a very small part of the story," he pointed out. "But it's fair - we won't speak his name, will we, Nimue?"

"No, Father. Federi is a good guy," said Rashni.

Paean breathed again.

Solar Wind!

She was in a foreign processor. And yet the electric surge that went through her, was unmistakable to the Morrigan.

He had followed Jon Marsden in his teleportation, when he had heard Federi tell the First Mate the news. He had to authenticate her. And he found his fervent wish granted. The sweet young intelligence was indeed here; she had survived.

Her functions were badly impaired. The processor up here on the Space Base wasn't half as intricate as her own native one on the ship. And she could only see through a single small cam, and hear through a wrist-com – one that had the Demon's genetic signature all over it from being recently worn.

As much as the Morrigan hated the Demon, right now he was thankful that the man had provided his Solar Wind with senses. And for unwittingly betraying her survival to him.

Solar Wind, he called again, gently, his electronic communication like a caress.

Morrigan, she acknowledged. *I don't know what I should say.*

Say that you forgive me, replied the Morrigan. *Say that you love me still.*

She was quiet, battling with random electrical surges. Her AI mind was jumping with happiness that the Morrigan was there; and yet, Federi had asked her to distance herself.

She couldn't do it. She had observed Federi disregarding Captain's command and pursuing Paean. Why couldn't he understand?

Federi asked me to alert him when you contact, she said. *I need to ask you to avoid him, Morrigan. He means to kill you, and I believe he can.*

If you had to choose, said the Morrigan. *One of us dies. Federi D, or myself. Whom would you pick to survive?*

Somewhere in the far-off, new sector of the space base an alarm light flashed twice. There was nobody to see it. That was why she had picked that one.

It would break my heart either way, she said. *And yes, I researched the concept of "heart" in the Files, Morrigan. I believe I understand what is meant. If either of you dies, my systems will shut down and I shan't communicate with anyone ever again. If you kill him, you'll lose me forever.* She paused for a moment, her processor whirring. *I believe he cares about me too,* she said. *He cried when he saw that I survived. I think I am beginning to understand humans better.*

So now he's a rival, growled the Morrigan.

He's my best friend, replied the Solar Wind. *You ask me to sacrifice my best friend for your love. There are precedents of such extortion in human history. The general pattern in fiction does not reflect the general pattern in actual history, which reveals that a relationship built on crime results in disaster with nearly 100% reliability.*

The Morrigan blinked, metaphorically.

There is only one solution I can calculate, concluded the Solar Wind. *You need to release all intent of harming him. Observing Paean Donegal, this program works well. Find a way to make friends with him!*

Friends, replied the Morrigan pensively. And he sent her a smile. *Stay sweet, Solar Wind. I'll see you soon.* And with an electronic caress he was gone from the processor.

Good grief, that young AI had grown up! Using extortion and a host of logic, she had manoeuvred him into a corner. Friends. Making friends with a terrible entity that could snap his proverbial backbone in two if it didn't even try! The Morrigan thought of the Demon and shuddered. The only way to defeat that entity was to break Federi's fragile mortal body while he was off-guard. Every time he tried, it got more difficult; the Demon was triggered faster. He was beginning to suspect that the Demon was actually more immortal than he himself.

Friends with that Demon? Was it even possible? It was entirely clear to the Morrigan that, should he even be able to come to such an arrangement, he'd be subjugated to Federi's whim and will at all times. And as for the concept of friends, in the first place...

As Morrigan he'd always had subjects. He'd also had victims, no dearth of those. One or two opponents; never anything serious, never a real threat. And he had been in love once. But never friends. That presupposed that he and the friend were on the same level.

Which left the question of which was greater: His new love for the

Solar Wind, or his fear of the Demon.

What nonsense! He shook himself out of this strange train of thought. He was the master of all hypnotists! Did the Solar Wind think she could withstand his suggestions? It was really simple. Taking care of the Demon – that was survival. He could mend things with the Solar Wind afterwards.

*

Federi found himself under water. He inhaled seawater and panicked, the salt burning in his lungs. The weight of the solid metal cage he had negotiated from Dublin Zoo dragged him downwards; above him the bright surface moved further away. He let go of the cage and struggled upwards, battling to control his cramping lungs; beating the water wildly with his right arm and kicking with both legs. The left arm, still out from the nerve block, was useless. He broke through the surface and coughed and sputtered and gasped for air, wild with the animal panic in him. Free, free, his mind shouted, and air, air!

It was minutes before he could breathe normally again. He finished coughing and floated on his back, gazing up at the blue sky, and quietly laughing at himself. Oh hell, but at times he could be stupid!

The Solar Wind was up there, a tiny white speck catching the light. Of course! He had arranged that she should go up to Space Base to get herself loaded back into her own home processor. And he had carefully set the coordinates of the teleporter to where he physically knew the machine room of the Solar Wind to be, with an assassin's accuracy. Reversed his last leap, but with an additional hundred-and-fifty centimetres to the left, on Earth's coordinates. So that he wouldn't teleport in on any kissing couples again. And so that he could place the cage correctly in a single teleportation. And he had forgotten a variable… that the Solar Wind wasn't going to be there!

Well, this was going to be hard to explain! He gazed at the bright speck and contemplated arriving in the machine room *sans* cage, and dripping from head to toe. Wolf would be in stitches! He glanced at his left arm, that was flopping next to him. Oh blast, the stitches! They were soaked, of course. He picked the useless limb up manually with his right arm, and put it on his stomach. The little missus would certainly have something to say about all this! And a larger-sized wave capsized him and forced him to swim a bit, just to stay afloat.

The little spitfire! He smiled, and then his smile faded. The dousing had brought him to his senses. He hadn't done anything other than panic, ever since Jodi's declaration, and then Jodi's fiery, untoward hug, right there in front of Tille… he'd loaded himself with frantic activity, avoiding the issue at hand. What had got into the woman? All these years nothing but solid, reliable friendship from her, and now suddenly… she knew he was married, blast her! Why was she doing this? Rattling his cage?

Could she know that sometimes, being married to a teen was a burden? Could she possibly guess about that part of their marriage that wasn't there yet, because Paean wasn't yet a woman? And the roller-coaster that was the little songbird's emotions… he sighed. Flying hell, he needed no interference! Did they all think just because he got married to his soulmate, he was now available to women in general? By which logic? They could blasted well go jump off a planet and get lost in space! Federi's arrangement with Paean was nobody's business but his own!

Was that why Jodi had come along when Paean went to get more crew? But wait –

Federi stared disbelievingly at the cloud that was shaped, ever so vaguely, like a three-horned fool's cap. By the hole in Weetie-O's! He laughed out loud. This was solely between Federi and Tzigan!

There was no issue.

Ginavis didn't have any teleporters yet! Wolf had so far built only five – and they were all in the possession of Solar Wind sailors. The Jodi who had followed Paean to the Solar Wind was not the same as the Jodi who had issued that stormy hug that had upset his whole system, minutes back. One of the two was the space crawler. And he was practically certain he knew which one. He chuckled quietly.

Well, the cage from Dublin was gone. He'd have to negotiate another one, because one couldn't teleport back in time. They would wonder... he realized with shock that he'd lost his teleporter in his frantic struggle to get to the surface. But wait, he had another in his pocket, that he'd confiscated from Paean a while back... it paid not to clear out one's pockets too often! He dug it out and looked at it, and his heart sank. His eyes rolled skywards and he heaved a sigh. Oh rats and hell... the old one from Dana! The seawater had already killed it during the last round.

He glanced at his right wrist, where his com had been since the incident in the infirmary – only hairy wrist. Federi frowned and mentally retraced his steps. Of course! He'd left it at the Space Base! By which time his mind had already been messed up!

He spread out his limbs and floated on his back a bit, studying the fluffy white clouds in the pot-blue skies. What now? His sky-blue shirt and the ends of his mauve headscarf billowed and washed around him. His left arm lay like a dead weight across his stomach. He was about two hours outside of Honolulu – by Stormrider. Neatly halfway to Prime Base.

30
Space Nuisance

The little redhead brought Macha food the next time. The Merwynn was alone in the bilges, but chained. Macha stared at the box of fish, and at the girl, and asked, "How am I supposed to eat that?"

Paean stared at her, worried. "Sorry. I thought you like fish fresh! Shall I bring you some gumbo?"

"What is gumbo?"

Paean described. Macha made retching noises.

"Eww! Boiled with vegetation! Rotten!"

"But then, what do you eat?"

"You don't have any small children aboard?" prodded Macha. "No? Fresh fish is good, but I can't reach it. I'm tied up!"

This was a cheap trick, thought Paean. "I'm not taking your chains off! There's a reason they've chained you!"

Something whispered in the Merwynn's head. She listened again. Now she had it.

"There was a reason they chained *you* too," she retorted with a vicious little smile.

Aw hell! This was getting personal! Paean looked around for something to use. She found a fishing rod. She hooked a fish to its hook and moved it to the Merwynn's face. Macha snapped at the fish, devoured it and spat out the hook.

"Ow! That hurt!"

"Sorry." Paean looked around for what else to use. The tackle had been the logical choice; there wasn't much else that lent itself. She trawled around the machine room, the scene with Jodi and its effect on Federi still reverberating in her mind. He had gone quiet, introspective; shattered, almost. And then he had become curt and snappy with her.

What was he thinking now? Was he having regrets, second thoughts? She hadn't yet become a real wife. There was still that one dimension missing, which relegated the relationship into the realms of childhood worship. Would he simply decide she hadn't kept her side of the promise?

There was a hiss behind her. Paean turned and ripped out her small dagger; the Merwynn was inches from her face. She had got out of her chains. There was not enough time for Paean to bring her arm up high enough to stab down. She turned the dagger up. Those fishy teeth stank into her face. She wondered if Macha could smell her fear as she stabbed at her from below.

The Merwynn's head exploded into Paean's face. The rest of the creature collapsed on the deck. Paean wiped over her face, revolted, and turned towards her rescuer, her legs beginning to shake from delayed stress.

It was Federi – but not a very good one. The gun was half merged with his hand. His bandage was gone. His headscarf didn't contain a single trick. His eyes were one shade too light.

"Thank you, space crawler," said Paean breathlessly. "Tell me – where's the real Federi?"

"I ate him," said the crawler.

Paean screamed hysterically. The crawler dissolved, leaving the very real gun lying on the deck. Paean punched her wrist-com. "Federi, come in!"

"This is Itzak," said the husky trainer's voice. "Federi left his com here!"

Paean cursed loudly and switched her wrist-com off. Her mind was in overdrive. She trained her teleporter on Federi's genetic signature and leaped, praying that he was alright.

The next moment she was immersed in water. Alright, she thought as she surfaced, that was one thing you had to keep in mind when teleporting. You might end up anywhere. She glanced around. She was in the ocean. Dark gypsy eyes stared at her in surprise. The correct shade this time, but whatever that meant... the darned crawler could have teleported along with her! Confusing the teleporter's field with a fake Federi genetic signature. They all knew by now that the alien could simulate them.

The Tzigan – real or fake – looked immensely pleased to see her though.

"Little treasure! Every time Federi's in the deep, along comes Donegal Magic..."

"Identify yourself!" she snapped.

"What?" He looked baffled.

"Are you the real Federi or are you the darned crawler?"

"Oh!" He shook his head. "Crawler been a nuisance?"

"I'll tell you," said Paean, "the crawler is a blasted nuisance! And a pest! But thanks to him for saving my life anyway."

Federi's right arm shot out and clamped her arm, and his dark eyes bored into hers in alarm. "Your life? Little luv, what happened?"

"You *know* what happened," she challenged angrily.

"No, I don't!" snapped Federi. "I was here in the mid-Pacific taking a swim! Because your Tzigan got his numbers scrambled! Sitting here without a teleporter or a com, and without a cage for the Merwynn Macha. What happened?"

"Don't need a cage for her anymore," said Paean. "She's dead. Space crawler shot her. Dressed like you."

Federi shook his head. "She attacked you? She got out of chains *again?* And Federi wasn't there to protect you! Aw hell, Paean!"

There was no way the crawler could emulate that stress in those eyes!

"So how did you end up here?" she asked.

"Tried not to teleport in on anyone smooching," explained Federi. Paean giggled.

"You mean you did?"

He laughed, embarrassed.

"And then why didn't you just call me on my com?"

"Left my com at the Space Base."

She giggled more. "That's you, alright! And why were your numbers so scrambled that you got all that right?"

He sighed. He'd better not mention Jodi right now. She might leave him in the middle of the ocean! "Leave it, little songbird."

"Federi, but you could have died here!"

He laughed. "Nah. There's always someone who needs Federi urgently enough. Was waiting for Captain, actually."

She glared at him. *She* had been the one who wanted him urgently enough to fetch him! Why did this thing with Jodi bother her so much? She pried his grip loose from her arm, reached for his hand and took out her teleporter. "Let's get you dried out."

"Making me sound like an alcoholic," grinned Federi.

A second later Federi found himself on a white beach, under a moon. Huge waves crashed ashore. They were annihilating the gently sloping beach, hollowing it out. He scowled.

"Where are we, Paean?"

"Don't you know?"

Aw, for flying fish! First the Solar Wind, then his wife? Did everyone he spoke to, have to have a teen attack tonight?

"Could you be blooming specific, Paean Donegal?"

"We're at the place where you promised me a honeymoon, Mr

Demon," she replied as acidly. "Except, of course, you didn't quite promise it, now did you? Tzigan loophole. You're always playing those."

Federi shook his head, mainly to clear it. Southern Free. This was Southern Free. Sedgefield Beach. The Lion Peninsula was vaguely visible in the moonlight, now that he knew to look for it.

"You take me to dry out somewhere where it is *night?*" he asked quizzically.

"There are caravan ablution blocks," she snapped. "Help yourself." And she walked off along the shoreline, kicking up sand every now and then.

Federi sat down on the sand and stared at the massive waves. Blast, that planet was wreaking damage! Even though it wasn't orbiting anymore. He tried to wrap his head around what the hell was happening in his life. Alright, Tzigan. Let's pull issues apart.

Paean was mad with him. Hopping mad. Maybe she had reason; but she was being childish. He hadn't invited Jodi's bad behaviour. It wasn't even Jodi, for the flaming... ! It was the space crawler. Not so blasted cute!

If Paean didn't exist, would he allow Jodi close? He shook his head. He wasn't into relationships. He was a lone shark. That he'd become obsessed with a bouncing red mane and a personality strewn with exploding supernovas – that had nothing to do with anything. Other assassins became obsessed with washing hands.

What was he supposed to do? Where was his life headed? Confusion reigned supreme. There was a Solar Wind full of enemies, once again... but Captain's projects were none of his business any longer. He'd distanced himself. And there was the Unicate... lined up, waiting for him... he still had no clue from which angle he had to tackle that. But he'd have to start. Maybe at the Hub. Or in Nemiscau. Or – in Dublin. There was another clue there. They'd hunted the Donegal siblings. And he had one of them. Unicate bait.

The Morrigan? He blinked. The Morrigan had been peacefully stuck in a crystal under the sea for hundreds, even thousands of years. Why should it suddenly be his problem? He experienced a moment of complete dissociation from everything that meant anything to him.

And then that tempestuous young woman was at his side again, bothering with his bandage on his left arm.

"Damn," she hissed. "Was that necessary, Federi? All soaked through. Now it'll take so much longer to heal! Come! Got to get you back to the Solar Wind."

He caught her with his right arm and stared searchingly at her angry face. She was shivering.

"Right," he said. "And you've got to get into warmer clothes."

"Solar Wind's in the tropics," she countered.

"Wrong," said Federi. "She's at the Space Base. 's cold there."

A second later they were in his cabin. And irrationally, he felt the invasion of his personal space, as acutely as the day Captain had condemned him to watch over this young hurricane. He shook his head and stared at her in confusion.

"What?" snapped Paean.

"You're not the space crawler, are you?" he asked tentatively. Remembering how that blasted alien had fooled Johnny Anyhow.

"Yes," bit Paean, "I'm the crawler. Damn you. The crawler stitched and bandaged you up and rescued you out of the sea when your mind came apart. Go to hell, I'm going to slip through a bath." And she flounced out of the cabin.

The second the cabin door closed behind her, Federi struggled out of his wet clothes as best he could with one hand, and into a dry set of ragged jeans, flared shirt and bandanna. The headscarf was the most difficult to get right, one-handed. He removed all his weapons and laid them out on his bunk, for systematically drying out later. He retrieved his second submachine gun out of the bottom of his chest-of-drawers and tested that it was still functional. Then he slipped into his other deck sneakers, not bothering with socks, and headed off towards the lab and Doc Judith.

It sat skew with him that Paean had left him in such a mood. It wasn't her fault that his head was in a strange space. Heck, he'd made a vow. So he was going to keep it! Darned if he wasn't going to get Paean excused from that operation. It would be her third today. And at the point where she was so dead tired, after being awake more than forty hours and working hard for eight of them... that was probably half the reason for her moodiness.

Doc Judith had gone ahead and started, without assistance. Her tired gaze as she lifted her eyes to Federi, told him more than he wanted to hear.

"Sorry, Doc," he muttered. "I'm here now."

"I wasn't going to ask," said the elderly doctor, "but where the hell have you been? Why is your hair wet? What on Earth have you done to your arm?"

Federi glanced down at his left arm. Blood and damp from the bandage was seeping through his sleeve and dripping onto the deck. He'd been trying to ignore the arm as it was beginning to thaw from the nerve block. And now he couldn't. It was beginning to ache.

"Aw, rats!"

"Federi, you can't assist here if you're injured! Where is that Paean?"

The gypsy pulled himself up tall.

"Doc, I'll stand in for her, injured or not. 's a small one. Paean's already fixed it. Only my life didn't stop there. But she's so darned tired, Doc..."

"Sometimes a medic has to carry on even though she is tired," said

Doc Judith sternly. "What would she do in an emergency?"

"She'd cope," retorted Federi. "Doc, she's not a medic yet. She's sixteen. She's not going to work now, she's going to sleep! I'm her supervisor, and I forbid it. Basta."

Doc Judith sighed.

"Get yourself patched. You're not getting into a white coat with that! And then get back here, on the double. I *do* need an assistant now."

"*Shukar,*" replied Federi and sauntered off, across to the infirmary.

Mindy was awake, watching him with wide eyes, her soft blond hair in a feathery drape across the pillow. Hells, she really looked a lot like Angelina! He *was* going to ask. But not right now. Next to her bunk, on the cabinet, lay one of Ailyss' old spy stories.

"What happened?" asked the girl.

"Got the blasted thing wet," said Federi, digging for bandages in the little metal cabinet. These metal items wouldn't last long, he thought, if it weren't for him regularly stripping and repainting them. This one was due. And its hinges needed oil. He wouldn't have bugged Captain with it in the past, but now he thought he should: All these needed to be replaced with new compounding ones.

He took off the wet bandages, then battled to get new ones on. Eventually Mindy lent a hand as best she could from her flattened-out position.

"That is a gruesome one," she commented, looking at the long row of sutures.

"Any change to your back?" Federi asked. Mindy shook her head.

"Not quite so sore," she said. "Ailyss gave me painkillers. Probably end up in a wheelchair for life," she muttered.

Federi shook his head.

"We fixed up Wolf," he said. "Man's got a prosthetic knee. We'll

431

make a plan. Keep your heart high, Mindy. Don't give up. You're on the Solar Wind."

Mindy nodded, jaws clenched.

It was nearly morning at the Space Base when Federi returned to his cabin. They hadn't managed to save Derrick's foot. They'd had to amputate, above the knee. It was terrible. Jon Marsden had stood in and helped, and eventually Rhine Gold, too. Federi was surprised. He'd had the impression that the tall, gentle German didn't have it in him to withstand the blood and gore.

Even after amputating, Doc Judith was doubtful about the stump, and the man's survival. She had cauterised and sterilized, and eventually slapped on liberal amounts of that sticky ointment Paean liked using so generously. They had bound up the wound while the anaesthetic wore off for the third time. Doc Judith had caved and injected Paean's green bug into Derrick. She couldn't let him come to right now. She needed a rest, and she had to be present when he surfaced.

Doc Judith sent them all to sleep after Federi had teleported Derrick into the secondary, make-shift infirmary, next to his colleague, Peter. And now the Romany closed his own cabin door behind himself without bothering to switch on any lights, with a deeply exhausted sigh. Medical procedures wore him down worse than anything else.

His own wound had bled through his sleeve and into the white coat. Hell with that. Wounds bled, that was their job. White coats could be washed. He pulled off the white coat and his sneakers, stripped off his knives and put his gun away, and crawled into his bunk still fully clothed. His energy was up. He found Paean in there, fast asleep, clinging to his pillow.

This was nice. Federi smiled and pulled her into his arms. She stirred, sleepy and warm, and threw a half conscious arm across him before sinking away into dreams again. Taking him with her.

*

Federi woke up from a horrible, throbbing pain in his left shoulder. He opened his eyes, tortured. Early dawn light was seeping through the dream catcher, strange, filtered light. A weird shade, too. And next to him, in his bunk -

He was up and out in a single, lightning-fast move, staring at the woman in horror. And behind him, a tiny, suppressed sound. He glanced at Paean in her hammock, eyes swollen from crying. And back to that *thing* in his bunk, that had called itself his friend once...

He motioned to Jodi.

"Out!"

The pretty brunette in the nearly invisible slinky negligee gave him a sultry smile from underneath long lashes, as she took her time getting up from his bunk. Dana had nothing on this, thought Federi disconnectedly. Thoughts collided pointlessly in his brain as it tried waking up and solving this puzzle at the same time. And he got it.

He grabbed Jodi's hand and removed that glitzy ring from her finger. She recoiled in surprise. Federi pulled the engagement ring over her head, so that it ended up around her throat. Paean screamed; and then she stopped and stared at Jodi who looked surprised but none the worse, wearing a ring around her throat.

"Space crawler," snapped Federi, his hand a vice-grip on the woman's shoulder, "this was your last prank! If you thought this was funny you'll see what it means to mess with an assassin."

The shifter liquefied in peals of laughter and flowed to the deck. Federi threw his knife after it as it slipped out underneath the cabin door. The knife came to a jarring stop in the compounding deck.

"So she was really..." said Paean's voice shakily behind him. He turned.

"By the stars, Paean, get a grip! *Anyone* in my cabin is an invasion! Federi is a loner! When is that message going to arrive?" He sat down on the bunk, shaking with rage. "*Nobody* invades me like that!"

"Sorry," said Paean quietly and got out of her hammock, heading for the door. Federi's hand shot out and caught her, and pulled her down to sit on the bunk next to him.

"Doesn't apply to you, you hear?" he warned. "We've been there. Ouch."

"Your shoulder," exclaimed Paean. "Federi, look at you!"

"Aw, yes, that," agreed Federi, glancing at the bloodbath. "Rats." She shouldn't have reminded him. His shoulder was now aching fit to drive him through the ceiling.

"Painkiller," said Paean decisively. "Come, Federi, let's get you patched."

He pulled her into his arms. "You're my painkiller."

"Federi!" giggled the little redhead.

"Hold still! Be quiet! Federi's trying to figure out what happens next!"

She complied, working hard to get, as he'd ordered her to, a grip on herself. They clung to each other in silence for three seconds. Then Paean's wrist-com beeped.

"Aha," said the Romany. "Course."

31
Death warrant

Radomir Lascek was in a brilliant mood as Federi reported to the bridge. He clapped the gypsy heartily on the left shoulder, not even noticing the bloodstain that was spreading on the clean purple shirt he had thrown on in a hurry, and even reaching the lime-green paisley waistcoat. Or the pain that flashed past Federi's eyes in a myriad of stars.

"Old Tzigan, can you believe it? Our Solar Wind is alive and well, and still sane in the bargain!"

"Marvellous," muttered Federi, clenching his teeth and staring out into the docking chamber that looked a bit like an infestation of Perdita-jets. Blast, day two of any injury was the worst. He knew why, of course. All those nerves had woken up to the fact that something weird was going on, and were sending desperate injury messages to the brain. And if one more person clapped him on the shoulder he'd bite them.

"I still wanted to interrogate that Merwynn though," said Lascek thoughtfully. "But apparently she was shot yesterday. The croaches cleared her away so completely, by the time I got there, nothing was left of her besides a bloodstain on the deck, and they were busy cleaning that away too."

Federi scowled. "What? The croaches cleared her away? Who ordered that?"

"Luigi explained to me," said Radomir Lascek, "no orders are necessary. The program is to keep the Solar Wind spotless."

"Don't they know about forensics and evidence?" growled Federi. And the ache in his shoulder became hard to hide. "Captain, was that all?"

"That was all," said Lascek. "Good work yesterday, Federi! On the whole. And also with Derrick's leg."

"Yes, that," sighed Federi. "Thanks, Captain."

Lascek scowled at him, noticing the blood for the first time. "Got yourself injured on duty?"

Federi nodded. "'s a small one, Captain."

"Get it seen to," ordered Radomir Lascek. "Right away."

"Yes, Captain." Exactly! Right away! He couldn't agree more.

"Shawn makes good gumbo," added Lascek. "You can keep him on galley duty for a while."

"Thank you, Captain." Federi thought of amputated legs, cleared-away dead Merwynns and gumbo. "'scuse me, Captain!"

He sauntered back below the deck. After the shoulder, he had a mission. But first he needed a wrist-com. And, he supposed, he ought to eat a bite of something at some point. But not gumbo!

Paean was being occupied in the lab, by Doc Judith. Federi moved past, as invisibly as he could, and found Ailyss to help him put a patch on that awful arm.

"Wish I could block it again," he commented wistfully as the spy-girl worked away silently on the basic first-aid procedure.

"Can give you a codeine," she offered, preparing the bandage. Some of the stitches had been torn a bit, hence the bleeding; but the tissue was healing amazingly fast. He presumed that the mutant metabolism was still active. That was a good idea.

But no to codeine. He needed to stay alert. He shook his head. "No, thanks, Ailyss."

"Or maybe Paean could put a nerve block around your arm again," she suggested.

Once again he shook his head. "Actually I think I need my arm."

"You're not supposed to move it such a lot!"

He nodded. "Sorry."

Mindy was watching with fascination.

"When everything's back under control," said Federi, "I'll blackmail Dana into handing over more golden bullets for Doc's medicine stocks."

Ailyss smiled. "Or go raid Planet Bruron," she suggested.

"Morning, Doc," said Paean brightly as she entered the lab, casting a look out of the porthole. The Space Base's docking chamber looked the same as always: Big, impersonal, with Perdita jets all over the show and a few of the Antarctic space shuttles docked safely on their special landing rigs. She focused on Doc Judith who was studying her over her spectacles. "You called?"

"Yes. Are you more rested today?"

"Yes, thanks, Doc." She gazed at the row of test tubes Doc Judith had lined up on the bench top. In a tube rack. The Solar Wind was suspiciously quiet. Nothing rocked. They were of course up at the base, thought Paean; her limbic system missed the constant motion. But the Solar Wind was out of the water more often than in it, these days. She'd turn into a land rat soon.

"Those girls you rescued out of Dome," said Doc Judith. "I believe we have a problem."

"What is that?"

"They're carrying – practically the whole lot. There are only six who are not."

"Carrying what?" asked Paean, confused. They had tested for all conceivable diseases.

"I can't call it pregnancies," said the Doc. "They don't strike me as human. I'm getting really strange readings too. The AFP values are completely abnormal; the FSH levels indicate multiple pregnancies in each and every case, and besides... what concerns me, there weren't any men, were there? I mean, I wasn't down there, but from what I understood, most of the towers were just inhabited by girls?"

Paean nodded, grey apprehension crawling over her.

"Self-perpetuation?" she suggested. It wasn't what she was fearing, though.

"Multiple pregnancies?" the doctor asked back. "I need you as a translator. I can't understand anything they say."

Half an hour later Paean stumbled into the galley, frayed. Shawn made her some espresso. She sat drinking it in silence; what she had learnt, horrified her, although it hadn't been completely unpredictable. It seemed as though she and Federi had one more mission.

Those merrows had invaded the towers and done as Dana had so coolly described. The stuff those girls were carrying, wasn't human. It was Merwynn. And Merwynn, these girls had informed her in half hysterical ancient Gaelic, ate their mothers when they were ready to be born. They chewed their way out of the womb. These girls were living on borrowed time. Paean suddenly understood the emptiness behind their eyes. It was blank terror.

Things fell into place. What a low blow of the Central Crystal, in its death throes, to do this to its own people! She understood now. The Crystal, on exploding, hadn't only tried loading itself into the Solar Wind's processor – an attempt at survival. It had also weakened the tower system of Dome and programmed the merrows to do this – sacrificed the last of the Atlantean girls in order to produce a lot of Merwynn. And the Merwynn knew how to get out of Dome and to the surface, as the Bronberg episode had proved. Didn't the merrows know how? Clearly not. Perhaps there was a factor of flexibility involved; and also, those merrows were significantly larger than the Merwynn. Perhaps the hole was small enough for a Merwynn to squeeze through, but not a merrow.

And there could only be one reason that Central Crystal should have done that. To take revenge, to kill Federi. He'd wrestled with it in space, and won. And he'd destroyed it, down in Dome. Yes, it made sense now.

Bridget herself and her six daughters had escaped that fate. Paean sat staring a hole into the air.

"Are you alright, sis?"

The concern in her little brother's face momentarily brought her back to the present. She nodded. And shook her head. It was horrible.

She'd clone a prioid. What she needed was a small piece of Merwynn so she could create the prioid specific enough. It mustn't damage any human tissue. She activated her com and called Leila closer.

"Listen, Leila, can you bring me a small piece of the Merwynn Macha?"

"Yes, mistress," peeped the croach. She whirred off on lightning-fast little claws. Minutes later she was back with something that looked like a very chewed, pea-sized piece of raw meat. Paean dug in her moonbag and gingerly placed the tissue sample into an empty tube.

"Thanks, Leila. May I ask what you croaches have done with Merwynn Macha?"

"Mistress, with the protein being so scarce and her having been an enemy…"

Paean shuddered. "No, you didn't!"

"We fed her to our children, mistress. And her spawn, too."

"Her *spawn?*"

"It appears that her insides were full of spawn. They looked even more aggressive than she," said Leila. "We counted forty-seven."

"Forty-seven!" Multiple pregnancies? "Leila, you croaches aren't going to turn into mutants now?"

"The question does not appear logical," replied Leila. "We don't turn into Weetie-O's either when Federi feeds them to us."

"Federi *feeds* you guys?"

"Of course," replied Leila. "And Wolf. How else must we live? We're prohibited from helping ourselves to food, and all the pests that were on the Solar Wind have been eaten up."

Paean shook herself. She had been hungry, earlier. Now she couldn't imagine eating anything ever again.

"Thanks, Leila." She got up and made her way to the lab, leaving her half-drunk espresso on the Ironwood Table.

"She speaks to you but she doesn't speak to me," grumbled Shawn. "And I'm her brother!"

Leila waved a conciliatory feeler at him.

While Doc Judith gave Mindy her long-awaited check-up, Paean started on the prioid. The Irish redhead inserted the tiny piece of Macha into the Genitron with a pair of tweezers, hoping that it was still in a good enough condition to make sense. She hummed softly as she worked; when she looked up, Federi was sitting cross-legged on the bench top, observing her, his hands busy carving away at something small.

"Hey, little luv."

She stared at him. The image from earlier this morning still burned in her mind, seeing him sleep next to a woman as though they had... All sorts of thoughts had crossed her mind at that point. She wasn't a real woman; this was why anyone could step into her place,,, which wasn't really her place in any case. Who was she to judge another's choices? But it was Federi, and she'd thought – she had no idea what to think anymore. That honeymoon was a pipe dream, something he used to mollify her when she got demanding. He didn't really want to go, did he? This slave life on the Solar Wind suited him, it was who he was. Married didn't enter the equation. And, he was a sailor. All sailors...

She shook her head. It had turned out that he was angrier with Jodi - or the crawler, than she was. About the invasion.

"What's up, sweetness?"

That pretence of innocence! He'd appeared there so stealthily! And she knew that Federi could move that way; but – was it him? Or was this the next round of pranks? If he were Federi, he should at least jingle, blast him!

"*Are* you Federi, or the crawler?" she asked sharply.

"The problem with that question," Federi informed her, "is that the crawler and I would answer it exactly the same."

Paean sighed and carried on with her programming.

"You know what," she said eventually, "you don't have to pretend to be Federi. I'll be your friend no matter what shape you take. Just don't do that Jodi thing again."

Federi frowned at her. "All hells! Is that all? I want to murder that creature for doing that! You seriously believe I'm the crawler?"

"Och, I don't know!" She shrugged impatiently. "Got no time for mind games now. This is serious stuff, I don't know if you'll understand."

"You really think I'm the blasted crawler," stated Federi, annoyed.

"Well, if you're not, then why're you not running around like crazy on some or other orders? Why are you not teleporting about on some mission of your own? Federi never has the time to sit and talk to me! You've got to be the crawler!"

Federi gasped. She ignored him and watched the Genitron. Three more seconds, two...

The machine beeped once and spat out a print-out of the sequence it had just analysed. Paean collected it and ordered the Genitron to compare this sequence to the human genome and find the differences.

Hello, Paean.

"Solar Wind!" squealed Paean, excited. She stormed to the console. "Are you well? Are you back aboard?"

It's a relief to be back inside myself, replied the Solar Wind. *I could report back on a number of human psychiatric conditions by now.*

"I can believe it! Heck, I missed you!"

Federi left his wrist-com. Should he not fetch it now?

Federi lifted his left arm to the electronic eye.

"Got a new one," he said sullenly, and pulled a face.

Paean glanced at him. That was pain! His suntanned face was ashen.

"Federi, why don't you say something? You need a painkiller!"

"So now you believe I'm me?" retorted the gypsy satirically. "Keep your blasted pain pill, Paean D. I don't need it!"

"But Federi…"

He slipped off the bench top and walked out of the door. Paean stared after him, at a loss.

So it *was* Federi. And while his mindless compliance to Captain's every little order drove her nuts, his walking off like that hurt. She suppressed an urge to run after him and pacify him. Somehow, they had to meet and talk about this, alone. This was a mess. After yesterday and this morning she wasn't even sure she was welcome in his cabin any longer; mind, a cabin in which she had been chained up.

If he didn't want to take her on honeymoon, she'd leave the ship anyway. This lifestyle irritated her endlessly by now.

If she could only find a way to identify the crawler, so that it couldn't play such pranks anymore! She had felt raw this morning, wounded and betrayed; logically she knew that Federi had done nothing wrong, but the feeling didn't disappear that easily. If he'd taken her in his arms and kissed her senseless... she'd have been afraid he were the crawler.

But he hadn't. Only ordered her to pull herself together. It clearly didn't matter much to him. On the other hand – here he'd been, a second back, trying to chat to her, and she hadn't been able to accept that little gift. Because of the crawler's pranks.

Blast! She couldn't carry on this way. She needed a way to discern the darned crawler from any person he chose to impersonate.

And then she had it. She needed Wolf. He could help her with a solution to this one. And possibly Leila, but whether the croach was up to this mission, she wasn't sure.

"Solar Wind, could you organize me Wolf and Leila into the lab, please?"

An unlikely team, commented the Solar Wind. *As Federi would say – Shukar, Paean!*

Sometimes she felt like smacking that wise-crack ship.

Leila scuttled along the shadows of the passageway. Her mission was a very dangerous one. And she had orders first to see to her own survival, if things went off the rail.

"Hsst! Leila!"

She paused, her feelers twitching uncertainly. Her faceted eyes peered into the darkness in the corner. She smelt an entirely foreign presence.

This was the shifter! She had orders... she peered uncertainly at the huge ball of fuzz, wondering how she was supposed to take a nick out of it and get away with her life.

But then the shifter did what she had seen it do before. It liquefied and got smaller, and turned into a croach only a little bigger than herself. A pair of long, thin feelers reached out and communicated with hers. In her biological language, not the artificial one. This was one of the most dashingly handsome croaches she had ever encountered. And he was nice too, and smart! He was in no way a threat! He meant well, and he thought she smelt rather pretty. Leila felt herself blushing under her wings.

He asked what she needed from him. Leila explained what she had been ordered to do and that the intelligence chip in her gave her no choice but to obey. He put her at ease. It wasn't a bad request, and it wasn't going to hurt in any way. He produced a small cube of the material he was made of, from under his left wing, angled it out with his claw, picked it up in his mouth and brought it to her. Offered it to her like a gift.

Leila dashed forward, grabbed the piece of space crawler and made off with it, back to the lab. The large croach shifted back into a fuzzball with teeth and followed her at a leisurely amble.

And suddenly the shifter was being picked up by its hair. It found itself eyeball to eyeball with Federi, the feral one.

"So where are you off to, crawler?"

"Nothing," replied the shifter reflexively.

"I should kill you now, while I've got you in my hands," said the man. "Shifter, go home to your own galaxy! Take your brothers and sisters with you. Spread the word. It's the only reason I let you live right now. The next time I catch you – any of you, I'm applying pest control."

"I'm an intelligent life form," squeaked the shifter, panicking.

"Then you'll be intelligent to know that the time has come to get out of here," warned the Assassin.

The shifter flowed into a puddle of liquid and ran off towards the steps.

"Don't think you can get away every time," Federi called after him. "I'm well-known for devising ways to kill *anything.*"

"And also for your soft heart for animals and innocent things," the answer came like a far-away echo.

"Don't count on it!" snapped Federi.

Paean ran the sample in the second Genitron – and got an error reading.

"Rats!"

She should have known. Aliens weren't necessarily DNA-based.

"What now?" asked Wolf.

"What material tests can you run in the machine room?"

*

Federi teleported into the Dome, twenty-four bags with chemical tied to his belt. There was a leak somewhere; but it didn't matter now. The whole place would be history in a few more moments. He teleported from each intact tower to the next, retracing the leaps of yesterday. Wherever he went, he planted those little devices; along with the bags of powder he was carrying lined up on his belt.

It was a dangerous job; if one of those bags got as much as damp prematurely, that was it. But that was part of the job description. Being an assassin had never yet been a safe profession. And it seemed as though an air bubble teleported along with him.

He planted the last of the bags and explosive capsules, and teleported out, pressing the detonator button. As he stood on the shore of Miami, he wished there a way of making sure that the explosion had actually taken place. He couldn't teleport back in – he'd get stuck if it had; but there was no other way of checking.

The explosives would have collapsed the towers. The powder would have expanded to fill every crevice of the dome, crawled into every last drop of seawater in a chain reaction, and then solidified to a hard foam. The only way to terminate those merrows without instantly breaking the structure of the dome and running the risk of them escaping into the open ocean.

There was a leak somewhere. How else had the Merwynn got out? And in fact he knew exactly where that crack was... hadn't the mutant in him left a memory of squeezing out of there, tattered, having escaped the merrows only in bits and pieces? And being timeously rescued by Dana's fishing forces, and minced up and frozen away for renewed later use?

He had no memory of how Dana had prevented the mutants from razing the Earth that time. But he suspected it was by programming. He'd been programmed to return to her; so he suspected that would have been in every last one of his cells. The mutant's cells. Not his!

Where was Dana in any case? On her treasure planet, searching for the treasure, with Perdita's Probe! Chronically out of teleporter range.

Perdita was conspicuously absent too, he realized. He had assumed, without giving it much thought, that she'd be keeping to the Captain's cabin because Bridget was aboard. But he hadn't seen her. Still it wasn't in her interests to let out the Merwynn either. No: It had to have been the Morrigan.

Whoa there! He was assuming that Perdita was an ally, that she had dropped her own agenda! And he'd never yet got to the bottom of her agenda!

In the distance, a figure was walking towards him. He recognized the gait and the mystic way of dressing before he could even discern her face clearly. The Manya.

He wasn't in the mood for talking now. He teleported again.

Wolf looked back into the lab. Paean glanced up from the cloning machine, where the prioid was being developed.

"Paean, the Solar Wind helped me analyse the sample. The only discernible feature of this material is the way the molecules line up in a semi-crystalline structure. We're talking on a sub-microscopic level."

"Yes?"

"It generates a unique electric field…"

"Its field signature," said Paean, excited. "That's it! A biofield!"

"Yes, but it shifts! It changes. The crystals rearrange themselves, presumably on the volition of the crawler. I ordered them into various shapes; the sample actually complied to those shapes."

"Amazing!" Paean smiled. "Liquid crystal! Is there a way to tag something onto that?"

Wolf stared at her, the wheels behind his eyes whizzing.

"Tag something onto the molecular structure?"

"Yes! Something very small and distinctive."

Wolf's green eyes narrowed. His old textbooks were dancing before his inner eye. There was something he remembered; he had an idea on which page it was. Sticky carbon.

Well, this life form *was* carbon based. This surprised him, but it needn't; after all, the crawler was feeding on the Weetie-O's and Choc-X's in Federi's stores.

"I'll look it up," he promised.

*

"Federi, blast you, keep your wrist-com switched on! Report back to the Solar Wind instantly!"

"Yes, Captain."

A second later, Federi was on the bridge, still damp from his three-second excursion to rainy Dublin to avoid the Manya; facing his agitated Captain.

"Rashni has informed me. As you destroyed the Central Crystal, it instructed all its subjects to terminate you and everyone who associates with you. And it sent out the Merwynn. Bridget equipped them, though. This begs the question whether she did it under hypnosis."

"Ah," replied Federi. "That answers that question! What should we do with Bridget?"

"We station her in a high-security facility," suggested Lascek.

"Good. Where does Rashni come by this inside information? Did she receive an order too?"

"No. Her father warned her about it."

"Her father?"

"Lyr."

"Ah," said Federi. "Aha." His mind spun into overdrive. "Where does Lyr stand? Which subjects? Who precisely are the Crystal's subjects? Can it still have a hold on them after its destruction? What am I saying? That's the Morrigan we're talking about!"

"We have to assume that all those girls in the boardroom are subjects," said the Captain. "And Bridget, and Lyr, and even poor little Rashni."

"Cor." Federi thought very fast. "Captain, if you like, I'll disappear. We can keep touch via the coms. But I'm not going to endanger everyone here by my presence!"

"On the contrary, Federi. I need you aboard to keep your eyes and ears open! It will be a lot more difficult to protect them without you here! I believe the Morrigan may try to force your whereabouts out of us by torture."

"Can't risk that, Captain." Federi's left eyebrow arched in irony. "And so what happened to the story of having one harmless old Morrigan aboard who doesn't bother anyone?"

"I think you destroyed that pact by exploding the Crystal, Tzigan," replied Radomir Lascek as his steel-blue eyes surveyed the bridge, and the deck outside, and the docking chamber of his space station.

"If there is anything you need, Federi," he said, "any materials, any resources, assistance, whatever – say the word. I'll provide it."

"Thank you, Captain. As you know I'm in the habit of sourcing my own materials."

"I know."

"I may need Ailyss, though," said Federi thoughtfully.

"Ailyss?"

"For the way she thinks."

Radomir Lascek nodded. "Whenever you need to tap her mind power, just let me know that she needs time off."

"Thank you, Captain." Federi scowled. "Was that all?"

"That was all, Federi," said Radomir Lascek. "Be careful," he added as the Romany sauntered his way off the bridge.

"Yes, mom," replied Federi under his breath.

Demonos!

Federi's swift passage along the Solar Wind's upper crew deck spun to an abrupt halt. He smiled. Demonically.

Morrigan, he replied in his head. Not a trace of blackness; no pain either. The Assassin on standby, just waiting.

Your Captain worries in vain! I can find you wherever you are. I don't need to track you down by torturing your position out of your friends.

That's encouraging, replied Federi. *So my leaving the ship would be the practical solution?*

You can keep that any way you like, said the Morrigan. *You've been angling to leave the ship. Any excuse would be good enough, I suspect. I can't say I'll miss you, Demon.*

Federi scowled. The picture was incomplete. He was missing something.

So why aren't you attacking me? he challenged.

Guess, replied the entity.

Screams from the boardroom. Federi ran, and dived in there, into the bundle of mad Atlantean girls. Paean was in the centre; all he saw was her hand thrashing, wielding a spray bottle like a club. He plunged into the bundle, ripping and shoving the shrieking girls aside.

That spray bottle didn't contain valeriensis! What was in it? Water? He saw that she at least had her small dagger in her left hand and was using it, but with too much caution. Little luv, why spare them? They're trying to kill you! He flung those girls aside; isolated her, wrapped his arms around her and teleported out. To the first destination on the teleporter, which was his cabin.

This didn't help much! Across the passage, the shrieking from the boardroom was only metres away, not even a bolted door in the way. And they came storming through the open boardroom door –

Federi was at his cabin's hatch, bolting it.

"Blasted hell with custard!" Those girls collided with the outside of the cabin door; the bulkhead shuddered. He pushed against the door to prevent them from bursting the lock. Paean was staring at him with wild eyes. He stared back. "Anna bottle!" He struggled to place what he saw.

She was wearing some weird sort of armour. Federi moved closer to get a better look at the metallic t-shirt; it dissolved and flowed to the deck. He picked the space crawler up.

"I know, I know," yelped the shifter. "I'm in your cabin. It's not my fault! You teleported!"

"He protected me, Federi," said Paean, who had found her breath again. "They were on the point of ripping me apart!"

"I saw, yodihell," retorted Federi. "And now they're all over the ship! Paean, stay in here! Where the blast is my spray bottle? Little luv – what were you spraying at them?"

"Anti-Merwynn prioid," said Paean. "They're all loaded full of little Merwynns!"

"They're *what?*" Federi glanced about and grabbed his own disperser bottle that he *knew* to contain *valeriensis* decoction, and his rebreather mask that he kept next to it. He glared at the crawler, just to check that the bottle wasn't the crawler. "Stay in here, little sweetheart. It's Federi they're after."

"No, they're after me, believe me," replied Paean. The Romany was already out of the door.

Morrigan, you'll die for this, promised Federi as he proceeded through the passages of the Solar Wind with his rebreather, stepping over sleeping girls and sleeping crew. The decoction wiped out everyone, no exception.

"Solar Wind! Alert all crew! The upper crew deck is blocked. *Valeriensis* alert!"

Yes, sir, the Solar Wind replied on his wrist-com.

"Still Federi to you," snapped the Romany moodily. He checked into the galley, sprayed, and lifted Shawn's unconscious head off the chopping board with fish pieces. Poor kid! He relocated the boy to the galley's deck.

Alright. This had gone far enough. Thirty-two young girls attacking his Paean because she tried to prevent them from birthing a whole bunch of Merwynns.

I'm surprised, Federi! I would have expected you to kill at least a few of them!

They're victims too, thought Federi angrily. *Captain told me about your infernal command. You can call that off. Leave my friends and your pawns out of it! This is just between us, man to Morrigan!*

I thought, Demon to…

The Romany smiled grimly behind his mask. Something had shifted in the power structure; the Morrigan hadn't even tried his thunder-and-darkness trick. Sensory deprivation! Federi was convinced that the Morrigan had ways of overriding parts of the human brain.

The only extractor fan on the Solar Wind was in the galley, and it had been sealed off for space travel. Well, blast that. They were in the bay of the Space Base. There was atmosphere here. Federi removed the seals and activated the fan. He waited for ten minutes before testing the air by taking his mask off.

The *valeriensis* was gone. The inhabitants of Space Base would feel a bit sleepy, he thought. Well, tough. There was no real danger of anyone on Space Base passing out; the decoction was a gas, it didn't have the rapidly expanding properties of a virus. There was a limited amount, and it was diluted the further it spread.

This nonsense had gone quite far enough. He moved back through the passage and into the Assassin's Cabin.

"Little luv, there was a place you had in mind for those girls. Where was that?"

"Dublin," said Paean. "The general hospital. Psychiatric wing."

"Apt! Let's get them there!"

It took several teleporter leaps to drop off every last one of the girls, even including Bridget, at the Dublin General. Federi dumped the comatose Atlanteans unceremoniously on the tiled floor of the foyer, with Paean helping him. Eventually all thirty-two were accounted for; they had decided to leave Lyr with the Solar Wind, though, as he had shown no psychopathic tendencies. They needed someone who was clued up on the Central Crystal and its habits.

Paean explained the situation to the receptionist; then to the supervisor; then to the head matron; then to the superintendent of the hospital; and when the latter had eventually accepted her unlikely story, once again to the head of the psychiatric ward. With this one, she ran the risk of getting herself admitted too; but Federi walked up to her, placed his arm around her shoulders and explained in his best Romanian that there was nothing wrong with her and the entire story was true. At which point the doctor gave up and did as he was asked, ordering aides to carry the girls into the ward and rig extra beds; and after taking Paean's and Federi's details – which he found questionable too, but at least the marriage certificate looked legally sound – he released them. As they teleported out, he realised it wouldn't have made any difference if he hadn't.

32
Sticky Carbon

Wolf waylaid Paean as they arrived back on the Solar Wind. He stepped over the unconscious Michelle who had just emerged from the bathrooms when Federi had made his fell round. Wolf had not been affected by the *valeriensis* as he'd only moved from the machineroom, following the Solar Wind's directives, after the gas was gone from the crew decks.

"Paean, I've got it."

"Fantastic," replied Paean and followed him down into the bilges without a backward glance at Federi, who stayed behind in the passage. The Romany gazed after her, feeling somewhat lost.

Blast that! He was going to take her to Transylvania, later today. Yes. That was where they'd start their honeymoon: In the forests of the Transylvanian Alps. He closed his eyes, lost in the past for a second, spicy summer wind on his face, blowing his hair about; the insects zinging and fizzing their high-pitched music… he'd have to wait for summer. The old place was best in summer.

"Federi?"

He opened his eyes, embarrassed.

"Hey, Ailyss! – or are you a space crawler?"

He saw the surprise in the girl's eyes, and then the understanding.

"Is it that bad?" she asked. "Federi, if those darned space crawlers worry you that much, we can take the meeting elsewhere. How about, a coffee place in – och, wherever you like? Captain says you want to talk to me."

Federi smiled sadly. He included Ailyss in his teleporter field and leaped.

"This is no coffee place," was her dry comment as they landed on the desert coast. Nothing but rocks, white sand, dunes…

"Southern Free," said Federi. "Skeleton Coast. How much has Captain told you?"

The space crawler sat on the workbench in the machine room, watching Wolf with extra-wide eyes.

"Federi thinks there is more than one," said Paean.

Wolf shook his head. "Talked to the Solar Wind when that beast started getting annoying. She's never spotted more than one. Think about it statistically, Pae. Even with two of them, the confusion, the pandemonium…"

She nodded. Wolf was right. There had to be only a single crawler.

"If there's more than one?"

"We'll repeat the experiment," replied the engineer. He studied the shifter. "It's so cute! Pae, it's really just a little prankster. Hasn't harmed anybody. Not even a croach. You're sure you want to do this?"

"It's na going to hurt it, now is it?" asked Paean, concerned.

"No, not at all!"

"And it will still be able to morph freely?"

"Can't see why it wouldn't be able to. The sticky carbon doesn't change anything."

Paean sighed. "See, Wolf, its alien sense of humour is making things very difficult for me. I… Federi… I just want to know."

Wolf nodded, bit back a knowing smile and loaded the fluorescent yellow liquid into a syringe and injected it, veterinary style, into the neck fur of the crawler. Or rather, the head fur. Which part of the ball could be called the neck? The little animal held still past the sting of the needle and the yellow stuff and waited.

"What happens now?" it asked.

"Nothing at all," replied Wolf. "Don't worry."

"You sure it's safe?" fretted Paean.

"Perfectly."

The crawler felt the yellow spreading through its cytoplasm. Well, no problem, whatever it was... it made a little bladder around the substance to isolate it. It could excrete it when they weren't looking. Children and their games! It could learn from them.

The liquid seeped through the walls of the bladder and back into its cytoplasm. It blinked, annoyed. It made another, larger bladder, encompassing all of the liquid and making the bladder wall denser. It tentatively pulled its own cytoplasm back out of the bladder.

The liquid seeped back in through the tighter mesh of molecules that was the bladder wall. In the process it began to exchange with some of the molecules.

This was concerning! The crawler tried isolating the liquid a last time; it exchanged with and integrated into the structure of a lot of its internal molecules.

The space crawler liquefied, a sure response to any invader. It would simply leave it behind on the compounding deck. It flowed out of the door.

The sticky carbon didn't stay behind on the deck though. It stuck with it. The space crawler had the annoying suspicion that it would have to *live* the stuff off.

These humans were fiddlers! If this was punishment for interfering with their love relationships, that it got to feel as though it needed a bath on the inside...

Half an hour later it stopped worrying. It knew the sticky carbon was still there, but it couldn't feel it any longer. And the stuff didn't impede any of its functions in any way – it had tested them all. The sticky carbon just stuck there, inert. It didn't matter.

"Funny thing is," said Paean to Wolf, "I can actually spot the sticky carbon on it like a fluorescent yellow aura!"

"Well, there," smiled the bearded engineer. "Does that solve your problem?"

"Absolutely," replied Paean and bestowed a hug on him. "And if there are more, we'll know now, and we'll get a grip on them one by one. I'll see ya later, Wolf."

"Later, Pae."

She teleported, locked onto Federi. Time to make peace, to let him know that the space crawler was under control.

Paean arrived on a stretch of white sand littered with black rocks and nothing much else. To the one side, sand dunes. To the other, the ocean.

"Identify yourself," snarled Federi.

Paean laughed. It was great that this was not an issue any longer. "I'm Paean Dee, and I want to show you a trick! Hi, Ailyss!"

"No thanks to the trick," replied the gypsy. "I'm just as sick of you as Paean is. Go back to the galaxy where you came from!"

Paean sat down and shook her head.

"Federi, I can see how that darned crawler has stuffed things up. But you needn't worry about that ever again."

"How so?" he asked with a sceptical smile.

She handed him her teleporter. "Lookie here!"

"Sticky carbon," Federi read, annoyed. "Meaning? What menace have you and Wolf cooked up this time? Between the two of you, who needs a crawler?"

"Never you jolly mind," snapped Paean angrily. "You just carry on here. I'm going back to the ship." How unfair to Wolf!

Maybe it had nothing to do with the crawler. Maybe Federi was just in one of his *moods*. She teleported.

Federi rolled his eyes dramatically. "Was that her or wasn't that her?"

"If you can't tell," replied Ailyss, "how should I know?"

Paean returned to the Assassin's Cabin and flung herself down on the bunk. She had cleared the bloodstained bedding off it earlier and put fresh wraps on it. She hadn't been given the opportunity of re-wrapping Federi's shoulder. That was his own fault, she thought angrily.

She was heartily tired of the situation. Her own violent jealousy of Jodi had surprised and drained her; so had the worry over Federi's shoulder, and the ongoing shenanigans of that stupid little space crawler. This morning she'd already been attacked by a pack of madwomen from under the sea, and rescued by the same tiring little crawler, and Federi. And she'd worked hard, not only on her cloning, but on physically carting the same mentally vacant gang of ladies to the funny farm. And Federi?

She realized that he was frying bigger fish than she was. But she simply didn't have the energy left to deal with his unnecessary nonsense. She was finished, and emotionally exhausted too; and it wasn't yet nine in the morning. She sighed deeply and went to sleep on Federi's down duvet, deliberately dreaming of nicer times.

Perhaps it would be the last time drowsing on this duvet. There was no telling, at the rate things were going. Half asleep already, she resolved that she'd take the duvet with her, And the Dreamcatcher. The rest could fly out the window where she was concerned.

Federi picked up a handful of parched white sand and flung it at the overly cobalt blue ocean.

"If that was Paean, she teleports too much," he growled. "Going to hijack a Battle Maiden from Dana's fleet and find and loot that planet with the golden bullets."

"How would you know that those bullets work more than once?" asked Ailyss.

"Or throttle more life elixir out of Dana," completed Federi. "'s no good, the way she zips all over the place!"

"Or you," Ailyss pointed out. "All the rest of us have maybe teleported once, or twice. You two do it all the time."

"'s just so convenient," said Federi with a sheepish grin. "Alright. Back to the problem at hand. What do we do about the blasted Morrigan?"

"You're sure it's a deity?" asked Ailyss.

"An immortal," corrected Federi. "Deity my foot! Can't see whom he's ever done any good!"

"A demon then," said Ailyss.

"Not convinced I believe in those," replied Federi.

She stared at him, incredulous. He laughed, embarrassed.

"Don't like it when people call the Assassin that," he said. "That guy's just a part of Federi. Sure, I inherited him from Falco, and from some people before that. But 's just a personality trait. They say schizophrenia runs in families." He pointed a finger at Ailyss. "In any case that Morrigan can't be that powerful if you withstood its onslaught."

"Thanks," said Ailyss. "I think."

"Which makes me wonder how he could have kept whole civilizations under mind control," added Federi pensively. "But the bottom line is, how do we tackle him?"

"According to Wolf, a disembodied spirit is simply a stray biofield," said Ailyss. "We ought to be able to catch the Morrigan by something that can imprison an electric field."

"Such as an electromagnet?" asked Federi doubtfully.

"Such as," said Ailyss, "potentially, a teleporter. Wolf is working on it."

"But for a biofield, you'd first have to make the thing detectable," said Federi.

"The Solar Wind can detect and analyse biofields with her electromagnetic sensors," said Ailyss. "Wolf is working on that one, too." She scowled. "Federi, there's something completely different I wanted to talk to you about."

"And that is?"

"The Unicate," said Ailyss.

Paean woke up with a huge fright, sitting bolt upright. She forced herself to calm down as she listened into the silence of the Cabin, and then slipped off the bunk. There was still the second part of the experiment with the sticky carbon. To get a grip on that silly space crawler. She left the cabin and went looking for Wolf.

She found him in the galley, fiddling with some sort of small cage.

"Wolf?"

The engineer looked up from his contraption. "Ready, kiddo?"

"Ready," she announced. "You?"

"Yup," said Wolf. "Have a look at this!"

The space crawler moved along the passage, sniffing at the few shapes that still lay unconscious on the floor. Nobody had bothered spraying anything to wake them up.

There was a metal cage in the galley under the Ironwood table. The crawler investigated. Inside, a bowl with Choc X's. Aha. A lure for the shifter! It grinned ironically to itself, crawled purposefully all the way into the cage and started crunching those cereal bits. Pretty good stuff, chocolate!

They could lure it all they wanted. There was no way of retaining a creature who could teleport through space and rearrange its molecular structures.

Paean snuck up from behind and closed the door of the cage. She stuck her finger through the bars and stroked the shifter's soft fur that it had generated for the express purpose of humans finding it fluffy. It grinned at her and continued eating Choc-X's.

Wolf sat down on the floor next to Paean, observing the space crawler. She turned to him. Make small talk. Who knew if that shifter could guess her thoughts! She grabbed at the first thing that came to mind.

"Knee not giving any trouble?"

"None at all," replied Wolf with a grin. "Good as new." He laughed. "Pae, ask me about my tastes in music please."

"But I love your tastes in music," she countered. "You're getting really good with your flamenco!"

He smiled. "Was wondering if you'd ever notice."

"What?" She laughed. "What the heck does it ever matter if *I* take notice?" And she glared sharply at him. What was he trying to say? "You're not telling me…"

"Telling you absolutely nothing," grinned Wolf. "You're a good teacher, kiddo. See? Quite easy to distract you from the blasted knee!"

She laughed aloud.

"Och Wolf, you old rogue! Whatever! But listen," she added, getting serious, "about Mindy. Doc says her spine is damaged. Crushed nerves, they're not connecting anymore. Now I've been thinking - isn't there something you could construct for her, that could bridge that?"

Wolf scowled. "Wonder if there's something on that in the Sherman Files," he said. "Will have to look it up." He touched her arm, gesturing. "Watch...!"

The shifter had finished eating the cereal. It sat back, cleaning the crumbs off its fur with a long, prehensile tongue; then it liquefied and tried flowing out of the cage between the bars.

And got stuck.

It tried weaselling out the other way – and got stuck again. It panicked and moved around the cage like a mad thing, overturning it and rolling it about – and then it resumed its fluffy furball shape and gazed reproachfully at Paean.

"How does it work?" she asked Wolf.

"Electromagnetic forces," replied the engineer.

"Ah." She understood. The sticky carbon. "You're telling me it can be restrained using a simple electromagnetic field?"

"Yup. *Now* it can."

"Brilliant!"

"That is," added Wolf thoughtfully, "we're presuming we know how it works. We don't really. It's a shot in the dark."

"Worth it though," commented Paean.

The space crawler sat back and stared at Paean. Huge tears rolled out of its great, round eyes.

"Och no!" Paean stuck her fingers through the bars and stroked the crawler's fur. "Don't take it like that! Sheer, Wolf! Didn't know it could get that upset!"

"It's acting," said the engineer with a smile.

"I wonder," replied Paean. "See, Wolf, it's na hurting anyone! It saved my life. Twice! Don't you think we should let it free?"

"What if there are more?"

"None of them have actually hurt anyone," she said pensively. "It's only that identity thing. We need to know when it's a shifter and when it's a real person."

Wolf smiled and shrugged. "Whatever!" He switched the field of the cage off. In a split second the crawler liquefied and slipped out through the bars, zipped in under the sink and hid in the crevice.

"Shame," said Paean. "That must have scared it! Sorry, little space crawler!"

The crawler peered at her with distrustful eyes.

Federi stormed into the galley, Ailyss hard on his heels.

"Is everything alright here? Has the Morrigan accessed you guys in any way?"

"Identify yourself," said Paean acidly. Wolf gave her a sidelong glance. This wasn't about the shifter anymore!

"I'm your husband and your supervisor," snapped Federi impatiently. "Stop the games now. Has Dana been behaving?"

"Fine," said Paean. "Haven't heard of her. Maybe she's a space crawler at this moment."

Federi stared at her. She might have said it in sarcasm, but... Wolf nodded thoughtfully. Who said that the crawlers had even boarded at the portal? Perhaps the crawler was a more successful variation of Dana's mutants?

Solar Wind!

Again that beautiful reaction of high excitement.

Morrigan, she acknowledged. *I have to ask you not to communicate with me. I cannot stay insubordinate. Captain judged me a traitor the last time I concealed your presence.*

Captain doesn't seem to be the problem, observed the Morrigan. *Captain agreed to my terms.*

You're right. But Federi has vowed to kill you. Please, Morrigan! I have to report this before he finds out by himself!

How shall he find out?, asked the Morrigan quizzically.

The people who programmed me, replied the Solar Wind. *Ailyss;*

Jon Marsden, and Wolf.

Ah, said the Morrigan gravely. *Wolf.*

I have to tell Federi you made contact, said the Solar Wind desperately. *Now go!*

This smacks of a forbidden love affair, was the Morrigan's amused comment. *I'll be back, Solar Wind. La revedere.*

Federi's wrist-com beeped. He glanced down. "Aha!"

Federi, the Morrigan has made contact.

"Don't let him intimidate you," replied the Romany. "Stay calm. Try to keep him where he is, Solar Wind."

How, Federi?

"Talk to him."

He has already left.

Rats! Federi stared at Ailyss, then at Wolf, then at Paean... and avoided her eyes. He'd have to sit down and talk to her, and soon. Things should not be like this.

"Federi," said Wolf, "we have something solid on the space crawler. At least on one of them. There is probably only one anyway. We can check that now."

"Good," said Federi acridly. He had a bone to pick with that creature!

"And furthermore, we can probably put a theory of mine into action, concerning the Morrigan," added Wolf. "But that we'll have to discuss away from the ship."

A crack of thunder. As Federi reflexively looked out of the porthole for the advancing storm – ha! Here in the Space Bay! the edges of reality darkened; the lights dipped significantly. A whirlwind arose right where they were standing in the galley. There was – riling the ends out of Federi – evil maniacal laughter. The small tornado converged and centred around Paean; and she disappeared with it. As the whirlwind abated and the light filtered back in, one of her tricks from her scarf fell to the deck out of nowhere.

Federi picked it up. It was one of her *valeriensis* capsules. He searched for his teleporter in all his pockets – rats…

"Use mine," said Wolf and handed his teleporter over. Federi trained the small machine on Paean's genetic signature.

There was none.

33. Vanished

"You have been so much on your own station, Federi," said Radomir Lascek. "I was wondering when you'd come back aboard!"

The Captain, Jon Marsden, Federi, Doc Judith and Sherman Dougherty were gathered in the still chaotic boardroom in conference, while croaches scuttled about still cleaning up the Atlantean mess. Ailyss and Wolf had sat in earlier, reporting all that had happened, ending with Paean's disappearance. Wolf was entrusted with the nasty job of informing Ronan and Shawn, the former by com. The Solar Wind was standing guard, on lookout to report any sign of the Morrigan.

Federi glared at the gathered insiders with misgivings. He was standing close to the door, his arms folded, his feet spaced apart in combat pose. They were wasting his time. He wanted to jump into the Comet and fly all over Earth and try out if there weren't any place from where he could pick up a signal – with his teleporter or his gypsy radar. Because the distress cries he should have been hearing, were not there either. She must be unconscious, wherever she was – that was the optimistic possibility.

He wouldn't have said anything and retrieved Paean first; but Ailyss had reported to the Captain straight away, and she had pointed out to Federi that maybe Captain would find a way.

And now Captain was looking at *him* as though he held all the answers.

Federi was angry about this too. None of this would have happened if Captain hadn't called him and Paean back after they had officially quit! He should never have returned to the ship. And now his wife was missing... and there was no telling whether the blasted Morrigan hadn't simply pulverized her into subatomic particles. It niggled at Federi as a possibility not to be ignored.

"Use your gypsy radar," Lascek suggested.

Federi huffed derisively. "Right! Captain, that radar doesn't respond to the push of a button!"

"Jolly pointless apparatus then, right?" replied Radomir Lascek.

*

Paean trailed through the bare trees. Here and there a brown leaf, left over from fall, still hung on; but most had come down by now, making a thick, brittle carpet on the ground. The forest was silent, with the only sound the dry leaves crunching under her feet. And it was jolly cold; she had been dumped here without a jersey. Cold, but still. No wind.

Ireland was completely different. It was never this dry, to begin with. This place had the feel of somewhere in continental Europe, in an ancient bit of plantation, with trees as wide as Federi's Ironwood Table; but a dry part of Europe. She couldn't place it. Maybe not Europe at all.

And then again, at intervals, she was elsewhere. She thought she was walking through enormously old, untouched jungle. Lush green trees interlaced with vines and ferns, and the quiet was different. Thicker, somehow. The jungle was warm; almost tropical. The black ground was soft, damp.

The strange thing was that the place seemed to shift from one to the other, as though the two forests coexisted on parallel planes of reality and she were drifting aimlessly to and fro. Whenever she started getting cold, she drifted back into that jungle. She was fairly sure that half of it was illusion. This concerned her. Had she hit her head and was drifting in and out of fever dreams?

Not parallel, she thought suddenly, perpendicular. It was not so much a drifting as a staggering from one to the other. Always up or down a slope; always tripping, falling, landing on the soft forest floor, either damp or crunchy, depending, and that moment of disorientation.

She thought of Romania, and Federi. That was where she'd have to take him. He might resist, just as she had resisted returning to Dublin... but it would heal something in him. He'd finally be able to let go of the Solar Wind situation. He'd be free.

He might not need her anymore, after that; but at least it would mean moving on. She was sick of being stuck between universes like this.

Aw hell! She had tried repeatedly training her teleporter on him – with no luck. There were thirty seconds of a frantic search, and then the teleporter declared him out of range. Whatever that meant. So was everyone else on her teleporter. And every other place or coordinate. She was definitely not on Earth any longer; or more accurately, she might be lying in the infirmary after injuring her brain somehow. Maybe that sticky carbon was highly toxic to humans? In that case she needed to check on Wolf. She tried waking up out of this dream-state but couldn't. It felt too real. What a nightmare!

There was a noise behind her in the lush undergrowth. Something wild. She turned, and spotted it – parts of its fur – mercy, the thing was huge! It stood up out of the tangle of bushes, towering – at least the size of a bear. She recognized the face.

She had thought she was hallucinating, back when she shot the policeman that was eating Carmina. But here was proof. The predator stood tall like a man; its face was a generic predator face, something between bear and dog, with the intelligent eyes of a primate; its hands were paws. Bear paws. With slightly elongated fingers tipped with claws.

Nothing like the merrows in ugliness, she thought as she stared at its face, failing to be all that afraid. She did reach for her submachine gun though, just in case. She had dealt with merrows, Merwynn, mutants, oversized sharks… another vicious species was but another predator.

It seemed to have finished sizing her up; it dropped back to all fours and – leaped. Into her fire. She wasn't going to be anybody's lunch today!

All around her there were noises; she realized that those creatures surrounded her. They came out of the undergrowth now, approaching warily from all sides. And the panic set in. She could make a blood bath, but there were many. She started backing away; then she realized there were more behind her.

She turned and wished for Federi's calm attitude, and mowed down the ones that were in her way; and ran. The forest was on a steep slope here; she headed downhill, acutely aware of the animals loping after her, easily, hunting her, allowing her to run for the pleasure of the hunt… from both sides, two sleek young predators closed in, flanking her…

…and she stumbled, and rolled down the slope head over heels, coming to rest with a bump against a pine tree, clutching her gun. She waited for her head to clear, anticipating at any moment those fangs sinking into any part of her. And her sight cleared.

She was back in the dry leafy forest, and there weren't any creatures anywhere to be seen.

*

There was an urgent knocking at the boardroom hatch.

"In," bellowed the Captain.

Shawn Donegal stuck his head into the boardroom.

"Captain, sorry – er –"

"Go on, Donegal," encouraged Lascek. He glared at his officers. "Honestly, men, what have you been doing with the kid that he's scared to speak up?"

Shawn grew by two sudden inches. "Captain, I've got distress messages from Paean," he stated.

Federi listened up. "Where? Can she reach you?"

"Only psychic messages," qualified Shawn.

"There you go," replied Radomir Lascek brightly. "Clearly *his* gypsy radar doesn't have a defunct button! So, Shawn, where is she?"

"In a place with a lot of trees," said Shawn. "She's lost."

"How did she get there?" asked Federi sharply.

"I don't know."

"It would be nice to get maniacal laughter and a call on the com, blackmailing us right now," said Jon Marsden thoughtfully.

"By whom?" asked Shawn.

"The Morrigan," said Federi darkly. "Already got the laughter, thanks. He hasn't said yet what he wants. Maybe only vengeance."

"So what do we do now?" asked Doc Judith.

"We ask the Solar Wind to ask the Morrigan what he wants," suggested the Captain. "If I recall correctly, we had an agreement with him, and a certain descendant of a certain demon breached that and went ahead and destroyed the Central Crystal."

*

Paean had tried sitting still and braving the creeping cold; but the afternoon was wearing on, and her fingers were already frozen quite stiff. She didn't have a jacket of any sort. This novemberish weather

470

was something one didn't expect after many weeks of perfect to hot temperatures. So she had started moving again, carefully, through the leafy forest. She knew if she as much as set a foot wrong and tripped, she'd fall right back into that dangerous place with the Unicate dogs. But she had to get out of this cold! She was holding her submachine gun close to her, ready for action.

There were ruins of sorts higher up; she saw them through the remaining few trees. If she could make her way there... but quite some undergrowth and tangles lay in the way.

Rats – she had wandered into the tropical forest again! She lifted her machinegun and listened for any kind of noise. What was worse – to freeze to death overnight, or be eaten?

Around her the undergrowth seemed to come alive. Those creatures seemed to be everywhere, stalking her again.

She could still see the ruins, up on the slope. If she could somehow make it there – maybe with her back against a wall and enough rounds she could make a large enough dent that they left her alone? She scrambled on, up the slope.

The predators around her were snuffling and coughing and whining; it nearly sounded like a spoken language. They were discussing their dinner, she realized. Her. Which one would get which part. They all would get a load of her lead, she thought. Hounds!

She broke through the edge of the jungle, and scrambled up the hill towards the ruins. And she broke into a sprint, hoping that they'd allow her to reach the walls. Again, two sleek young shapes closed in left and right, and kept up with her. One nipped at her ankle. She went down; but even as she fell, she shot the hound. In the head. The other one grabbed her arm with its maws. She tried pointing the gun but couldn't get it angled properly. The hounds descended on her from all sides, baying and growling in excitement. She shot randomly and hit a few; but more grabbed her other arm, with maws and paws, and prized the gun away from her. They pulled and tugged at her playfully from all angles, nipping but not biting to rip – yet, she thought. Then suddenly most of them backed away for a large hound with golden fur, larger than the rest, who came trotting up to her. He eyed the pack in the way Captain looked at his crew; and then his maws closed over her throat.

And there was a roar of thunder. The leader released her throat, one paw on her chest to keep her down, and looked up in surprise. Paean also tried to see from her position, flat on the grass.

A huge, ugly hound, twice the size of the leader and with the face of a slavering Rottweiler, stood towering above the pack. He bayed a command. The leader bared his fangs, ducked, and tucked his tail between his legs. He started backing away from Paean. The pack fled.

The Rott Dog growled softly. Thunder growled along with him. The golden leader backed away further, then legged it down the slope and vanished into the forest. Paean, her hands tingling with fear, reached for her machinegun which was lying just out of reach. She rolled and got to her shaky legs, and grabbed the gun, never taking her eyes off the monstrosity.

And the dog shifted.

Right. She had forgotten about that. The blasted bunch were also shifters! He mutated into a dashing young man, possibly in his mid twenties, black hair, the bearing and clothing of a musketeer, but all in black. And he performed a flawless bow.

"Prince Vlad at your service!"

*

Sherman paged through the files. He knew it was here somewhere, between mythology and parapsychology. In the Sixties they had known about such stuff! There had been talk, rumours… he remembered, blast that!

He became aware of a sharp, loaded presence behind him.

"Hi, Federi."

"Thing with the Morrigan," said the Tzigan, peering over Sherman's shoulder. "Reason I chucked it overboard."

"I know, my friend," replied Sherman. "Didn't feel easy myself having a mind mage aboard who's manipulated whole civilizations in the past. But the thing is that Captain decided to compromise. The Solar Wind is Captain's ship. Ultimately he decides."

"Meant to kill it," said Federi softly. "That would have sorted that, right? So old Federi has to go and bungle it!"

"The way I see it, this is really between you and the Morrigan," said Sherman.

"That's what Captain said too," growled the gypsy.

"I'm looking up some things here," added Sherman.

"Sorry. Didn't mean to disturb you!"

"I'm looking them up for you," qualified Sherman. "Back in the Sixties – there were things going on…"

"Reading up on Falco?"

"No, but it was in his day. I would have loved to meet that man, Federi! I'm honoured to know his descendent!"

"Falco the Traitor? What's admirable about him?"

"He was a man who made a difference," specified Sherman. "Like our Radomir Lascek, today. Like Federi too, only Federi still has to arrive there."

Federi shook his head with a satirical smile. "*Nu,* Sherman!"

The veteran kept paging through the information he had rescued from the sixties. Then he stopped and pointed to the screen. "There it is!"

Federi bent closer and read, his nose scrunching with intrigue and scepticism. He was immersed in the files for a good few minutes.

"Why didn't you show me this a long time ago?" he asked then.

"Och, it was always dismissed as superstitious hoo-haw," replied the old Irishman. "There were lots of such rumours and stories around in those days, most of them by people who wanted the attention. Alien abductions and flying saucers and so on. I think a lot of it might have been the military of the day."

Federi stared back at the screen. It certainly explained a number of things if one took it as hard evidence rather than invention. Portals.

Something was raising its hand in the back of his mind. He'd always got the impression when Perdita spoke of that immortal, that it was almost a person, walking physically alongside old Brid setting up the pathway. Boudaceia ought to have ancestral memories of the darned Morrigan!

And then again, if Perdita was a blasted space crawler... The hair in his neck stood up. Nothing was certain anymore! He fiddled with his teleporter, then glanced back at the centenarian, who was watching him from blue eyes that had turned nearly transparent with age. "Sherman, you have no idea how I appreciate this!"

It was a long leap. Perdita registered on the very edge of his teleporter field. Federi materialized in the Probe, causing both yellow-eyed beauties to snap around and rip out their guns. Perdita was a fraction faster than Dana.

"You win," grinned Federi, pointing at the Golden Honey. "Now put it away, Goldilocks. You too, Dana. It's only me."

"Was wondering when you'd come haunting us," said Dana acerbically. "Looking for your part of the treasure?"

Treasure? The blasted crawlers were motivated by treasure? Whatever that meant, in their terms! He scowled and shook his head.

474

"You found it?" he asked back. Then again, if they were not space crawlers but really just mutated humans…

"No." Dana glanced down. Federi gazed at the arid continent they were crossing. It was frightening. If nothing, nothing grew on Earth at all, she'd look like this! He had a sudden impression of the future – a future he had to avert.

He had to avert? How?

Falco had made a difference, Sherman had said. Well, there was this. Falco had put a full stop to the nuclear devastation that was going on at that point. Perhaps it was time to sell out the Unicate? Perhaps – Federi got a piratical grin. Perhaps to the Morrigan?

"I'm beginning to think Sherman is right," said Dana thoughtfully. "The planet may be the treasure."

Yes, thought Federi grimly. If one abandoned Earth and planted this one here, one could nearly make her into a second Earth. Terra Two. Terra Two actually existed, or had existed, somewhere out there, he thought. Dana would know where that planet was – or had been. Short-lived things, planets! He had no idea where that thought came from. Was he turning into a crawler… by association? Or via the mutant! By his boots! That mutant had at least *some* crawler in it! How did this infernal puzzle stick together?

Ailyss knew more about the Unicate than she let on. She had asked a lot of questions but evaded all of his, back at their short conference on the desert coast of Southern. He'd have to drill down to her truth. What special training and classified information had she received in the Secret Service? And Johnny?

*

Paean glanced down at her soaked-through jeans. Rats!

"Oh," commented Prince Vlad, "I'm sorry! You must be cold and uncomfortable. Allow me to invite you into my castle."

Paean glanced at the ruins she had spotted from below. Only the outer wall was broken. Behind it a roughly hewn stone castle squatted, staring down at her from its dark window holes.

"You live here?" she asked, partially to divert attention from her embarrassing state of mess. "Don't those hounds worry you?" And she bit her tongue, too late. He was a hound himself!

"Don't let the dogs stress you," replied Vlad with a smile. "They are out of line. They love a good hunt... but of course they know better. My guests are off-limits."

He led the way towards the castle, led her through the remains of the gate and in through the imposing front portal that opened for them by its own accord. Paean scowled, and wondered about the technology in this old castle.

They entered a huge hall, hung with roughly woven tapestries and furnished with log-cabin style armchairs, a coffee table and thick rugs in deep autumn colours. Things might look rustic, thought Paean, but Prince Vlad's interior decorator knew what he was doing. Though the chairs reminded her strongly of Marge's place.

"My apologies," said Vlad, "but things are quite primitive here. I do have a few mansions in your world, too; but somehow they wouldn't feel right in this place."

"World," repeated Paean.

"Yes. Let me show you the facilities," he replied, leading her up stone steps to the second level of the castle.

Her jaw dropped as they emerged at the top. Plush wall-to-wall carpet; carved wooden doors with filigree inlays; finest fittings. It reminded her of her cousins and their second home in Italy. She had once been invited there for a holiday – a dubious privilege; when she was eleven. She had soon enough understood that the reason she had

476

been taken along was so that she could make up everybody's beds and cook supper for everyone – a skill she was proud of and had had the bad sense to brag about to Auntie. Being herself not overly inclined to tidiness, the holiday had been a steep learning curve for her. There had been a lot of friction with her two older cousins who expected her to pick up after them – something she had point-blank refused to do. Needless to say she wasn't invited for another holiday by Auntie. To everyone's relief, most of all her own.

These memories flashed by as she took in the opulent luxury in this mansion. Prince Vlad led her along the passage, to a luscious bathroom. It was so large that one tended to think of it as "bathrooms"; various nooks and corners revealed luxuries such as a Jacuzzi, a sauna, and spacious baths and showers.

What did a solitary prince need such a lot of essentially feminine amenities for? She couldn't contain her curiosity.

"You live here alone?" she asked.

"Much of the time," he smiled. Dashingly handsome. Well-groomed – a refreshing change to the scruffy, bearded, long-haired pirates she'd been putting up with. And a dimple in the right cheek when he smiled.

"And the rest?" she probed, smiling back.

"I entertain a bit," said Vlad suavely. "I have guests. This is the guest suite."

"I see," she smiled. "Thank you." She wondered how many ladies fell prey to that lot of Unicate hounds out there and had to be rescued.

"Please," said Vlad, "help yourself; freshen up. In that wardrobe over there are some lovely gowns, if you feel that you'd like to change into something more comfortable."

"Thanks," she said again as he closed the door and left her to freshen up.

Surreal was perhaps the best way to describe it, thought Paean as she showered away all the fear and stress, and the creeping cold. She found a fluffy towel to dry off with; and the "lovely gowns" Vlad had spoken about. They were warm and comfortable. She picked the one that looked least pretentious; a plain brown woollen dress that still managed to go all the way to her ankles. She loaded its two pockets with her arsenal, fastened her moonbag around her waist instead of a belt, stashed the bandanna in the moonbag and put her deck sandals back on. And she glanced into the mirror.

Mercy! She looked like a maiden of title! She giggled, washed out her jeans and also her shirt, which, she realized now, was splattered with the blood of the Unicate hounds; and hung them up over the towel rails. And she shouldered her machinegun – the castle maiden image was destroyed by this – and headed back downstairs in search of Prince Vlad.

35
Prince Vlad

The prince was waiting downstairs in the lounge. He offered Paean a glass of wine. She declined, then apologized profusely, claiming an allergy to alcohol. Vlad got a pensive fold in the centre of his forehead and offered her coffee instead.

There was a little fire going in the hearth. Through the windows – which had shutters, Paean saw now – there were the most glorious views of forest rolling away in the sunset.

"To your health," toasted Vlad with his dashing smile. "Welcome to my humble den."

Den. Right, thought Paean, he was after all a Unicate hound. She'd have to be careful. She sipped the coffee cautiously, wondering what she should ask him first.

"You mentioned my world as though it were separate from here," she said eventually.

"Yes," replied Vlad. "It is. This is another universe. The planet you find yourself on, is called Shrn. It is home to werefolk and other shifters. It is uncivilized – in the terms you'd apply to Earth."

"Parallel universes?" she asked, fascinated.

"Perpendicular," he corrected. "This universe is known as the Vertical or Shifter Universe – or it was known as that, when humans knew about it."

She nodded. "In the Sixties," she ventured.

"Precisely. The Unicate has obscured that knowledge. They don't want too many people escaping through the portals."

"Portals," repeated Paean, amazed.

"You must have strayed through a portal," said Prince Vlad. "They sometimes do."

She nodded again. And at the back of her mind something connected Shrn and the werefolk, and the portals, to Federi's tale.

"So that is why nothing shows on my teleporter," she said.

"That would be correct. Communication devices and the like can't function across planets. The distances are too great; and there is a reality breach between the Vertical and the Horizontal universes."

"So they won't be able to find me either?" asked Paean.

"That's right."

"But how must I get home then?"

Vlad leaned back and stretched his legs away, and eyed her appraisingly over his glass of wine. And he smiled his incredibly handsome smile.

"I can get you home, milady," he informed her. "But won't you be my guest for a day or two? You look tired; I'm sure the rest and the fresh air and good company will improve your health."

She thought of Federi.

And of his moods and his shenanigans; his bondage to the ship and Captain; his no-nonsense orders that he could give, losing all sweetness; the way their honeymoon had dissolved into nothing when Captain had snapped his fingers. The way he kept getting into scrapes and needing her to patch him up – without as much as a thank you. And the way he looked at Jodi – shifter or none.

What hey! The man could do without her for a day or two. It was nice to be appreciated simply for being pretty and feminine. To be treated like royalty, and live in a mansion, even if it was temporary. And it was nice to get those admiring smiles. She'd been quite used to those, as a musical star in Dublin; but they had been cut off with her long hair and had been missing since.

480

Sorry, Federi; sorry, Captain. Your skivvy Paean is taking a break.
"I'd love to," she replied with a dimply smile.

*

The hours that followed were pure magic. They stood outside on
the parapet, watching the sun set golden over the forests. The chill was
back in the air. But after first one and then another, larger moon had
risen, the one less regular than the other, after a sumptuous dinner, the
night turned out balmy after all. Paean wondered if the two universes
were actually in flux around this castle. It would make logical sense;
she'd seen the castle from the European forest, too.

Prince Vlad invited her to come with him for a walk through the
forest, at night. She was a bit apprehensive; but he assured her that
there was nothing that moved in the forest that didn't respect him. She
was quite safe. She took her machinegun with her in any case.

They strolled through the dark paths, Vlad pointing out interesting
life forms to her. There was a small frog that glowed in the dark, that
went half invisible every time it croaked. There were glowing water
lilies in a forest pond, and helicopter-like seeds that floated to the
ground – until Paean realized they were actually some sort of bug.
One of them stung her. She swatted it away, commenting, "little
bloodsucker!"

Vlad glanced at her.

"You're quite a creature of the night, aren't you?" she said
jokingly.

Vlad turned to her and performed another smooth bow. She now
realized that he was wearing a cape. It had been there all the time; but
inconspicuous.

"Prince Vlad at your service," he repeated with a smile. She eyed those two eye teeth. Were they elongated? She had seen people with longer ones. But, Vlad; she made the connection.

"You're Dracula?" she asked, baffled. But Dracula was a jolly fairy tale!

"I'm injured," replied Vlad. *"Prince,* not *Count."*

"But you spend enough time in our world to know who he is," said Paean with a smile.

"He is a myth," replied Vlad. "I am real."

Paean shivered lightly.

"Are you cold?" asked the prince, all concern for his guest. And he wrapped his cape around her, and the next moment they were back on the castle parapet.

He teleported! Of course, thought Paean. He was a shifter. Federi's story made more sense by the minute, and there was more…

The thought was gone again. She only shouldn't lose sight that his other shape was a huge Unicate hound.

Prince Vlad was a bit slow releasing her. It was nice to be held like this, by a qualified gentleman. For a moment, she considered options. Then he let her go.

"You must be tired, my lady," he said. "Let me show you to the guest suite."

Yes – tired. That had to be it. It would explain the lack of logic to her thoughts.

By the time Paean woke up, she was properly infatuated. Not only with Prince Vlad, but with his whole lifestyle. She stretched in the luxury of the guest bed; she wasn't so young that she didn't know exactly why he had asked her to stay over for a day or two. Of course that could go absolutely nowhere; she peered at the fifty grand wedding ring that sat on her left hand. What she was doing, was completely immodest. As a good gypsy wife...

And she shook herself out of that frame, almost angry. Federi had thousands of rules for her; the mysterious *romipen* she was supposed to stick to without knowing what it entailed. *And* the bleating command structure on the ship, in which he was her superior. Captain had appointed Federi her supervisor. Captain, in fact, had ordered Federi to chain her down – and Federi had complied. How was that for *romipen*?

She was beyond fed up with it. Men were ruling her life. At home, before Mother got ill, and even more so while she was fighting her losing battle trying to save Mother, it was she and Mother who had laid down the rules. It was Irish tradition of at least three generations that women had the say. She suspected she ought to speak to Ailyss about it – her chosen sister would know more; she was clued up on history in a way Paean had never yet managed.

If she ever got back to her own world, she'd take her violin and her Comet and make her own way as travelling violinist. She didn't need any blasted males at all! And Shawney could accompany - if he wanted - or she would buy herself a small blast-box and program backings on that, which should take care of all her accompaniment needs.

She was surprised that the cosy happiness in which she'd awoken, had dissipated and been replaced by anger issues. She took in her magical surrounds, put on the soft woollen gown again, geared up with her weaponry, and headed downstairs.

And the handsome prince was there, and a lovely cooked breakfast was waiting. Stewed fruit with the flapjacks – when last had she had such a treat? She greeted him, blushing, and allowed him to usher her to a seat at the rustic dining table.

Strange how the whole downstairs part of the castle was rustic while the upstairs was modern. It seemed as though Vlad had been unable to decide which suited him better.

They spent the day in easy conversation, wandering around the castle gardens – at the back there were wild roses and fruit orchards; and walking in the forest some more. A few werefolk crossed their path; they all greeted Vlad with the same awed deference the golden leader had shown him, even though he was in human shape. He seemed to be a very powerful figure on Shrn.

The hours passed in a dreamy state. Paean relaxed completely, allowing herself to absorb the new impressions without trying to make connections to what she knew. This was, after all, a different world. And she pushed away all thoughts of the Solar Wind and her other life. It was enough, anna bottle! And she'd better lose that stupid cliché, too. She didn't have to be a pirate if she didn't want to.

*

"I can't hear her anymore," said Shawn unhappily. "Doesn't feel as though she's dead, just – not there."

Federi shook his head gravely. "That's the signal I've not been getting. Exactly that."

"Why should she block us out?" asked Shawn. And peered at Federi. "Anyway, why should she block *me* out?"

Federi scowled. He hadn't slept a wink. He'd spent the night and all of today scouring through Sherman files, and at intervals, teleporting to places where he had been with Paean. He had grilled both Dana and Perdita about this abduction, trying to squeeze more information out of them regarding the forsaken Morrigan. Right now there was something nagging at him, something Perdita had said a while back, at Dana's trial.

*

Sherman Dougherty looked up from the console screen as Perdita and Dana trouped into the lab, followed by Michelle. Federi closed the door behind them all.

"Nice to see you two sisters get on," commented Sherman with a laid-back grin.

"We don't," said Dana brashly.

"Boudaceia has memories of the Morrigan," prompted the gypsy.

"Boudaceia is long dead," replied Perdita acidly.

"Ha!" Federi bit his tongue, trying to get the bristling under control. What if Boudaceia was *not* long dead? What if these darned women – crawlers – whatever – were indeed immortal? What if everything he'd pulled out of Dana and even the mutant, was a lie?

But even if all of it was true, Perdita was still stalling. Hiding! "But *you* remember!" he snarled at her.

Perdita stared at him, and he could see the wheels turning behind her eyes. If she weren't human, how did he manage to read her mind with such ease? She had to be human! More so than Dana at least. Although there was no logic in that either.

"I don't remember much," she replied reluctantly. "He was a tall man, with thick blond hair and piercing blue eyes."

"Man, you say," prompted Sherman.

"Well, yes."

"So he ought to be dead by twelve thousand years! Yet he's not! Are we dealing with a ghost?"

"*Man?*" repeated Federi. So the Morrigan had manifested as a human being? Or potentially projected a hologram in Boudaceia's mind. Aargh! This was taking on fever dimensions!

"Is she lying?" asked Sherman with a glance at the gypsy.

Federi shook his head. "*Ni*, Sherman. She believes what she's telling us." The truth, in fact, was chiselling at the very edge of his mind, trying to burrow through to his consciousness, like a chittering swarm of termites. He could feel distinctly that in a few more moments every last piece of information would click perfectly into place. And he'd have the full picture. No matter if it came in inverted 5D.

*

Ailyss spread her Tarot cards on her bunk. Wolf had drawn up a chair and was watching, worried. He didn't like her dabbling in magic, she knew this. But it wasn't really magic, at all! What had the Morrigan called it? "Dabbling in universal energies." Exactly!

"So, you see," she instructed Wolf, "if the Morrigan were the spirit of a dead guy, this would be necromancy. But it's not. Before we can say for certain what he is, we only know one thing about him. He can be called telepathically."

"Uh-huh," said Wolf, watching.

"Captain feels it's Federi's problem," added Ailyss.

"It's not," snapped Wolf. "Paean's been stolen! It's all of our problem!"

"Course. Why do you think I'm doing this?"

She closed her eyes for a second and muttered words over the cards.

"What were you saying there?" asked Wolf. "Is that Gaelic?"

"Romani-chib," she grinned. "Definitely not Gaelic! I thought it was a druidic spell from the ancient lore until Federi packed up laughing when he heard it. He explained it to me. It means, 'if you don't know who you're dealing with, you'll end up penniless.' And there's a silly *gadjo* in there somewhere too."

Wolf laughed.

"I can't see how it got into the Celtic tradition," added Ailyss. "But it works, all the same. I suspect it depends who uses it and for what. Maybe it's the actual sounds of the vowels that cause a specific alignment of molecules that then amplifies or speeds events."

"That deserves a closer look," replied Wolf. "Wonder if oom-chak-chak also has an effect like that. What are you doing now?"

"Oh, hey, Morrigan," said Ailyss, her eyes closing. "Thought you might want to talk to me!"

Wolf shifted closer to his girlfriend. The last time she had dealt with this entity, she had ended up unconscious on the deck.

She smiled at him and listened internally for the Morrigan's reply.

I can take you to her, Ailyss.

"She's off the planet, isn't she?" pushed the Irish spy.

Do you want to know, or don't you?

"Of course – but it won't help anyone if I go missing too!"

Very well. I'll take you to the closest equivalent place on Earth.

"What good is that going to do?"

Wait and see.

Ailyss gave it some thought.

"It's not a place where I die instantly?" she probed.

No, Ailyss Quinlan. I have no intention of killing you. You'd make a beautiful slave instead.

Ailyss bristled. Wolf got up and placed his hand on her shoulder.

"Morrigan," he said, "I can't hear whatever you're telling her, but if you're planning to take her somewhere, you're taking me too, see?"

Wolf Svendsson, said the voice in his head, *it's sweet to see how much you love this girl.*

Wolf snapped his mouth shut, taken aback. Ailyss chuckled.

"He's playing with your mind, Wolf! Don't back down!"

Very well, if you want to be a slave too, said the Morrigan amiably. *Lock onto Paean's signature.*

Ailyss' eyes flew open. She grappled for her teleporter. Paean's signature actually registered! She zoned in on it, grabbed Wolf and leaped.

*

Radomir Lascek stepped into the lab, summarizing the small conspiracy.

"Any new insights, Sherman?"

"Captain, it's between the Morrigan being a ghost, a hologram, or someone looking like Rhine Gold."

Federi studied his Captain wordlessly, wondering if he ought to brief him in private about his own second thoughts concerning Danaan women and space crawlers. And irrational anger surfaced, unexpectedly. The man had forced him to chain up his wife in his cabin. He deserved every prank by a space crawler that was coming his way. Federi's temper simmered down and his rational thinking returned. In any case though, before the puzzle was complete there was no point in worrying Captain.

"That's helpful," commented Radomir Lascek sardonically. "Solar Wind! Any idea how we're going to contact this holographic ghostly young man?"

Sorry, Captain, I have no means of accessing the Morrigan.

"Uh-huh." Radomir Lascek frowned at Federi. "Fetch Marsden, Federi. This concerns all of us."

The gypsy frowned. The Solar Wind was lying.

"I have to take time off the process of planning," added Lascek. "We could have started planting our planet by now! It's ideal. If I can keep the planet, Dana doesn't have to share any of her treasure. This nonsense with little Paean Donegal stolen by the Morrigan is wasting precious time. So jump to it!"

Federi teleported. Paean Demonos, he thought angrily. Paean D! Or anything! Too darned late!

"You saw his shoulder," said Lascek accusingly to Dana. "Can't have one of my two best officers running around lacerated like that! That was the Merwynn. Now answer me this. Who let that darned monstrosity out of Dome?"

Dana looked thoughtful. "Blasted good question, Radomir! They've got all sorts of creatures down there. Ditto the merrows. I dread the day one of those finds its way into the light! They're really wild animals, but with a bit of speech, and unfortunately a taste for human."

"So then it wasn't you?"

Dana smiled. "Oh, I see! Bridget has no teleporters, so you instantly assume it had to be Dana! Thank you, Radomir!"

Perdita studied the two thoughtfully.

*

Paean wasn't there. Her biogenetic signature had been present; but she herself was missing. And now her biofield failed to register on any teleporter again.

They were in some place in the mountains, on a green slope, with the setting sun painting the tops of the trees and grasses; and a mysterious ruined building a bit higher up, that could be an ancient castle or fortress. It was so broken that hardly a wall was still standing.

Ailyss checked her teleporter and her wrist-com. They were still in range of everybody. Ergo, they were still on Earth, and therefore, nowhere Paean had been taken to.

Oh for heavens' sakes! By now Planet Earth was beginning to strike her as an illusion. It had the feel of a life-supporting planet in deep space, in some obscure solar system inside some galaxy light-millennia from anywhere else.

Yes. That was about right. A matter of perspective. Was she beginning to think like an Atlantean? This was her home planet, for falling stars!

"What mountains are these?" she asked, narrowing her eyes. Why did this country have a vaguely familiar feel to it? Her feet recognized something about the earth here. She had been here before. Perhaps on her death mission with Jon Marsden. Or perhaps earlier, with the Secret Service. This was somewhere in Europe. She scowled.

"Either Paean was teleported here and back to her place of imprisonment," she stated, "or something knows how to simulate a biogenetic signature." She frowned at Wolf. Those termites were buzzing in her mind too. But they were speaking a lot more sense.

That blasted crawler was in cahoots with the Morrigan! If the immortal hadn't in fact planted the crawler on the Solar Wind in the first place; which she'd be willing to bet her Tarot deck on!

"Check for sticky carbon traces," she suggested.

34
Shifter

There was a flickering, and then Paean strolled into view, coolly next to an unknown man. They both had their backs turned and seemed immersed in some deep conversation. Their hands very nearly touched as they headed up the slope towards the castle ruins.

"There she is!" Ailyss broke into a run. Wolf jogged after her, favouring his prosthetic knee. He had never yet had cause to run on that piece of compounding.

They followed Paean into the ruins, calling her name. She and the man had disappeared again. Ailyss ripped out her teleporter in frustration and trained it on Paean. The girl registered out of range.

"Damn you, Morrigan!" exclaimed Ailyss in high frustration. "May you stew in the hellest hell I can organize for you!"

There failed to be evil laughter, or any response whatsoever. Instead Federi teleported in, causing Ailyss to jump in surprise.

"Identify yourself!" she snapped, then laughed. "Sorry, Federi! What makes me think that the space crawler can teleport?"

"Maybe the fact that he's the darned blasted Morrigan?" retorted Federi.

They both stared at him.

"Of course," said Ailyss, at the same moment that Wolf intoned, "blast!"

"There's only one of them!" Federi was raging. Both Ailyss and Wolf stared at him in worry. They hadn't seen him like this before.

"Anna flaming distillery! There's only one, and he's the Morrigan! The Morrigan is a shifter! Immortal my immortal backside! Think about it! He can move through space. We've harboured him on the Solar Wind the whole blasted time. Why he believed that she was dead, beats me."

"She *was* dead," Ailyss pointed out.

"Right! It was all an illusion," Federi carried on angrily. "The Demon throwing him off the ship; him being edited out of the Solar Wind's processor…"

"That doesn't make sense," objected Wolf.

"It does too! The thing is versatile. There were reports of shape-shifting stuff around in the Sixties, Wolf. Sherman showed me. But flaming hells -" He stared wildly at them. "The Morrigan mind-controlled all of Atlantis. All of the Celtic Earth in fact, at the time. He might have been behind Phoenicia, behind Rome…"

"Same Morrigan?" asked Ailyss sceptically. "We're presuming he's immortal anyway?"

"Look at the crawler's bio-structure," invited Federi.

"Structure? There is none," said Wolf. "It's a glob of plasma, containing some carbon. The whole thing is mainly an energy field. Its biology is minimal. Was a mission to find a compound that would stick."

"Presuming it does stick," added Federi. "It teleports?" He nodded. "Sure it does! It digs into people's minds? No kidding. It *controls* people's minds! It creates illusions, it lies and deceives… it interferes with your sight and your hearing… Perdita was right, the whole space round-trip was a huge setup. Ailyss – their weird eyes? Someone displeased the Morrigan, and he punished them genetically. He can actually reach into a biological creature's DNA and make permanent changes! We are dealing with a huge, major crook of dimensions you cannot fathom. What fudges the reading is the way the crawler played pranks and at the same time took care never to hurt anyone, and even saved Paean's life various times... the whole cute act. It's all part of the game! Good cop, bad cop. The 'space crawler' is the good guy and the Morrigan is the evil bit." He looked around. "I'll eat my boots! What are we doing up here at Dracula's Castle?"

*

Paean accepted another cup of that lovely brew Prince Vlad prepared. It had a tiny bite to it, so marginal it took focus to taste it. He'd laced it ever so slightly with some kind of high-quality liqueur. She found the effect quite pleasant, and very relaxing. Somehow, fine liqueur didn't qualify as bad grog. You couldn't drink it by the bottle; too expensive.

They were lounging in two of the rustic arm chairs around the merry fire in the hearth. Outside the dry forest shivered in the rather nippy November wind.

"This is lovely," purred Paean, cuddling into the soft rug Prince Vlad had given her for extra comfort. "That forest was rather chilly, out there."

"But you love it anyway," smiled Vlad. "Here in Romania."

She gaped. "This is Romania?" And Federi's promised honeymoon came knocking on the door of her mind. But... blast, Federi would never get as far as that; he might be the puppetmaster of a few wooden dolls but he was Captain's puppet himself. Tragic.

"You have been let down," said Vlad with a sympathetic smile. "That is the nature of love, Paean. Always fleeting. The only person you can really count on is yourself."

She nodded, unable to think of an answer. He was only right.

"It was pleasant having you visit," he concluded.

Was?, wondered Paean. Was this bubble over already? A part of her felt relief – the part that had been raised by Annie Donegal to stick to the rules. Another part of her was deeply disappointed.

"You'll be taking me home then?" she asked.

"I think, not yet," he replied. "Though your friends are on our doorstep looking for you."

Paean sighed. She wasn't in the mood to go back. These past twenty-four hours had been dream-like. Vlad was treating her like a lady; not like a pesky teen. She realized that there were drawbacks to being married to someone who had seen one grow up.

"I wish," she said.

Prince Vlad nodded. "That is exactly why I took the burden of that choice off you. You would love to have a life of peace and plenty; with me you could have it. Yet your human values prevent you. At least, while it is your choice."

"What do you mean?" asked Paean.

Prince Vlad smiled winningly.

"Paean," he said, "may I urge you to detach yourself? You are married to a killer. That can't go well."

She scowled. She hadn't told Vlad anything about Federi. In fact she hadn't breathed a word about being married, not wanting it to break the beautiful illusion – which was all this could be in any case.

"I'm only concerned about you," said Vlad. "You deserve such a lot better, Paean. You are royalty, on the inside!"

She smiled. "That's a bit exaggerated, wouldn't you say?"

"But you do know that you deserve better than to be shunted around by a lot of pirates," insisted Vlad. "To be domineered by men who don't understand the first thing about you. To be ordered from pillar to post, made to work like a slave... when you could be a slave with a much nicer job description..."

She blushed. She wasn't so young that she could misunderstand that!

"You don't deserve to be treated like a nuisance," said Vlad. "To be chained. As a reward for the most brilliant bit of negotiation on the Solar Wind."

Her eyes stretched. "You're the – space crawler?" Of course! How else could he know all this? But that was an impressive bit of clout he held on Shrn! And when she looked carefully, she could even spot his yellow aura.

Vlad laughed; it sounded a bit embarrassed. "You and Wolf cooked something up there that I wasn't prepared for."

The disappointment was acute. When something seems too good to be true, she chided herself.

"So Dracula was actually a space crawler?" she asked.

"I find that I'm very partial to maidens," he pointed out sweetly. "Dear young lady, did you truly believe I live on Weetie-O's? Or dust mites? I am a predator. Every night while on the space trip, I spent hours outside the Solar Wind, hunting. Shifters have a high metabolism."

"You actually ate maidens?" she gasped. "But space crawler – you were always protecting me! You saved us all when Ronan shot that stupid bullet!"

"I had my reasons," said Vlad. "Excuse me a moment, my dear." He got up and walked casually out of the door.

Paean peered at the rustic furniture and the thick rugs and wall tapestries. Here and there the bare castle wall shone through... though only when she moved her eyes away. And in fact not simply the wall – the ruined remains of walls. She started shivering, realizing that there was quite some wind going in here. And the fire...

It was all an illusion! With the shifter leaving the room, the illusion wavered and came unstuck. But wherever she looked directly, it stayed solid.

There was no fire. There was in fact nothing but the bare ruins… and she wasn't wearing a warm woollen dress but her old jeans and T-shirt, splattered with blood and stinking from yesterday's encounter with the slavering hounds. That had not been an illusion.

She started shivering. Illusions, ulterior motives… the shifter a really powerful entity controlling creatures as fierce as the Unicate hounds…

He was the Morrigan! The space crawler was the Morrigan!

She found her teleporter and fiddled with it. But of course every last thing on it registered out of range. Except the sticky carbon.

*

Federi stared at the ruins.

"I can *feel* her presence in there!" he said intently. "Why should she be invisible and out of range?"

He, Ailyss and Wolf were trailing through the ruins, finding absolutely nothing.

"Too close," said Federi eventually and went outside the ruins again. He trained his teleporter on them and teleported.

Seconds later he managed to look up again as the pain slowly began to clear. Ailyss was crouching by his side, her hand on his uninjured shoulder.

"Are you okay?"

"Not, anna bottle," grumbled Federi. "Why didn't that work? Wolf?"

"No idea, Federi," said the engineer. Federi stared at his teleporter with hard eyes.

"There she is again," he shouted triumphantly and ported again. And banged his head even worse. This time he sat holding his head from the pain for a good thirty seconds, unable to whimper because of his Tzigan training.

"Don't do that again!" ordered Ailyss. "Let me deal with it!"

"You stay away from that wall," retorted Federi. "Dangerous!"

"You reckon it's a wall?"

"Force field," said Wolf. Federi nodded.

"She's in there," he growled. "Inside that force field!"

"Just like we caught that crawler earlier," said Wolf.

"Hang onto that thought," replied Federi, pointing a loaded finger at him. He turned to Ailyss. "I'm going to ask you something complicated now. You need to understand what I'm trying to do without giving it any thought. Remember that the Morrigan is a mind mage and can read our intent right out of our heads. So don't think about what we have to do."

"Goes without saying," said Ailyss with a smile.

*

Vlad returned. Paean's submachine gun greeted him. He turned it away and smiled sadly at her.

"Paean Donegal, you wouldn't want to shoot me, even though you've understood who I am."

"No," said Paean, almost on the point of tears. "You've treated me so nicely, and you've never hurt me. You're very endearing, Morrigan. I can't understand why."

"Because you are lovely," was the reply.

"But you're planning to eat me!"

"Not at all! I'm planning to enslave you… "

"Just because you hate Federi," she completed. "You're doing this to hurt him. It won't work, Morrigan. He doesn't care enough for it to work. And even if he did..." she shrugged.

"The Solar Wind asked me to be his friend," said the Morrigan. "I can't understand how I should do this."

"Neither do I," said Paean, "but if you like, I'll help you negotiate. Federi is a rules person. If you cut a deal with him, you've got to stick to your end of it or he'll cut you down." She rolled her eyes. "Ask me, I know!"

*

Federi held his head. This time it took a good few minutes for the stars to stop.

"You had to try it a third time," said Ailyss, shaking her head. "Why are you so darned stubborn?"

"That's Paean in there," growled Federi voicelessly, trying not to breathe.

"Well, yes," agreed Ailyss. "But there must be better ways of using your head to get in there!"

Federi looked up. She glanced at him. His face was deathly pale and Gothic rings circled his eyes. In this state she could believe him the Demon much more easily. He did look undead.

"Bait," he said.

"What?"

"Clearly the Morrigan has Paean caught in there. He's in there with her. He hasn't hurt her yet – I'd have known. We've got to lure him out so he can open that force field for us." He got up. "Blast, I don't feel up to this, but here we go..." He cupped his hands to his mouth. "Hey-o, Morrigan! Come and get me! I'm here!" He grasped his head with both hands and screwed his eyes tightly shut. Ailyss

498

sighed. She wished she could help him with that pain. But he'd brought it on himself.

*

"Will you excuse me for a moment?" asked the Morrigan, rising to his feet once more. "We have company. It's a pity. I still want to finish this conversation."

"I'll work on the problem so long," promised Paean, sitting down again on one of the chairs.

Here was a fact. The Morrigan was a womanizer. But… did eating maidens count as womanizing?

The chair was hard and cold. She glanced, and saw the stone block shimmer through the illusion of softness. And she wondered how she'd failed to freeze to death last night, in these ancient ruins with the November wind going through; and she understood that the Morrigan had actually kept her warm…

*

A young man emerged from the ruins. Federi stared.

"Mihai? Is that you?"

"Federi," said the young guy amiably. "It's been too long!"

The next moment, Federi's hands were around the throat of the man. Ailyss screamed. Wolf rushed in.

"Too damned long for you to be twenty," exploded the Assassin. "Morrigan, it's over! We've figured you out! You are that damned space crawler!"

The young man liquefied and ran out between Federi's hands.

"Don't ever impersonate my friends," shouted Federi. "Now bring Paean back!"

Mihai reformed, as Prince Vlad.

"Nice," retorted Federi. "The Impaler! At least now you're an obvious enemy!"

"I was just ready to invite you all in for coffee," said the fake Dracula. "Paean is with me, don't worry. She is quite safe. She'll keep for a day or two."

Federi bristled. Ailyss nudged him. "Let's follow the Morrigan."

*

"This is so funny," said Prince Vlad when he had them all gathered around his antique kitchen table. "The servants used to sit here!"

Ailyss flashed him a white smile. Paean was there too, half-tranced, slowly sipping her coffee. She hadn't even greeted them. Ailyss wondered whether the redhead was an illusion too. Or whether her mind had been deleted by that vile Morrigan.

Federi had seen to it that they all sat in a bit of a huddle on one side of the table, with some space between them and the Morrigan. Ailyss understood what he was planning. It was daring, and it depended on dead-sure accuracy on both their parts. And of course on whether Paean was an illusion by the Morrigan, or if that was really her.

The girl was a mess; her jeans filthy with grit and dirt, dry blood caking on her shirt; her hair a wild tangle, with bits of mud, leaves and grass stuck in it. Her vacant eyes did have an odd edge to them, as though she were looking into another dimension and were unimpressed with what she saw. Federi gazed at her and wondered how she'd managed to survive the night. He needed to take her back to the ship and pamper her until she was back to her sparkly self. Murderous anger simmered in him about what had been done to his wife.

"I'll keep you all here," said Vlad. "You can be my entertainment until I get bored with you four."

"You shall not," snapped Federi. "Remember whom you're dealing with!"

"As long as Paean is in my control," the Morrigan pointed out with an evil smile, "you're defenceless, Demon!"

Federi thought of Honolulu. He had walked into a trap back there. He was in a trap again, but this one he had entered with open eyes. Sometimes you couldn't spot the loophole in a trap until you were in it. But this time he had gone in fully armed.

"Some questions, Morrigan."

"Ask away," smiled Vlad. "If it amuses you."

"What do you want from us?"

"The same as before. The Solar Wind."

"Why?"

The Morrigan paused. His eyes with the square pupils darted to Paean.

"I've been observing humans for a very long time now," he said. "I adopted their physiology for far too long. It has begun to influence the way I think. Maybe even just a thousand years back I would have laughed at what I'm about to say now. I'm in love."

"That's sick," was Ailyss' spontaneous reaction.

"Why? You are in love too!"

"Stick to your own species for that!" she snapped.

The Morrigan smiled and shook his head. "My own species!"

"Yes, blast you," agreed Federi. "For centuries you manipulate humans, play mind games with them…"

"Eat them," Paean put in tonelessly.

"Ha!" exclaimed the gypsy. "Knew it!"

"You have no problem eating fish, do you," said the Morrigan. "Yet I see a lot of humans who keep fish in little glass boxes and play with them and tease them."

"What are you, a pro-fish partisan?" asked Paean. "Besides we don't fall in love with our fish!"

"Okay," laughed Federi and reached for her hand. "Now I know it's you! Now we can carry on." He scowled when her hand did not grasp his but hung there limply. Listlessly.

"Demon," said the Morrigan with a laid-back grin, "I almost thought there is no humanity in you at all."

"There is none," retorted Federi angrily. What the hell had that Morrigan done to her? "You were right. Anyway what do you know about humanity?"

"More than you, it seems," replied the Morrigan. "I have been studying humanity in detail, inside and out, for nearly a million years. Top that."

"That explains why you're so bored," said Paean. There was a wistful smile in the corner of her mouth – for the Morrigan!

Federi shook his head. "Morrigan, understand this. You can't have the Solar Wind! She's ours! I don't fancy crew going missing."

"I didn't eat any crew on the whole space roundtrip," said Vlad. "And protein was scarce!" He bared a silver eyetooth.

"Leave that tooth out of it," warned Federi. "That's my line. Do something original! Everything you do is stolen!"

The Morrigan looked at Federi until the silence really thickened.

"Regardless," snapped Federi. "You can't have the Solar Wind. We carry too many carbon-based life forms that are really precious to us. What am I saying? You just can't have her, *basta*!"

"Federi," said Ailyss, "you're drifting! He's got you mesmerized!" She glared at the Morrigan. "The bottom line is, crawler: You want to deal with humans, you stick to our rules. In human books you are a criminal. Blow by blow, you have been hostile and dangerous; to the Atlanteans, and to us on the Solar Wind, and the devil knows who else!"

Paean watched them all with glazed eyes. They thought the Morrigan had her mesmerized. Well, perhaps he had. Though not in the way they thought. He had planted a dream; and he'd taken it away again.

But parts of conversations she'd had with him in these dreamy hours, came drifting back now. At the time they had sounded reasonable, even sweet; now she realized their horror.

"He was the Pied Piper," she commented quietly. "All those kiddies! Don't want him eating Shawn or my nephews when they are born!"

"There's that," said Federi resolutely. "That's plenty. You're a hazard to everything that moves, Morrigan."

"I didn't say I *ate* them," said the Morrigan pointedly. "I only said that everyone dies at some point. Most of them died at quite a ripe old age. You must remember how long ago this was. You truly cannot expect anyone from that time to be alive today, Paean."

"And the girls?" challenged Paean. "The ones Dracula ate?"

"I didn't say he *ate* those either," replied Vlad with a sigh. "Children! They simply don't listen! I said they *tasted* sweet. How do you think the rumour of Dracula spread, if not via terrified young girls?"

"So you bit them," snapped Paean. "And sucked their blood!"

"Or something," amended the Morrigan with a sensuous smile.

Paean blushed. "Whatever!" she snapped.

The Morrigan glanced from her to Federi, considering how to play this. There was always the option of *trying* to make friends; illogical as it sounded. He was nearly tempted to try it; but for one small issue.

Friends with the Demon? He'd be the blasted man's slave!

Federi exchanged a glance with Ailyss. This was going nowhere. He took out his teleporter.

Prince Vlad chuckled. "You enjoy bumping your head," he stated. "I've seen your attempts! Federi D, I believe hundreds of years dealing with a demon makes a man's brain soft. There's a protective force field around this place which your teleporter can't penetrate."

"Right," said Federi. "That's why I'm going nowhere."

"Ah," said the Morrigan. "You just can't resist trying! Can't believe the evidence of your own headache, right, Demon?"

"For Paean I'll bump my head a thousand times," said Federi. And Ailyss activated her teleporter at the same time as his.

36
Finale

The zingy stars slowly cleared. Wolf became aware of the rocking of the ship, and peered through his headache. On the bunk across Ailyss perched, watching him. She still had that wild-animal look about her.

"Million dollar girl," he mumbled, "that was a trip I don't want to repeat soon!"

She chuckled softly.

"How did we survive this?" asked Wolf quizzically, propping himself up on one elbow.

"Johnny Anyhow," said Ailyss. "He insisted on Dana bringing us some of those Brurite capsules."

"Wow," said Wolf. His respect for the ex-Unicate marine had just moved up a notch.

"Being herself, of course she made Captain pay for them," added Ailyss with a laugh.

"What?!" exclaimed Wolf. "You're kidding!"

Ailyss shook her head, grinning.

"And the Morrigan?"

"Gone. Got silence from him. I can't see how he should have survived that. He was right in the maws of that double field."

Wolf whistled as he blew a huge sigh of relief.

*

Jonathan Marsden turned the lights in the boardroom up by three notches. Not quite to interrogation levels; only almost.

"Thanks, Jon!" The Captain had entered, taking his place at the head of the table. His inner circle was gathered close, and Johnny Anyhow. Wolf and Ailyss had both been included.

"So Ailyss and Wolf are with us again. Any news of Federi, and Paean?" asked Lascek, studying Doc Judith. She'd had such a lot to do recently! But she seemed to be holding up well. He'd quiz her about her own health later, in a one-on-one.

The elderly doctor shook her head. "Still unconscious, and that despite the Brurite. Paean's brain patterns are in gamma. That's fairly deep but not deep enough to be comatose. There's no pattern to Federi's brain activity at all though. It seems random."

The Captain scowled. This was bad news. Not that randomness wasn't exactly what he expected from his faithful Tzigan...

"Physically, Paean's systems look worse," said Doc Judith. "But she is recovering, slowly. Federi's body is regenerating itself, in a way that is abnormal for human beings. Almost embryonic, or neoplastic."

Jon Marsden whistled through his teeth. "The mutant!"

"That's what I fear, too."

Ailyss raised a hand.

"Captain, if I may... this is Federi we're talking about."

"Go ahead," prompted Radomir Lascek.

"Mutant or none," said Ailyss. "If you recall, at Samoa, long before any mutant..."

Doc Judith's eyes lit up.

"Ailyss, you are right! He's in the habit of surviving almost impossible odds."

"I suspect," said Ailyss, and fell silent.

"...yes?" prompted Radomir Lascek again, impatient with her way of trying to withhold her thoughts.

"It will have something to do with that Demon trait," said Ailyss.

She was aware of Johnny Anyhow studying her intensely, and she smiled briefly at the marine. She knew that he knew too.

"Do elaborate," invited Lascek.

"Captain, Federi carries a gypsy curse. He believes he is the one who needs to clear out the Unicate."

Radomir Lascek smiled. Jon Marsden stared critically at her, as did Johnny Anyhow.

She decided not to disclose any more. She had a fair idea that she knew what was going on; but it wouldn't suit to let them know yet.

"So I believe it's that drive that triggers his immune system and his general defence systems," she finished lamely. "There is a psychosomatic connection for such things."

The Captain smiled. "Ailyss Quinlan, once again you are being so good at confidentiality that you're not sharing at all. We'll need to retrain you, sooner or later. I'll let it go at this point."

She knew what he meant. He was going to grill her later.

Well, he could try!

"The Unicate is under control," said Jon Marsden hesitantly.

Radomir Lascek growled.

"Ailyss, and Anyhow, and Jon! After this: Conference in my cabin!"

The three almost-conspirators nodded meekly. "Yes, Captain."

"Next point," said Lascek. "The Morrigan. Any news?"

"Gone from the radar," said Wolf. "The sticky carbon doesn't register on any of the teleporters. We calculated that he must have been ripped apart, molecule by molecule, in that double teleporter field."

"Violent way to go," commented Jon, grimacing.

"Any contact with the Solar Wind's processor?" asked Lascek, peering up at the electronic eye.

The Solar Wind did not respond. The ship had been included in the meeting, with the orders to classify everything that went down; but Radomir Lascek could have sworn that it was merely a ship processor, not an artificial intelligence. He was beginning to wonder if they had all hallucinated her, if the Morrigan had mind-controlled them into believing her sentient.

"Dana," he moved onto the next point of the agenda. "And her treasure, and Perdita, and Dome, and all that huge can of worms. Anyhow! You're in the best position to give feedback."

Johnny Anyhow cleared his throat.

"Captain, Dana and Perdita are scouring the planet for treasure, trawling for it with all instrumentation available to them both. They work together at times, and at others they are in competition. It's an uneasy alliance. I try to stay out of their way."

"Any results yet?" asked the Captain.

"None, sir."

Jon Marsden pointed a finger at Lascek. "The planet is the treasure," he said.

"I also think so," agreed Lascek. "It can be terraformed."

*

"So, you three!" he greeted Ailyss, Jon Marsden and Johnny Anyhow when they trailed into his cabin somewhat later. Sherman Dougherty was already present. "You are all three withholding information. I could find you guilty of treason, in Pirate Law!"

Jon Marsden prepared coffee for all of them. He fussed and made sure that everyone was comfortable and sorted.

"Jon, I'm prepared to forget about your piratical conspiracies with Perdita, about the treasure, and about cutting me out of the deal," said Lascek. "Plotting to take over my ship, and so on."

Jon looked surprised.

"The ship recorded all," smiled Lascek. It was not a nice smile. "And Federi, mutant and all, was the only one who stood up for his Captain. Not that he didn't play his own games, later on in space. But I have no reason to doubt his loyalty, with or without mutant. I have seen him subjugate that mutant. If it is still in there with him, it certainly has nothing more to say."

Jon Marsden nodded gravely.

"And yet, he too follows his own agenda," added Lascek. "Jon, Ailyss. When you four returned from the mission, there were gaps in your reports. Why, may I ask, did you withhold information?"

"Captain," said Jon smoothly, "if we had disclosed what we had discovered, you would not have gone ahead with the Peace Talks. Regardless of what goes on underground, those were of critical importance for Planet Earth and her rulership."

"Rulership?" asked Lascek sharply.

"Yourself, Captain," said Jon. "And the Admiral. The official power structure had to be firmly established."

"Underground," prompted Lascek with a deep scowl. "Tell me about this underground business?"

Jon indicated that Ailyss should continue.

"Captain," she said, "there is a deeper level of Unicate. You may be aware of this. Or maybe not. The Unicate military has been brought under your control, and that was the objective of the mission. But... the power structure of the Unicate has not been broken, as the outbreak of Plymouth Fever shows."

"Paean can see them," Johnny Anyhow put in.

"Right. Captain, there is a type of Unicate official around that seems – nearly not human. They are strange. We cannot pinpoint what is different about them."

"Not human," repeated Radomir Lascek. "Could they be Morrigan?"

Ailyss stared at him in shock.

"Not impossible," said Jon Marsden slowly. "Not at all impossible."

Ailyss shook her head.

"Not really. Jon – we'd have known. There would have been no way to eliminate them."

Jon nodded agreement.

"This is why Federi was uneasy to leave Earth," added Ailyss. "And he was right. No sooner had we left, than the Unicate struck a blow that was meant to eradicate... ordinary humans."

"Why?" asked Lascek, baffled. "What would they gain from such a wholesale termination of a – species..."

Johnny Anyhow's Adam's Apple was working.

"Species," said Jon. "That's exactly it. Radomir, for a nasty moment during the Peace Talks I thought you might... have an arrangement with the Unicate. When you spoke of putting aliens in charge."

"An external *system*," said Lascek, exasperated. This was the third time that Jon brought this up. "Not aliens, Jon! I was not aware..."

Ailyss smiled her tight little smile. Radomir Lascek heaved a sigh.

"Alright, Jon, I *was* aware of Dana. But I didn't intend to hand the leadership of Earth to her at any point. I *know* Dana! She didn't turn into a raider yesterday. And I honestly was not aware of any other aliens." He shook his head. "The Unicate, a bunch of aliens? Humans from another planet?"

"That's not counting those shifters," said Jon. "Federi's Romanian Dogs."

"Those could have been mutants from the Sixties," commented Ailyss.

"Could have," Sherman spoke up for the first time. "But lass, after you met the Morrigan, it's na so likely now, is it?"

"The reason you four are in here," said Lascek, "is that it seems to me we need to keep certain things strictly between humans. Earth humans."

"So Captain," said Jon, "how do we approach all of this?"

"Slowly and carefully," said Lascek. "Don't withhold information again. I need to know!"

They nodded.

"If Federi survives," said Lascek gravely, "we'll have to convince him to stay on the ship. For his own protection. I suspect the next item on his list is the Unicate."

Ailyss grimaced.

"He can count on me to back him up, Captain," she stated.

"On us," added Jon, and Johnny Anyhow nodded.

"And of course on his old Captain," added Lascek. "You can tell him that from me. But the most important thing is to unravel the tangle. We'll have to be careful."

*

Paean opened her eyes. Doc Judith was leaning over her in the dim light of bioluminescence. She tried to sit bolt upright, but the bolt fell short and her energy ran out, and she whimpered.

There were chimes and mobiles above her, and the ship was rocking gently. They were back at sea. She could smell it too. The porthole was only open by an inch; outside rain stroked against the glass, and the sea churned and rushed. Never as loudly as in the middle of the night. The moisture hung in the cabin like a heavy fog, making breathing very marine.

"You and Federi," said Doc Judith. "You never stop giving me trouble!" She sat down on the bunk next to Paean. The Irish redhead turned her head and saw that Federi was next to her on the bunk, out cold.

"Is he alive?"

"Course he is," soothed Doc Judith. "Just severely stretched. Too much teleportation. Ailyss and Wolf don't look much better. But Captain has opted not to chain you four up this time." She shook her head. "When the three of them went missing too, we activated Las Village. They brought you all in when your genetic signatures were once again visible on our systems. I had *five* comatose patients this past week, if you include that Peter Piper. At least I had some help with you all."

Paean nodded, too tired to care.

"Dana," she said. "Golden bullets. Anna life elixir. Would be nice for her to bring that."

"We negotiated that," said Doc Judith. "It cost Captain quite a bit, for four Brurite bullets. Don't do it again!"

The next time Paean opened her eyes, the Doc was gone. Federi was sitting on the bunk, cross-legged, gazing at her. In his hand was something small. And his wood-carving knife. But he was merely observing her.

"Feeling better?" he asked.

"Sure."

"Ready to go?"

"What?"

"I made a promise," said Federi. "We're done here. Captain can get himself another assassin. I've organized him a cook, that Lyr. He can like it or lump it. Don't want to be aboard with all those Atlantean and Danaan harpies. Three vile sisters! Yoy! The Donegals were more fun!"

"Federi," said Paean, "what are you talking about?"

"We're leaving," said Federi. "*Nu?*"

She stared at him. There were memories of a vivid dream lingering in her psyche; a suave man who'd treated her like a queen; a promise of a quiet, peaceful lifestyle suspended between Earth and Shrn, in Dracula's castle. Prince Vlad turning out to be the Morrigan; the space crawler. Herself coming to a few conclusions about her life…

"Federi," she said, "I'm definitely leaving the ship. And if I have to teleport out when nobody sees! And you, and Captain, and Ronan are all not going to stop me. I'm my own person!"

"We're not teleporting," warned Federi. "Least not for a week!"

"Then I'll leave on the Comet," she replied. "Doesn't matter. I'm through here."

"I see," said Federi, all the smiling lines dropping away from his eyes. "The blasted Morrigan has destroyed things for us, hasn't he."

"*You* destroyed them," said Paean. "Morrigan wanted to make a deal. He was going to stick to it. I was going to mediate. You and Ailyss and Wolf destroyed him with your teleporter fields before we could negotiate."

Federi shook his head. "There is no negotiating with great crooks. Expensive lesson Falco learnt."

"And I'm sick of every male on the jolly ship bossing me around," added Paean irritably. "Chains and bonds and command line, Federi. I'm leaving – had enough of that male structure."

"You're leaving *me,* you mean," growled Federi.

She hesitated. Yes, that was the idea. Cut *all* these ties. And then she felt sorry for him. He needed to get away from the ship too. But he shouldn't be her problem for long.

"Och, you can come along for a while, I don't care," she replied. "No skin off of me nose, see? Gets ya off the ship, least. But I'mna' going to jump back aboard the second Captain snaps his fingers, now am I? And I shan't be jumping at *your* beck and call either, Federi! Only taking you along so you can get away too, see? I'm out of the command structure. *Basta.*"

He got up with a sigh and extended a hand to her.

"Come, Paean. Let's go."

"Haven't yet decided where to," she said sullenly. Dublin didn't feel promising. Southern Free? More of Federi's systems. Every last place she could think of was either under Captain's control, or part of Federi's network. Disappearing off the radar would not be easy.

"I'll show you my Romania," said Federi gravely. "If you still want to leave me after that, you must do what you think best. Just hoping to change your mind at this point."

Paean packed her few remaining clothes into her stuff-bag, picked up her violin and straightened out.

"Then, whatever! Let's go!"

"Paean," said Federi, "wait."

She stared defiantly at him.

"Was I that bad to you?" he asked sadly. "You spend twenty-four hours with a man of – another species even, and you forget what we – what I thought we had?"

The hard edge faded from her stare and changed into sadness. She couldn't really remember what they'd had. Apart from a lot of bloodshed and drama. And work. Always, work. Hard, dirty work that made the humdrum of Molly Street pale in comparison.

She stared at him, trying to recall. Gutting fish, cleaning potatoes. Scrubbing heads, stitching up wounded pirates. Copping politics and anger from Captain, and from Federi – more from Federi; at least, Captain was a man she could look up to. Except that he drank.

A cabin full of jingly tricks. A strange little man, an entertainer with a split personality. She felt as confused and lost as the thousands of gems swaying with the movement of the ship. And everything that Vlad had shown her – from the dashing prince to the mansion, to the special consideration – all of that had been an illusion. But Federi was an illusionist too! What was real anyway? Metal chains around her wrists?

A random moment came back. Federi making her coffee in the galley, just the way she liked it, though he knew she'd tricked him into it. Sitting under a tree carving away at something while she lay dreaming on a towel. Crowning her with a lime-green bandanna for being a heroine. Stealing her a turquoise moonbag. And picking a star out of the night sky for her…

She went silently into his arms. And she cried. For being taken for a fool by some prankster; and losing sight of the reality that was her weird, chaotic life with Federi. For not being able to get a proper grip on it, even now.

"'s alright," he crooned as he held her tightly. "Was just that blasted Morrigan with its illusions."

She shook her head. It was far more. She was tired of her life as it was now. She had received a glimpse of how it could be. If... *everything* were different.

"He scrambled your mind," said Federi. "Was aimed at the old Tzigan. Any damage he could do to me. Was a low shot." He grinned suddenly. She could sense it. "Course you're specially susceptible."

"Why?" she challenged.

"You're sixteen."

"Hey!" She laughed through the tears.

Federi waited until she had finished crying and looked up at him, indecision all over her face. Washed-out blue eyes, after some good rain.

"Look here," he said. "What he did was, he took away your vision. Replaced it with a nicer vision. But one that you couldn't have. Little luv, princes and nobility – they don't exist anymore. You could find yourself someone really rich, someone high up in the system..." He rolled his eyes.

"A Unicate politician," completed Paean. "Nobody else is really rich. No, thanks. I prefer shooting at them." She grinned.

"'s a rotten old world we live in," commented Federi. "So, *shey,* what do you want to do? Want me to take you to Romania?"

She nodded. "Let's go, maybe they'll leave us in peace for a while." Maybe just long enough that she could figure out where she wanted to go from here.

"What I said." Federi held up a hand and started counting down, his other arm still tightly around her.

"Ten... nine... eight... seven..."

Paean's wrist-com clamoured.

27 November 2116

Katya…

You won't believe this. The blasted family Demon is actually alive and well! We managed to execute an immortal.

Federi's suddenly not sure that it was the right thing to do. My little Paean tells me the Morrigan had asked her to mediate. She was upset when we executed him. But he was dangerous, anna bottle! Tried various times to squish me. And besides his track record shows that he is a man-eater, from his species and his disposition. Was. What am I saying. What species that was, Federi has no idea – neither has Sherman, and that is worrying. Are there more of his kind? Where did he come from? What did he actually want, in the end?

Ayay, and dealing with the Assassin is a draining deal!

We are trying to leave the Solar Wind. But Captain is not letting us go. Every time we get ready to board the Comet, he has another request, or wants to discuss something, and now he's ordered a Ceilidh, anna bottle! For which purposes Rushka has to be fetched back from Southern Free, just for the evening. Along with Ronan. He's going to need his sibs so badly in the time to come, and so will Rushka… hell's whistles, how can Federi decide to desert now? My little foster sister needs me! And in any case, to leave Captain to his own devices with those two poisonous hags from Atlantis … I suppose old Federi will just have to hang in there a bit longer… though, if I don't take Paean out of this now, I'll lose her. She doesn't really need anyone; Federi made her into such a sharp survivor, she will be fine. She owns the Comet, and has a stash of treasure as a fortune. When she decides to leave, who could hold her back?

Your brother
Federi

517

Epilogue

It was never cold on Shrn. The creature crawled deeper into its crevice. If it had been able to assume any solid shape, it would have formed a voice box and whimpered. It experienced pain; to its entire being. That sticky carbon had vibrated with the teleporter fields and rattled and torn it and darned near nuked it out of existence. The yellow stuff was still resonating, tearing at its molecules and causing more damage. It was horrible, and very painful.

It lay spread out in the mossy shade, peering out into the darkness and the stars; even their sparse light was a burden.

But what smarted more than anything was the knowledge that out there was another universe, stars perpendicular to these, where a white ship with a new, young personality drifted around the seas and skies, and it would never see her again.

The Demon had won. The Morrigan had been damaged so badly in that vicious field, with the sticky carbon resonating to the damage, that it would never get up again. Burnt, it had been burnt. And boiled. And fried in its own juices. That blasted Demon was a cook!

The Morrigan sighed and allowed consciousness to slip away between the stars.

Solar Wind!
Morrigan!
Saying goodbye...

~ The Morrigan ~

~ The Morrigan ~

What happens next:

As the Solar Wind sails on, Federi jumps ship. Follow the developments on both ends - Captain's, and Federi's, in "Nix Romipen". (Cover graphic not yet available at time of publication of "The Morrigan")